BEAR TALES

Adventures of an American Original

DF GARLAND

This is a work of fiction. Names, characters, places and incidents are either the product of the author's imagination or are used fictitiously, and any resemblance to actual persons living or dead, business establishments, events, or locales, is purely coincidental.

BEAR TALES
Adventures of an American Original

COPYRIGHT © 2013 by DF Garland

All rights reserved. No part of this book may be reproduced in any manner whatsoever without written permission of the author, except in the case of brief quotations embodied in critical articles or reviews.

ISBN-13: 978-1491099322

ISBN-10: 1491099321

Dedication

To my wonderful Grandson, Trevor and to my friend, Charlie, who was the first to read these stories.
Thanks for your ideas.

Thanks to Demi and the YOTB writing group for your suggestions.
I couldn't have accomplished this without you.

TABLE OF CONTENTS

Introduction

Recipe for a Talk Show
Troops
Graduation
Callie
Rabid Raccoon
Memorial
Bear Signs
Getting Grilled
Setup
In Your Dreams
Wobble
A Better Bear
The Root
The Check
Toi
And Matt
Hello

INTRODUCTION

To the readers, thank you for taking time out of your busy schedule to read this book. A hint, if you get hung up in a story, which you do not like or feel that you cannot finish, skip ahead to the next story. You may find it is totally different.

DF Garland

RECIPE FOR A TALK SHOW

Ingredients;
One old curmudgeon writer
One attractive young talk show host
One aggressive talk show producer
One simple-minded neighbor

Mix appropriate quantities of the above ingredients together and bake under the spotlight of a show stage in the Big Apple in front of a live audience to make one award winning talk show episode. If you have questions about proper mixing techniques and baking temperature to be used, well, just refer to the following to glean any pertinent details that you may require.

I had to interrupt the afternoon game on television and get off my favorite, old easy chair to answer that damn phone without spilling my beer. I grabbed the phone and practically yelled "Hello" even before the receiver was at my face.

I heard a feminine voice hesitate and then ask, "Hello is this Mr. Bear?"

"No", I replied strongly, "it is Bear – not Mr. Bear and who are you?"

"Well, I am Julia Brown and I am a producer on the *Sunshine Show* and we would like to invite you to be a guest on a future show. Miss Jacky Mooney has a great show and it would be the perfect opportunity for you to discuss your books….."

I cut her off sharply in mid-sentence and said, "Yeah, I know who she is".

"Oh, do you watch the show, Mr. Bear?" She responded happily.

"No, I don't watch that talk show," I barked, "but I don't live in a cave all the time. I do sometimes hear things about people. It is Bear not Mr. Bear, Miss Brown".

"It is Mz Brown," she replied.

"Okay, Mzzzzzz Brown", I replied. I made a serious effort to drag out the Mz. I heard her sigh.

She took a few seconds to collect herself and then asked in a very serious and proper tone, "Bear, are you interested in appearing on the Sun and Moon segment of the Sunshine Show with Miss Jacky Mooney to discuss your books and short stories now that one of your stories is up for an Emmy for a television mini-series and one of your books was made into a movie so......"

"Stop, I know all that", I cried. "Why would I want to be on the show?" Before she could answer, I glanced at the television and noticed that the Yankees had just scored a run, which I missed because of this call so I asked, "Mzzzz Brown (*drawing out the Mz again*), if you will give me your phone number, I will consider your offer and let you know."

She sighed again and gave me her phone number, which I wrote on the back of an old score card. I hung up without saying bye-bye or something all these young people like to say today.

After watching the Yankees lose and then watching the end of the Cubs game against the Pirates, I went to bed after having too many beers and not much food.

In the middle of the night, I awoke with an idea (*and a sour stomach*) about appearing on the talk show.

My agent was adamant about me promoting my works and he usually referred to an obscure paragraph in my contract, which read I must do book signing tours. Also, I would appear on national television at least once or be in violation of said contract. He would even say I had signed the aforementioned contract. He would gladly send me a copy!!!

Now I would cut off one of my appendages before talking or appearing in front of a group of young, giggling women talking about mundane topics (*like why did I write that or what did I mean by that or where did I get the idea for*). But my sleep was interrupted with a creative way to be on the show and satisfy my agent and the publisher.

Yes – yes – yes, I could do it my way and it would be great or beyond great, why I might get an award for the stupid talk show.

Sleep wouldn't come so I got up and made coffee and scribbled out the script for the talk show on the edge of some junk mail, an advertisement for a credit card.

I fell asleep in my favorite easy chair. I slept till eleven a.m. I got up and got dressed in jeans and a tee shirt and sandals and went to see my neighbor and good buddy Bench. As I was leaving, I noticed I had spilled some beer on my favorite easy chair last night. I stopped to admire the pattern that the spilled beer made. I liked the way the spill blended with a prior coffee stain, which covered other artistic stains. (*God, I'm good*).

I walked in Bench's side door and found him stretched out asleep in his easy chair, which was much newer than mine and hadn't yet obtained that total-lived-in look. I went to his refrigerator to look for something to eat, but all he had was some ketchup, mustard and spoiled yogurt, which had been there since Snoopy first appeared in a comic strip. Bench did have a couple beers in the fridge, but it was before noon and my stomach still felt uneasy. I had a seat on his old torn sofa, which had a lot more character than his new easy chair. I removed the remote carefully from his hand and switched the channel to find a game on his idiot box. I found the golf channel and was sitting there watching the golf when Bench woke up.

He remarked, "That was a great shot that tall golfer (*I can't remember his name*) made back on hole number five. He made the ball bounce off the raised rim of the sand hazard and it went in the hole for an eagle."

Then the announcer said, "Now let's watch a rerun of the shot just made on hole number five for an eagle by...."

I glared at Bench because it was just as he had described it! How had he known since he was asleep the whole time and the television was on the food channel?

Bench only chuckled!

I asked Bench if he wanted to go get something to eat, it was my treat.

He said he would but only "if I combed my hair" first. Oh boy!

Bench himself wasn't much to look at. He is a big guy, well over 6 feet tall and 230 pounds, I guessed. He wasn't fat, just solid looking although he never exercised, but he was a lot younger than me. He didn't work at a steady job yet he always seemed to have money when I asked him to go fishing, hunting, and golfing or to see a game at the stadium. However, he never turned down friends or neighbors who needed help with moving furniture, building something or with yard work. He also never turned down my offer of going out to eat and he always showed up just as I finished cooking on my barbeque grill. What aggravated me the most was he was always drinking my beer!!!!

After walking home together, I drove my custom car to Old Joe's Café. Bench ordered the all-you-can-eat breakfast of eggs, sausage, bacon and pancakes. I had a smaller meal of scrambled eggs, fried potatoes with cheese and whole wheat toast (*and yes, they serve breakfast all day*).

Over a second cup of coffee and while he consumed a third helping of everything, I filled Bench in on my plans for the talk show. I said I would arrange it so he received a free trip to Atlantic City, another one to the Big Apple, and a thousand dollar fee for appearing on the show. He said it all sounded fine, but he hoped it wouldn't interfere with his busy schedule, which caused me to choke on my coffee.

After dropping Bench off at his house (*he doesn't drive or own a car or have a schedule*), I went home to call Mzzzz Brown. I finally found her phone number on the old score card under my easy chair.

She answered after the phone rang a couple times and said, "Hello, this is Mz Brown speaking". I said, "Mzzzz Brown".

She sighed and said, "Hello Mr. Bear er... just Bear".

I said, "I have decided to be on the show".

She interrupted me (*can you imagine that?*) and practically purred "Oh marvelous".

I said, "Whoa Mzzzz Brown – hold up there. I will appear on the show, but we have to talk first about how I am going to appear on the show. First, you are not to tell anyone AS IN ANYONE ANYWHERE ANYTIME I am going to be on the show and we must meet to discuss everything about the show. It will be marvelous (*I tried to mimic the way she said it.*)"

She replied, "I do not understand".

"Yes, I know you do not understand. I have written a script for my appearance on the show, which will knock the socks off the viewers and will win you an Oscar if you do it my way. But this will all be for naught if you leak even one word I am going to be on the show. If you do let it out, then we might as well just do the usual normal-boring-middle-of-the-afternoon show appearance. But I can assure you an Oscar if you do it my way".

She came back with, "It's an Emmy, not an Oscar." She sighed and collected herself and asked, "What do you have in mind, Bear?"

"Reserve a suite with two bedrooms in Atlantic City for me and a friend under your name for one night. Then you come down there to meet with me in the morning so no one would know we were meeting. It has to be ultra-secret and I expect you to pick up the tab for the hotel and our meals".

She replied, "I can't do that without getting approval from my boss, the executive producer."

I then asked her, "How many levels of management would need to approve this, Mzzz Brown? I can assure you an Oscar if you do this my way. It will be the talk of the entertainment world."

To which, she gave a sigh followed by another sigh (*I was very happy. It was my first double sigh*).

"Just the one level above me is all that would be required to approve this. Can you give me a hint of what you have in mind for your appearance on the show, Bear?"

"No can do, you have to hear about it in person and once you do, you and your executive producer are going to love it. It is all legal and it does not involve nudity or foul language or anything else that is banned on network television. (*With all of that going against it, I wondered how I could get Bench to appear on the show*!!). Remember my plots in my literary works; I am a creative genius so I can do this (*now I was making myself feel woozy*). Can you say Oscar, Mzzzz Brown?"

I must be slipping since she did not even sigh. We proceeded to decide when was the best time for us to arrange this little get-together in Atlantic City.

I expected a call back from her or her executive producer to question my sanity, but she only called back to confirm the date and hotel in Atlantic City.

On the check in day, I picked up Bench and his small suitcase and we were off to Atlantic City for our big television adventure. He made me stop and buy him a meal at a fast food joint – well, actually it was three meals. That seemed to hold him until we were half way there when he wanted to stop again to get something more substantial to eat. But I forced him to abstain from further gluttony as we rode along listening to a sports all-talk radio channel.

Checking in was easy, but it took an act of god to keep both of us out of the gambling arenas. Bench wanted to charge the gambling tab to the room, but I flat out refused. I figured I could never live long enough to write enough books to pay off the gambling debt the two of us could run up in one afternoon!!

In the room, we ordered from room service – it was two steak meals for Bench and one for me along with a couple six packs of beer. (*Would you believe it they didn't have my favorite on the preferred beer list?*) We found a baseball game between San Francisco and San Diego on the all sports channel.

It took two waiters and two carts fully loaded to bring up room service the next morning. Then we showered, shaved and changed clothes (*at least I know I did, but I wasn't too sure about Bench's attention to hygiene*). We both waited for the producers to show up.

Bench told me our guests were here. I opened the door just before they were about to knock, which surprised them, but not me since I knew Bench. He was always doing that.

I figured out later how Bench was able to surprise people. He has exceptional hearing. He heard them talking just like he heard me before I entered his house. I will test you later, Mr. Bench. I will

Mz Brown was a short, dark-skinned beauty with short black hair. She introduced me to her boss, one Mr. Clapper, who was a tall and distinguished looking bald man (*boy was I going to have fun with his name*). I invited them in and asked if they wanted coffee or rolls. They said they were fine and could we proceed. I made sure to look at Bench and mouthed the word "no" before he could say he could eat something more.

I introduced my colleague as Bench, which is the only name that I knew he had. Standing close, Mz Brown looked up at Bench in wonder.

We all had a seat and I laid out how my appearance on the show would go and what Bench's part was.

I asked for them to provide another two night stay in New York City in a two bedroom suite for us (*with meals provided, which is important if you are traveling with Bench*). I asked that Bench be reimbursed $1000.00 for his appearance on the show.

Mz Brown looked up at him sitting beside her (*yes, he is big even when sitting down*) and assured me that wouldn't be a problem.

I demanded they maintain the strictest secrecy and even the host couldn't know who the guest was. She was to introduce me as a special secret guest. She could be given clues on what to do or say by use of the teleprompter once we were on stage.

Mr. Clapper said, "I do not think that we can do that – we must let Miss Mooney know about this since she is well, the hostess!"

"Listen Mr. Crapper, you will not get the anticipated level of spontaneity out of her if she expects or anticipates any part of this. You do want an Oscar for this show don't you?"

He sighed one time and said, "I hope we do not get fired for this but ok, fine, we will do it your way. Also, my name is Mr. Clapper and it is an Emmy, a day time Emmy!" He practically yelled the last part.

A few days before the show was scheduled, I took Bench to a clothing store to get him ready for his part of the show. He seemed in awe of all the clothes. We selected a black tight tee shirt to show off his biceps and chest, a pair of pleated black trousers, black belt, black socks and a new pair of black shoes. I finally relented and purchased new underwear and a new jeans and tee shirt for traveling also.

We stopped at a hair salon to get his hair cut since it looked ragged and uneven to me. I paid a small fortune to have the stylist look at his hair and trim a quarter inch off the one side and fluff it up and admire how good Bench looked. She couldn't seem to keep her hands off Bench's neck, back, and his face (*talk about sickening!*). I won't even go into how much it cost to feed him before and after shopping or how much it cost to feed him while on the way to the Big Apple.

The day of the show arrived and I was feeling a little nervous but not as much as I expected. I had written the script after all. Nothing could or would go wrong. To sneak in the studio without attracting attention, I was given a ticket in the audience. I didn't stick out too much as I was the only old fart there in the middle of lots and lots of young pretty giggling, clapping, yelling, and talking women.

At a pre-arranged time, I left my aisle seat and walked to the back where I was met and escorted to a dressing room. Bench was there already. He looked massive yet trim in his black tight uniform, while I looked old, gray, small, wrinkled and frail. Also, I was getting crankier by the minute.

The hostess, Miss Jacky Mooney, who was petite, pretty, perky, bouncy, young and blonde, started with her patented announcement, "Next on our Sun & Moon segment on the Sunshine Show, we have a special guest. I do not know who it is – no, I do not know who it is but I am told that he is a national figure of renown that other talk shows have been trying to get on their shows for ages. So without further ado, here he is."

That was the cue for us to go into the act. We hesitated for a minute for effect, I let out a yell like a banshee and Bench picked me in a bear hug so my front was facing him. He pushed aside the curtain roughly and walked out on stage. All that time, I was struggling to get out of his grip and trying to breathe while I moaned and groaned and shook my hands and arms and waved my feet around since Bench was holding me too tight.

Replays that aired on all entertainment and news shows later would catch the extreme surprise and shocked look on the hostess's pretty face as Bench carried me over and placed me in the empty chair. While he did that, he had his back to the stunned audience and I sneaked a peak at Miss Jacky Mooney, the hostess, who was shocked and speechless. Keeping a giant hand on my right shoulder, Bench walked around behind me and stood there looking formidable and serious in his tight black uniform. He moved his hand to atop my head as I struggled to escape, which I really was. It was even worse than I had even expected. I cannot stand being in front of an audience.

Finally, the hostess glanced at her monitor which gave her instructions on how to proceed. She was cautioned to act surprised while introducing everyone to Bear, the famous writer.

She said, "Look everyone it is Bear."

Then she listed all my recent works and what awards may be forthcoming for me. She went on to add (*without being prompted*) I was apparently scared of being on stage.

She glanced at me and added, "It is ok to be scared, I was my first time." She looked back and up at Bench and asked who he was. She seemed to be sizing him up with a look a dog would give a ham bone.

I finally was able to utter, "His name is Mr. Bench and he was hired to make sure I fulfilled my contract to be here today. I will never get used to being on stage. I am unaccustomed to being in the public eye. In fact, I detest anything to do with being in front of people or to be recognized by anyone."

The hostess followed her instructions on her monitor and I was able to manage making enough small talk in a squeaky voice to keep the show moving for about ten minutes. But those questions finally came up from audience members about *why did I write that or what did I mean by that or where did I get the idea.* That was when I made my break for it by shifting to my left towards the hostess so Bench moved that way to go with me. I jumped up and went right and ran off stage before even the stunned Bench could stop me. The audience went crazy as they now thought all this was scripted and was a part of the show.

In the dressing room, I was given a cold soda and was able to lie down before Bench came in the room. He saw how white I was so he went to the sink and dampened a cloth and put a cold compress on my head. He was able to stop everyone from coming in to see me except for the producers, Mzzz Brown and Mr. Clapper.

They both seemed genuinely surprised at my condition. I was in such dire straits I couldn't even think of a thing to say to them that would elicit a sigh. I was invited back on stage to talk informally to the hostess and her audience after the show was over but I just couldn't do it.

The audience was given my latest book. I did agree to sign the books but I insisted on doing it in the hall outside of the stage. The sight of the doors to the outside gave me courage enough to sign the books and receive congratulations on the best talk show episode ever.

Bench kept me company there. But it seemed like every young lady in that audience stopped to chat and flutter their eye lashes at Bench or to touch him on his chest or his biceps. The line past Bench was so slow the guards threatened to call in the National Guard to evacuate the theater.

Later in the day, the news programs and entertainment shows all raved about the Sunshine Show. There were many clips of Bench carrying me struggling on stage and my running off the set. The talking heads on those shows just talked and talked and talked about my performance. Some brought on experts in the field of phobias and tried to analyze everything about the show.

Bench and I had a good meal (*Bench only had one meal but he did have three desserts*) and a couple beers in the hotel restaurant.

I had told Bench what I had to do next so he turned the TV on to watch the Red Sox play the Yankees in Boston.

I called my agent on his super-secret-cell-never-call-me-there phone.

He answered, "Hello, this is Cliff Loews, Agent to the Stars" in his smooth yet nasality made-up voice as he tried to articulate every syllable. I would love to hear him say syllable.

I said, "Hi, Mr. Lewis."

He sighed and said, "Oh, it's you, Bear. I must admit I am quite disgusted you didn't let me know you were going to be on the Sunshine Show. I am quite upset with you!!"

"Well, how did it go? Was it ok? Did I satisfy the legal requirement to be on a talk show to promote my books, Mr. Lowest?"

He hesitated and sighed and said, "I guess you did meet that requirement, but you still need to go on a book signing tour. But you are now the talk of the entertainment world. Quite frankly, I didn't think you had a performance like that in you."

Before he could go on and on and on, I stopped him by saying, "Mr. Lois (*Lois Lane from Superman fame*), I will need an advance now for my next book. I expect it to exceed six figures".

He responded, "Do you think today's performance on national television will pave the way for that much money for your next book?"

"Yes I do. Definitely! Now let's put that money in perspective. Six figures could be like 36 24 36 and to exceed that would be maybe 38 24 36. But we both know that isn't going to happen so how about $101,000.00, which is over six figures. It is my only offer. Take it or leave it, Mr. Last Chance".

He sighed again (*but only once*) and said he would let me know tomorrow. "Make it early, I'd like to have the check in my pocket when I leave tomorrow," I replied.

I had instructed Mz Brown and Mr. Clapper not to bother me or to tell anyone where I was. I had had all the attention in front of cameras I could stand for like, well, forever.

As Bench consumed three donuts after breakfast the next day, the phone rang.

It was my agent, Mr. Loews, Agent to the Stars. He asked if I stop over to his office to transact some business.

Bench, in his newly glorified black uniform, and I took a cab to the office. The cabbie recognized us from the Sunshine Show and loved Bench's performance. He said Bench had a real future in acting. That cabbie ignored me so I only gave him a $5 tip, which was designed to teach him manners.

With my agent was one of the publishers, one Mrs. Teller, whom I had met before. She was a plump mother of a brood of children. She positively gushed over Bench. She barely looked at me as she handed over the check.

While she was so distracted, I decided to ask her a question about the book signing tour.

"I would like Bench to accompany me on the book signing tour. The price to you in publishing would be for his travel, lodging and food (*if only they knew about his food consumption!*)."

Mrs. Teller thought about it for only a second before saying, "A lovely idea" in a very distracted and confused voice.

We thanked them and left.

Bench and I went home before packing to go on tour. I had coordinated the book signing dates with baseball schedules so Bench and I could attend games at every city we were going to. I wanted to see the most major and minor league baseball games we could fit in.

Of course, I had to pay for the tickets to the games for both of us. The beer and food was on a voucher to my publisher, who had agreed to pay for Bench's travel and living.

After watching Bench consume more hot dogs at the first game than was gobbled down at a hot dog eating contest by all contestants, I told Bench we would only be allowed to have two each of those $10 hot dogs at each game. So we stopped to eat before the game, then he ate his two doggies and my two doggies at the game and then we stopped so he could eat after the game. Both the pre-game and post-game food consumption was at fast food restaurants to hold down the cost. I still hoped the publisher would pay for Bench's participation on this tour.

I was upset at how the book signings went, however. After watching us on the Sunshine Show or on the various entertainment news programs about the Sunshine Show, the people showed up in droves to get autographs. But the people insisted that Bench sign my books also so a seat would be found for Bench and a line arranged for him. The young and middle aged and most of the older ladies were all in Bench's line. They were all so giddy just to talk to him and to try to his touch his hand as he handed them back the book (*my books*) he signed. They all tried to give him their phone numbers by saying something like "just sign it to Ellen the love of my life 717-555-1212". My line contained only older ladies, men, and possibly a few librarians. It was the same at all the locations, which aggravated me to no end.

In Seattle, it was pouring down rain and Bench's line still went out through the front door and down the street for two blocks. All of the people in line were soaked to the skin. It looked like a wet tee shirt competition at Spring Break. Each lady showed Bench their obvious delights while they smiled expectantly!!

To add insult to injury, my line consisted of only three little old ladies and two men who were probably older than me. One of the men even asked me to sign another author's book (*written by a Mr. Fox*). Of course, it was very enlightening and entertaining watching all the ladies in Bench's line.

After the whirlwind of travel and ball games finished, Bench and I came home. A couple days later after confirming that the publisher's check didn't come back for insufficient funds, I walked over to give Bench his $1000 payment.

I walked right in his house and there on that old worn and torn, comfortable sofa was Bench and a lady in a passionate embrace with body parts almost visible. They were both moaning and groaning and touching each other on my favorite sofa, where I could never sit again.

I was so shocked and stunned I voiced an epitaph, which caused them to stop briefly what they were doing. The lady looked up at me, while panting. It was none other than Miss Jacky Mooney of the Sunshine Show. Her face was red and flushed and she was on top of Bench. After regaining some feeling in my body, I left just as fast as I could on these two ancient legs, which were feeling older by each step.

After dark and while I was on my first beer to try and wash that sight of them out of my mind, Miss Jacky Mooney and Bench walked in hand-in-hand. They wore rumpled clothes. Miss Jacky Mooney hair was a mess, not something that she would want her fans to see.

They did not apologize but both sat down.

Miss Jacky Mooney said, "I have invited the Bench man (*did she say the Bench man?*) to be a permanent addition to my show. He will add so much decoration to the set of my show and he can stay in my apartment. We both can come here to Bench's little house for peace and quiet out of the public's eye." She practically purred all of this in a dreamy voice as she gave Bench a wicked look and with an almost feline set to her eyes.

I added, "If you want to be out of the public and media's eye while staying here, you need to enclose Bench's backyard with a solid fence."

Bench said, "I can build that fence and install the locks myself".

I said, "Bench is quite handy with his hands"

Miss Jacky Mooney of the Sunshine Show of national television looked at me and replied, "You will never know the half of it. I hope I do not have any marks on me - you know Bench marks" (*did she say Bench marks?*) She pulled up her sleeves to look at her arms. She chuckled to herself as she massaged him on the back.

After they left hand-in-hand and with Miss Jacky Mooney giggling like a school girl, I was sinking into a deep funk and knew I would be quite grouchy for a long time. But I thought of a way to cheer myself up so I called my agent.

When he answered, I said, "Hello Mr. Lewd, Agent to the Farts".

He sighed!! It works wonders for me. Now which type of a pizza should I order and what teams are playing ball on the ole' boob tube tonight!

If you are considering appearing on a national talk show, you may use any part of the above recipe free of charge. The author, Bear.

TROOPS

The ringing of the phone interrupted me while working on my latest book (*or should I say while I was having a brain cramp and not being very productive at all*). I answered with a plain "Hello" instead of a usual sharp "WHAT?"

The deep male voice said, "Hello, my name is Norman Ghant and I am a counselor for MBCI, MSMBCI... (*and a bunch more letters, some of which ended in .com*)."

I hesitated. I had to write down the current time and his name on paper and prepare my thoughts. (*I had to keep him off balance, since I did not want him to get up a head of steam, if possible, since he is a lawyer after all and you know how they can talk*).

He finally asked, "Are you still there?"

"Si, oh, yes, please be patient while I turn down the volume. Ok that's better. Did you say c i or s e?" I asked. (*I spelled it for him.*)

He hesitated again and said, "What, ci or se, huh?"

"Yes, was that ci or selor?" I asked again.

He sighed and asked, "Could you please repeat that again?"

Very methodically, I said, "Ci as in council of or selor as counselor for?"

He jumped on that right away, "Oh yes, counselor for, I'm an attorney for MBCI, MSM......".

I interrupted him before he got his sail unfurled in the wind, "Thank goodness that you got that straight. If you are attorney, then you have a license to practice law, right?"

"Of course, I am licensed in New York, Connecticut and Massachusetts".

"Fine, what is your license number?"

He started to sputter, "My what? Are you asking for my license number to do what?"

I said calmly, "I would like your license number to practice law just to ensure this isn't a scam. It was on your network just last week that unscrupulous people will try any means to capture data from unsuspecting people so I want to be sure you are who you say you are."

"I do not have that license here at my desk since my clerk sends in for that license. She files it".

"Oh, ok. Then look on one of your cards. It is bound to be listed there," I suggested.

He responded, "No, it is not listed on my cards".

"Well it would be a good way to ensure that someone is really dealing with an attorney if the law license is printed on their cards, don't you think?"

"Mr. Bear, you can be sure that I am an attorney. You can trust me".

"That is just what they said on the program - the scammers say you can trust me." I hesitated before asking, "Did you pass the bar exam?"

"Yes, of course right here in the state of New York."

"Good, now we are getting someplace. What year did you pass the bar?"

He hesitated and sighed and then said, "What would that prove?"

"I'm just trying to be sure you are who you say you are, Mr. Gent".

"I am Norman Ghant, spelled G h a n t, and I am attorney. I passed the bar here in 1988, I think. Yes, I'm sure that it was in 1988".

Time to redirect his attention so I asked, "Do you know that I live in the Commonwealth of Pennsylvania? You did not say you are licensed to practice law in PA."

"There is a reciprocal agreement between Pennsylvania and New York so I can practice there and a lawyer in PA can practice in New York".

"When was that signed? Do you have a copy of it, Normal?"

He said with extreme patience, "My given name is Norman, I'm not Normal."

"That sounds about right", I happily responded. "If you want to talk to me, you will need to furnish me with proof you are an attorney representing the Board of Directors."

He replied, "I do not work for the Board but directly for the President, Mr. Jay Tylers".

"Really? Is Mr. Tylers at the same address as you?"

He gave me his address in the Big Apple and confirmed that his boss was at the same address (*which was a big mistake. He gave me too much information!*).

I apologized by saying, "I'm sorry I cannot continue this conversation since you cannot confirm who you are. It's too bad since we have been on the phone for over 35 minutes. Are you always this confused?"

I hung up.

It should be noted we had been on the phone for 43 minutes.

My day wasn't productive anyway so I decided to take the rest of the day off and make plans for golf for tomorrow. I warmed some coffee in the 'wave and retired to the swing on the sunny porch to contemplate the phone call with the attorney from MBCI. I know the way I handled the call may appear sophomoric to some people. It was designed to be that way since I wanted and needed any advantage if I was to win my appeal against MBCI, which I had filed with the PA PUBLIC UTILITY COMMISSION.

The appeal was designed to get the members of our military serving in the Middle East some media coverage. It just galls me to no end the broadcast media doesn't provide any coverage of the wars in Iraq and in Afghanistan.

I am not a war monger but we have somewhere close to 200,000 military personnel over there putting their life, limb and future on the line and the media does not seem to care. The media giants must be concerned about their ratings or something. In addition to the troops over there, let's not forget their families and friends back here who are worried about them. Plus the rest of the taxpayers need to be kept informed about the situations over there.

I suspected a lawsuit against the media giants wouldn't get too far in the court system since the Constitution provides for Freedom of the Press. But the appeal to the PUC could work since they were the licensing agent for the state and there are stated requirements, which must be met. I just might win this appeal if my plans worked. At the very least, I could make the situation more public. I had just completed the first step.

Now I had to call Reets to make arrangements for golf, which wouldn't be easy since I had learned the subtle word play-by-play from Reets. Reets is the all-time master so here goes nothing. I won't bore you with all the details of the call, but I want to give you excerpts you may find interesting *(or not)*.

Reets answers, "Hi, This is Reets and not a recording. Please call back a better time since I am taking a nap."

"Reets, you never take a nap. This is Bear. How about playing golf tomorrow?"

"Bear, is it? What is the weather supposed to be tomorrow?"

"Sunny and low eighties".

"Oh, I am not interested in playing golf in that much rain!!!"

Now I know Reets has good hearing so I ignored the last comment.

I replied, "I'll pick you up at eight a.m. and we will stop at Old Bob's Café for breakfast. I'll pay for breakfast if you pay for golf."

"Who is this again?" he asked.

"Just be ready at eight in the morning to play golf", I intoned and hung up.

I had a thought I needed to implement so I left the porch and went in to my laptop computer and drafted the following letter.

Mr. Jay Tylers
President Mega-Broad-Cast-Inc.

Dear Mr. Tylers,

I had a most disturbing telephone call from a Mr. Norman Ghant, who claimed to be your attorney. He was quite confused and had trouble convincing me he was in fact both an attorney and that he represented MBCI. He rattled incoherently on for over 40 minutes.
It is so sad to see someone progress to this point. If he is your attorney, maybe you have been working him too hard. I have heard stress can cause conditions such as he displayed. Your corporation should maybe send him to a retreat for rest and relaxation.
If he is not an attorney, and does not represent your company, then you should start an investigation to see who would attempt a scam based on your company's good name.

Bear

I mailed the letter to the President of MBCI as I was on my way to pick up Reets. I won't bore you with the golf results especially since Reets plays a great game and always beats me. Everybody beats me…hmmm…is that why I never have problems getting partners to play golf with?
On the way home, I asked Reets, "Are there any devices that could be used to determine if someone was recording a phone call?"
He chuckled and said "I have one of the latest and best. Would you like it?"

I replied "I would like to borrow it."

He said "No, you can't borrow it but I will give it to you". (*So it goes when talking to Reets!*)

Before retiring or as he liked to say, in his prior life, Reets had been an engineer who designed various and sundry devices used to eavesdrop or record or what-ever-you-can-think-of by our CIA, NSA, other secret agencies, etc. He claimed he was still on retainer.

He led me into his lab, which looked like a cross between a rock quarry and a space laboratory. Some tables were covered in slates and chalk. A few of the slates had been written on in what looked like Latin or hieroglyphics or pictograms or a combination of all three. The rest of the basement had lots of high-tech-looking equipment I can't even begin to describe. It's sad I can appreciate slate/chalk more than current or future technology.

Reets went on a scavenger hunt to end all scavenger hunts with items of hardware and nuts and bolts and what-have-you flying around before he said "Ah ha" and handed me a small round device, which would fit on a phone receiver. He explained it was a special sound magnifier, which could determine if a phone call was being recorded.

Before putting it on the ear piece of the receiver, I was to push one button, which would record the current Meridian time the call started. I was to push the same button when the call was over.

I listened to the device, which he called a sniffer. If I heard beeps, the call was being recorded either at the other end, by a hacker on the line, or a bug at my end. If I suspected a bug at my end, Reets would come to my house and sweep it for more bugs. I found that greatly reassuring!

A few days later, I received both a notice from the PA PUC the hearing had been scheduled, and a call from another of MBCI's attorneys. He said his name was Mr. Jekesen. I asked him to hold on a second and pushed the button on the sniffer to activate it and put it awkwardly on the phone.

I put my face to the phone and said, "I'm ready now, Mr. Jekesen".

"Hello, Mr. Bear. My name again is Jake Jekesen and I am an attorney with MBCI. I would like to talk to you about your appeal you filed with the PA PUC. Can we talk about it? Are you sure you want to go ahead with that?" He ended the last question in a menacing tone but I had noticed he took his time and talked in a very direct and evenly paced way. (I *wonder why he thought he had to speak to me like that.*)

"Yes, we can talk about that, Mr. Jekesen. In fact, I am led to believe that the PUC has allocated all the time we need to talk about that on the 17th at 11 am in Harrisburg." I replied.

I hung up because I had detected the steady rhythms of ticking on the sniffer, which would indicate the boys at Mega-Broad-Cast-Inc. were illegally recording this call.

I set about finishing some correspondence using the old paper, envelope and stamp method and even the current e-mail. I did not want my friends and fellow veterans and other interested parties to miss out on the upcoming hearing.

I called my attorney, one Maude Klein. She is a short, pretty woman, who has been my reluctant attorney for a few years in spite of her young age.

She said to me in her sharp twang of a voice, "Hi, Bear. I'm glad you called about the hearing. You know I have not done anything other than some procedural reviews per your instructions. I do not want to go there and have my head or butt handed to me on a platter."

"Do not worry, Miss. Klein. We are going to be fine. Shall we meet to ride up together?"

"Good idea – we can discuss the appeal on the way. Let's see, the hearing is at eleven in the morning so we can meet in York at ten a.m. and be there in plenty of time."

"That is not a good idea since I would like to stop and get breakfast on the way. Suppose we leave York by 8:15."

"Do you need so much time to eat?" she asked.

Well, usually I take an inordinate amount of time reading the menu at Old Bob's Café just to aggravate Alice, the waitress, but Miss Klein didn't know this nor did she know what might happen at Harrisburg on the day of the hearing.

I simply said, "Yes". We finalized the place and time.

I made the rendezvous with Miss Klein right on schedule but after looking at my car, which I call the tank, she said she would gladly drive. The tank is a massive sixties GM car I have had all these years.

These days, Bill goes over the car every few months and replaces whatever is needed. He even washes and waxes it. Sometimes Bill would scavenge and modify parts so while the car looked and ran great, it seemed oddly strange to the cultured or discriminating eye. But I will keep it forever since it was the only car my wife and I purchased the old fashioned way (we saved and paid cash for it). I anticipated changing my will so Bill received the tank after I died.

As Miss Klein started to drive on I-83, a car passed us. It appeared to be full of women and had a sign on the side and the top of the trunk, which read "Mothers for Coverage." This caused Miss Klein to take her eyes off the road and glare at me. She didn't take her eyes off the road after that as the expressway was unusually busy. The vehicles were a mix of vans, cars, buses and hummers. They all appeared to be full and had signs such as "Veterans Demand Change", "Respect the Military", etc, etc.

Miss. Klein said to me over her shoulder and with gritted teeth, "What have you done, Bear?"

I said innocently, "Me, little old me?"

After that, she was too busy driving in all the traffic headed to Harrisburg. We finally arrived in the downtown area. It was a holiday atmosphere as the streets were very crowded with people walking around with signs draped over their bodies (front and back) or they carried signs. These signs pretty much said we should do **responsible reporting** for the military, where ever they were deployed.

The first big hotel on the left had signs hanging outside almost every window. I knew the American Legion had tried to rent every room in the hotel and had a rally planned in the common area on the first floor. The second hotel on the left was being rented by the VFW, who tried to outdo the first hotel. Every room in the downtown area was probably rented by some veteran group or relatives of the military. They all had signs outside the windows.

The city police, the state police and the National Guard were out in force directing traffic. They even tried to direct the foot traffic since there were so many people present. We could hear the sound of a marching band playing military marches and patriotic songs in the distance. The bands must have been on the river front walkways.

Miss Klein finally was able to drive her car to the parking garage besides the PUC building but the garage had a "full" sign out front. She issued a curse and started to drive past until I told to her to pull part way in and stop at the sign. She looked at me as if I was crazy but she followed my instructions.

I slowly got out of the car and walked over to the attendant. He started to say something but I interrupted and said, "I am Bear. Are you holding a parking place for me?"

He smiled widely and said, "Si, Senor Bear, park there." He pointed to one spot at the front. "I will personally watch your car".
Miss Klein parked her car after the attendant removed the sign. We both started to walk out of the garage. I was wearing my old, worn and shiny blue suit with a new red tie and a new white shirt (a weak attempt at red, white and blue) while Miss Klein looked very pretty and professional in a snug fitted gray suit and moderate heels. She carried a slim briefcase and I carried a folded newspaper.

As we hit the street, the parking garage attendant pointed at me and yelled "Bear". All the people on the street stopped and the chant started "Bear" and then "Bear" again but louder. The chant went on until I put my hands up and out and waved them down slowly.

The attendant walked over and told us to head to the diner across the street and tell Selma he sent us. Selma wanted to buy us a meal as a way of thanking me for thinking of the military personnel stuck in harm's way.

I was unprepared for all this. Well, yes, I had notified all the veterans groups, the Pennsylvania National Guard, and many military support groups about this hearing but I never expected this turn out. The reception plus celebrity status for me was not necessary. Luckily, Miss Klein appeared to be speechless. I expected her to rip me into shreds as soon as she got her composure back.

Selma, a middle aged, bleached blonde with obvious delights, went overboard by trying to give us everything on her breakfast menu, but we finally convinced her to serve only one breakfast each with coffee. Orange juice appeared magically however. Selma thanked us profusely. She even hugged me and kissed me on the cheek. I blushed.

We tried to sneak out of the restaurant quietly but the Bear chant started up again. It continued after we were inside the PUC building. As we went through the x-ray machine, the guards apologized many times for treating us that way. Both guards were veterans and were busy thanking us for filing the appeal.

Once inside the PUC building, I insisted on going to the men's restroom so Miss Klein went to the ladies room. I hesitated, watched her go into the ladies, and turned around and went to find the legal offices, which supported the PUC. It was easy to find so I walked in and asked to talk to a lawyer. I was introduced to a slightly overweight, blonde guy with a shaggy blonde mustache named Mr. Schmidt. I asked to speak to him in private.

I told him my suspicions about the lawyers from MBCI and suggested we have a private meeting to discuss the ramifications. He said PA had the Sunshine Law and all discussions should be held in open session but in this case, maybe a short private session would be appropriate. He sent a clerk to get both of the MBCI lawyers and Miss Klein.

Once the five of us were in his office and after introductions were made, he said he wanted to have a private conversation before the hearing. He reminded everyone he was not trying to avoid the Sunshine Law. If after hearing what was discussed, everything could always be talked about again in the open hearing.

Mr. Schmidt indicated I should speak. As I stood up, I glanced at my lawyer, Miss Klein, who now tried to shrink down in her chair and hide her face with her hands since she knew me well and knew this could not be good for all concerned.

I said, "On the first day of the month at 2:23 pm, I had a very prolonged phone call for 43 minutes with Mr. Ghant, who is here since he is an attorney for MBCI. He was confused and incoherent. He had trouble making any sense whatever. He couldn't even confirm who he is and what he wanted to say to me."

At that time, the chubby, balding Mr. Ghant jumped up and started to sputter about how he had trouble with understanding me. He tried to say I was the problem. My lawyer kept sighing and tried to hide down in her chair.

Mr. Schmidt stopped all the talk and confirmed he would make sure the hearing went smoothly. He indicated I should continue.

I did by saying, "On the tenth at 11:23 am, I had a call from the other MBCI attorney present here, Mr. Jekesen. We only talked for 5 minutes because he was recording the call without my knowledge. I was never asked for my permission to record the call".

I glanced over to see the young Mr. Jekesen slide down in his chair. He was turning pale as he looked at Mr. Ghant and said something, who hissed back that he should be quiet. I wasn't sure I should bring this up as maybe the sniffer wouldn't work but after their reaction, I knew the sniffer had worked and they had secretly recorded the call. My attorney, Miss Klein, glared up at me in daggers.

Mr. Ghant jumped up and yelled, "I object, they have no evidence".

Still standing, I pulled the sniffer from my pocket and said, "Oh yes, I do. This is a sniffer used by the CIA and other secret agencies to detect recordings on phone lines. It doesn't record the call but it kinda' magnifies and captures the sound of the recording device."

I showed them how it worked and played it back for them so they could hear the clicks.

I looked at the young Mr. Jekesen, who was almost to the point of tears as he saw an end to his legal future. He was facing disbarment and criminal charges for illegally recording a call.

"Mr. Schmidt, since this sniffer is probably not admissible in a court of law, we will push that no action be taken if Mr. Jekesen will excuse himself from this hearing and refrain from appearing at any other PUC activity in PA".

When presented with an easy out, Mr. Jekesen jumped up and said, "Mr. Schmidt, Miss Klein, and Mr. Bear, I apologize for any hint of impropriety, which may have resulted from my actions. I will remove myself from this hearing. I also terminate my employment at MBCI. I never wanted to work there anyway. I plan on starting a small legal practice in my hometown in upstate New York. I promise to walk the narrow legal path in the future."

Mr. Ghant was so overwhelmed he did not even think to jump up and object.

The attorney for the PUC took charge then by saying, "Now there are two final things to discuss. The first is we accept Mr. Jekesen's heartfelt apology with the understanding he better keep everything legal in the future or face proper punishment. The second thing is all of us agree this meeting NEVER took place."

We all verbally agreed.

Whew, I had made it through that hurdle. I needed to use the divide-and-conquer strategy since those lawyers presented me with the opportunity, but it was risky. I expected my lawyer, Miss. Klein, to expound about it – as soon as she got me alone.

We left the legal room and I beat a path to the men's restroom to avoid my lawyer and, well, I really had to go now. Stress seems to cause us older guys to need to go a lot and more often! We are just like little boys!

The official hearing started as soon as I was out of the restroom. The hearing room consisted of a table on a raised dais for PUC members, their lawyers and staff. There was a seat for a stenographer. There were chairs for the MBCI lawyers and a couple for us. Behind us were seats for an audience and behind the audience were reporters and cameramen from all the networks.

The audience section was full and noisy while the reporters were talking quietly into their microphones. This was live and the real thing. For all those people serving in uniform in dangerous zones around the world, I had to succeed.

After the hearing was called to order, we were given the first opportunity to address the PUC members. I put my left hand on Miss Klein's right shoulder to hold her down and I stood up and introduced myself as "Bear".

I was instructed to proceed.

"I could quote from MBCI's own web site, or from their license filing with this august commission, but I will paraphrase. All broadcasting stations in the Commonwealth of Pennsylvania are required to cover the news events impartially here in the States and around the world. They should be responsible to both themselves and their viewers and to the community. I submit to you that MBCI has failed in that objective.

"Since I filed this appeal, I have watched over 26 hours of news broadcasting on the local MBCI station and in all that time, only 23 minutes of reporting has been shown about the military serving in Iraq, and Afghanistan. That is not counting a few instances in which the President included references to these conflicts in his talks. This is such a minuscule percentage, it is not worth mentioning. We have some 200,000 troops serving in those two areas alone. Over 6,000 of those troops are from Pennsylvania. Each one of those brave people has many friends, families, and neighbors back here that worry about them.

"Also, the taxpayers such as you and I deserve to know how those wars are progressing and what problems and conditions are faced over there. How many people present have friends and family over there serving in harm's way?"

Looking around, I noticed almost every member in the audience raised an arm. I noticed no one from the media in the back raised a hand so I asked, "How many of you in the media in back have friends and family in the military?" A few raised their hand.

"So it is easy to see MBCI has shown a total disregard for all those brave men and women by not properly covering their service in war."

I sat down.

Now it was time for Mr. Ghant to speak, who represented MBCI. He jumped up and started to bellow and spit and sputter "Ladies and Gentlemen of the PUC, we have the constitutional right to free press in this country".

I jumped up and interrupted by yelling, "And Freedom of Speech".

Mr. Ghant added, "Yes, and Freedom of Speech'" He realized who had trumped him so he hesitated and stared hotly at me so I sat down. Then he got his wind back and went on, "You cannot control or direct the actions of the press as we have the right, nay, the obligation to broadcast whatever we want as long as it does not libel or …."

The Chairman of the PUC stopped Mr. Ghant, "We understand your position, Mr. Ghant".

Mr. Chant couldn't believe his turn to speak was cut so short but he sat down.

I rose and asked if I could speak again and I was approved by the board.

"Yes, we have many Freedoms in this country including Freedom of Speech and of the Press. Those Freedoms were won in battle by the brave men and women who serve in the military. All I am asking in this appeal is the media give back to those troops a respectful and responsible reporting of the wars underway in Iraq and Afghanistan. If combat isn't significant enough, then coverage could be of their living conditions or even of their families here at home. Far be it from me to try to tell someone what to report. But reporting should be done."

With that, the chairman of the PUC made the following statement. "I move we censure MBCI for failure to do responsible reporting of the military, which are in harm's way and that we revoke MBCI's license in thirty days if corrections in broadcasting aren't accomplished".

When a second wasn't voiced, the chairman said, "My motion dies from want of a second".

Mr. Ghant sighed happily and smiled at this recent development.

Then the lady to the left of the PUC chairman stood and proclaimed, "I'm ashamed of myself; I did not raise my arm when the question was asked about family members serving in the wars in the Middle East since I wanted to appear neutral. But I have a niece over there I think and worry about a lot. Therefore, I move we censor MBCI immediately and we revoke their license to broadcast in five days unless they change their ways. They have until Monday at 12:01 a.m."

There was an instant second. The chairman asked if there were any discussion. There wasn't any so he asked for a vote. It passed unanimously. Mr. Ghant put his head in his hands, devastated.

Before the PUC could leave, I stood up and said, "Pardon me please but I have more appeals to present to the PUC". I handed them towards the commission. I glanced back at the other reporters and cameramen as I said, "These appeals are for the other networks – they have been as negligent as MBCI. Since you have representatives from those networks present, maybe ask them what their plans are for responsible reporting of the military overseas."

The whole room went silent as a grave as my words were digested. Then the various and usually eager reporters flew out of the room in a rush. There were arms pumping and people pushing and shoving and yelling as the reporters left. It looked like there was free food and liquor being served somewhere else. Then the cameramen realized they were the only members of their networks left in the room and they exited stage right and left and middle.

I chuckled because I suspected the cameramen never had time to turn off their cameras. I would love to see what was captured on those cameras.

The audience in the PUC went wild. There was applause and laughter and chanting "BEAR BEAR BEAR!!!!!" You could hear the crowd outside pick up the chant also. Even the bailiff came over to shake my hand with a large smile and say, "Thanks so much. I am a veteran. We really needed someone to bring this to the forefront."

As we stepped outside, there was a roar of more BEAR chants. I looked around to find all traffic was stopped and people got out of their cars to join in the cheering and chanting and clapping. The police and the National Guard, which were there to direct traffic and for crowd-control, joined in the levity.

I pumped my arm in the air with the chants until I realized I could get arrested for inciting a riot so I stopped. The crowd parted. Miss Klein and I walked to the garage. There was a pretty young National Guard woman standing in front of the garage. She grabbed me and hugged me tightly and then kissed me on my expanding forehead, which the crowd loved. I enjoyed it also. I like to see pretty women in uniform.

The crowd parted so Miss Klein could drive us out of Harrisburg and towards home. As soon as we were moving south on I-83, Miss Klein started an expected discussion, "Does that sniffer work? Does it really detect recording on phone lines?"

"Yes, it does."

"I hoped it did. But let me tell you something, Bear, you will never ever accuse anyone and especially lawyers of anything at any time without discussing it with me first or I will strangle you. Do you realize what could have happened to you if things had turned out differently? Do you understand?"

"Yes, I understand. I knew it was a gamble going with that strategy but…" I replied.

She sighed. (*I have that effect on people – even when I do not try sometimes.*)

Since it was approaching lunch time, I suggested we stop at a favorite donut place of mine to get a maple iced donut and coffee. Miss Klein agreed. She knew just how to get there too, which surprised me.

The donut shop was close but the roads are tricky. You need to make left turns at places without a traffic light. It always seemed to me to be quite difficult to drive there. But the shapely and yet trim Miss Klein knew an even better way. She looked like she never had a donut in her whole life but she sure knew the best way to get off of southbound I-83 and make it to that donut shop in record time. Who would have suspected?

Miss Klein ordered when I went to the restroom.

I joined Miss Klein at the booth. I sipped on the good coffee and munched on a delicious maple iced donut. I could hear the TV set in the background. It was broadcasting the events in Harrisburg.

That was when the chunky girl behind the counter came over and asked if that was us in Harrisburg. She asked if I was that Bear?

"Yes, that was us."

The counter girl grabbed me and pulled me into a standing position and she hugged me and kissed me on the forehead. She turned her head and called back to the kitchen "Rani, come here".

Out came a tall black lady wearing an apron covered in sugar and flour. The counter girl explained who we were and what we had done at the PUC hearing. Rani grabbed me and pulled me into her ample bosom and began kissing me on the forehead. She alternated between kisses by telling me about her son and his service to his country. Luckily she released her hugging when she talked so I could breathe since I am short so my head was right between her boobs.

I was finally released and I stood there getting my breath back with flour and sugar all over me, when all three women started laughing. I felt the heat in my face and knew I was blushing. You would think at my advanced age I would have grown out of blushing, but I guess not! Yet again.

The counter girl brought me over two bags of donuts and apologized about being out of the maple iced donuts, but if we cared to wait, they would make more for us.

I thanked her and told her we declined to wait. We left.

During the ride, Miss. Klein asked, "Do you know what 'pro bono' means?"

"Yes."

"There will not be a bill as I am doing this 'pro bono' since you did all the work anyway and it is a very worthwhile effort. I applaud you. But if you ever accuse someone like that again, I will….. (*She gritted her teeth*)."

I left her by saying, "Be sure to watch the national news tonight."

She raised her eyebrows with a questioning look. She waved goodbye as we departed on our separate ways.

The drive home was uneventful. I pulled into my driveway past the borough police car and put my car, the tank, in the garage. I

34

went back to the front porch and joined Chief of Police, Dulie Andrews, who was seated on my porch swing.

"How many reporters have you chased away?"

He replied, "This is the first one" as a media van pulled onto my front yard and a female reporter jumped out with her microphone in hand.

Chief Dulie sighed and got up and sauntered over to intercept the reporter. He held up his right hand to stop them and went into his best John Wayne impersonation, "Whoa there, Pilgrim. Can't you see that No Trespassing Sign?"

The young perfectly coiffed reporter said hurriedly, "Yes, but I really need to interview Mr. Bear. I want to get his opinion on all this."

Chief Dulie replied, "If you continue to invade this private property, I will arrest you and turn you over to the State Police."

"But?" she asked.

He replied, "There will be an interview at the borough activity center at 7 p.m. tonight but it will start at 7 and no one will be admitted after that."

The reporter wasn't happy but she left after seeing the stern look on Chief Dulie's face.

My buddy Reets, tall and cadaverous and ancient, came walking around my house while using his five iron as a cane.

Chief Dulie said, "Deputy Reets is watching the back to chase away any paparazzi, who may attempt to invade that way."

Reets joined us on the porch and showed me his toy badge, which was pinned on his shirt.

I made coffee. We shared donuts while Chief Dulie and non-Deputy Reets chased away reporters. The reporters were all informed about the planned event that evening.

The donuts were the best kind, free and delicious. It is the same with beer; the best kind is the free kind!

At 6:30 p.m., we adjourned to watch the national news broadcast. The news anchor of MBCI did not fit the usual mold for a

TV reporter since he wasn't tall, good looking or pretty or cute. He was squat with an elongated misshapen face and a crooked nose. I never knew how he made it to the forefront unless he did it the old fashioned way by earning it.

He began, "We here at Mega Broad Cast Inc. want to apologize to all the viewers and especially to all those who currently serve and to those who have served in the United States Army, Air Force, Coast Guard, Marines and Navy and to their families and friends. It took an appeal filed with the Pennsylvania Public Utility Commission by a little known author, simply called Bear, to show us the error in our reporting. Bear filled this appeal by saying we here in MBCI have not properly and completely provided coverage of our military in the war in the Middle East."

They showed clips of my presentation in front of the PUC followed by the response of the audience.

He continued, "As Bear so artfully stated, we in the media forgot to give back to the troops, which give so much and ask for so little." He chuckled and went on, "At the end of our hearing, Bear presented more appeals against the other networks and asked the reporters present from the other networks to answer questions in behalf of their companies and this is what transpired".

Clips were shown of the mayhem as the reporters and cameramen vacated hastily the hearing room at the PUC.

He chuckled again and went on seriously, "At the same time that this hearing was taking place in Harrisburg, similar appeals were filled with every PUC and PSC across this great nation. There were crowds of peaceful demonstrations in front of and surrounding every PUC and PSC as these appeals was filed."

They showed some of the crowds and their signs. The signs usually referred to a demand for responsible reporting.

"MBCI will now switch to our reporters in Iraq and Afghanistan. First in Iraq is……"

I interrupted him to start to fume and fuss about that "little known author" stuff. Who did they think they were?

Chief Dulie and non-Deputy Reets laughed out loud. They said goodbye and went to handle an expected unruly crowd of reporters at the community activity building.

I was told later that the interview went as follows.

Chief Dulie and non-Deputy Reets went into the community building and locked the doors promptly at 7 p.m.

Chief Dulie jumped on the stage and made the following announcement, "Attention everyone, the interview will start promptly. The doors will stay locked until 8 pm. You may leave any time after that time."

This brought a round of lots of comments you could not hold the media as hostages and they would all file suit. Chief Dulie reminded all of them about the sign on the door outside that read, "The doors would remain closed for one hour starting at 7 p.m. tonight. If you want, I can show you a video of you all walking past that sign." He pointed at a smiling non-Deputy Reets (with the toy badge) holding up a camera.

"Now then, all of this was never about Bear. It is not now nor ever been about him. Any of you who persist in bugging Bear for an interview will probably be arrested and charged with criminal trespassing and/or other crimes. It is best for your well-being if you leave Bear alone.

"All of this is ONLY about our valiant and brave military personnel and their families, who have given so much and expect so little. With that in mind, let's bring out your guests here today."

He introduced a WWII veteran, who was helped on stage by his wife. The third person was a young looking mother and her son, an amputee who served in Iraq. The next person was a young reservist who was on his way to Afghanistan. There was a veteran of Vietnam who had cancer, which he suspected was from handling Agent Orange and two Marines who had been on the front in Korea. Lastly, there was a married military couple and their kids to talk about problems, when both parents are serving in a war zone.

Chief Dulie and non-Deputy Reets left after unlocking the doors. We heard later the news media spent a lot of time there and everyone was pleased about how tastefully the forced interviews went. The response from their viewers was positive also. I had prayed the self-serving reporters wouldn't have snubbed the veterans and military personnel by just leaving in a fit of anger.

Chief Dulie and non-Deputy Reets spent the night with me at my house to ensure I wasn't bothered. Since they were both going to guard me anyway, it was decided the best place to do the watching and protecting was on the golf course. We played 18 holes each of the next two days and enjoyed ourselves. My good buddy Bench even came to town to help protect me. He filled out the foursome. Bench had to make the ultimate sacrifice and leave the love of his life for a few days to do so. His main squeeze is, of course, Miss Jacky Mooney of the Sunshine Show, an afternoon talk show and she is gorgeous!!!

GRADUATION

By now you have probably figured me out. I am known simply as Bear. I am an award winning writer of stories, articles and books. The awards are too numerous to list. I have also won an Emmy for the Sunshine Show on television. If you GOOGLED Bear properly, you could also learn my true identity and the infamous part I have played in the history of this great nation. I could tell you about that now but I think I will save that for a later time.

I avoid the media at all costs, but my agent and publisher are constantly pushing me to appear as often as possible so that they can make more money off of my writing. They view it this way; the more appearances I make, more of my books are sold and the more money they make. If the truth would be known, more people buy my books due to the weird circumstances, which occur as a direct result of my extreme attempts to avoid the public and the media.

The media calls me a reclusive celebrity. The truth is not only do I detest talking in front of an audience, but also I fear talking in public. The fear is magnified twenty times when I have to be in front of a camera on stage.

I'm telling you this since I must be the keynote speaker at the upcoming graduation ceremonies at my alma mater.

I had the following conversation with the graduation coordinator, Florie. Florie is short for Florida; some first name right?

Here is how the call ended.

Florie said, "You will be the keynote speaker, Mr. Harvey ….?"

"No", I interrupted her loudly and sharply. "My name is Bear, just Bear. If you call me anything else, or print anything other than Bear, I will gladly sue your esteemed college." I huffed and puffed, while I caught my breath.

The phone went silent for a moment, and she said, "Okay, I guess we can agree to that condition."

"Also, you must agree to my way of giving the speech."

This made Florie stop to think since the keynote speaker always stands in front of the graduation gathering and does a thank-you/spiritual-save-the-world speech. They start by telling the graduates to thank all of the people, who provided financial or mental assistance. Then the speaker progresses to the part about where it is up to the graduates to make the world a better place and to give back more than they have received. I intended on covering both parts of the speech but in my own way, the Bear way.

Florie said, "No problem, I think."

I asked, "I will need a small private room to get ready."

She agreed.

To carry out my plan, I required someone with sophisticated camera skills; you will understand why later. I knew just who to call to obtain said cameraman. My good buddy, Bench is the main squeeze of Miss Jacky Mooney of the Sunshine Show.

I called using my new-fangled cell phone, which should have all of the numbers in memory, but who knows since I am technologically challenged.

Bench answered in his deep masculine voice, "Hello, Bear."

"Hi Bench. How are you? Getting over to the stadium to watch the bombers playball much?"

He chuckled and said, "No, I'm much too busy to get to many ball games."

I ignored his reference to being busy since he appears on the Sunshine Show as just a prop, a big silent prop standing with crossed arms (and biceps showing) in the background, but I guess the ladies find him easy to look at.

I asked, "Is Miss Jacky there? I'd like to speak to her."

"Sure thing."

A minute later, she said, "Hello, Bear. How are you doing?"

"Fine, Miss Jacky. It is good to talk to you. But I need a favor. Do you know any cameramen who are quite good at what they do and not too expensive? Old Bears don't have much money, you know."

She ignored my comments about lack of funds. She probably knew I was doing quite nicely from the royalties.

She asked me for specifics about what I required. I told her.

She said, "Yes, there is a good man by the name of Croc. Mention my name and he will probably do it cheaply."

I thanked her and talked to Bench awhile before I ended the call.

I called Croc's number and made the arrangements for the graduation day ceremonies. We agreed on a price, which included his travel, hotel, and food.

(*By now, you are pretty much confused, I'll bet.*) Why do I need a cameraman to do a speech at a graduation? Especially when I fear being in front of cameras as much as I do talking in front of a large gathering of people.

I had it figured out. There was one way I could do the speechifying while in front of a camera and I would not be bothered much by doing it.

On the day of the ceremony, I put my college robe and mortar board (the ones I had worn to my own graduation eons ago) in my car. I had the robe dry cleaned and pressed but after wearing it for ten minutes, it would be wrinkled and rumpled. This was just the effect I had on clothes.

I met Croc, the cameraman, at a pre-arranged spot. He was short and squat with lots of curly, reddish hair. He did not talk much on the way to the college. He just sipped his coffee.

We arrived at the campus. I met Florie, a dazzling beauty about six feet tall with brown cascading locks and dark rimmed glasses. She was in a robe and mortar board. She led us to the private room for us to use. She never once asked who Croc was or what he was doing here. I did not volunteer the information either. The less said the better.

Croc and I went over everything and he set up his equipment. He went outside and viewed the podium where I was to give my speech; while he was there he hid both a speaker and a microphone.

We sat down and waited.

Finally, it was my time. The introduction of a York College alumnus by the name of Bear was quite flowerily with all kinds of compliments. This came, of course, after the invocation by a local pastor of note.

I was standing in the private room under a spotlight. I was in front of the special camera and I was wearing the cap and gown. After a fashionably late interval, Croc turned on his camera and my image and voice were projected back to the podium and right behind the microphone. I cleared my throat and then we could hear the oohes and aahes as the audience understood.

They were watching a hologram of me dressed in my cap and gown, which I expected to be fairly stable except if a light breeze sprang up or someone walked directly into my silky image. I started to speak by thanking all of the dignitaries, graduates, parents and friends, which were in attendance. I went first into the thank-you phase of the speech.

We could hear a giggle or someone talking once in a while but besides that, everything was going fine until I hesitated at an appropriate time to let the content sink in. Then my remote audience roared with laughter and applause. I gave Croc a quizzical look but he quieted me by rolling his hand for me to continue. I did.

Everything went as I had planned except for the roars of laughter whenever I hesitated in my speech. Finally, the speech was over, thank goodness!

I thanked everyone again and the crowd went crazy with laughter and applause. I was totally confused by this. If anything, those people in attendance at this august ceremony should have been upset I was making a mockery of the whole important event, instead they were laughing.

Maybe now would be a good time to explain. I knew I couldn't stand in front of all those people and make an hour-long speech. I came up with the idea of having my image and voice projected to the podium. I thought I could handle the speechifying this way.

I sipped a glass of water before making the long walk to the stage since I was to be on stage to shake the graduates' hands after they received their diplomas.

I walked boldly upon stage with a prop in my hand. Once on stage, I held the prop in front of my face. The prop is a carved face of an angry bear on a handle. I could hold it in front of my face whenever I wanted to. My buddy, Bench had made it for me in his workshop.

I expected laughter now but all I could see was every graduate holding up an exact copy of my bear mask in front of their faces. I glanced around the stage and everybody was also holding a bear mask in front of their faces. The audience went ballistic.

People were rushing around taking pictures and laughing. After an exceedingly long time, the Dean of Students called for quiet so the commencement could continue. I lowered my mask and everyone followed suit, which helped to restore order. I had noticed that the other masks were an exact paper copy of my mask. Also, their masks did not have handles.

It was time to hand out the diplomas. The first name was called. The young lady came on stage and shook hands with everyone except for me. She stopped in front of me and put the mask in front of her face. I lifted my mask up in front of my face. We shook hands and turned to face the audience so pictures could be taken of just the two of us, Bears with the same face. That same protocol was followed for every graduate. At the end of the event, the graduates threw their bear masks in the air and made quite a ruckus.

Finally, the event was over. I shook hands on stage and murmured bathroom and made a hasty exit stage right. I received many thank you's, endured endless handshakes and back pats before I was able to get away. I stopped at a men's room and took care of that business first, of course.

I was finally starting to breathe easy as I walked back to my private camera room.

I opened the door and found an empty room. It was completely bare except for the table and chairs it contained when we entered. The room even looked like it had been cleaned. I couldn't figure out where Croc had gone. His specialized equipment wasn't too heavy or bulky but I couldn't picture him carrying it a long distance. Plus I hadn't even paid him yet.

I left the room and went to my car and drove to where I had met Croc. His car was gone. Interesting?

On the way home, I stopped and picked up carry out Chinese food. At home, I made a cup of green tea and consumed my late lunch.

I stayed inside in social hibernation even though the weather was warm and sunny. The constant ringing of the phone almost drove me crazy.

I wanted to venture outside in the glorious weather but I expected to see lots of media vans filled with paparazzi out there. I endured the ringing, which were probably more reporters.

I tried to write on my next manuscript but finally gave up and sat in my favorite old easy chair and watched the golf tournament on television. I dozed off there since I had had a very restlessness night. I was consumed about my appearance at the graduation exercises.

The next morning, I made coffee before venturing outside to grab the newspaper. I now wish that I did not read the Sunday paper. The college graduation ceremony was on the front page with a special insert covering it.

The front page headline was LOCAL COLLEGE GRADUATION IS BEARABLE. It mainly showed pictures of everyone including me, the dignitaries and the graduates. All holding up bear masks. But at the bottom of the page, it showed me in my cap and gown as a hologram behind the lectern. Then it showed similar pictures except they all were weird as if I was standing in a house of mirrors.

In the first picture, I was triangular with the pointy end at my feet and wide end at my shoulders with another triangle for a head. The next showed me as a shimmering disappearing image. The third ones were a series of photographs that showed me disappearing from the top down and reappearing from the bottom up. I opened the insert quickly and counted twenty different weird images of me as I talked. That would account for all of the laughter; the audience was viewing these miscues as I paused. Could this have been a flaw in the broadcasting equipment or was it done on purpose to humiliate me? After all, I continue to made enemies.

I refilled my coffee cup and turned on the TV news. My distorted images filled every news channel. The reporters laughed a lot at all of those weird holograms. The shows all concentrated on my appearance at commencement and did not once mention any of the other ceremonies, which took place on the same day across the country. The President was at one in his home state, but the media ignored it. The media was doing its usual story de jour. They would show this and analyze it and discuss it until everyone was sick of it.

I then gasped as I realized that all of this was on the internet; people across the world would view all of this and laugh. But would they laugh at me or with me? Who knew?

I turned off the television and called Croc, the cameraman to get his spin on what caused the distorted images of me to happen. He answered in a rough and uneven voice, which did not sound right.

I said, "Croc, this is Bear. What happened to your equipment yesterday? I looked terrible. I thought this was supposed to be uneventful."

"Nothing happened to my equipment. I wasn't there yesterday", he replied slowly.

"What?" I hesitated. "Yes, you were there."

"No, I wasn't. You called me about two weeks ago and told me to forget it."

I was confused.

I asked him, "Are you short and overweigh with lots of red curly hair?"

"No, I am 6 foot 4 inches and weigh 180 pounds."

"What?" I asked again only more sharply.

"Well, ok, I only weigh about 175 pounds. I am a string bean and I am losing my dark hair. There is no red hair here", he admitted.

That totally floored me. I was speechless.

I asked, "Do you know any media technicians who match that description, short, fat, red hair?"

"Come to think of it, no, I do not."

"Did you recognize the voice who called you on the phone?"

"Again, no. I am a video man, not an audio man. Ask your friend Miss Jacky Mooney to describe me. Did you pay him?"

"No", I admitted.

"Well there you have it. I would never leave without getting paid. Not yesterday and not ever." Then he said with conviction, "I do not ever discuss business with anyone but the customer. I am ethical to a fault which is why you were referred to me and not to someone else." He hung up.

I did not have any ideas at all now. I was totally stumped. I made my coffee warm and looked out of the front picture window just in time to see a line of media vans slowly idling on the street past my NO TRESPASSING signs. They must have learned not to stop when those signs were up. After a while, the media would go off and pursue another hot story and forget about me.

I warmed up leftover Chinese food for brunch and contemplated this situation. I wanted to call Miss Jacky Mooney of the Sunshine Show to get her opinion about who may have been responsible for setting me up with a substitute cameraman, but I wasn't ready to discuss this with anyone. I have made many people angry at me over time. I would not be able to narrow down the list easily. This would take time and luck.

I did not suspect either Bench or Miss Jacky Mooney of the Sunshine Show of arranging this though. I have only a small inner cadre of friends and they have all proven their steadfastness time and again. If not them, then could my house or phone be bugged?

I had a way to determine if that was the case since one of my friends is Reets, who had worked for some of those alphabet clandestine services for many years. He still dabbled in all of that stuff. I looked out the window to ensure that the slimy reporters were not around. Since I did not see any, I went into the garage, started and backed my large old 60's model custom car out of the garage and went to Reets' home.

Reets was like me, an aggravating old man. He would help me but I had to feed him first. He ate whenever there was food in front of him, just like I did. I arrived at his home and parked by his large work shed. I went in the door to find a cluttered shed that probably contained everything from slate and chalk to more ultra-modern spyware.

I saw Reets, who is tall and gaunt. He was in the back of the shed working on something.

I yelled his name.

He answered without looking up by saying, "Go away. I don't want or need anything."

"How about supper?"

He turned and brightened up and exclaimed, "Let's go."

I said, "Not so fast, kemo sabe. I need some help." I described what I wanted. He found it quickly and we got in my car and left.

I asked, "Why didn't you lock the door to the shed?"

He replied smugly, "Anybody trying to get in my shed or house IS IN FOR A BIG SURPRISE." He chuckled to himself.

I did not ask what that was all about. I guess that I did not want to know. We stopped and had supper at Old Bob's Café. Bob had been a Navy cook. He ran his greasy spoon just like he had run his galley on board ship. He would not tolerate any problems like the media trying to bother his customers. It was safe to eat here. I just wasn't sure it was healthy to eat here but that is another issue.

At my house, Reets first silenced me by putting his finger to his lips. He used a tiny device about the size of a golf ball to check for bugs. He did not find any.

He asked, "How did you call Miss Jacky and the cameraman?"

I held out my cell phone and said, "On this."

He smiled with a crooked smile and took the cell phone from my hands and removed a chip from it. He laid the chip on the counter and walked into my garage. He laid the cell phone on the garage floor and took a hammer off of my work bench. Reets smirked at me and then he pulled the hammer over his head and swung the hammer down and broke my cell phone into pieces.

I yelled, "No".

Reets looked up at me and admonished me, "Do not ever conduct sensitive conversations over a cell phone Bear. Has there been any strangers lurking about?"

"Hmmmm, let me see. There was one man who walked down the alley a few times, I guess. But that was some time ago."

Reets said, "It wouldn't take a professional much time to record your calls, Bear. Do you have any beer?"

So that was it. My calls had been listened to and I had been set up. Reets interrupted my thoughts as he went back into my kitchen and was helping himself to my beer.

I joined him. He said, "Take this chip to the store. It contains all of your saved contacts. At the store, they will load this into your new phone."

Changing subjects, he asked, "Isn't there a game on television now?"

We sat and watched the game and finished off my supply of beer or should I say that Reets finished off my supply. I only drank one since I had to drive Reets home.

Sleep didn't arrive easily so I got up and contemplated this strange turn of events. Finally I took out a piece of paper and a pen and tried to analyze the situation. My thoughts and writing about the graduation ceremony went this way.

Was what they did to me illegal? No. Was it unethical? Maybe. However it was not in good taste to make a mockery of such an important event like a graduation ceremony. It could even be thought this applied to my activities with the camera as well as to the way my image was made comical.

I thought about why someone would arrange this. Was it done for some purpose other than to make fun of me? What could anyone gain?

Then it hit me.

All in all, this episode would just add negative publicity about me. Publicity could make more people want to buy copies of my writing, which would increase sales of my books and articles. The only people who would make money from the sales of my writing other than myself would be the publisher and my sneaky agent, one Cliff Loews, self-proclaimed Agent to the Stars. It would be just like Cliffy to arrange this so he would make more money to waste on trips to the French Rivera or to Un-holly-wood.

I had arrived at the correct answer; I was sure, since he was one of the few people who knew my cell phone number. Now what to do about it? I wasn't sure exactly but I did decide to keep a wary eye on the Cliffster until I could prove it. I would just have to give him rope enough to let him hang himself, I guess.

Tomorrow after breakfast at Old Bob's Café, I would go to the cell phone store and purchase a new cell phone. It would be just my luck the style of cell phone had changed enough so I would have to purchase a new charger. It was a technique employed by the cell phone suppliers to ensure they took more of our money.

Yes, I know, I am still a cheap old Bear.

The added publicity due to the many people worldwide laughing at the web broadcast of the disappearing and shimmering Bear at the graduation ceremony would only add to the mystique that is me, an old reclusive Bear.

CALLIE

I went to bed at 9:30 p.m. and fell asleep before my head hit the pillow. Now I know that 9:30 is early, but I had been deer hunting. It was the last day for deer in this license year and it was a cold and windy. When old farts get inside after being out in the cold, we can't stay awake long, but I managed to stay awake until after 9. Oh boy!

I came awake with a start and glanced at the bedside clock, which said that it was after 10 p.m. There was a light on in my kitchen and I could hear the sound from the TV.

Strange! I had only given my keys to two people. Bench has one but he isn't expected back in town for a couple weeks and the other is Chief Dulie, the chief of police of this borough. Well, maybe he got in trouble with his lovely wife and she kicked him out to teach him a lesson so he came here to spend the night. That must be it. I peeked around the wall of the hallway.

I was surprised to see a young girl, a teenager, sitting in my glider. She had my remote in her hand and she was switching stations. I turned and went back in my bedroom and took my 20 gauge double barrel shotgun from under the bed. I loaded both barrels with number 6 shot.

I stood up and said in a confused and sleepy tone, "Is that you Bench?"

I walked to the dining room and raised the shotgun so it was pointed directly at her alarmed face.

She had started to stand up and answer, "No, I'm Callie Bonnet and I'm....." and then her eyes focused on the business end of the shotgun pointed at her head. She went white and slowly sank back in the chair.

"Who are you and what are doing in my house watching my TV?" I demanded.

She stammered and seemed confused. Now might be a good time to describe who or should I say what she was looking at. I am a skinny, short, frail-looking old man and my remaining tuffs of white hair were sticking out at all angles. I was wearing my favorite blue micro fiber shiny pajamas with the big yellow smiling face on the chest and I had that shotgun pointed right at her head. Also, I was trying to look as serious as I could. (*To tell the truth, I was close to laughter as I watched her surprised and scared reaction. But she needed to be taught a serious lesson about breaking into someone's house uninvited especially in the middle of the night!*).

"Come on, out with it, who are you and did you steal anything?"

She started to regain her composure and said, "I'm, I'm, well, er…, I'm C-C-Callie Bonnet and I came to get an exclusive interview with you for the school paper, the Tattler. You know it is the early bird that gets the worm, right? So how about that interview?" She started to get up off my glider.

"Not so fast, Missy! This breaking and entering stuff could get you in jail or worse, it could get you dead. Don't move," I yelled at her, while keeping the shotgun within a few feet of her face.

I finally found the cell phone but then I had to search for Chief Dulie's phone number.

Callie said, "Oh, no. You aren't calling the police are you?"

"Damn right, I am. You can either shoot someone who breaks and enters or you can just turn them over to police."

"But I only wanted to get an exclusive interview for the school paper. I wasn't going to steal anything. Honest. I did not break anything to enter; I, just, well, picked your locks and came in." She pleaded and almost sobbed.

I had found Chief Dulie's cell phone number and I called it while maintaining the direction of the shotgun right at Callie, who looked devastated.

Chief Dulie answered on the first ring so he must have had night duty.

"Hi Chief. I've got a problem with a burglar. I have a gun on the suspect. Can you come here?"

He replied hurriedly, "Don't shoot anybody Bear. I'll be right there."

Callie just sighed and started to weep silent tears.

She mumbled, "Now I have really done it. I'll get expelled."

I saw the flashing lights in the front of the house, so I walked over to the door to the garage, opened it and hit the opener so that Chief Dulie could come in the house through the garage. He practically ran in. But he stopped suddenly when he saw that the burglar was a typical teen age girl of about 15 or 16. She had medium length brown hair, and was wearing a Penn State sweat shirt, jeans and dirty tennis shoes. She had her head in her hands and was weeping while still sitting in my glider.

"OK. Bear, what happened?"

"I was asleep and woke up to find her in my chair and watching my TV. Not knowing who or what it was, I got the shotgun to come out to confront the intruder."

She had raised her head and was watching us talk.

"Who are you? What are you doing here?" Chief Dulie demanded.

She shook her head and began, "I'm Callie Bonnet; I'm a junior at the high school. I thought I could get an exclusive interview with Mr. Bear since he is SO famous now. I could get an A in English composition and show up all those self-righteous rich kids. But when I got here, the house was dark and I let myself in. I couldn't work up the nerve to wake him up. I just had a seat here to decide what to do. In a few minutes, he came out with that hideous GUN and pointed it right at me. Then he called you. Oh, I am in SO much trouble."

Before the Chief could ask any more questions, I made a suggestion, "Chief, I would like to put this shotgun away so please put this dangerous felon in hand cuffs." I winked at him. He slowly took out his hand cuffs and put them on Callie. I took my time in lowering the shotgun and removing the shells, which I sat on their bases right there at her end of the table. Her eyes were wide open in fear and wonder both at being hand cuffed and at seeing those shells.

"How did you get in?" Chief Dulie asked.

"Oh, I'm naturally good at stuff. I just seem to know how to pick locks especially the older models like this house has. It didn't seem like a big deal at the time since I was determined to get the interview," she said dejectedly.

"Bear, make some coffee. I'll check outside," Chief Dulie said slowly. He went back out through the garage and I set about making coffee. I heard Callie mutter something but I did not turn around to ask.

Chief Dulie came back in and asked Callie, "Is that old bicycle outside yours? Is that how you got here?"

"Yes, it is. I live just down off of Forrest Oak Avenue."

"Oh, I know you now. I've seen you riding that bike around town. I will call your mother, I guess", he said.

"We do not have a phone and Mom probably forgot to charge her cell phone. We do not have anything", she said quietly.

I turned to get the coffee and heard a hiss from Chief Dulie and a giggle from Callie. I turned around and Chief Dulie pointed at the back of my pants, which has another smiling yellow face across the rear.

He exclaimed, "Pull up those pants, Bear. We are seeing more than we want to." (*That is the trouble with having a skinny old butt; my pants keep falling down*).

I hurriedly pulled up my sagging bottoms. I turned to get the coffee and served all three of us coffee with my favorite flavored creamer. Chief Dulie wrote something on a piece of paper and handed it to me. The paper read she doesn't have a criminal record, which he had checked while he was outside.

Callie had to use both hands, which were still handcuffed together to sip the coffee but she seemed to really enjoy it.

She remarked, "I have never had such good coffee before. This is great."

I got up and made her a peanut butter and jelly sandwich with chips. She was almost like a hungry dog, which has food put in front of it. The dog will just gulp it until the food is gone. That was the way that she attacked that sandwich. I made her another cup of coffee with creamer.

Chief Dulie and I must have both been thinking the same thing so I said, "Do you realize you could have ended up with a criminal record for breaking and entering? Or worse, that I could have shot you for illegally entering my home? A criminal charge would always be on record so you could forget college, or getting a good job. Do you have any idea about all that?"

She replied in a very quietly and subdued manner, "I have no present and no future. Mom is always so depressed. She just manages to make enough money for us to stay in that old house and to feed us. I don't think she cares much about me or about anything. I learned a long time ago how to care for myself and how to come and go as I want. She probably doesn't even know I am not at home now. College will NOT happen for me." She sighed.

Chief Dulie asked, "Don't you have dreams?"

She replied "I want to fly" and she pointed up.

"There are ways to at least try to get you flying, but first, we need to address this breaking and entering thing you are facing," I said. "Are you prepared to work hard at trying to succeed at something or are you positive you can't get there? It is all up to you."

"What do you mean? I do not understand," she said

"First, we ask the good Chief here not to arrest you, although he should. Then we put together a plan to get you in college, and maybe, just maybe, if you work hard you might have a chance at flying. But you must always, always, always keep out of trouble. Excel at school and graduate first. Talk to me before you contemplate doing something this stupid ever again. How are you grades?"

"Mostly B's and C's. I do not need to try much to get them."

"That is the first step then. From now on, you must get A's."

I remembered something I had read about in the local newspaper.

I asked Callie "What is your school project? Don't you need one to graduate?"

"I don't have one. I haven't even thought about it" She quipped.

"Well, that has to change. Let me think about it. Also, I could use some help around here after school so you could earn some spending money and make use of my internet connection to help with your school work. What should we tell your Mother about this?"

"She might not really notice since she doesn't get home from work until after 6 p.m."

Chief Dulie admonished her, "I will keep a record of tonight's events. The statute of limitation doesn't run out on B and E for six years so you must keep yourself out of trouble or I will find you and arrest you. I know Bear and once he makes his mind up, he gets what he wants, but he can be wicked to those who have offended him so keep that in mind. I'll put your bike in the trunk of the cruiser and take you home. You better listen to my buddy, Bear!!" he said as he removed her hand cuffs.

"Be here after school tomorrow. Bring your books to study. Leave your Mother a note if you think that is best. We will discuss how to handle her so she approves of the new Callie and of her reaching her dreams and goals", I said. "N o m o r e t r o u b l e." I spelled it out very seriously.

As she left with Chief Dulie, she looked back at me with kind of a questioning look on her pretty round face as if to say, "What is happening? What have I got myself in for? Is he real? Does he really believe in me?"

On the next afternoon around 4 p.m., I was sitting on the swing on the front porch enjoying the unseasonably warm sun and the light breeze as I contemplated my writing while I sipped on some coffee.

I am a writer but I live almost like a college student. I eat carryout or at the local café, I drink coffee and beer (too much coffee but not much beer), and my clothes are in various piles of unclean on the bedroom floor.

Callie actually arrived on her bicycle. I was curious if she was going to try to uphold her end of the bargain, which was reached last night. She jumped off the bike in the middle of the driveway and started to walk towards me when I interrupted her by saying, "Put the bike off to the side there in case someone pulls a car into my driveway." (*I did not know who that someone was but I wanted to start off with her by getting her to think of someone else first!*) She moved her bike and then brought her books over and laid them on the bench and plopped down. She looked kinda' gloomy.

I said, "There is pie in the kitchen; please cut me a piece. If you want one, bring yourself a piece. Fix yourself coffee if you want it. There is that flavored creamer in the 'fridge. Let's enjoy it out here in the pretty weather." I had made a run to pick up groceries this morning. I suspected she did not eat much.

She brought out the pie for us. Then she went back in and brought out her coffee.

I asked, "Did you wash your hands?" She glared at me.

"I know what you are thinking. That is what the in-crowd at school would say to you to make you feel bad and small; to make it seem like they are better than you. But I only asked because this is about you and I and we must be honest with each other if this is to work at all." That made her think some as we sat there sipping coffee and eating cherry pie.

"I won't ask you how school went as I expect nothing but A's and no trouble of any kind. But I will answer any questions you might have. Do you have any, Miss Callie?"

She shook her head side to side sadly.

"What time should you be home?"

"Seven or so."

"Ok. Do you need to use my internet connection to do your assignments tonight?"

"No", she replied quietly.

"If you can do your homework at home, then you can start to work now."

"Ok", she murmured.

"The first thing we need is a contract. Call it a mentoring contract. Think about what you expect and we will agree on the terms tomorrow afternoon. We will both sign it.

"Can you fold clothes? I can't. I used to try to fold clothes for inspection when I was in the Army. After I got married, my wife Midee (*pronounced mydee*) did all the laundry. But she has been gone for many years. Now I have piles and piles of clothes. It would be great if you helped me with that. Please put these dishes in the dishwasher after rinsing them."

We went inside. As we walked past my computer room, I asked her, "Do you do all this new technology?"

She was caught off guard. She asked, "Huh?"

"Do you know computers, cell phones, printers, voice recorders and digital cameras? I can't seem to get them to work at all."

"Yes. All that stuff is easy."

Spare me the youth and their command of new technology, but maybe Miss Callie might save me a lot of grief and heartache. I smiled at her and winked. That seemed to cheer to her up.

"Forget that laundry for now. I can never find any phone numbers, I only remember three phone numbers and one of those is 911. Can you program numbers in this cell phone? When I have trouble with something like cell phones or laptops, I just go buy another one and have the sales person set it up for me."

Callie spent three hours as she cleaned up my latest cell phone and laptop (*it would have taken her only a few minutes but I kept interrupting to ask questions*). She loaded the phone numbers that I call the most. She then instructed me on how to use the cell phone. This was going to take a lot longer than I thought. I waved good bye with the cell phone as she left. Over the next few months, Callie would often have to redo my technical devices, after I messed them up. Again.

When she showed up the next afternoon, she seemed a little more relaxed and not as gloomy. We shared coffee and donuts and we started to discuss the contract. It finally ended up like this;

Mentoring Contract between Bear and Miss Callie Bonnet.
Bear agrees to mentor Miss Bonnet. Mentoring will include but not be limited to providing advice, assisting with homework and the senior project, and providing incentives for Miss Bonnet's success in the future. Bear agrees to pay $2 for each A on her report card. Miss Bonnet agrees to maintain or improve grades and finish her senior project. She agrees to do part time work for Bear (for pay if agreed to prior to the work being done). Such work would constitute household duties and other jobs that are agreeable to both parties. Miss Bonnet agrees to be cheery and pleasant at all time and to stay out of trouble. Nothing that is illegal, illicit, explicit or sexual will be permitted at any time. Honesty between the parties will be the norm.

There was a section at the end of the contract for Callie's mother to sign her approval and there was a place for Chief Dulie to sign as an overseer.

Chief Dulie stopped by so the three of us signed the contract. We also discussed how to get Callie's Mother to sign it. After Chief Dulie left, Callie started to work on mission impossible, which is cleaning up my laptops. She told me it would be possible to reload word processing on my old laptop so I could write all my books and stories on that laptop since it had a larger keyboard. It would not be connected to the web and would be password protected. I could backup using a flash drive.

I informed Callie, "You have already earned your way. I have wanted to have that done for a long time. I need to protect my manuscripts.

"What is your schedule for Saturday? Maybe we could get started on those piles of clothes then. I can pay you $10.00 for work on Saturday."

She shuddered in distaste but said she could be here by noon.

"Noon is not acceptable. Be here by 8 am for breakfast and we can get started early." (*If what I had planned for her worked out, she had better get used to early starts and long days and cleanliness!*)

"How do we present this contract to your Mother? She should be aware and agreeable to this mentoring contract."

"I don't know. I'll think about it. See you tomorrow Mr. Bear."

She was late on Saturday by 21 minutes. I asked her, "Should I dock your pay for being late?"

Miss Callie responded, "Why? I'll just stay until the laundry is finished." (*She would soon learn why!*) We had coffee and leftover donuts and got started on this hideous task.

We agreed to wash everything. Callie knew even less than I did about laundry so we started by separating everything into various colors. We made a pile of clothing, which needed to be thrown away. I am too old to be embarrassed about my underwear but Callie seemed to be embarrassed by all the old underwear I had left simmer in the piles of dirty and smelly clothing.

It took both of us to decide how to use the washing machine. We succeeded in washing and drying everything. Callie folded my clothing but she still needed practice, which I would gladly provide in the future. We had pizza for lunch. I paid her the $10.00. Yeah, I know I should have paid her a lot more since she obviously needed the funds, but I'm not like our governments who believe throwing money at a problem will fix it.

Callie was given Sunday off but she showed up anyway. We started to work on my late wife's clothes. I hadn't touched any of her clothes since the time of her death. I just couldn't find the courage to do so.

Callie separated the clothes into ones to donate to charity and ones to take to a consignment store to sell. I stayed in the background and tried to maintain my composure. I did not want to break down in front of Callie. I suspect that she knew how close I was to tears. Callie knew of a nearby consignment store. It is open on Sundays so we loaded the clothes into the tank. That's my large old custom mixed-heritage car and took the clothes to the store.

The plump, tall lady there knew Callie. I let them handle the sales arrangements. It sounded satisfactory. For her help, I suggested that Callie pick out some jeans and tops for herself. The sales lady put the charges on a tab, which would be deducted from the amount the clothes sold for. Callie seemed happy with the new-to-her clothes.

We stopped and had fast food on the way home. I asked if she had plans for the rest of the day. She declined to answer. I suggested that we go to the golf driving range. (*I suspected Callie would need to know more than what she learned in high school if she was to succeed with my plans for her college future*).

Callie tried her best but she had trouble with keeping her head down while she tried to hit the golf ball. It is problem all golfers need to suffer through, but she persisted and didn't give up. I would have to explore getting her a set of women's clubs.

Every day, I kept Callie busy with various and sundry chores. I tried to enforce the rules especially about being punctual, clean, and cheery.

One afternoon, I happened to catch the reflection in the living room mirror of a state police cruiser and another car as they pulled into my driveway. I grabbed the cell phone and went into the bathroom. I turned on the vent and called Chief Dulie. I made use of the number Callie had programmed in the cell phone. I could never have done that.

He answered, "Hello."

I said, "Chief, there is a state police car in my driveway."

At that time, Callie knocked at the bathroom door and said, "Mr. Bear, there is someone at the door."

"Let them in. Invite them into the dining room and ask them to have a seat. Make some coffee please."

She responded, "OK".

Chief Dulie had listened to all that and finally said, "They are here about Callie, aren't they? I'll be right there."

I flushed the commode and turned off the vent. I walked out to see a big old cop (just like in that country song) and a pretty, curvy, middle-aged black woman seated at my dining room table. I held up my left hand with the palm out to stop them from speaking. I went to the fridge and took down the mentoring contract and handed it to the black lady.

"After you have read it, I will answer your questions."

The huge policeman started to get up from his chair due to my rudeness, when the pretty lady held up her hand to stop him while she read. Then she arched her eyebrows and handed the cop the mentoring contract.

Callie was watching all of this.

I asked the lady, "How long have you been a social worker?"

"A little over seven years, Mr. Bear. My name is Miss Jones. Miss Jice (*rhymes with nice*!) Jones. I've got to say I wasn't expecting this contract. This is a first for me."

Chief Dulie came walking in like he owned the place. He does have a key, however. Introductions were made. Chief Dulie knew the state policeman, who was named Sergeant McKeon. It looked like they might have discussions at a later time about why the good Chief of Police of this borough wasn't included in this visit.

Miss Jones asked, "Chief, is that your signature on this contact?"

"Yes, it is."

She continued, "I am pleasantly surprised at this contract. As I was telling Mr. Bear, I haven't seen a document like this before. But hopefully I will see it more often. Maybe we should ask Miss. Bonnet to leave the room as we discuss this issue further."

I replied, "No, this is all about her. She needs to be here. We can't expect to raise responsible adults, who will make wise decisions if we keep them in the dark about everything."

Miss Jones sighed and said, "OK".

I asked Callie to serve us all coffee including herself and join us at the table. Having Callie here was probably another first for Miss Jones.

Miss Jones thought for a minute and started to talk, "Chief and Sergeant, you both may leave to go handle your important police work. You will not be needed here."

Chief Dulie got up to go but Sergeant McKeon remained seated and gave Miss Jones a questioning look.

She responded, "Please go Sergeant. This situation here is under control. Thank you again".

He got up also and left with Chief Dulie. It was now just the three of us at the table sipping coffee.

Miss Jones asked Callie, "Do you have any problems with this contract? Have you been asked to do anything that you shouldn't be expected to do?"

She replied, "No ma'am, but I REALLY don't like folding clothes." She rolled her eyes when she said that loudly.

Miss Jones chuckled, "I agree. I do not like that either. How about you Bear? Any questions?"

"Well, I have tried to think of a way to get Callie's Mom to sign off on all this; to make sure that she is in full agreement, but she doesn't want to talk to me. I guess she has had bad experiences with salesmen or other people who want something from her.

"She really loves Callie and has done an admirable job in raising her in spite of the hardships of being a single parent. She has been lax, however, in not pushing Callie to set personal goals and then to try to meet them. That is where I come in. Also, Callie has really helped me a lot around here. She does do a great job of folding clothes. Maybe I can let her help you also, Miss Jones."

Callie shuttered and said "PLEASEEEEEEEEE".

We all laughed.

Miss Jones asked the most significant question, "Mr. Bear, would you care to share your plans for helping Callie set those goals?"

"Yes, I can. First, she needs to stay out of trouble and get all A's on her report card. Then she needs a have a senior project to graduate. Plus she needs to have a school project to put on her college application. For the senior project, I am going to suggest working every weekday all summer at the senior center in town here. She could ride her bike there. She must be punctual, clean and cheery. I suspect she is going to like it about as much as she likes folding my clothes, but she will learn a lot about life there. I have talked to Mabel who is in charge and she would be glad to have the help.

"For the project in high school, I was thinking about the yearbook committee, which would be something she could do during study hall and any other free period. If she needs to use the internet, she can always access it here. If it is necessary, I can pick her up at school.

"Here is where I will need your help, Miss Jones. I will try to arrange it so Callie receives a nomination to the Naval Academy. I am assuming she could not afford college, and she wants to fly. What would be more exciting than landing and flying off of a carrier while it is rocking and rolling in the ocean? Also, the Naval Academy is nearby so she can come home to see her mother.

"I intend on contacting Buzzcut's office just as soon as I see Callie's report card for this semester."

I looked over and saw a kind of wonder in Callie's eyes. I glanced at Miss Jones, who had confusion in her face until she blurted out "By Buzzcut, you mean Representative Buster Cottle? I have never heard him called that. I have heard him called other less glamorous names though. He is going to be a hard sell. He is one tough cookie."

She laughed and said, "It will be my pleasure to help. You both need to fulfill that contract. Callie, there will be no guarantees, but both of us will do our part. The rest is up to you. Do not give up. Also, I want to meet with your Mother to get her approval" (*I couldn't have thanked Miss Jones more as she said exactly what I wanted to say.*)"

I said, "Miss Jones, if you need to keep an eye on me! There is way to keep both of your lovely eyes on me. Why don't you go out to dinner and a movie with me?"

Miss Jones looked flustered while Callie piped in, "He just asked you on a date." She giggled. Miss Jones was speechless.

Miss Jice Jones finally got her breath back and replied, "I'll let you know about that, Mr. Bear. But it is against policy for me to date a client."

"So you would date a dirty old man like me – if the circumstances were different, huh?" I asked in a light-hearted way.

The three of us had a good laugh. Callie left with Miss Jones to visit Callie's Mother. Miss Jones had to keep working on the problem. She really wanted to get Callie's Mother approval.

I had already organized my ancient and customized big, old car, the tank, with the correct shooting equipment so we left as soon as Callie arrived the next afternoon. We stopped and purchased coffee and doughnuts on the way to the range.

As I drove, I asked Callie how it went with her mother yesterday.

Callie responded, "Mom isn't sure about all this. She is still under the impression you are doing this for some personal gain. I must agree as I can't see why you are doing all this for me."

I changed the subject slightly by asking, "What did your Mother say to Miss Jones? Is your mother upset?"

"Mom agreed to let Miss Jones and Chief Dulie, who Mom respects, to monitor the situation. Mom appears somewhat satisfied although she is sure I will NOT get that appointment." (*Let's just leave that to 'ole Bear, I thought smugly.*)

I asked then, "Are you ready to learn about the proper way to use and shoot firearms?"

"Yes, I guess so. I will be around guns in the military. Is that why we are doing this?"

"It has been proven that military personnel who have prior training with guns do better in shooting. Also, I enjoy putting holes in paper at long range. So it serves two purposes."

When we arrived at the shooting range, there weren't any other shooters present, which would be good for our lesson. I showed her all of the safety things, which must be remembered, like always treat guns like they are loaded, always keep the muzzle pointed down range, etc. I showed her how to disassemble the rifles and told her what all the parts were called.

Using ear and eye protection, we spend the afternoon shooting 22 caliber rifles. She shot very well for a first timer. Callie also remembered the safety instructions so maybe she was good at everything, just like she said. We cleaned the rifles and departed.

When I dropped her off at my house, I asked her to bring some old clothes tomorrow so she could help to work on my old car, the tank. She gave me a questioning look but she was starting to understand I wasn't going to give her advance warning about anything.

As she prepared to put on her riding helmet, she said, "Thanks, Mr. Bear."

It was the first time she had said that word so I answered, "You are welcome. You know, that is the reason."

She hesitated, "Reason for what, Mr. Bear?"

"Thanks are all I want from you for helping you out. You just paid the bill in full with one little word."

A smile was on her face as she rode away. Then she stopped the bike and waved back at me. (*Actually I am quite selfish as I was doing this for me as much as for her. It just felt good to help someone who needs it. Also, I am a lonely old man, who was enjoying all of the time with a youngster. I was also enjoying the thought of the upcoming confrontation with Buzzcut.)*

I had my wife's cousin, Bill the mechanic, drive to my house the next afternoon. He was to give Callie some instructions on the mechanical aspects about cars. Also, they were going to install a bike rack on the tank so I could drop Callie and her bike off at her house and I wouldn't have to put the bike in the trunk. I figured if she was going to fly complicated machines, now would be a good time for her to start to learn something about a simpler machine. I still hadn't decided if I should teach Callie how to drive a car!

Her after-school activities with me were spend shooting (rimfires, shotguns, high powered rifles, and pistols), or at the driving range, unless my newfangled gadgets developed problems.

Callie was always cleaning up my laptops, cell phone, digital camera, or printer. I usually messed something up while I was using it so Callie had to correct what I had messed up. Also, Callie spent a couple afternoons on refurbishing her bike. She changed the tires, painted the metal, and put on a new chain. I had to admit the bike came out looking good.

We both talked to Mabel at the Senior Center and had everything arranged for Callie to start there the day after Callie finished her junior year in High School. I told Callie about her swimming lessons I had arranged at the local swimming club. They would be three days a week; usually after her time at the Senior Center. If she was going to be in the Navy, she needed to know how to swim.

I still couldn't figure out how to teach Callie to dance. The way I thought about this was that the Academy would have social events. Callie being the attractive and smart young lady she is would get invited to go to these social events. Therefore, she would need to be able to dance and have the confidence to handle herself with young men. I knew I was forgetting a lot of other necessary skills, but I couldn't figure out what to do about them either.

Callie and I both kept in contact with Miss Jones. She seemed happy with the progress we were making. She even let me call her Jice (*did I tell you that it rhymes with nice?*) but she still hadn't accepted my offer of a date. But I persisted; sometimes to her apparent dismay!!

Callie had almost all A's (she had a B in Calculus) so I paid her the $2 for each A.

Finally, I called Representative Cottle's office to start the process of getting Callie an appointment to the Naval Academy.

I rang his local office and a young lady answered, "Representative Cottle's office. How may I help you?"

"Is he in, I need to talk to …er… Mr. Cottle." (I *almost called him Buzzcut, but maybe I better not aggravate the beast just yet*).

"Representative Cottle is not available now. Can I help you or would you like to speak to one of his aides?"

I replied, "I will talk to an aide please."

"I'll connect you to Mr. Vladovitch. He goes by Vlad." (*Just my luck, I'll get to talk to a machine, which I will probably mess up also.*)

But a man answered, "Vlad here. How can I help you?"
"Hi, my name is Bear and I have an outstanding young lady, who would like to receive an appointment to the Naval Academy."

"Mr. Bear, did you say? What is your address, Mr. Bear?" (*Here we go again.*)

"No, I am just Bear", and I gave him my address, which is in Buzzcut's district.

I waited a couple of minutes while he GOOGLED Bear on the web. He came back to reality slowly as if he didn't know how to process the information. He was maybe shy about how to ask the pertinent questions.

I helped him out by saying, "Yes, I am THAT Bear, the one who filed the appeal at the PUC for the benefit of those brave members of the military, who are serving in the wars overseas. I am also the Bear, who was on the afternoon talk show with Miss Jacky

Mooney. I write books and short stories. Since we have that out of the way, please take my nomination request."

Well," he said slowly, "all the appointments have been made for this year."

"That is why I am calling now since Callie is a junior. She will be ready next year. Write this down," as I gave him Callie's name and address.

He responded as expected by saying, "Those appointments are in demand. They are just not handed out. It would help her cause if you would agree to provide support to Mr. Cottle's next campaign; talk at rallies and that kind of stuff, you know."

"I have no plans to provide campaign support at this time. But you can assure Mr. Cottle that I WILL NOT run against him in the next election if he gives this nomination proper consideration. I could really siphon off a lot of votes if I ran as a third party candidate. Think about it."

I went to the Senior Center for lunch once a week. Callie seemed to be adjusting well to the drudgery, but she did seem to brighten up whenever I was there. Plus I really enjoyed the extra helping of desserts Callie would sneak on my plate. Mabel confirmed that Callie was doing a good job and was usually on time.

After Callie had worked at the Senior Center for three weeks, I met with her and Mabel one afternoon.

I asked Mabel, "How is Callie doing?"

"Fine. The people here really like her", she replied.

"Great, then they will sign this petition I intend on sending to Buzzcut's (er, Representative Cottle's) office to try to get Callie an appointment to the Naval Academy."

"I'm sure every one of the seniors will sign it. They will probably volunteer to get their families and friends to sign also," she added.

I gave her a few copies and one to Callie for her Mom and their relatives to sign.

After one week, we had over two hundred signatures. I faxed those petitions to Buzzcut's office.

I asked Callie if she could help me at a booth at the local fire company's carnival. I made it sound like the booth was so I could autograph my books and stories while collecting donations for the fire company. There was that, but really it was all designed to get more signatures for Callie.

Seating was arranged at the carnival so Callie was on my left. After the people came in my right side to get autographs, they had to depart past Callie. She had a sign in front of her, which she had made (at my suggestion). The sign showed ships and planes and said she wanted to attend the Naval Academy and asked people to sign her petition.

I instructed Callie to smile a lot and to talk to people. It must have worked. Some people brought their children and we had the kids sign the petition also. I have to tell you I really hate this kind of event. I just do not like signing my name to people I do not know but I did it so Callie could get more signatures.

After the carnival was over, I faxed in 1100 more signatures to Buzzcut's office. That afternoon, I answered the phone.

"Hello, this is Vlad."

"I'm so happy that you are glad. How may I help you?" I pretended not to know who was calling and why.

"No, this is Vlad at Representative Cottle's office. What's with all these petitions?" he asked.

"I am SO sorry but we thought you would want to know all these voters think she is the best candidate for the Naval Academy."

He asked, "Did you really have kids sign these petitions? They can't vote."

"No, they can't vote now, my main man Bad, but they will be voting in future years. If Mr. Cottle is like all the other politicians these days, he will still running for office when these kids are of voting age. He might still be running for office when their kids can vote."

70

He sighed and thanked me for the petitions and said good bye.

Now was time for the next part of the plan. Callie and I went to a VFW rally at the fairgrounds. I had called ahead and was able to get us on their agenda. Again it was about to kill me but I intended on building up my courage and appearing on stage before all those veterans to ask their support in getting Callie an appointment to the Naval Academy. Callie had a speech prepared also.

Somehow I made it through a short speech in front of what-seemed-to-be thousands of screaming fans, who remembered me from the PUC appeal. Need I say that Callie is a much better public speaker than I am? The people loved her.

Callie and I asked them to fax, e-mail, call, and/or petition Buzzcut's office to get Callie nominated.

The next day, I emailed the American Legion, and other veterans groups asking for their help in getting Callie an appointment to the Academy.

Three days later, the phone rang. I answered it.

The cultured voice said, "Hello, Mr. Bear. This is Representative Buster Cottle."

I was able to contain myself so I just said "Hello." (*I really wanted to jump on him and call him names but I used proper restraint.*)

"If I may ask, what is with all this correspondence? We cannot keep paper in the fax machines, the phone lines are constantly in use, hell, our operators can't even fit in lunch or bathroom breaks, and the emails just keep coming in."

I asked innocently, "What is causing all that?" (*As if I didn't know*).

"It is all about this Miss Bonnet and the Naval Academy. Did you have something to do with this?"

"Now would I do that?" I lied easily. "But does she stand a chance to get the appointment? She seems like a very smart and capable young lady."

"Well now, it would help if you would promise to go on the campaign trail with me next fall," he countered.

"It is like this, Mr. Cottle. If you give Miss Bonnet a fair chance at that appointment, I promise NOT to run against you as a third party candidate. Just think of the votes I could siphon off if I did run. After that PUC thing, I would get all the veteran's votes plus all their families' votes. Let's not forget other supporters and every little old lady, who watched me on the afternoon talk show. Plus I would get the support of the librarians due to all the books and stories I have written. Hells bells, I might just beat you."

I was sure he did not like it one bit but he seemed confused so he hesitated before he said something like "I'll think about it" under his breath.

The next day, I called Vlad at Buzzcut's office. I was put right through.

After identifying myself, I asked, "Gladdy, how goes it? Does the people's candidate have a chance of getting that appointment?"

He sighed and said, "Well, it is like this. She will not be considered unless you promise to help to get Mr. Cottle elected for the next term. It wouldn't be much – just appear at rallies and make a couple commercials in which you proclaim that Mr. Cottle is the candidate you endorse. It is called quid pro quo and Mr. Cottle is an expert at its use."

I had expected him to say, "Yes, she stands an excellent chance of getting appointed. Mr. Cottle would be a dummy not to appoint her in light of the support of his constituents."

I asked, "Doesn't he think that I could make his chances of a re-election difficult if I ran against him as a third party candidate?"

"I guess not. He hasn't shared his thoughts with me" he said.

It was time for plan B. I had it in mind already, but I had hesitated to put it in motion. Now I had no choice but to implement it and let Buzzcut fall where he may.

I walked down to the senior center for lunch. I had been going there more often since Callie was helping. Over lunch and an extra dessert, I made the decision to proceed with plan B.

When Callie stopped by after work at the center, I asked her to start work on a website called electbeartocongress.com. She hesitated as if she wanted to question me but she had learned not to ask me questions so she started to work on the web site. I had already written the required petition to get on the primary ballot, but not as a third party candidate. Since I was registered as a Republican and Buzzcut was a Republican, I was going to be a candidate in direct competition against Buzzcut. (*Or so I wanted him to think since I had no intention to actually run for office.*)

I could see Callie was concerned so I explained this was all part of the plan. She had to do her part and keep helping at the center, improve her swimming, stay out of trouble and keep good thoughts and everything would be fine. I knew even if she did not get the appointment to the Naval Academy, she could still sign up for the Navy or Air Force as an enlisted person and work her way up, but I wasn't prepared to suggest yet. I asked Callie to start to get signatures on the election petition tomorrow. I was sure that Mabel wouldn't have a problem with that.

The next day, I needed to find some props so I called Chief Dulie and asked him to meet me at Old Bob's Café for breakfast and, yes, I was buying again!!

Over breakfast, I asked if he knew where I could purchase an old, obsolete piece of farm equipment. I had asked Chief Dulie since he lives outside of the borough on a small farm and he had contacts in the farming community. Like Callie, he wanted to know what in my weird-world I wanted with something like that, but I played dumb and ignored his question. (*It is easier for some of us to play dumb than it is for others!*)

He thought he knew where one was to be had. Therefore, I made arrangements to have him pick me up at the end of his shift and go see the farm implement. It all worked out fine. I paid the farmer and had it moved to Reets' place. (*Reets would charge me and arm-and-a-leg for storage but it would be worth it.*)

At home later, I started to make the second prop. It involved making copies of money, loads of money, multi-colored greenbacks, on my printer. Callie helped a lot, but she sure seemed concern I was planning on trying to spent it or something. I hushed her and proceeded to have her help me cut some plywood into the shape of a sailboat. It ended up being about five feet long with a sail about six feet high. Glue came in handy for the next step, which was covering the boat with the fake paper money. It was crazy looking but it really looked like a sailboat. Callie is good at everything she tries once she sets her mind to it.

We painted a yellow sun above a turquoise ocean on some plywood. The paper-money-covered-sailboat was mounted in the foreground in such a way that it looked exactly like it was sailing on a beautiful ocean under a bright sun. All of this was made in such a way it could be folded so it would fit in the trunk of my old behemoth of a car.

Thank goodness, Callie did not ask me anymore questions, because I wouldn't really know how to explain it to her. But I could sense that she was very confused. I got more of that confusion factor when I asked Chief Dulie to hook his tractor to the farm implement and move it to an old shed in one of his fields close to a back road.

At home the next day, I made signs using word processing on my computer. I taped the paper to cardboard.

Plan B was finally coming together so I called Representative Cottle's minion, Vlad to set it in motion.

The receptionist answered my call and transferred me to Vlad.

He said, "Hello, this is Vlad. How may I help you?"

"Vlad, my boy, this is Bear and I have good news for you. I have decided to throw my support behind The Honorable Cottle's re-election campaign. It will be the talk of the town. It will put The Honorable Cottle on everybody's ballet. He will be guaranteed to be re-elected. This is WAY better than speaking at a rally. WAY BETTER."

"Are you sure?" he asked. "Mr. Cottle doesn't like surprises."

"Well, then, he should see a demonstration for himself before he decides. When can you guys come down my way to see it? I could send you pictures but it will be well worth your travel time. I can assure you of that."

"Mr. Cottle is busy but he likes to meet with his constitutes so we should be able to arrange it. He has an opening in his schedule next Tuesday afternoon, say at 1 p.m.?"

"Fine with me. Make sure you bring a camera so that Mr. Cottle and his staff can savor this experience and plan where to use it fully. I wouldn't invite the media just yet though. It will be better if this is showcased in front of the media at just that exact moment so it generates the most positive exposure."

While all of this was going on, I met with the VFW and the American Legion to get more signatures on my election petition. (*I hated to lead them into thinking I was actually considering running, but, of course, I would never run for office – even if my life depended on it. I had had a prior bad experience with politicians*).

Tuesday came and I got dressed in my most un-wrinkled and semi-clean clothes of shorts and golf shirt. I met the fancy limo that The Honorable Cottle and his staff arrived in. I walked up to the limo and asked they follow me to where the exhibit was and we could do introductions there. So the limo followed me in the Bear's tank to the field in front of the old shed.

I got out and met Vlad who was tall and slim and wearing a sharp suit. Mr. Cottle was of medium height. He made an attempt to stand erect but he gave the impression that it was forced. He also appeared soft so he might have been wearing a girdle. He did not fit my nickname of Buzzcut as he was balding (even more that I am) and his remaining hair was combed over. It looked like it had been painted on.

Buzzcut grimaced when we shook hands so I smiled as wide as I could as I held his hand tighter and for far longer than I wanted to. It was all to further aggravate him.

I said, "Now is a good time to show you the demonstration." I led him into Chief Dulie's old shed.

I watched Buzzcut as his face went white and his jaw sagged as he looked at the manure spreader and the sailboat coated with money in front of a shining sun on a beautiful light blue-green sea. Vlad coughed and I heard a shuffle behind us and I noticed the limo driver watching this take place. He was a chubby guy in a limo driver's suit and cap. He was trying not to laugh out loud. He was really enjoying it.

The kicker, of course, was the signs in front that made all the difference. The first sign said "RE-ELECT BUSTER COTTLE FOR ANOTHER TERM IN CONGRESS", and the second sign said "BECAUSE HE REALLY SPREADS IT THICK IN WASHINGTON AND ELSEWHERE". This sign was in front of the manure spreader, of course.

The third and last sign was in front of the sailboat. It had written on it "IF ELECTED TO ANOTHER TERM IN CONGRESS, HIS GOVERNMENT PENSION WILL INCREASE BY $12,312 A YEAR. HE CAN THEN RETIRE WITH A PENSION OF $154,399 A YEAR SO HE CAN SAIL INTO THE SUNSET AND AVOID RUNNING FOR THE CONGRESS AGAIN AND AGAIN AND AGAIN".

I wanted to upset Buzzcut more so I said, "I am thinking of placing this display along the major roads in this district to enlighten the voters since I am running against you in the primary. Some farmers want to pay me to let them put this in their fields. Also, I already have a significant number of signatures on my petition."

Vlad added, "But independents are not in the primary." He must have remembered my threat to run as an independent candidate.

I responded, "Yeah, I know but since I am a registered Republican, I decided to just run on the primary against old man Cottle here.

"If I do that, I will add a figure of a bear painted with THE STARS AND STRIPES. In front of that, a sign will say something like "BEAR FOR CONGRESS. HE WILL NEVER FORGET THE CONSITUTENTS, JUST LIKE HE HAS NEVER FORGOTTEN THE MILITARY AND THE VETERANS. The wording in front of that sign needs work."

Buzzcut appeared to gag so he grabbed Vlad's arm and pulled him towards the limo. The bemused driver opened and held the door for both of them. As he closed the door, the driver gave me the thumbs up below the level of the window and winked at me as he walked around to the driver's door and got in.

Yeah, I know. I had just ended Callie's chances of getting her appointment to the Naval Academy, but an old Bear will only put up with so much before he fights back in aces and spades. I decided to put this together and try to shock Buzzcut some more. You just never knew where the chips would fall. (*I did not know what hornet's nest I may have stirred up, however*).

I folded the signs into the trunk of the tank and went to Old Bob's Café for coffee and a piece of pie.

I wasn't feeling too well since the day at the display at Chief Dulie's farm. I was worried and concerned about Callie. I had all but led Callie to believe she had a chance at getting that appointment. She was still helping out at the senior center faithfully and cheerfully. She was spending her spare time with me at the driving range and the golf course, taking swimming lessons at the YWCA or shooting lessons at the range.

She excelled at everything. She beat me at golf EVERY time we played. She even beat me when she teed off at the white tees and I went from the gold ones. (*She could probably beat me with one hand tied behind her back, and blindfolded. Someday, or someplace, I will beat someone at golf. It just has to happen!*)

She discussed how to write her senior project and how she was actually looking forward to her last year in high school. She even asked me questions about the life in the military since I had spent three years in the Army. To say I was in dire straits would be putting it mildly. To top it off, I was fresh out of ideas. I, Bear, winner of various and sundry awards for creative writing for books and short stories, was all out of ideas and almost out of hope.

I considered letting the social worker, Miss Jice Jones in on my dilemma. She talked to Callie, Chief Dulie and me weekly to ensure that nothing inappropriate was happening and that we were all adhering to the mentoring contract. I just couldn't bring myself to tell Miss Jice Jones of my failure; not just yet anyway.

My worrying continued for a little over a week, when I was interrupted about 11 a.m. but a loud knock on my door. I opened the door to a tall dark haired attractive lady, who held up a badge with her right hand.

She informed me, "I am Agent Hernandez with the FBI. I have some questions to ask you, Mr. Harv…..."

Before she could say anymore, I interrupted her and murmured, "Come in." I turned and walked into the dining room. (*It was probably rude not to hold the door open for her but I needed to think for a couple minutes.*) I could hear her shut the door and follow me into the dining room.

I pointed at a chair at the table and said loudly and forcefully, "Have a seat and my name is Bear, just Bear" as I walked over to the coffee maker and poured a cup for her. I took my cup off the table and filled it also. I did all of this while she watched somewhat surprised.

I opened the fridge and took out my tasty flavored creamer and said, "Have some coffee please. It is my current favorite blend. I like it with this creamer."

I still hadn't given her a chance to talk and I wasn't about to. "Do you have a card, Agent Hernandez?"

She had to open her handbag and take out a card so I asked, "What office do you work out of?"

She replied "I work out of the York office. Here is my card," she said as she handed it to me.

It listed her first name as an S. I asked, "What does the S stand for?" Then I decided to stretch it a little as I asked, "And how did you get assigned to the little York office?" (*I was letting her know I suspected that she had messed up somewhere so she was sent here as punishment. As she thought a second about that, I took another look at her. She was tall and attractive with a slight hook to her nose and some gray in her straight black hair so she wasn't a kid. She had to be over 50.*)

She regained her composure after taking a sip of her coffee and answered, "The S is for Sole. Now I get to ask the questions, Just Bear. How long have you felt Representative Cottle is not the right man for his position?" (*Now I knew how to proceed. Happily.*)

"Why? Does he feel intimated by a little old Bear?"

"I would say he feels threatened by you. Did you or did you not, threaten him?" she replied matter-of-factly.

"Well" I said slowly, "I guess I did threaten his chances of getting re-elected so he might construe that to be a personal threat. But before we waste any of your valuable time with questions, it would be faster and more effective if I could show you what transpired. To do that, you will need to ride with me in my car to a farm about three miles from town. Since you do not know me, it might be better if you called Chief Andrews, who is the Chief of Police of this borough for a reference."

I pulled up Chief's phone number from my cell phone and asked her to call it. She was having second thoughts but she called Chief Dulie anyway. I guess it was so unusual to have a suspect tell her to call another officer of the law. She couldn't resist. He answered.

She explained who she was and where she was and why she was there and why she was calling him.

You should have seen the look of wonder on her face as she listened to Chief Dulie. She held her cell phone away from her face and asked me "Where are we going Bear?"

I replied "To an old shed on Chief Dulie's farm to see an election demo that I made."

She informed Chief Dulie and said goodbye after exchanging cell phone and office numbers. (*I would really have liked to have heard both sides of the phone call. The good Chief and I are friends so he probably laid it on thick.*)

We went outside and I backed the tank out of the garage. She gave the tank a thorough once over with her eyes. She must appreciate old cars since the tank is one-of-a-kind. It is a mix of parts from various years and makes. My wife's cousin, Bill, keeps it in perfect running condition and Callie finds time to wash and wax it so it looks in mint condition. (*It is too bad that I could not be rebuilt to look and run that good.*)

I held the door open for her to get in. I got in and drove to the senior center where Callie was helping out. On the way, we made small talk about the weather and the traffic.

I said, "You might as well start at the beginning so let me buy you lunch."

She started to protest but I assured her we must start this dog-and-pony show there. Also, I told her I would introduce her as Miss Hernandez and not Agent Hernandez.

As we walked into the center, the people there started to cheer me and there were comments I heard like "Bear has a girl friend." and "She is a looker". These were followed by "Sit with us".

I declined and selected a table for two. Agent Hernandez had heard all of those comments and probably some I hadn't heard. She had another confused look on her pretty face.

Callie delivered the plates of food. She walked past me while giving me a shoulder squeeze. She walked behind Agent Hernandez and gave me a quizzical look as if to say "Who is she?"

As Callie served us, I said, "This is a friend of mine, Miss Hernandez, who just happened to stop by." Now Agent Hernandez was giving me a quizzical look behind Callie's back. I continued, "This is Callie. She helps me around my house in her spare time."

They exchanged pleasantries but Callie was busy serving. She did manage to get me an additional piece of cherry pie, which everyone else in the center noticed. They all chuckled at that.

I made sure we left as soon as we finished eating. On the way to the car, I started to explain, "Callie is the child of a single parent. I took on the task of trying to get her prepared for the future. Part of that future is to try to get her an appointment to the Naval Academy, since her Mother couldn't possibly afford to pay for college. That is why I approached old Buzzcut, himself."

She thought some before she asked, "And Buzzcut would be Representative Cottle?"

"Yes, he would be. He controls the appointments for his district. Ah, here we are."

I pulled in beside the shed. "Please help me set these up" I asked her as we took out the signs and the sailboat. Then I arranged all the props and stood aside. She started to chuckle as she looked at everything. She took out her cell phone and started to photograph the demos.

I warned, "I hope you are not going to publish those, are you?"

"No, but my boss will want to see them. Now sit over there on that old bench and tell me everything, which transpired in all of this." She took out a notebook to write everything down.

I told her about meeting Callie (but not about the break-in), and about the mentoring contract. I included the fact that Miss Jice Jones, a social worker, was monitoring us. I talked about the petitions, the faxes, etc. I explained I promised I would not run against Buzzcut if he considered Callie for an appointment. When Buzzcut demanded I work for his re-election, I lost my senses and devised this demo. I explained about the Bear sign that I wanted to add and my petition to get on the ballot.

I also said, "I wanted to add another display; one of a casket on a desk with the sign saying that Buzzcut might continue to run until he died in office, but that might be considered threatening so I did not add that in."

She started to laugh and said, "For some reason, I believe you. Bear. I believe all of this. My boss is NO FAN of Buzzcut. I'll bet she will have some thoughts on all of this. Are you absolutely SURE you never threatened him with bodily harm?"

"Yes, I am sure I would never threaten anyone with bodily harm. I'm sure that you have checked my record so you know about that little episode down in Baltimore. I was never charged with a crime there. But Buzzcut figured that with a record like mine, well, he could convince the FBI I was a serious threat to his life, I guess."

She agreed.

After that, we put the foldable prop and signs back in the tank's expansive trunk and I drove back to my house.

She got in her car to leave and I walked over to the driver's side door so she rolled down the window.

I asked, "Are you married Miss Hernandez?" She gave me another look this time; a different look. She shows a lot of emotion on her face.

"No, I am not."

"Is there a significant other in your life?"

"You are a nosey Bear aren't you? Yes and no. He is assigned on the West Coast. Why do you ask?"

"I would like to ask you out to dinner and a movie. I think that single people still date like that, don't they?"

This caused here to drop her jaw a moment, and then she got a big dirty-old-woman smile on her face.

She replied, "Not only are you a nosey Bear but you are a fast old Bear. I'm going to have to watch you closer. But thanks, and no thanks, for now."

"So maybe after I am no longer a suspect, huh? Maybe?"

She shook her head and started to drive off when I stopped her by waving both hands. She gave me a look of exasperation and stopped the car.

I walked over and said, "Be sure to include the limo driver in your questioning. I suspect he heard everything said at the demo. The only other person I have talked to in Buzzcut's office is Vlad, which is short for something, but I forget what. Will you let me know when your investigation is finished and I am cleared of all suspicion?"

She replied, "Yes, of course" and drove away. (*I would date her or Miss Jice Jones but not my lawyer, Maude nor would I date a politician or a reporter. Even a Bear has some standards!*)

The next day, I went golfing with Chief Dulie. We enjoyed the 19th hole over burgers and beer (which I bought; of course). I told Chief Dulie what had happened with the pretty FBI agent. We both agreed it would be best if I did not contact Buzzcut's office until all of this was settled. However, Chief Dulie promised to make a follow up call to Agent Hernandez.

I still held out hope Callie would somehow get the nomination. I did not mention anything to her but it was weighing heavily on my mind, until I had another visit from Agent Hernandez. It was about 11 a.m. again when I answered a knock at the door. I was still in my bright blue micro fiber lounge wear with the big yellow smiley faces on it. I only opened the door a crack to see who it was. I was about to greet her loudly when she put her fingers to lips to indicate silence and handed me one of her business cards. She had written on the back "I want to buy you lunch. Let's go. Keep quiet."

I hated to do it but I opened the door a little more so she could see me in my lounge wear, the sight of which has caused strong and brave men to go running and screaming down the street in absolute terror.

She just giggled and whispered, "I'll be in the car waiting for you, you cute little Bear" or I thought that is what I heard.

I got dressed in my rumpled Bear skins and left the house. I almost forgot to lock the door since I was confused.

I got in her car and she looked at me and said, "You look better in blue and yellow, Bear."

"Where are we going and why?" I asked.

"I'll explain on the way. But first, where can we have a quiet meal?"

My usual haunt, Old Bob's Café isn't the best for a quiet, romantic lunch so I picked an old fashioned open air, ice cream parlor. I gave her directions and she started to talk.

"I met with my boss, who loved the pictures by the way. I questioned Vlad and Buzzcut, but I think I learned the most from Pete, the limo driver. I met him in a private place so no one else would know we talked. He had heard things at the display and in the car which supports your testimony. He also suspects your house and phone may be bugged but we have no proof of that. Even if we found bugs, we couldn't prove who put them there. That is why I suggested that we eat out someplace.

"My boss met with Buzzcut yesterday in private and suggested it would be better for him if he just appointed Callie to the Naval Academy and we all could forget this. Then she showed him copies of her pictures of your demo and threatened to post it on the web, which would embarrass old Buzzcut to no end since he has a lot of enemies. My boss just happens to be a single mother like Callie's Mom and one of his biggest enemies. Posting these pictures might shorten his political career. He went ballistic but he finally calmed down and agreed to the appointment. Will you let this end here if he does make that announcement soon?"

All of a sudden, I was feeling a lot better. Callie was getting her appointment and I was having a burger, fries and a milkshake with a gorgeous woman at an outdoor ice cream parlor in the country. It was sunny in the mid-eighties with big puffy clouds in the sky. Life is good.

"Of course, I will gladly drop everything including my petition for the primary. I guess I can site health issues and time constraints, since I am planning on continuing to write. I have a friend who has worked with intelligence agencies in the past who will sweep my house and phone for bugs. Thank you, Agent Hernandez. Is a date in my future?"

She laughed and said, "You do not give up, do you, Bear? No, I can't date you since my boyfriend is being reassigned to Philadelphia within two weeks. I can't wait to see him again."

"I hope he knows how lucky he is."

"He will because I intend on helping him remember", she said.

Callie was notified by Christmas she had won an appointment to the Naval Academy. She was ecstatic. She tried to thank me again but I told her she had already thanked me once, which was more than enough. I still had not talked to her Mom. Strange!

Miss Jones was very happy also but she still declined my offers of going out on a date. (*That wasn't strange since Miss Jice Jones is a smart lady; much too smart for me!*)

The expected phone calls started to come in from Buzzcut's office. Thanks to the cell phone with caller id, I was able to just ignore those calls and messages for months and months until after Callie had left for the training at the Academy. By then, I was at the end of my rope with all this so I took a call from Buzzcut himself.

"Hello", I answered roughly and curtly.

"Mr. Bear, this is Representative Cottle. I have been trying to reach you. I need your support with my next campaign. After all, I did you a little favor and now it is your turn to help me. That is the way that it works in politics. I wash your back and you wash mine." He seemed so sure and full of himself as he said it.

I replied, "Do NOT push your luck. I still have all of the parts of the demo stashed away or I can re-create it. If you have read any of my writings, you know how fiendishly creative I can be if pushed. The pen is definitely mightier than the sword. I hope we do not talk ever again!!!"

I hung up the phone and sipped a cold beer to wash the bad taste out of my mouth.

RABID RACCOON

1st Garbage Day.

While I sipped my coffee and contemplated my daily activities, I watched the world go by through my picture window. It seemed to be just another Tuesday. Everybody had put their trash and recycling by the curb for pick up and the flowers were starting to bloom. The birds were flitting around and chirping away amorously.

As I turned to leave my perch, I realized my trash bag was NOT there. Also, my paper recycling was gone. This really made me wonder since I had just placed it curbside about one hour ago. Scanning the street, I determined my items were the only ones missing.

After finding my cell phone, I called my buddy Chief Dulie and asked, "Have you enjoyed breakfast yet?"

He replied, "I'm on duty but I could take a break at ten. What do you have in mind, Bear?"

"Pick me up at ten and I'll buy you a snack at Old Bob's Café."

"Ok. See you then," he replied.

He showed up at a little after ten a.m. and we went to the café. We made small talk about the weather and the best day and time to get together to go golfing.

At the café, we sat at the counter and were served coffee by Alice, the usual waitress there. She brought us menus, but we both ordered without reading them. This caused her to raise her eyebrows.

We both ordered the breakfast item named after me. It is called THE DAILY GROUCH and is made with scrapple, egg and cheese. Did I say that it is delicious?

After we finished eating, I was glad Chief Dulie had a few minutes to chat so I asked him, "Did you notice anything different today?"

"Do you mean you did not read the menu or that you did not put out trash today?"

Now I guess I do spent a lot of time reading the menu to be sure nothing new has been added and especially to bug Alice, but I had been sure nobody noticed. I was wrong about that. But I was also wrong in that I expected the good Chief had NOT noticed the early trash pick-up.

I began, "I put my trash and recycling out this morning as usual. It was stolen before the trash men arrived. Has other trash been stolen? Or am I the only lucky one?"

"Well, I wouldn't rightly figure it is a crime to steal someone's garbage, which they have abandoned at the curb. The ultimate destination is burning at the incinerator. It doesn't have any monetary value. I think a judge would probably throw that out of court. Also, I haven't heard about this happening before here or anywhere else, for that matter."

He received a police call which demanded his action so he apologized and departed.

I left a tip and paid the bill for both of us and started to walk home. While I walked, I kept a watchful eye for the trash and recyclables, which were along the street. I couldn't see where any was missing. It made me wonder a lot. Well, I better get home and get back to writing. My expensive agent was bugging me to finish a new book. He says the publisher will want the advance back unless I finish this book sooner, rather than later.

2nd Garbage Day.

On the next scheduled trash pick-up day, I varied my routine. Usually I put out the trash before I make coffee, but today, I started the coffee maker and then put out the trash and picked up the paper off the driveway. Back inside, I added creamer to my coffee and sat at the right side of the curtains at the picture window. I was in an ideal spot to watch my garbage bag at the curb. As I sat there reading the paper, I would glance up frequently to make sure that my garbage bag hadn't disappeared yet.

The coffee intake forced me to go to the bathroom to take care of outflow. Well, you guessed it; my bag of trash was gone by the time I got back. I did catch the back of a dusty blue car leaving the street. Just my dumb luck!

I still did not have an idea what was going on but my interest was peaking now. So I devised a plan for the next scheduled day of trash pick-up.

3rd Garbage Day.

There was recycling as well as trash pick-up today. After taking out my items, I switched my paper recycling with the next door neighbor's paper recycling and I switched my garbage bag with the bag from across the street.

I watched the street off and on. Finally my patience was rewarded. The paper recycling and trash bag from my spot were both gone. My trash and paper recycling were still there safe in front of the neighbor's houses. Whoever was stealing my trash and paper recycling was persistent, I'll say that. Now let's see how they handle the next problem I have planned for them.

4th Garbage Day.

Trout fishing season is in full swing. I allowed myself to go fishing instead of concentrating on my writing. Yes, I'm an award winning author.

Luckily, I got three nice trout. Usually I bury the entrails and heads in the garden (use it for fertilizer like the Indians taught the Pilgrims), but I had a better plan for this stuff.

I put the entrails and heads in a plastic bag to ripen in the garage before I added it to the garbage bag. I punched holes in the bag to allow the stinky goo to seep out before I added it to the trash. Whoever opened that bag was going to experience an enduring smell.

I watched my trash while I sipped coffee and was rewarded when an older rusty and dirty car pulled up and stopped. A man jumped out and grabbed my precious trash bag and threw it in his trunk and drove off. I took pictures of him using my new high-tech digital camera.

Chief Dulie stopped by later in the day and I showed him the pictures of the trash thief. You couldn't make out too much detail due to the distance and the fact I took the pictures through a window pane at an angle and into the sun. But there wasn't any doubt that someone had just purloined my trash.

He said, "Yes, it does look like someone is targeting your trash. Do you have any idea why?"

"No. But it would sure be nice to know."

He admonished me, "Bear, I know you. I know that you are not going to give this any rest; just do not do anything stupid." He shook his head side-to-side and chuckled and left to go home to have supper with his lovely wife and kids.

I took the memory card out of the camera and went to the store and tried to enlarge and increase the definition of the photographs of the trash thief, but it just wouldn't work. The pictures were still blurry and grainy.

On the way home, I stopped and picked up a road-killed opossum using a flat shovel and a hoe I carried along strictly for this purpose. I put the deceased critter in a plastic shopping bag. It was recently killed and hadn't started to smell yet. Hopefully it would stink a lot by the next trash day.

At the local post office, I rummaged through the trash can beside the door. Many people who pick up their mail either at the desk or at their boxes drop any mail they do not want into that bin as they exit the post office. I had an excuse prepared if anyone asked me what I was doing. I would just say I was looking for a coupon since I had already used mine. But nobody asked.

5th Garbage Day.

The trash and paper recycling were ready. The mail from the post office was placed with my paper recycling. The dead opossum was in the trash. It was too bad it wasn't ripe, but it was a bloody mess anyway.

The thievery took place within an hour and fifteen minutes after I put the trash out. I tried to run outside through the garage to get better pictures but the trash thief had left by then.

6th Garbage Day.

I made a run to the local sporting goods store and purchased another digital camera. This one is a trail cam and is designed to take pictures of wild animals usually at a baited spot. The bait was, of course, my valuable waste and the game was the thief of trash.

I made some additional road tours until I found a dead squirrel and a smashed rabbit. I also stopped and picked through the trash bin at another post office to scatter in my recycling to keep the thieves guessing.

I got up early before I might be noticed by the thief to arrange the trail cam on the oak tree, which is on the property line. The camera was head high and would be activated by motion so I would capture a lot of vehicular and walking traffic, but it had a lot of memory space. I turned off the flash.

My trash disappeared as usual so I went out and took down the trail cam. I deleted shots of cars driving past and people walking by until I got to the thief and his ugly blue car. He was caught trash-handed.

He appeared to be youngish looking, average height and was wearing a baseball cap. There was wispy hair sticking out from under the hat. Rumpled jeans, dirty tennis shoes, and a sweatshirt finished out his attire. But I still did not who he was and why he was stealing my trash of all things.

I had more discussions with Chief Dulie who seemed amused by the whole situation.

7th Garbage Day.

I built a support for a hanging basket out close to the street. I put the trail cam on the wooden support. I wanted to capture the license plate this time. I must admit it looked a little weird seeing that hanging plant close to the street, but my neighbors thought I was strange anyway.

The trash was populated with a deceased groundhog this time and mail from a York post office trash bin. He came right on schedule and removed my trash and put it in his trunk. The only problem was his car and license was so dirty I couldn't read his license number. Drats!!!!

I made copies of all the pictures and made notes to document all the events on this case. I included times, dates, and the added delicious tidbits like dead animals or entrails, and other people's mail. I put the notes and pictures in my gun safe, just in case.

8th Garbage Day.

This time, I was planning on being more personally involved. Not to worry though since I was not planning on anything dangerous or physical.

I prepped my garbage with a dead black snake and a couple ripe carp, which I caught at the local reservoir.

I put on a light jacket and a hat and walked across my back yard and down the street. I turned and walked so that I could start up my street from the direction the thief usually came from.

The dirty blue car was parked close to Mr. Armis's garage. There was just room enough to squeeze the car there and not block any part of the street. The man was in the front seat so I waved at him as I walked past. I went on up the street past my house until I reached the convenience store, where I purchased two cups of coffee and two donuts in separate bags.

I walked back down past my street while sipping from one cup of coffee. When I reached the car, I held out the other cup of coffee towards the car window. The man inside turned on the switch and rolled down the driver's side window. I offered him the coffee and one donut by saying, "If you are on stake out, you could always use a coffee and a donut".

He responded with a crooked smile, "Yeah, on stake out, heh, heh. Thanks."

He accepted the coffee and donut as I asked, "Who are you watching? What did they do? I always wondered about a few of these people which live around here. Or can't you divulge that information?" (I gave him an out in case he was slow witted!).
He grinned and said, "I ain't supposed to say".

He sipped the coffee as I studied him. He had pale stubble on his plump cheeks and on his almost non-existent chin. He appeared to be wearing the same hat he wore the last time. There was a long odd shaped boxy thing on the front seat beside him. I wondered what that was.

Since I did not want to wear out my welcome or have him identify me, I said, "Good bye and good luck" and proceeded to saunter along sipping my coffee. I tried to read his car license as I passed his car but it was really grubbed up – probably on purpose to hide his identity. I walked along and made the turns back to the street behind my house. I went in and changed into a house coat and took out my garbage while yawning as if I overslept.

He showed up within ten minutes and swiped my trash and left in a rush. The who and the why still haunted me.

The night after 8th day Garbage.

I had the perfect plan. I would catch a couple rats in a box trap. I knew a couple of farmers. They would be happy to let me catch all the rats I wanted.

I would transfer those feisty critters into a plastic box made with a thin spot on one side. I would rub bacon fat on the outside of the thin spot before I put those boxes inside the trash bags.

By the time the trash thief reached his destination, the rats would have chewed through the thin spot and be raving mad when the thief opened the bags. Talk about scary. I could see the look on his pale face as he screamed in surprise.

Another plan was even better. Put a snake in the garbage bag and watch the reaction, when he opened the bag and the live copperhead lunged out at him with its jaws wide open and fangs extended. I could see the beady eyes of the thief bug out in pain and terror as his face became swollen and he couldn't breathe as he choked to death.

These dreams came easy after a couple beers while watching the Marlins play the Red Sox. I awoke in a sweat after the nightmare left me shaking.

I had to figure this out somehow. It was making me jumpy.

9th day Garbage.

The plan came to me while shopping at the local hardware store. It was a great way to further aggravate the trash thief so I purchased this great new toy.

It was really foggy for the today's trash pick-up, which was great weather for this idea. Of course, I still sprinkled my trash and paper recycling with other people's mail and smelly, bloody dead critters since I did not want to make any radical changes.

I took my fancy new tool, which is an air compressor for blowing up tires. It is compact and looks just like a cordless drill.
I went out back and circled around to the other street so I could walk up on the passenger side of the car. That way he wouldn't see me in all the fog.

I snuck up to the back of Mr. Armis's garage and got down on my belly and crawled around to the front passenger side tire. I removed the cap and put pressure on the stem, which let out all the air slowly. I crawled back to the passenger side tire and let the air out of that tire also. I made sure to put both caps back on. I figured he wouldn't have two spares and also he wouldn't have a portable compressor.

It was tough for an old fart like me to get down on my belly and crawl around so much. I know I did it many times while I was in the Army but that was many lifetimes ago.

I really wanted to crawl to the back of his car and rub off the dirt from the license plate so I could read it. But I thought I would be in a dangerous position lying behind his car. Especially if he started the engine quickly and backed up since I do not move fast.

After crawling around the garage, I got up and walked home in the reverse circuital path and put out my trash.
I walked back around on the same street again just to watch his reaction to those two flat tires.

I saw him open his driver's window and raise that long box above his car and look in at the bottom. It was a homemade periscope so that was how he could see above the rise in the street and determine if I had put out the garbage.

Seeing the trash was out, he laid the periscope back on the seat beside him and started the car and put it in gear. The car only went about five feet before he stopped the car and got out and walked around to check the tires. I could see him react. He raised his arms and looked around to see if someone had done something. He couldn't see me clearly in the fog since I was hiding behind some shrubs. He walked towards my house and then he walked back to the car. He waved his arms around and leaned against his car. He reached in his car and took a drink from a bottle of water.

He took a cell phone out of his car and made a call. I thought maybe he was calling a friend to bring a portable compressor. He started to walk up the street. I watched as he walked pass my house and my trash. He was probably going to the convenience store to get some coffee or something to eat. This was the perfect time to finish my plan. I ran over and pumped up his tires using the fancy new portable compressor.

I went back behind the shrub to watch. After about half an hour, he came back carrying my trash and leaned it against the front side of his car. He got in the front seat and waited. I was glad he never once glanced at his tires on the passenger side of the car.

Soon a sharp little foreign sedan pulled in behind his car. A young girl with long brown hair, a short skirt and high heels got out. He opened the door of his car and got out.

She walked around to her trunk and took out a hand pump, which she handed to him. They talked and she gestured to his car. They walked around to the passenger side of his car and found both tires had pumped themselves back up all by themselves. Really! He looked around again (all around) but still couldn't see anyone.

Things really got interesting as she yelled at him, "I'm about to lose my job since you called about tires, which needed to be pumped up. I had to stop and buy a pump. I was worried if I purchased the correct one. Now you say those same tires are back at full pressure. What about that? How can that be?"

She gestured and waved her arms around and yelled some more. He just put his hands on the back of his head and pulled his chin towards his chest in retreat. He leaned against his car trunk with his head down and didn't move as she jumped in her car, slammed the door and sped away.

He slowly looked at all the tires again. He walked around his car a second time while muttering to himself before slowly putting my trash in the trunk and getting in his car and driving away.

I waited awhile before I walked to Old Bob's Café for breakfast. I did not want to walk directly home in case he was somehow watching me. I took my usual long time reading the menu (*much to Alice's chagrin*), and I walked a longer haphazard route home while humming to myself.

It all became clear on the way home. I figured out what was happening. I couldn't think of who might be doing it, but I now knew why.

At home, I turned on the old laptop which Callie had set up for me to use exclusively for book and story writing. This laptop was not connected to the internet and it was password protected – both of which is important to protect my manuscripts. It also has a larger keyboard for my use.

I found the instructions Callie had prepared for me. I set about scanning a recent short story into my computer. I had recently read and enjoyed this story.

It is called LOWER SIDE by Torry Pynts. This story has a quite unique plot, which would be important for what I had planned.

I sat at the laptop and edited the story, which I now called Bottom Drawer. I added and substituted words and phrases but maintained the same plot. I printed out the new version, which took five pages. I took a red pen and manually edited to make it look like I was struggling with getting this manuscript exactly correct. I made sure my pen name of Bear was not on this manuscript. I deleted the word document for Bottom Drawer from my laptop. I deleted it from the waste bin. I did not want anyone to know I was responsible for this plagiarism of the LOWER SIDE by Torry Pynts.

I turned the manuscript over and used the back of the first page to make a grocery list; some of the items I crossed out and some I put sizes and quantities next to. On the back of the second page, I sketched out what I would plant and where in my garden. I just doodled on the back of the third page as I watched the local weather. The back of the fourth page was used as a score card for the Indians-White Sox game, which I watched that night. I tried to project who would win all the majors in golf for the year on the back of the last page.

I scattered these pages in among my paper recycling. One page was folded, one was crumpled, the one with the scoring was folded in with the following days' sports page, etc.

10th day Garbage.

I put out the recycling with the trash and watched until Mr. Confused in his dirty and rusty blue car swipe both my trash and paper recycling.

The next Saturday.

I hosted a venison barbecue with Chief Dulie, Reets, and Callie. My good buddy Bench wasn't there since he is off seeing the whole wide world with his new love, Miss Jacky Mooney of the Sunshine Show.

After eating and sipping beer (not Callie since she is a minor), I brought up the subject of my premature trash removal problems. I wanted to brain storm to try to determine who and the why about all this. (*Actually I wanted to see if my friends would come up with the same reason that I had thought of.*)

I explained the ongoing problem but left out the things I had added to my trash like the dead critters and other people's mail, and the mystery of the tires going flat (I left the comments open ended).

Chief Dulie asked, "So this is still going on? Why haven't you asked me to do something about it before this?"

"I thought that you couldn't do anything about it," I replied. (*I wanted to solve the mystery and have some fun first, but I didn't tell him that*).

"But it sounds like harassment and it could have gotten dangerous. I will send him on his way on the next trash day. I will find out his name and will check his record in the law enforcement data bases."

Callie asked, "I wonder why it is being done. I know you would not put anything of value in your trash".

Reets chuckled and said, "Ole' Bear doesn't waste anything. He wouldn't throw anything away. Heh heh."

Then all three looked at each other and nodded as it hit them.

Callie announced loudly, "They are after your manuscripts, aren't they? But wouldn't that be plagiarism?"

I added, "Not if they published before I did. Then I would be the one guilty of plagiarism." (*I did not let them know I had already put out bait to identify and catch the perpetrator*).

Chief Dulie obviously wasn't happy as he said, "I am going to grill this guy to find out everything I can. This stops now. Bear, I suspect you know more than you are letting on. I just hope you did not let your head get your ass in trouble over this!!"

"Now would I do that?" I responded innocently.

This brought a groan from Chief Dulie, a giggle from Callie, and a shake of the head and a wry smile from Reets. (*It looks like they knew me much too well.*)

11th day Garbage.

Chief Dulie told me later how the traffic stop went since I wasn't there for the entire procedure. Chief Dulie is just an average sized guy with a baby face. He doesn't look very intimating but don't let that fool you. He knows how far he can expand the law without going too far.

Chief Dulie parked his car beside a house and right in front of a garage and behind a tree so he could watch the end of the street without being too noticeable. He watched the dirty blue car arrive. Then he called me and instructed me to put my trash out. He watched as the trash thief used his home-made periscope to check for the presence of my trash. There was another police car at my end of the street to make sure there would not be a chase situation in the borough.

As soon as the dirty blue car started to move, Chief Dulie put on his siren and lights and sped up behind the car. He stopped behind it, turned off the siren and took his time getting out of the police cruiser. He slipped out of his car and approached close to the side of the blue car with his hand on his revolver. Then he asked the man to get out of his car with his hands in plain sight and to move very slowly.

The trash thief got out very reluctantly. He raised his hands about head high; both hands were empty.

He asked, "What did I do?"

Chief Dulie commanded, "Hand me your driver's license, car registration and proof of insurance. Then we will talk about your moving violation."

"My moving violation? I was barely moving."

"We will do this my way. Hand me those three documents and be slow about it. Make no fast moves."

Chief Dulie kept his hand on his gun and maintained his serious, you-may-wish-you-were-dead, cop face.

The young un-tidy, surprised man reached in his back pocket and removed his driver's license from his wallet. He was given permission to reach in his glove box while standing outside the passenger's side door. After rummaging around in there for a couple minutes awkwardly, he produced his registration and insurance card.

Chief Dulie had him stand firm while the documents were reviewed. Chief Dulie went back to his car and checked for warrants, priors and anything else the data base would show. Nothing came up except for a couple speeding tickets.

By then, I was walking down the street towards all this commotion.

Chief Dulie said to him, "OK, Mr. Tikes, I will give you a ticket for your license plate. It is not readable. In fact, you will be required to clean the plate before you can drive your car further. Can you do that while I write the ticket?"

It looked to Chief Dulie that Mr. Ed Tikes relaxed then, since he was only getting a ticket for an unreadable license plate.

Just as Chief Dulie was presenting Mr. Tikes with the ticket and having it signed, I showed up.

I demanded, "Chief, it is about time you captured this thief. He has been stealing my garbage and paper recycling. I want him arrested and convicted with due haste!" I practically yelled the last two words.

With that Mr. Tikes turned and looked at me with a mixture of surprise, recognition (from the coffee and donut event), and fear.

Chief Dulie said coolly and calmly, "Now Mr. Bear, I'm sure that you are mistaken. Why would someone steal your garbage?"

I presented them both with copies of the pictures with dates printed on them, which showed the trash thief stealing my trash.

Chief Dulie scowled at Mr. Tikes.

Chief Dulie snarled, "What about all this? Is this correct? What are you doing here? Is that why you were waiting? Were you targeting Mr. Bear's trash for theft? What is that illegal contraption that you were looking in? Think about all the trouble you are in now, boy."

Mr. Tikes almost collapsed and his face lost all its color, but he took a deep breath to regain his composure and replied, "I have been making money collecting people's trash so a marketing analysis can be done to determine people's buying patterns. We select people randomly – sometimes based on their age for instance. It is not illegal to examine people's garbage. The police do it all the time."

Obviously he had been trained to say all this. He had practiced it since he wouldn't know a marketing study from study hall.

Chief Dulie thought a few minutes, then he admonished Mr. Tikes, "That may be so. But I will turn this over to the District Attorney for his review. It will be up to his office to determine if you have committed any crimes like harassment or hate crimes or identity theft by targeting older people, or whatever. I will personally accompany other law enforcement officers if the DA issues an arrest warrant for you and I'll hope you resist arrest. Do you understand? Now you better not let me see you here in this borough again or I will pull you over and examine that car and find something to hold you on; even if you are only going one mile over the speed limit. I am also going to let word leak out to the other police forces in Pennsylvania to watch out for you."

Chief Dulie returned the documents. He asked, "May I see that periscope?" When it was handed to the Chief, he issued a receipt for it and said, "I'll give this to the DA as evidence."

Mr. Tikes did not like it much but he relented. He appeared totally overwhelmed. He cleaned off his license plate with a nervous twitch to his hand and got in his car while bumping his head and slowly drove away. He made a long stop at the stop sign and turned left. The other police cruiser followed him quite a long ways.

Chief Dulie turned off his flashing lights and I rode along for breakfast.

Chief Dulie remarked, "I hope that finishes that. It is too bad we will probably never know the person or people behind the stealing of your trash. Tikes doesn't appear bright enough to be the brains behind all this."

I agreed as we had breakfast. Before I left to walk back home, I was cautioned, "Maintain vigilance. Call me or the state police if anything looks out of the ordinary."

Two Months later.

All was back to normal. The trash collection was actually being done by the collection people. The DA decided not to press charges. The periscope was returned to Chief Dulie, who kept it locked in an evidence room.

I would inquire about Mr. Tikes and Chief Dulie would say that he was keeping an eye and ear open for any dirty deeds done by Tikes, but he had been clean.

I kept an eye open for the telltale article called the Bottom Drawer. It finally appeared in a magazine. It was called Below the Bottom and it was written by Ricky 'Rabid Raccoon' Roberts. It was almost exactly as I had edited it. There wasn't any doubt about it.

One Month later.

Since there hadn't been any news about the plagiarism, I called my agent, Mr. Cliff Loews, Agent to the Stars. It is one of the phone numbers I have memorized.

He answered in his nasally yet monotone, smooth voice and I said, "Hello, Cliffy."

He said, "Oh it is you …. Bear. Are you calling to tell me that your book is finally finished?"

"No, but I expect to finish by next week. The book is in its last days, I fear."

"Good."

I asked before he could hang up, "What does the industry do about plagiarism?"

"Oh no! Don't tell me that you have been copying other writer's works?"

I maintained my cool and said, "Not me, but I did notice a similarity between LOWER SIDE by Torry Pynts and BOTTOM Drawer by Ricky 'Rabid Raccoon' Roberts. Both are short stories so it might not matter."

He replied in a very serious tone, "It does matter immensely. Are you sure about this, Bear?"

"Read them both yourself and decide, Diffy. Let me know please." I hung up.

Three weeks later.

The writers' trade journals were covering the latest gossip about a plagiarism case brought by one Torry Pynts and her publishers against Ricky 'Rabid Raccoon' Roberts and his publishers. Since that short story probably did not generate a lot of money, the settlement would probably be quick and soon forgotten. After all, money talks and nobody walks. Money settles all.

One month later.

I was on my front porch enjoying a cup of coffee while I tried to think of a finish for a short story when a new shiny, red, two seat sports car pulled in my driveway. A slight middle aged man with a paunch climbed out and smiled at me and waved. He asked if he could join me on the porch since he wanted to talk to me. I waved him towards a seat on the swing.

He said, "I am Ricky Roberts, better known as the 'Rabid Raccoon', and you are Bear. I have wanted to talk to you for a long time." He said all that with a lopsided grin.

I was getting antsy as I knew he knew that he had copied my manuscript, which was a copy of one written by Torry Pynts. He knew I had set him up. I also knew he had been sued over that same copy of a copy.

He said, "I now have a new job. I am an editor. Miss Torry Pynts liked my version of her short story so much I was offered a job to edit all of her upcoming work. She even dropped the lawsuit alleging plagiarism. This lucrative editing gig wouldn't have happened without your help. Thanks again."

With that he left the porch and waved at me as he drove off in his new fancy car. How about that? I edited the short story, which the Rabid Raccoon is claiming credit for. He gets the new job along with what appears to be lots of money and I get nothing but some raccoon crap left on my hands and the appropriate smell in the air!

I hope Miss Torry Pynts and the Rabid Raccoon are very happy together and I never see nor hear from them again. I also hope the Rabid Raccoon is adept at editing. He could maintain his new found job and wealth so he would remain happy and out of my hair. Thank goodness we did not shake hands while he was here! Yuck!

Now where is the cell phone as I gotta' fill Chief Dulie in on this development. I want him to keep his remaining eye and ear on the Rabid Raccoon. Then maybe we can play some golf tomorrow. I will be expected to pay his greens fee. Here it goes again.

MEMORIAL

I awoke to sound of that blasted phone ringing. Just let me doze off for an early afternoon nap and you guessed it, the phone always seems to ring. I stood up too quickly and almost passed out. It is tough getting old!

I made it to the phone and lifted the handset off of the hook to end the infernal noise. I grunted into the receiver before I slid down beside the cabinet and rested on the floor. I heard the ultimate feminine, silky, smooth voice. I'm talking of a voice here which sounded smoother than pure silk sliding over polished glass.

The voice said, "Hello, Mr. Bear, I am Makie from State Senator ..blah..blah..blah."

I dozed off to the sound of her voice.

She continued, "You are Mr. Bear, aren't you?"

I grunted in response.

The wonderful voice asked, "And you are in his district?"

"Whose district?" I asked.

"State Senator Crooner..blah..blah..blah."

Her voice made me doze off again.

"Are you still with me, Mr. Bear?"

I was able to grunt a second time.

Makie started talking again, "Well, anyway, he wants to nominate you to be the Pennsylvania state writer. You are the MOST FABULOUS WRITER currently residing here in the Commonwealth. It would be ..blah..blah..blah a great honor

..blah..blah..blah. OK? We will let you when ..blah..blah..blah and where. Bye bye."

I must have dropped the phone on the floor and dozed off there on the floor with my head leaning against a cabinet.

The next thing I remember was hearing someone close the door to my microwave and then the sound of someone chuckling. I slowly opened one eye to see my friend, Chief Dulie looking down at me. He was in uniform and he was just now removing a cup of coffee, my leftover coffee, from the microwave.

He had a mocking look on his face as he said, "Tisk, tisk, just look at the condition 'ole Bear has gotten himself into so early in the day. The wages of drink and wild women, I suppose. I could get a lot of money for a picture of you now."

I pushed myself and got on all fours before I was able to pull myself into a standing position. I glared at Chief Dulie. I put one hand on my back to straighten it out painfully.

I said, "My nap was quite rudely interrupted by the ringing of that blasted phone. But I just couldn't stay awake on the call. I guess I shouldn't have stayed up so late watching the Steelers-Browns game. Is there another cup of MY coffee left?"

He proceeded to fill a cup he found on the table. He popped it in the microwave before adding my flavored creamer to his coffee cup. He was still chuckling.

I said with a growl as I started to remember the contents of the call, "it was someone from a State Senator's office. They want to nominate me for the state writer."

He asked as he took my coffee cup out of the microwave and handed it to me, "you mean, you would be our state writer; kinda' like we have a state flower, bird, dog, and tree."

"Yes, I think so. But I did not get the total gist of the call since the caller had such a sweet and smooth voice. She kept putting me back to sleep."

The usually nice and good Chief said smartly, "I hope I never get so old that a great sounding woman's sexy voice puts me to sleep instead of, well, stirring my loins."

"OK. I get it. Leave it alone", I grunted in reply.

He said, "Thanks for the coffee. I gotta' go back on patrol. Just let me know where and when the ceremony is for this state writer award. I want to attend. You are bound to be a shoo-in, with your many writing awards and your past infamous history. I can just see you up there on the dais as you give your acceptance speech."

He said the latter with a chuckle since he knew I detest appearing in public in general and I have a deep-rooted fear of making speeches or appearing in front of the camera.

My face must have become white because he said, "You will just have to call in sick that day, Bear. But even if you attend, you will do fine. Surely even you can handle one little acceptance speech."

He set down his empty cup and departed through the garage. Maybe I need to re-think giving him my garage access password, although, he also has my house key.

I added creamer to my coffee cup and carried the cup to the picture window in the living room and watched him get in the cruiser and leave. I waved and he waved back before the cruiser backed out of my driveway and exited stage left.

I was heavy in thought as I contemplated my predicament. First, I did not have the phone number of the silky voiced young lady who called me. In fact, I could not even remember the name of the State Senator for this district. I am name challenged so this isn't a new problem to me. I would, however, be able to find all of this on the all-knowing-and-all-privacy-violating internet, of course. But could I stop this nomination from happening? Probably not; once politicians gets an idea in their heads, especially a frivolous one, there is no stopping them.

Secondly, it would be my luck I would win this nomination and be expected to attend and speak at a ceremony in front of a multitude of attendees and media cameras – gasp and gag and shake and shudder. Hmmm! There has to be a way out of this.

Today started out about like any other day. Since I wasn't playing golf or hunting or fishing, I awoke at about the same time as

I do every day even if I stay up late. I made coffee and ate a stale doughnut before sitting at my computer and writing for a couple of hours until hunger forces me to stop.

I changed into old jeans and an even older wrinkled sweater and walked to Old Bob's Café for my main meal of the day. I arrived there promptly at 11 am, just like most days.

I did not even go out of my way to aggravate Alice, the waitress, today. I ordered take-out broasted chicken with sides for my evening meal, since I prefer not to cook at all. At home, I read the paper and watched the news at noon.

Then my problem began with a simple phone call. Now I would not be able to continue to nap nor write; just contemplate and plan.

I logged on to the internet and checked on the state senate site for the Commonwealth. I found that my state Senator's name is Crooner and that one of his aids is named Makie. How appropriate that the Senator's name was Crooner since I suspected he could sure sing some pretty stories to his constituents. Just like Makie, the young lady from his office. Maybe that is a requirement to work at his office, being a smooth talker.

I called his local office in Leoberg and asked to speak to Makie. I was told she had left for the day, but was informed that I could call her back tomorrow or I could leave a message for Makie to return my call. As I thanked the lady who had answered the phone, I realized she had sounded vaguely familiar. I shook my head and tried to remember her name; was it Betty? Interesting, well, but probably not! If only I knew then what I was to find out later.

I got up the next day and made coffee. I shaved and showered as I prepared to go visit Senator Crooner's office to meet Makie and maybe stop all of this nonsense about me being nominated for the state writer. I made the mistake of turning on the bad-news tube and there was this report from MBCI, the giant media and news network.

This report aggravated me greatly. They vaguely showed where to purchase the ingredients to make the bombs. The kind used by terrorists to blow up airplanes. They even showed the effect a small bomb might have on a large aircraft. A hole was blown in the side of an actual airplane. Luckily, they did not show how to mix them, which was probably available on the internet.

They showed just enough on television to encourage terrorists to want more information. It is bad enough that all of this is available on the internet, but they did not have to show it in the morning news. DON'T ENCOUAGE ADDITIONAL BOMBING; what were they thinking?

So I decided to stop by the local affiliate of MBCI and complain about this breech of intelligence on their part. Usually I just call, which I do a lot. I even know their phone number by heart. Joyce who is the receptionist there doesn't take my calls well. She loudly hangs up on me. She has gone so far as to call me names or worse (*as you will see later*!).

I was finally ready to depart. I went into the garage and started up my car. I let it idle until it was warmed up before I slowly backed it out of the garage.

I backed out into the street before I remembered the new-fangled technology. I pulled back into the driveway and went into the house and found my cell phone. I should carry it along for emergencies since I am, well, quite aged if you must know. I even remembered to plug it into the cigarette lighter to charge the battery, since it is probably dead by now.

I just can't imagine that people have these things in front of their face or hanging on their ears all of the time. I wonder if scientists are trying to develop a microchip which could be implanted under the skin so people could communicate instantly without a cell phone. That microchip could be powered by the human body so batteries would not be required. It could even be developed so people could instantly see a keyboard and screen in the air in front of them so they could text at anytime, anyplace. They would just reach into space in front of them and start air typing or use their voice to access or answer.

What a sight that would create – people air typing and talking at any place or any time. Yuck, I better be quiet and not give anybody ideas!

I made up my mind about the route to take. I would stop at a diner on the way to the TV station on the Lincoln Highway. Then I would stop by the state senator's office and meet Makie. After that, I made plans to stop by the local big-box store to pick up essentials, like toilet paper, paper towels, dried fruit, nuts, frozen foods, and coffee; yes, lots of coffee. As you can see, I detest shopping so I make one trip a month and load up this car, which can hold a lot. I would also stop and pick up some of my favorite special beer. It is becoming difficult to find, but it used to be quite prevalent.

Once on the road, I drove slowly and carefully. I think that people in this day and age rush around way too much. They have forgotten how to slow down and enjoy the sunshine and flowers on a late spring day. Also, they have no patience; they do not save money to purchase anything like my late wife and I did to purchase this car. Everything must be quick like right now, this instant. Everything is on-demand.

After breakfast, I drove into the parking lot at the local MCBI station. I let myself into the lobby and noticed that Joyce was on the phone. I could see her talking into a receiver that had a cord attached to it; imagine that.

I looked at the many awards and photographs on the wall until I heard her hang up and say, "May I help you, sir?"

I turned around and she groaned quite loudly, "OH NO. Not you. Not today. What did I do to deserve you today?" Her broad face showed pure agony. Then she put her blonde head down and pounded on her desk. Did I hear her sobbing?

At that instant, a man in a suit opened the door from the studio and held the door for a smartly dressed woman. Instantly Joyce looked up at me and said, "I'll be with you in a minute sir."

She smiled sweetly as the couple asked a question. She answered and wished them a good day as they departed.

Her face instantly turned into a harsh grimace as she said, "ok, out with it, Just Bear. Let's get this over with. What can I help you with today?"

She picked up a pen and continued to give me a look which said she would rather do anything than talk to me; maybe a root canal without pain blockers would be more fun.

I said quietly and calmly and sweetly or as close as this old Bear can, "Joyce dear, please relax. I mean you or this foul station no harm. I just wanted to give you my opinion on the airing of that piece this morning which showed how to make and use a bomb to blow up airliners. The station should not have been so graphic. It was like a tutorial and it covered everything a terrorist could ever possibly want to know. Please do not encourage more misguided and disgruntled slime balls to try to blow up and kill more innocent people." I sighed slowly. "Will you pass that on please, Joyce dear?" I usually mispronounce her name to keep her attention fully on me, but I did not even do that today.

She groaned as she finished writing, but she kept her eyes on me the whole time. Those same eyes could have been quite lovely but they were boring holes through me as she said, "Yes, I will turn in your comments."

She hesitated and said, "Could you please go, Just Bear? Like now!" She pointed to the door. She obviously is someone else from this current society, since she appeared to be in a rush.

I waved gently at her and said, "Thanks and have a good day, Miss Joyce."

As I turned to leave, she called after me, "and please do not send me anymore of your flowers and candy like you have been doing for the holidays. I hate to even throw that STUFF in the trash since I expect it will cause devastating harm to the environment since it came from you."

"Why, Joyce dear, I was only trying to make amends".

She interrupted me by saying through a tight grimace, "You can never make amends. Every time I answer the phone, I am afraid it is you calling again to complain. You make my life a living hell. Now if you will excuse me, I have to go barf." With that she stood up and left the receptionist desk empty, something I suspect was not supposed to be done.

Joyce really appears high strung. Well, yes, I have been calling a lot, but I try not to take it out on her since she is only the message taker.

As I reflected on poor Joyce and what to do to repair the bad image she had of me, I drove to Leoberg to the offices of the esteemed State Senator Crooner. I had driven past this office many times but I had never noticed this was where his office is or who he is or what he does, if anything.

I expected a different reaction from the receptionist and I was correct. She had a longer face with a straight nose and brown hair. She smiled and me and asked, "How may I help you, sir?"

"Is Makie in?"

"Yes, she is. Is she expecting you? Oh, excuse me." She was interrupted when another lady entered the room. This woman was a short, plump lady with a round face and blondish curly hair. She smiled at me weakly and turned to her left to talk to the receptionist, but the blonde lady kept an eye on me while the conversation continued. Then she agreed to something and left. She opened the door and glanced back over her shoulder to look at me again.

The blonde woman looked familiar, but I couldn't figure out who she was or where I knew here from. Yet, there was something about her.

My thoughts were interrupted when I was asked, "Who may I say wants to see Makie?"

"Bear, just say Bear. She will want to see me."

"Ok", she said rather skeptically as she picked up the phone.

I won't bore you with the conversation I had with Makie because she answered everything with a positive twist. For instance, I said I didn't think I was well known enough to be approved as state writer. She replied I was well known enough to be the national writer. Yes, her voice was even sweet as honey in person.

When I stated the award should go to someone, who was an up and coming young writer to encourage him or her. She rebutted it by saying I should think I was still young and robust. Then she patted me on the arm.

Everything I said in the negative, well, she put a positive spin on it. She sounded like she was a career politician in the making because every time I communicate with politicians, they respond to my negative with glowing positives.

Makie asked me to wait and she would show me what had been prepared to ensure my becoming the state writer. Makie left and a couple minutes later, the chubby blonde lady came back out.

She introduced herself as Betty before she handed me a glossy pamphlet. It contained my picture with a bio of my writing career. It almost took my breath away since I am not a fan of myself. I think everybody takes themselves much too seriously.

Betty said, "We have provided this to all of the other state Senators so they can learn all about you and your accomplishments. You will definitely win."

I managed to say "thank you. " She said good bye and turned to leave me in the lobby.

As she opened the door, she turned and gave me a sly smile and a wink. I almost missed that. As it turned out, I should have used those gestures as a forewarning, but I was too overwhelmed.

I left the office and got in my car. My head was spinning both from my encounter with Joyce at the television station and now with Makie. I almost turned to go home but I remembered my other errands. I backed up and turned north to go pick up the supplies.

Since it was spring and the weather was turning nice, warm and sunny, I forgot all about this entire state writer stuff. I spent more time going to play golf or watching baseball games at the stadium and on television. I even tried to fit in some writing after I finished up lawn and garden duties.

One day right before I fell asleep for my early afternoon nap, the phone rang. It was Makie from State Senator Crooner's office.

She swooned, "Tomorrow is the last day of this session of the state legislature. They are scheduled to vote on your nomination. We thought you would want to be there to witness this historic event." She gave the last words an almost religious lift.

Oh well, I might as well go.

I told her, "Yes, I will attend. Do I need an official invitation or can I just watch from the gallery?"

She proceeded to give me instructions on parking and how to get to the gallery. I can tell you, a nap was out of the question now as I contemplated what affect this nomination could have on me. I finally gave up and went out to mow the lawn since I knew my creative side was out of commission now.

I actually slept fairly well that night.

After having coffee the next morning, I showered and put on my cleanest and only slightly wrinkled clothes and prepared to go to witness this historic event as Makie called it. I was soon going to wish I had stayed home or maybe moved to Guam or someplace even more remote than that.

The drive to Harrisburg was uneventful. I stopped and had an enjoyable brunch on the way. I parked in a garage and walked over to the Capitol. It was a lovely late spring day. It was nice to be out and about on a day like this.

The gallery was quite full, but I found a seat at a little after noon. The Senators were having lunch. I was able to locate Senator Crooner's empty seat on the floor. I looked slowly at my copy of the pamphlet about me, which I had brought along.

The Senators came back into the room and took their seats while talking and joking.

I must admit I did doze off a time or two as the Senators talked and argued about this or that or something else. Finally after four in the afternoon, the assembly went quiet. They still hadn't covered my nomination. Just then an aide came into the room and whispered something in Senator Crooner's ear. I could see him gesture back towards the podium. The aide held up both hands as if to say, "What can I do?"

Senator Crooner leaned over and whispered something to the Senator sitting beside him. That guy shook his head up and down and Senator Crooner left the floor with his aide.

The presiding officer said, "If that is it, I will accept any motion to adjourn for the summer."

The Senator who sat beside Crooner stood up and said, "We need to vote on this nomination from Senator Crooner, who was pulled away in a minor emergency. You all have copies of this glossy pamphlet."

The presiding officer said, "Ok, we can proceed. Do you all have copies of this?"

There were murmurs of accent. "If so, is there any discussion?"

One Senator stood up and said that he wanted to get home for the summer. There were chuckles and nods of agreement. He added, "I move that we change the state fossil to this Bear as per this pamphlet."

There was a second and then a multitude of "yeas".

At that exact second, two women over to my right stood up and cheered and danced around. They were quite loud and boisterous. Why it looked like Joyce, the receptionist from the local TV station and Betty from the state senator's office.

I must admit to be a little, no, a lot confused. (*I did not know there was going to be a vote to change the state fossil.*) I thought they were voting on my nomination of state writer. I let the crowds leave after the session adorned and was just standing when Joyce and Betty walked over towards me.

They both had wide grins and they were laughing and acting like their team just won the World Series and the Super Bowl or they just won ten million dollars, tax free.

Joyce said loudly, "Guess that we got you, huh, Just Bear? Now you are the state fossil, so there."

With that she dropped a pamphlet on my lap. I was still confused until I compared the two pamphlets. Their copy showed my face but it had been altered to resemble an actual bear. I had a toothy grimace and my face was covered in gray hair, lots of grey hair. It described how a bear's body was discovered in a cave in Western Pennsylvania. It detailed how the body had been preserved for so many years, etc. My copy called me the greatest author Bear.

I had been set up by Joyce and Betty. Come to think of it, they looked like each other in their faces and in body shape, and hair color. Where they sisters?

I was unsure if I should feel better since I wouldn't have to accept my nomination by giving speeches at many gatherings. Or should I feel anger at being set up. I slowly went back to the garage and retrieved my car and drove home deep in thought.

The other good thing about this strange turn of events was I hadn't informed my small circle of friends about the vote today. They would never let me forget that I was now the state fossil. I'm old but nobody is that old. Hmmmmm!

I stopped at a fast-food-chain restaurant and had proper Bear chow, a big burger, french fries and a chocolate shake. I was contemplating the whole string of events. I could understand Joyce though. She felt she had to get even with me.

I actually managed to get a good night's rest after watching the Mariners defeat the White Sox in a game that went extra innings. In fact, I even slept in until the phone rang at my bedside just after 8 a.m.

I opened one eye while I considered whether I should answer the phone or not. I detest a ringing phone about as much as I hate the paparazzi but I answered it.

The gravelly rough woman's voice said low and secretively, "Be in front of the farmer's market at two today."

"Huh?" I asked.

The voice got even lower in volume and continued, "You heard me, be in front of the farmer's market at two this afternoon."

The phone was hung up at the other end because I heard a dial tone.

I was really confused now. I knew I would not be able to get back to sleep. I got up and made coffee while I contemplated the strange and eerie message I had just received.

But you know me. I would have to go to find out what all of this conspiracy stuff was about. I would go there and get lunch and pick up some good meats and vegetables. I was fairly certain I was not going to be in danger at such a popular spot so I did not tell Chief Dulie about all of this cloak and dagger stuff.

I had a great lunch and shopped a little before I put my purchases in my car. I went into the market and purchased a cup of java, which I laced with flavored creamer.

I went out front and watched the crowds of people enter and leave.

I glanced at my watch a couple of times. It was now almost two fifteen, when I saw a tall attractive young lady walk slowly my way. She had her head down but she still looked familiar for some reason.

She walked up to me and said tearfully (*in a great smooth voice*), "I am so sorry, Mr. Bear. I do not know what happened to your nomination. It wasn't supposed to be any problem." Then she sobbed. I now know who she is.

"Makie, dear, do not worry. I've had worse things done to me. I might actually qualify as a fossil. Come inside and I'll buy you a cup of coffee, if you agree not to cry anymore."

I slowly took her arm and turned her around. I reached over and lifted her chin so I could see her pretty face. She had tears running down through her make up. It was not an attractive sight on such a pretty Asian face. In the movies, now would be when we both smiled and kissed. Yeah, like that is going to happen in real life to an old Bear.

She had a handkerchief in her hand but it looked wet and soiled. I led her into the market since I did not have a clean hankie in my pocket. I walked with her over to the restrooms and instructed her firmly to go into the ladies' room and clean up and come out with a smile on her face.

I went into the men's' room. She was outside waiting on me when I came back. She seemed refreshed so I asked her if she had eaten lunch. She shook her head no.

We walked over to my favorite deli in the market. We were fortunate enough to get a small table for two. After I encouraged her, she ordered lunch and I ordered a piece of raisin crumb pie.

After she sipped her soda, she seemed to gain some strength. She started to talk slowly and smoothly again. Oh, she was the smoothest talker. She could have had me pay her for the right to be nominated as the state fossil.

She remarked, "I'm sure Betty was responsible for changing the pamphlets which were sent to the other Senator's offices. I just can't figure out why she did it. Oh, she quit this morning also." Sigh. "I am so sorry, Mr. Bear."

"I think I know why, Makie. Does she have a friend by the name of Joyce?"

Makie nodded before answering, "Joyce is her sister."

I hesitated. I said, "I have apparently aggravated Joyce by my constant calls to the television station to complain about their poor news broadcasting so Joyce and Betty came up with this strategy to get even with me."

Makie looked at me before she attacked her lunch.

I enjoyed the pie, which was excellent by the way.

Makie said, "So that is it, huh? I had a discussion with Senator Crooner. He is in the process of letting it out it was all a prank our staff played on him. He has instructed the state printing office not to change any of the state lists or the web site. He has also asked a vote be held at the beginning of the fall session to cancel the prior vote. He anticipates this vote will be conducted with much humor. So that should settle that. I am still so sorry about all of this."

"Well, if you promise to forget about nominating me for state writer, well, then I will forget that this happened."

She asked, "What about Betty and Joyce?"

"Do you know where they are working now?"

She answered, "I heard Joyce and Betty were moving to Vegas to work as dealers. Will they cause you more problems?"

"Probably not. I have my writing password protected.. I also have friends on the police force. I suspect this episode is finished except we need to determine who is paying for this meal."

She chuckled and said she would pay but only if she could buy me a whole pie as a way of making amends. I agreed since state fossils really love raisin crumb pie.

BEAR SIGNS

I had been ignoring the persistent phone calls from my pesky agent, the self-proclaimed Agent to the Stars, one Cliff Lowes. (*Isn't caller identification a wonderful thing?*)
Finally, I answered his call by simply saying "hello".
He seemed so happy to talk to me, which made bells go off in my head because he is usually reluctant to talk to me.
He gushed in his smooth but nasally voice, "Bear, my man, my MAIN man, where have you been all of these past few days?"
"Oh, here and about Cleeffster."
"I have great news Bear. There is a job offer which is just beyond words. It has a myriad of possibilities; great salary, exciting locale, a chance to meet lots of celebrities, win more awards like Emmys and, also, need I add, great pay."
"Great. I hope you enjoy the new job. Don't worry; I'll find a new agent." I hung up. (*Yeah, I know he was talking about a job for me, but I just couldn't resist aggravating him. A Bear has to do what a Bear has to do.*)
The phone continued ringing and ringing and ringing. I fixed myself a cup of coffee with creamer and rum. I just knew I would need the extra kick of caffeine and alcohol before this was over.
I sauntered outside to sit on the swing on the front porch to watch the world go by in this great weather before I finally answered his call on my cordless phone.
"Hello."
"Bear, why did you hang up on me?" Cliff asked.

"Is that you Cliff? Wasn't I just talking to you?" I tried to give him the impression I was a little senile.

"Don't start that Bear. I know you better than that." He hesitated before proceeding. (*I hoped he would just give up but such would not be the case.*)

"Bear, you have a job offer. The powers-that-be in Hollywood have noticed your writing creativity and they want you to be a screen writer for a new comedy, which they are going to televise in the spring."

I interrupted him before he could proceed. I'm sure he had this call all scripted just like those paid callers do. If you can get them off their script, they get confused.

I asked, "I would be in living in Un-holly-wood and meeting all kinds of stars. I could play golf on those great coastal golf courses and go fishing for steelhead and they would pay me gobs of money. I would have nothing but time on my hands in sunshine to golf, fish and ."

He interrupted me, "No, Bear, you would have to work also. You would be part of a team of writers."

"Let's see then, Biffy. I would have to work with a team of writers, and have deadlines to meet. I would be working all hours of the day and night to have a script finished by late Monday so the actors could practice their lines for a couple days before filming the actual show on Friday for showing on Saturday. Is that what this is about?"

"Well, er, well". He was stammering now, "it is not that bad, Bear, and anyway, they only do 21 shows. So you would be able to do your other stuff the remaining half of the year. You would also have lots more money to enjoy your time off. You could travel the world with some young, pretty stars." (*Also, my agent would have lots more money to waste.*)

"Snuffy, just when did you ever get the idea this old Bear wants to work? Especially at a schedule set by someone else. A Bear can't just hit the creativity button at will. It has to be nurtured via fun time like hunting on a chilly morning in the mountains or chasing wily trout in a cold stream or playing golf on a sculptured green fairway. It helps also if one stops to watch the game at the stadium or on the flat screen while sipping a cold beer in my favorite easy chair. You gotta' let the ideas form; you can't force them. Also, being with those actors isn't healthy since they spend their time getting paid millions of dollars pretending to be someone they are not and then they forget who they actually are."

"Bear, no, NO, NO, you got it all wrong. It would be an ideal setting for you to expand your horizons. Your creativity would not know any bounds. Sharing ideas with those other writers would only help you to develop. You would love the interaction on the team."

"Let me get this straight, me, myself and I, who does not like talking about myself or my writing would enjoy working on a team and sharing ideas with others. I do not even want to talk to the lines of people at these forced book signings when they ask why I wrote this or that."

I laid on the sarcasm as I continued, "not only do I fear being in front of the camera but also I detest talking about my writing. It is what it is! Like my writing or hate it. I cannot control how readers feel about my writing."

I was hot now. I hung up.

Just then, a news van stopped abruptly in the street in front of my house and a young, pretty reporter jumped out of the passenger door. I just had time to pull on a rope which was lying beside me to force a sign to pop up on my lawn and right in front of that reporter. The sign said, "NO TRESPASSING" on two bat wings so it could be read by people coming either way on the street. It was easy to read by the reporter standing right in front of it. I hated signs so I designed this so it was visible only when I wanted it to be.

The reporter hesitated briefly as she glanced at that sign. She looked at me on the porch as I pulled out a three foot square sign from behind the swing. This sign was printed with the following;

NO TRESPASSING

NO PHOTOGRAPHS

NO INTERVIEWS
Under penalty of law

She yelled, "Hurry Cam. He is on the porch."

A tall man with short, blue hair and many ear rings pulled a camera out of the back of the news van and put it on his shoulder as I lifted a bear mask on a stick so that it was in front of my face.

I yelled, "No trespassing. Can't you read the signs? I will not give you an interview. I do NOT do interviews. Go bother someone else." The mask was made for me by my buddy Bench. It was carved with eye holes and teeth; it even had a long snout. Bench called it an angry bear mask, but I have used it at Halloween when I hand out candy. Even the littlest ghosts, goblins, and ghouls giggle at this mask so you can appreciate what it really looks like; maybe Yogi or Boo-boo or pooh bear. Just my luck!

But this reporter was not to be deferred from her mission. She said with much confidence, "No, I just want an interview. It will not take long." She started to walk towards me.

At exactly that second, one of the borough's finest happened to be driving by. He hit his siren briefly as he stopped behind the news van. He jumped out and approached the reporter and cameraman. The policemen in this borough know me and know I do not do interviews. I expected and appreciated their help.

This one is Pat and he is a chubby, balding youngish man, but he wears skinny, square glasses which only makes him look plumper. But I do not judge peoples' appearance since I am clothes challenged. I could put on the finest and still look like a rumpled and wrinkled old Bear.

He walked reluctantly towards the pretty, young, bouncy reporter.

I yelled at him, "Arrest these trespassers Pat. I ordered them off of my property."

The reporter gave Pat her finest smile and said, "But the press is protected by the first amendment to the Constitution."

I yelled even louder than I did the last time, "But I am guaranteed life, liberty and the pursuit of happiness by that same Constitution. Arrest them both, I say."

Pat shrugged and said quietly, "Mr. Bear is right. You are trespassing. Let me see some identification please."

I yelled again, "and have the cameras turned off.'

The cameraman dropped the camera off his shoulder and murmured something; "I never had a chance to start the camera."

The reporter and the cameraman walked to the news van to get their identification. I expected them both to jump in the van and make a hasty retreat, which might force Pat to follow in hot pursuit. But they reluctantly took out their id and came back and handed the documents to Pat.

Pat said quietly, "I am only giving you a citation for trespassing. You can pay the fine at the magistrate's office. May I have the owner's card for the van?"

"What, you are not arresting them, Pat? No hand cuffs? No conviction for trespassing?"

The reporter stared daggers at me as she turned and walked to the passenger's door of the van.

Pat took the owner's card and said, "I am also giving you a ticket for obstructing traffic. This can also be paid at the same office."

I yelled, "Give them an additional ticket for littering. They left slimy reporter footprints in my lawn. It might kill my perfectly manicured grass."

Pat just shook his head while the young reporter gave me her worse-wicked-witch of the combined east, north, south and west look as she got in the van.

After the van departed, I asked Pat to join me for a cup of coffee.

Pat pulled the cruiser into my driveway.

I went inside and made Pat a cup of coffee without flavored creamer. Who knew?

Pat sat down on the glider and asked me, "Do you really hate giving interviews or do you just hate reporters?"

"Both."

I changed the subject to baseball and the current status of the local independent baseball team. Pat received a call for action so he departed.

I went inside to freshen my coffee when the phone rang and I made the big mistake of answering it. It was the news director from the local television station. He talked so fast that I missed his name. (*I am name challenged also*.)

He asked, "Did you really try to have my reporter and cameraman arrested?"

"Sure did. It's too bad they were NOT arrested. Then they would have a criminal record and they would experience trouble getting jobs anywhere, except maybe in politics, where any criminal can be and often is elected."

He hesitated so I asked, "Did you lose a career contest?"

"What? What did you say, Mr. Bear?"

"Did you want that position of news director or did you lose a contest and have to agree to work in television news for five or ten years? You wouldn't willingly have made that career choice. It will stay on your resume for, like, ever."

He answered in a stuffy and self-important manner, "I most certainly did work hard to get this job."

"It is much worse than I thought. It is too bad. I am so sorry for you. Why your poor mother must make up lies when people ask her if you still work in television news. Tisk. Tisk."

"There is nothing wrong with our news broadcasts."

"Oh yes, there is. If you have a couple of hours, I will gladly share my ideas with you."

"Ok, shoot, Mr. Bear. What could possibly be wrong with OUR news?" he answered smugly.

"Get a cup of coffee and a long note pad and listen. You are, of course, encouraged to take notes.

"First, would be news de jour. It is like soup de jour. You take the current event and you talk about and then you talk about talking about it until everyone is sick of it.

"Second, you think that celebrity worship is news. This actor, athlete or even worse, a politician did this or said that or stopped to sniff a flower.

"Thirdly, your broadcasts are biased. Whatever.."

I stopped talking. Was that a click I heard on the phone?

"Hello. Hello. Is anybody there?" Just my luck, he hung up on me just as I was on a roll.

I sipped coffee and tried to relax. Finally, I settled down enough to get back to work writing. I continued that adventure until I stopped to make a PBJ sandwich and an apple for supper. After the evening meal, I sat in my stained but comfortable chair. Grabbing the remote, I went through the channels before I settled on a baseball game.

Later in the night, I awoke and turned off the TV before getting ready for bed.

Since it was misting outside the next morning, I wrote for a while until it cleared up before walking to Old Bob's Café for main meal of the day.

While walking back, I started to make a list in my mind of the supplies I needed to pick up at the big warehouse store. I was almost out of peanut butter, jelly, bread, granola, bananas, fruit, cereal, milk and everything else I consumed when I got hungry. Also, I could usually count on that store to have an ample supply of goodies there, like pie, cookies, and fancy edibles depending on the season.

I was still making the list as I turned the corner onto my street. Being distracted, I almost missed the large TV news van parked in front of my house. I made a hasty route change and turned to go around to the back of my house.

Luckily, the reporter must have been looking the other way since I didn't hear any yelled comments like "stop, we only want to interview you" or "there he goes".

Inside my house, I slowly moved aside the curtains and peeked out the front window. There was a well-dressed man standing in front of the van. He glanced at his watch and pulled at his clothes. Then he turned and said something over his shoulder, probably to the cameraman.

After watching him for a couple minutes, I became intrigued. Since the usual reporters were young and pretty, I just couldn't figure out who this middle aged man was and what he was doing in my street. He may have been a news reporter but he didn't fit the part.

I retrieved my bear mask and opened the door and stepped out. I held the mask in front of my face and beckoned the man to come over.

When his cameraman started to follow, I shouted, "No cameraman allowed. But you may come here." I pointed.

He hesitated and murmured to the cameraman, who turned back to the news van.

I shouted, "I will not allow any pictures or recordings to be made of me so if are wearing a microphone, please turn it off."

He opened his suit coat, and showed me his shirt.

He replied, "No bug or microphone here. After we talked on the phone yesterday, I wanted to come and meet you and get an interview."

Aww, he was the news director I talked to yesterday.

I pointed to my ratty old front porch benches and suggested, "Ok, let's sit and talk."

His face turned into a frown as he contemplated putting his impeccably tailored suit pants on my old benches. Since I had sat on my favorite bench, he removed his suit coat and sat gingerly on the other bench. He sat very rigidly, holding the suit coat folded in his arms. His back wasn't touching the back of the bench. In fact, he even glanced behind him to see if there was any dirt on the benches.

I chuckled and said, "The wind removed all of the dust so you can relax."

He countered, "Are you sure? Anyway, I only wanted to come here and meet you and discuss like rational people the prospects of my station getting an interview. So…"

With that I pulled the rope that popped up my 'No Trespassing' signs on the street.

I replied, "I do not give interviews, not now and not later."

I turned and glanced at the news van and was contemplating calling the borough police.

He sat quietly. He looked at me and talked convincingly for a few minutes. He tried every possible way to get me to relent.

I kept shaking my head side-to-side. I finally said, "No way."

I'm sure he was thinking how to get me to agree so I said, "You are wasting your time."

He finally stood up. He brushed off his pants and put his suit coat back on and faced me. He pulled and tugged at the coat until it was positioned to his satisfaction.

I stood up also.

He held out his hand and I shook it. At least, he was a gentleman about it.

As he walked down my short driveway, he stopped and looked at the signs I had pulled into an erect position. He laughed heartily and gave me a thumbs-up. He pointed to the sign and continued laughing.

After the news van left, I got up and started to go into the house when I had a thought. I walked out my driveway.

I was stunned. My 'No Trespassing' signs now proclaimed 'Reporters Welcome'.

I closely examined the signs. They fit to the backing just like they had been made for it.

My good buddy, Bench, had made the original signs. The plastic facade was incorporated into the wood.

Whoever had modified the two back-to-back signs had expertly covered the original words with these new ones. I glanced up and down the street as if whoever had done this would magically appear and say, "I done it. I got you."

Yeah, like that is gonna' happen. Also, it wasn't April Fools Day.

I went into the garage and took out my garden hose and gave those signs a good bath. But the new signs did not fade.

I knew Bench wouldn't have pulled this stunt. His humor was more subtle. But maybe I would need him to repair this mess. Let's see, he and his lovely significant other might be back in town in a couple weeks.

Could it wait that long? Guess it would have to unless I wanted to try to correct this injustice myself. But I might mess up these finely honed signs, although whoever did this hadn't left any telltale scratches or tears.

Also, who would do this? After some mind searches, I came to the conclusion it was a reporter. Someone I had made angry.

But when was this done? I had not been away from home recently. Hmm. Just another unsolved mystery, I guess.

GETTING GRILLED

I had to travel to the Apple to do a one-on-one interview with Sklyer Grille. You know him, the tall, handsome, blonde man, who does the television interviews in his calm, quiet voice.

I tried everything to get out of it, but to no avail. But if I did this, I would not have to go on the talk show circuit. This was the lesser of two evils. It would be one hour instead of much traveling and many, many, many terrible interviews.

I had already been through strike one with my agent about the screen writer's job, strike two with the recently departed reporter and her news director and now I faced strike three with this interview. Everything was going from bad to worse. My anxiety was increasing and I was going into a funk to say the least.

Well, they say if you must do something you really detest, then research if thoroughly and learn about it. I logged onto the internet and GOOGLED Sklyer Grille. I found his show was on for one hour on each weekday for 50 weeks a year. He sometimes conducted these interviews in other locales but usually in the Wormy Apple. His bio listed his accomplishments, which included awards won and a summary of his early gigs as a reporter, his time spent in the Marines and that he was an award winning quarterback in high school. It even listed his favorite brand of scotch and wine.

He was often photographed in the nightly hot spots in Un-holly-wood, and Lost Wages as well as in the Big Apple. The photographs showed him accompanying all sorts of the rich and beautiful or as I like to say the bitchy and spoiled.

I wasn't finding out what I wanted so I used my credit card and paid for additional information on him. I learned some stuff that he would never want distributed to the public. Interesting!

I searched the cable network site and I found everything I could about his show including the bios of his producers and writers.

I was feeling slightly better, but I knew I wasn't cool and calm in front of the camera. Even I did not know what I would do or say while there.

I somehow survived the sleepless night before my big interview. I tossed and turned and worried and thought about what to say. I only experienced a few shaving nicks, which I assumed the make-up people could cover. But I did not know what those people could do about my unkempt clothes. My hair, or what remained of it, would stick out at all angles no matter what I or they did to it, so there.

I hoped my car would break down on the way to the Amtrak station in Lancaster but it purred beautifully. This car is polished and babied. I knew in my heart it would not break down. Just my luck!

I usually enjoy riding on the train, but I was getting more anxious and nervous. I do not worry well. I could feel the butterflies forming in my stomach.

I do not remember most of the train or cab ride in the Apple since it went by so fast; much too fast for this old Bear. I kinda' came back to reality as the make-up ladies applied the cosmetics, and tried to tidy up my clothes. They must have sensed my fear. They tried to reassure me.

I was not introduced to the star, Sklyer Grille, before the show. It is too bad we did not meet as that might have changed the outcome.

After being installed in a private recording booth, which only added to my anxiety and nervousness, I could hear the Grillman's introduction. He seemed to really savor this part, but it only made me more upset.

Finally, I was led onto the stage and it was my turn to say something like "Hello Mr. Grille. It is so nice to be grilled on your show". But no, I said, "nice job you have here".

This brought a smug, wide grin to the Grillman's handsome face. He nodded his head up and down in agreement.

I said, "Yes, nice job. You only work about 39 minutes on each show due to commercials. So that means you make about one grand a minute plus bonuses."

His face started to sag a little.

I continued, "Also, you have two producers and five writers to prepare you for the show. I'll bet you have not even read any of my books or stories. Is that about right Griller?"

He said "what?" in an incredulous tone.

I was on a roll now. I said, "well, maybe if you would spend less time partying after the show and slow up the consumption of three hundred dollar a shot scotch, you could get more personally involved with this show. After all, this is your livelihood."

His jaw dropped and he could not even manage a comment. Looking back on this, I wondered why the director and producers did not stop the show then. But they did not.

My anxiety was slowing but my mouth wasn't. It was speeding up. I was doing exactly what I have criticized other people for; I had started my mouth before I engaged my brain. Also, I did not stutter, not once.

"And what about squiring all those young actresses around in Un-holly-wood and those show girls in Lost Wages? Doesn't your wife worry about all that? Oh, I get it; you are sexually challenged, aren't you? The old Grillman can't get it up."

He murmured "No, oh no" over and over again. He face was ashen and he kept shaking his head no.

I continued almost without taking a breath, "what a racket, working one show a day. I'll bet the make-up people work longer on you than you spend in front of the camera since you are getting pudgy, you know. That probably wouldn't have happened if you had stayed longer in the Marines. Yeah, I know you were given a medical deferment after serving only six weeks. What was your problem, a sprained ankle? Is that the same ankle that kept you from going to college on a football scholarship? You were a pretty good offensive lineman in high school in Cherry Hill, weren't you?"

With that he put his head down on the desk in front of him and just moaned. His bio, of course, bragged about him serving in the Marines and how good of a quarterback he was in school. I had just blown those two treasures of his.

I didn't miss a beat. I charged forward, "we shouldn't forget this old set that you insist on still using. It is getting quite dank and moldy. You should brighten this whole place up. Also, your producers and writers need more credit. They should get a raise for having to work with you, you phony.

"While you live in either your penthouse here in the Upper East Side or in a house on the beach in sunny California or in the super-secret apartment in Vegas that your wife doesn't know about, your staff probably lives in more modest places. You force them to stay in cheap hotels when they are required to follow you, don't you?"

He only raised his head to glance at me with wonder when I brought up that apartment in Vegas. Then he lowered his head and covered it with his hands. I must have guessed correctly about that place in Vegas. I again thought briefly why my full-in-his-face charge wasn't being stopped by the show's producers and directors. But the light in front of me never went out, which would signify going off-air.

I went on and on about him for the full show. I only gained momentum as I talked. Based on things I had found out about him on the web, I had made assumptions which would explain everything about the Grillman and his past. He was so shocked he did not even try to refute anything I said. When I was given the warning the show was about to end, I produced a little trophy I had made and brought along to give to him. It was a toilet seat covered with a grid from a portable grill, which read "I was grilled by the Grillman" and listed today's date.

I said, "Here is the Grillman award. You may wish to give these to anyone else, who has had the pleasure to be on your show."

After looking at it, he almost passed out as his head hit the desk in front of him. Then I got it; he thought I was presenting it to him, the Grillman. That wasn't what I meant. I was giving him a prototype of an award he could give to his guests. It was assumed by the media you had made it big time when you were invited on his show.

As the show finished and the on-air light went out, the door to the booth opened and a couple of the pretty, young assistants came in with big smiles on their face. One even had tears running down her cheeks. They both gushed over me. The shorter one hugged me and kissed me on the mouth. They hurriedly escorted me out of the show area and into the main television studio. The people I saw there were either laughing or had big smiles on their faces. The pretty young assistants just bundled me out and got me on the elevator.

One asked, "Where are you going now, Mr. Bear?"

"I-I-I guess, well, to P-Penn Station, and home. Eh. H-H-How did I do?"

They broke out laughing and said, "It was the best show ever. It is guaranteed to make headlines in both the trade magazines and the entertainment shows. It might even win an Emmy."

I thought, "Who knew?"

I got the shakes on the way down on the elevator. I also felt faint. Both of the young assistants grabbed my arms and held me upright as the elevator opened. They led me to a little cloak room and guided me into a soft chair. Then the one that had kissed me left the room quickly. She came back with a wet paper towel and a cold soda. They had to help me sip the soda since I just didn't have the strength or coordination to hold the can in my hands. They mopped my face with the cold paper towel.

I was asked quite a few times "are you ok, Mr. Bear? Should we call an ambulance?"

I answered "n-n-no" faintly to the ambulance question.

Finally, I started to relax a little and to breathe easy again. My hands stopped shaking. I realized I had somehow survived this interview. I started to relax for the first time.

You have to understand, I have an extreme fear of talking in front of people. This fear reaches an almost unbelievable level when I have to appear on television. I usually cannot speak at all so I guess that I had handled myself well on this show. At that time, I could not remember a thing I had said.

I assured them, "I feel fine now. Thanks so much for your help. Would you get me a cab?"

I heard, "are you sure, Mr. Bear?"

They both showed concern on their faces. I reassured them I was fine. I stood up by myself and started to walk towards the door. They walked beside me. Outside, one hailed a cab as the other held onto my arm for support. A cab stopped. The assistants held the back door open and helped me get in. One handed the driver some cash and said, "Penn Station please. Keep the change."

With that, I was on my way home. I glanced back as the cab pulled away and they waved at me. I grabbed a burger meal a fast foot place in the station. After consuming it, I really started to feel stronger. I had actually done it! I had finished the interview. Me, ole' Bear, I had made it through the Grillman show. That should show my publisher and agent! There!

I was on the train to Philly when I decided I had earned a nice cold beer to celebrate. The train would not have my favorite beer. I would have to make do with whatever they had. I walked back to the lounge car. I had to push and shove my way through a throng of laughing, talking and drinking people to get to the bar.

As I reached the bar, I glanced up at a television and saw they were watching me on the Grillman show.

I said, "beer please" just as the crowd slowly went silent as they recognized me.

The bartender popped the top off of a cold one and handed it to me and said "no charge". He was still laughing.

The people went back to watching the Grillman show. They would go quiet and then erupt in laughter when I made some statement about the Grillman's past. But it was then I saw how devastated that the host was. I had destroyed him. Just like a real bear, I felt I was backed into a corner and I charged out, straight at the closest adversary, who just happened to be the host, one Sklyer Grille.

He started out looking handsome, fresh and manly with his straight blonde hair, blue eyes and honest, smooth face. He ended up looking like he had been in a massive boat wreck with his make-up smudged and his hair askew. He had a scared look in his eyes and an agonizing expression. At the very end, he did not even look at the camera. He sat there with his face down on his desk and he was whimpering.

These people on the train thought it was hilarious; like it had been scripted. They offered to buy me more, but I declined since we were approaching the station in Philly. I finished the beer. I got up and thanked the bartender and worked my way through the crowd.

I heard comments like "great show", "the best interview show ever", "only a creative author like you could have written this", and "the Grillman is guaranteed to win the Emmy he has wanted forever."

I got off the train in the station and went into the restroom to wash my face. I was so stunned I almost walked into the ladies' restroom. I emptied my bladder and mopped my face with a cold paper towel. I almost soaked my sports jacket since I used so much cold water.

I somehow managed to find my way back on the train to Lancaster. I couldn't remember if I had carried anything on the train to the Rotten Apple so I did not know if I had left anything anywhere. Now all I carried was a newspaper under my arm. I tried not to notice if someone was looking at me.

On the ride to Lancaster, I tried to make some sense out of the whole terrible experience. It was, of course, my agent's fault since he insisted that I appear on as many talk shows as my contract demanded. He wanted to make as much money as he could off of my writing, which required me to do promotions. This was only natural. But there wasn't much I could do about any of that, except limit my personal appearances in the future.

Also, there wasn't much I could do about the show. It was in front of the world now. I could try to make an apologetic statement to the press about my performance or lack of performance. But I suspected that just might make the situation worse. I could try to contact the Grillman to apologize on a personal level. But I was not sure how to do that other than just call him to arrange a meeting; like he is ever going to want to talk to me again!

I am also challenged when it comes to the sensitivity of proper manners. Yeah, I know to say please and thank you or I'm sorry but that is about it. I also did not have anyone to help me. I could not trust my agent or my publisher. My late wife would know what to do now; hell, she would have made sure I never let myself get in this mess. She had tried to stop me from pursuing an avenue in my past; said avenue has made me into the Bear I am today.

Also, I could not rely on my limited circle of friends to help get me out of this predicament. I would have to figure this out for myself.

I continued to think about all of this as I watched the countryside roll past the train window, and one thought kept reemerging. That thought was the show's producers and director could have stopped this. They had arranged the broadcast so my dialogue wasn't interrupted much.

If the show was delayed enough for the commercials to be added in, then why was I allowed to continue? Of course, maybe the shows powers-that-be wanted me to continue, which left me totally confused.

As I left the train station, my insides were aflutter with a million butterflies. I was not sure I could trust myself to drive home.

I noticed another fast food restaurant so I ordered a milk shake. By the time I had finished about half of the milkshake, I felt well enough to drive home. I drove slowly. I spent the rest of the late evening watching the game between the Padres and Pirates while I sipped a cup of coffee. I was even able to fall asleep that night in spite of my recent experience.

The next morning, I managed to sleep in. The ringing of the phone awakened me. It was my agent. I decided not to answer it. (*Isn't it great to know who is calling?*)

I made coffee and retrieved my newspaper while it was still safe to do so. I expected to have a lot of paparazzi stopping by for interviews.

I put up all of the NO TRESPASSING signs around the edge of my property. I checked the signs to ensure that they had not been changed again.

I gambled I would not be disturbed so I sat on the front porch and read the newspaper. Well, I did not read the entire paper as I tried NOT to read anything about my talk show interview. I would probably not turn on the television news for a long time either since I did not want to know what they thought about the show.

As I sat and read the paper, I could hear my landline phone ring and ring and ring. My cell phone kept ringing also. It was too bad I had remembered to charge the battery in that blasted thing.

As I prepared to leave the house for my daily constitutional to get brunch at Old Bob's Café, I erased all of my messages without listening to them. I was still in a funk about all of my recent encounters with the media and celebrities. The constant ringing of the phones would not help my mood at all. (*Such is the life of a reluctant and reclusive celebrity, I guess. I sighed!*)

I turned off the coffee pot and brushed my teeth. I ran my fingers through my hair and I was off to get my main meal of the day. Expecting pursuit from the media, I went out the back door and around the block before taking a meandering path to the restaurant. It must have worked since I was not accosted for an interview. I waved and smiled at people as I walked past them. I may still be in social hibernation, but I would at least be civil and friendly to those people who continued to treat me the same way. I really do not enjoy being in social hibernation, but events in my life have forced me to stay in it over the past few years. Social hibernation was what caused me to create my Bear persona many years ago.

I sat at my usual seat at the counter in Old Bob's Café. Alice, the usual waitress brought me a cup of coffee and some flavored creamer, which they keep on stock just for me. I smiled and thanked her. She had a sly smile on her face. She must have watched the talk show yesterday but she refrained from saying anything to me about it. I gave her a break and ordered quickly. Usually, I make her wait as I take my time by reading and re-reading the menu before I order but not today. She took my order with raised eyebrows but again, she did not make any comment.

Just then Chief Dulie of the borough police dropped in the Café. He joined me at the counter while Alice brought him coffee also.

She asked, "Do you need a menu Chief Dulie?"

"Yes, please Alice."

He glanced at me and asked, "Would you like to see a good baseball game tonight?"

I looked sideways at him and asked, "Where?"

"At my son's little league game, it is the last game of the regular season. We will have burgers on the grill. Come on up and join us at six tonight at the elementary school. You will enjoy it." He said it all while sipping his coffee. He must have known about some of my recent ill-fated adventures but he never hinted at all. Come to think of it, he had never made any comments about my misadventures of the past and he has known about all of them, well, almost all of them anyway.

I walked a circular route home but I did not encounter any reporters so maybe I was going to get a media reprieve. I tried to work some on my next novel, but I was not in the creative mood. I mowed the grass.

I showered and walked up and watched a good baseball game on a bright, sunny evening. The kids made some ball handling mistakes but that was over-shadowed by their enthusiasm and their apparent love of playing the game. I really enjoyed the burgers, coleslaw and root beer the parents prepared and served after the game. It was good to be around people who did not seem to know or care about what mistakes I had made. It helped to improve my mood, but I still had a long way to go.

You will never believe it when I tell you that Sklyer Grille and I both won Emmys for the show. He looked so suave and cool with his long straight blonde hair and well-tailored tuxedo as he collected his prize.

He admitted he had wanted to win this award for a long time. It was a lifetime dream to win an Emmy. He thanked me for writing the show's script and for talking him into doing it my way. He thanked everyone on my behalf. He assured them I would receive my Emmy post haste.

I was shocked as I did not even know I had been nominated for the show. I knew that I had mentally destroyed him, Sklyer Grille.

Then I remembered a gold gilded envelope I had received but not opened. I found it under the sofa so I opened it. It was an invitation to the Emmy awards show. Who knew?

I guess I would no longer be on his radar. He had everything to thank me for and nothing to get even for.

The days slowed down considerably since I couldn't concentrate on writing and I was constantly checking for paparazzi, who wanted to be the ones to get the scoop. My tiny circle of friends had shrunk since Bench was off with his new main squeeze, the lovely Miss Jacky Mooney of the Sunshine Show and Callie was away at the Naval Academy. So that left Chief Dulie, who had a family and a job and Reets, who aggravates me about as much as I aggravate everybody else. I stayed in a funk.

SETUP

I finally made myself go shopping. I was out of almost everything including my two staples, beer and coffee. I jumped in my 60's custom car I call the tank and went to the town. I loaded it up with lots and lots of paper products, snacks, goodies and dry goods from the big-package store. I had lunch before I made a run to a distributor who sells my favorite beer. I purchased a couple cases and drove home while I listened to 60's music on the radio. I was in a better mood when I got home. I listened to more good oldies as I put all of the supplies away. I was just about to sit down with a cold soda when there was a knock at the door. I checked at the window since I did not want to be surprised by some sneaky reporter, but it was only a delivery guy, who was holding a long slender package. I know him. I gladly opened the door.

He said, "Good day, Mr. Bear. I have a delivery for you."

I said, "hummm, I can't remember ordering anything."

Then the smell hit me.

"What is that smell? Did you spill some perfume in your delivery van?"

He held out the slim package to me and raised his eyebrows as he said, "it is coming from your package."

It was. It definitely was. The smell was almost overpowering.

I took the package gently. I hoped I would be able to wash off the perfume from my hands.

He said, "Sign here".

I did. We exchanged pleasantries before he left.

The return address was from a florist in Philly. Interesting; very interesting! I laid that smelly package on the porch swing and went inside and got the soda. I wanted to let it air out a little bit! Whew!

I sat on the swing and contemplated the new package. I just couldn't figure out who would send me a package from a florist unless it was from some reporter hoping to get an exclusive. I carried the soda around my house to check for paparazzi. I found none. I walked around the other way to double check; everything looked quiet. Finally I sat on the swing and slowly opened the package. It contained one long-stemmed red rose and a note.

The note was written in a firm and looping feminine hand and read, "Lover boy, meet me at the L B Lounge at eight tomorrow evening. Do not be late. Signed S L." The initials S L were in the middle of a hand drawn heart.

I was way beyond perplexed and confused. This was flat out amazing. I contemplated the who, and the why that was behind this. My Bear mind finally clicked. I called Old Bob's Café and ordered broasted chicken and sides for two and closed and locked the house.

I got in my car and drove slowly to pick up the food before going to see my only contact in the clandestine world, Reets. I wanted to grease the wheels with food before I asked him for both his advice and his assistance with this problem.

I found him immersed in his shed, which is never locked. The shed was filled with everything from chalk and slate to the most modern equipment one could imagine. He was talking and humming to himself as he searched for something. He is a tall, almost gaunt older man; well, older than me by a long way.

I yelled "Reets. Reets."

He finally looked back at me and said, "Who are you? I do not want any."

I expected a similar response. I held up the food and said, "I brought supper."

He smiled and said, "Hi Bear. Let's eat out at the picnic table." (*Food always works for him and well, for me also since we both live alone and eat whenever we have food in front of us.*)

After we were through eating, he asked, "no dessert, huh? You must be the same cheap old Bear." He chuckled.

I laid the smelling package on the table. His face lost the smile as he slowly opened the package and saw the rose. He held up one finger as he left the table.

He was back soon wearing rubber gloves and carrying a magnifying glass. He opened the package fully. He examined the rose and the card with extreme care.

He asked, "Who is SL?"

"I do not know. I just received this today. Can you help me figure out who sent this to me? Also, where is the L B Lounge?"

He laughed as he said, "you do not know where the Leoberg Lounge is? It is one of the most exclusive country clubs in the area. How long have you lived here?"

"I live a sheltered life, I guess."

Reets chuckled and asked, "How often did you touch this card?"

"Some, I guess. Why?"

He replied matter-of-factly, "I want to get good finger prints from the person who sent this. I will need to call in a favor or two to have a couple of data bases searched to identify the writer."

"You can do that?"

"Sure can old man."

He proceeded to dust the card. He found a couple of finger prints that he wanted to compare against databases so he scanned the card into his laptop and send them off to a contact.

He went and got us both a cold beer. It was a fancy Mexican brand. It wasn't too bad but it wasn't my favorite. The beer seemed to help as we discussed the problem.

He seemed to have the same feeling I had about all of this.

Together we arrived at a plan of attack for tomorrow's romantic rendezvous. He was anxious to help. I was glad he agreed to help until he said, "you will have to pay for my food and drink at the lounge tomorrow."

He laughed.

"Just my luck."

The next day, I drove to the behemoth store that sells everything. I purchased a new shirt, dress pants, underwear and socks. I might as well look presentable for tonight's adventure. I had a good lunch on the way home. I had to keep feeding the inner Bear.

I shaved and showered before going to pick up Reets. He certainly looked dapper in his sports jacket and slacks while I still looked rumpled, even in new Bear skins.

I dropped Reets off at the door of the country club. I sat in the tank and waited and waited.

Finally, my cell phone rang at 8:24 pm. I wrote down the calling phone number before I answered.

I said quietly, "hello".

The youngish woman's voice said, "Bear, honey. Where are you? Please do not keep me waiting too long."

"I am running a little late. I should be there soon."

I saved her phone number in my cell phone just as Reets had shown. My new found lover had passed the first obstacle. She had to call me so we could get her cell phone number since the only finger prints found were the delivery people and mine, of course.

But she had my cell phone number. I do not give it to just anyone.

I parked beside the Lounge and checked out the cars as I walked up to the door. There were your usual collection of cars; nothing appeared out of the ordinary. I expected to be stopped as this was supposed to be an exclusive club. I entered; was not stopped.

It was dark and gloomy inside; it was designed that way so it would be cozy. As my eyes become accustomed to the low light, I looked around. Most of the tables were occupied by couples. There were a few men at the bar; my collaborator, Reets, was there. He glanced at me.

Just then a Marilyn-Monroe-wannabe in a tight sleek dress and long curly blonde hair approached with a small shriek of "hello honey". She had practically run in high heels across the room to hug me and then kiss me on the lips. Most of the other people barely glanced at us; I guess this kind of thing must happen here all of the time. But this was not something I was used to but I could get to like it, well, in other circumstances.

She took me by the hand and led me to a booth on the side of the room. There was a Champaign bottle with two glasses on the table. She guided me into one side of the booth. She climbed in beside me and pushed her body close to mine as she poured me a glass of that heady wine.

Before saying anything else, she said "cheers" and lifted her glass. I lifted mine but I let it slip through my hand and I spilled all of it out on the table.

I murmured "sorry" as I grabbed a napkin to sop up the wine. This was all planned since I could not drink anything she provided in case she had drugged it.

Luckily most of the contents stayed on the table, but I excused myself to go to the men's room to clean my clothes. She got up to let me get out. Reets followed me into the restroom, where I gave him a piece of paper with my new lover's cell phone number on it. I walked back to the booth and made her stay on the inside of the bench seat.

I signaled the waitress over and I said, "Bring me a beer in a bottle please." I told my young lover, "I think I had better stay with beer anyway. I do not like wine much."

She pouted her full lips a bit before she smiled and said, "No problem. Tonight you may have anything you want." She sipped some bubbly out of the fluted glass as I examined her. She appeared to be quite pretty under the heavy make-up.

The waitress brought my beer and I took a swallow quick, before SL could touch it.

SL made small talk as she ran her fingers up my arm and through my sparse hair before she started to urge me to get up.

She pouted and urged, "Let's get out of here. I know some place more romantic for us".

She placed a couple twenties on the table and grabbed my arm and molded her soft body onto me as we left the building.

As soon as we were outside, I directed the walk towards my car. She seemed more inclined to go the other way but I encouraged, "Let's take my car; it has a full front seat which is better for cuddling."

She finally relented. I opened the passenger door and helped her in the car. I got in the driver's door. She slid across the seat until she was tight against me. It was almost too snug for me to drive. I had almost forgotten how it is to drive with a lady that close but I managed to start the car and back up a little before I started down the access road.

I slowed the tank down as I said, "Blackmail is such an ugly word". Her head swung around to look at me as she disengaged her body from my right side. I say her head swung around to look at me but it was more like that camera thing they do in the movies when they show the head swinging sharply around from various angles.

I had stopped under a street light. She stared at me with anguish on her face. I examined her face. She was quite young and pretty under all of that makeup.

She managed to utter, "What"?

I was sure I was on the right track.

I continued, "I was thinking of taking you to a special bedroom that had hidden cameras to record our little adventure. I could blackmail you, but I think it would be better if I put you in all of your glory on the web. You would get your fifteen minutes of fame as people all around the globe watched you. You would be famous and could become an actress in a sitcom or in non-reality television. I would expect you to keep supplying me with money so I wouldn't tell anyone you planned to blackmail me."

She gasped and some tears ran down her face through the make-up. She sputtered as she asked, "What? What did you say? I wasn't going to blackmail you."

"Oh, yes you were," I thought.

I demanded "Who put you up to this? What did you plan on gaining by seducing this old Bear; maybe a shot at becoming an actress, Sarah?" I started to say Susan but changed it at the last minute. She looked like a Susan.

Her face went white under that makeup and she lowered her head towards her chest and said while crying, "How did you know my name? How did you find out about this?"

Her phone rang in her tiny pocketbook.

I said, "You better answer the damn phone, Sarah".

She looked up at me in surprise before opening her purse and taking out her phone. She looked at the cell phone. I leaned back so that I could see also. The phone showed a picture of the two of us at the booth as she was draped all over me.

Reets had done well. He had taken a picture of us from across the lounge. The picture was sharp in spite of the weak lighting. She moaned as she laid the cell phone in her lap. She glanced at me with a questioning look. Her phone rang again; she looked down at her phone. She opened it and hit a button.

I heard the speaker on the phone say in her voice, "I wasn't going to blackmail you."

I was wearing a wire so that Reets could keep track of me. He was recording everything and he could tell where I was by using GPS.

That must have been the icing on the cake so she said in a little girl's voice, "Let me out of here. I want to go home."

I answered, "I will take you back to the lounge as soon as you tell me who is responsible for this."

She hiccupped and said slowly, "I can't." She sobbed.

Since she was so young, I suspected she was being forced to do this. Or she could be just a young actress trying to get her foot in the acting trade. She had agreed to get me in a compromising position. I would be blackmailed into doing something I did not want to do; something like be a screen writer or appear on talk shows. Also, someone may have simply wanted to get even for something, like chasing away reporters.

I asked again more forcefully, "Who?"

"I can't. I can't. I just can't." She hung her head again and sobbed.

I let quiet reign for a while before I said, "You better leave the Big Apple behind. Go back home and enroll in a local college and take up a noble profession like teaching or nursing. Then you should meet a good man and raise puppies and babies. Will you do that?"

I waited a second before I admonished her, "If you agree, I will forget this ever happened."

She sighed and sighed louder again. She shook her head and said, "Yes. Yes. Oh, my God, yes!"

I turned the tank around and drove slowly back to the lounge. She was a beaten young woman with smudged makeup and short brown hair since she had pulled off the blonde wig. She now looked like a cheerleader with bad make-up. She got out of my car and stumbled slowly around to a small sedan.

She fumbled with the car keys as I leaned out of my car window and asked, "Who? I will make sure they never darken your door again."

She groaned and said loudly, "No, I can't tell."

She started the car and drove slowly away. Reets soon jumped in my car.

He said, "I can probably get friends in the spy business to access the rental records to find out who rented that car." He had written down the license number plus the make and model.

"Good idea. I would like to find out who put her up to this."

I took Reets home. Since it was just before ten p.m., Reets invited me into his shop. He looked up a number and called it.

After talking a couple of minutes, he hung up. He then told me, "The car was rented at the airport in Philadelphia to Sarah Lissen. Her address is Rampton, in upstate New York.

I used my cell phone to call Sarah's number. She answered the phone in a little girl's frightened voice, "Hello."

"Sarah?"

"Yes-s-s?"

"This is Bear. I know all about you, Sarah Lissen from Rampton, NY. You are to go home and forget all about acting. Follow my earlier advice, become a nurse or a mother. Forget acting. Now tell me who put you up to this?"

She just gasped, said a loud, "no" and disconnected.

Reets and I discussed this over a couple of his beers before he gave me his bar tab. It was for $145.00. I couldn't figure how he could have accumulated so much in such a brief time.

I paid him and thanked him and drove home. On the way, I tried to figure out who was responsible for this. Was it my ever-greedy agent who wanted me to do screen writing or was it some pesky reporter?

Uneventful days blended into other uneventful days. The reporters stopped bugging me for interviews. My agent did not call. I was able to get fully engaged in writing my next book as well as to play golf and watch some ball games on television. Everything was going back to a quiet and peaceful normal. My mood also improved.

I still hadn't figured out who was responsible for the planned seduction and possible blackmail of one ole' Bear. However, it was on my mind a lot.

Just when I had felt secure being outside, the reporters started to bother me again. I had to have them escorted off of my property three times. One young reporter yelled at me to ask how good it felt to win my second Emmy after being Grilled? (*I had also won one for the Sunshine Show with Miss Jacky Mooney*). I went back into social hibernation again. When would it ever end?

IN YOUR DREAMS

"Larry how is your wife?" I asked over the phone.

"She will be fine after the operation." He hesitated and then said, "But that is why I am calling you Harvey, er, I mean, Bear. She needs this now-routine operation to correct her problem. But I am scheduled to go moose hunting in Canada at exactly the same time she is having the operation. Therefore, I am trying to find someone to go hunting in my place. The lodge will let me defer till next year but they have a $1,000.00 deferment fee. I would sure hate to lose that money."

"Give me the specifics Larry. I might be able to go in your place."

He answered, "I am supposed to leave in three weeks to hunt at the Meandering Moose Lodge in Ontario. They have a great reputation; a bunch of guys from work gave me glowing recommendations for the guides and camp. It costs $4,500.00 for the week, which includes the license. Transportation to the camp, tips, and meat handling are not included."

He hesitated.

I asked, "Is there something else?"

"Well, yes. It is a muzzle loading hunt for bulls only. Flintlocks and in-lines with open sights are allowed." He then sighed.

"That is not a problem as I have two 50 caliber in-lines with open sights. Are there any restrictions on using the modern powders? They do not foul much so clean-up is a snap."

"No," he replied.

I thought a second. My latest manuscript was finished. I had the discretionary money so that wouldn't be a deterrent and I have always wanted to go off on a hunting trip to Canada or Alaska.

"I'll do it Larry. Give me your address and I'll get a check in the mail to you. Also, give me the names and phone numbers of the guys who gave you the recommendations. What gear will I need?"

After giving me the website for the lodge and the names and phone numbers, he proceeded to rattle off a list of things I would need for hunting in Canada in late October. The list included;

Waterproof and durable camo clothing suitable for layering
A quality pair of waterproof boots
Warm sleeping bag
Air mattress
Hat and gloves
Rifle with cleaning supplies
Ammo
Knife and camp saw
Back pack
Long underwear and warm socks
Passport
Camera

Larry said he would notify the camp that I would be taking his place. He had to cancel his own travel plans. He said, "If you want to arrive at camp a day early, get a bush plane to fly you from Sudbury. It will save you time and the discomfort from riding back to camp on a snowmobile."

"What did you say about a snowmobile? It might not be snowing then."

"They use the snowmobiles on dry land as well as on snow. If you do not fly into camp, they will meet you on provincial route 234 on the 3rd. Then you start hunting on the 4th. It's all on their web site." Since I did not have any more questions, he said, "Thanks again Bear. Have a good time." I barely had time to wish his wife good luck with the surgery before he hung up.

I thought about all of this before calling Jobo on his cell phone. Jobo is another friend I had worked with. He had also hunted at the Meandering Moose Lodge. He answered by saying, "Hello, old Bear."

"Hi, yourself, Jobo. You ain't no spring chicken either." We exchanged more un-pleasantries before I asked him about moose hunting.

He replied, "That camp is a great place to hunt for us older hunters. They use canoes, boats and snowmobiles to move the hunters around and to carry the meat back to camp. You will definitely have an enjoyable and memorable time. You shouldn't worry about going there." We went over my list.

After hanging up, I checked the camp web site to ensure I hadn't missed anything else I might need. It seemed that everything was in order.

After mailing the check to Larry, I called my buddies, Chief Dulie of the borough police and Bench, who lives down the street from me, when he isn't residing in the Big Apple with his main squeeze, one pretty Miss Jacky Mooney of the Sunshine Show.

They both know about my past. They also know I am an old, grumpy grouch. We made arrangements for them to accompany me on a shopping trip at a large outdoor store. After all, I had a bunch of equipment to buy and not much time. We selected a day that Chief Dulie had off from work.

On the day of the shopping trip, Chief Dulie parked in my driveway just as Bench walked up.

The tall, broad Bench looked at the Chief and said with a smirk, "Is Bear actually going to go on this trip? I'll bet that he chickens out. Bear has a yellow streak."

Chief Dulie looked at me and grinned as he watched me start to fume and fuss about Bench's remarks.

They both laughed loud and long. While they laughed, the Chief walked into my garage and opened the drivers' door of my restored sixties full size car. He climbed in and started my car. He knew I usually leave the keys in the car. He let it idle before he put it in reverse and backed it slowly and carefully out of the garage.

I went around to the driver's side door, but Chief Dulie wouldn't let me in.

He remarked, "If we let you drive, we will never get there. I'll drive." He snickered.

Bench kept laughing as he got in the back seat. They both knew I preferred to drive my own car at my own pace, which some people consider slow, quite slow. (*Okay, I understood now. They had put their heads together to distract me so Chief Dulie could get behind the wheel to drive before I knew what was happening.*)

With a firm grimace on my face, I climbed into the passenger seat in the front and sat. Chief Dulie put my car in gear and off we went. (*Actually it made sense to let Chief Dulie drive but I did kinda' resent the way I was set up about it. I soon relaxed.*)

We made small talk; about sports, hunting or fishing. Breakfast was enjoyed on the way, which I paid for again. Upon arrival at the large sporting store, we entered. I had discussed my list at length so we proceeded to shop. First, I tried on boots until I found a moderately priced pair that I liked. Then I selected everything else on my list. I did not pick the most expensive items.

Just as we were finished shopping, I noticed Chief Dulie nod and wink at Bench, k-ching. (*I guess that they thought I hadn't picked up on that exchange. I would just have to go along with this to see where it was going.*)

Bench suggested, "Let's look at those wild critter mounts over there, maybe we can find a moose for you." He gave Chief Dulie a straight stare. I followed Bench and we became engrossed with all of the mounted deer, elk, moose, etc.

Our contemplation and discussion of the mounts was interrupted when Chief Dulie called loudly to us from check out. Bench escorted me over to the register so I could give my credit card and a coupon to the casher. I signed in a rush and off to my car we went. (*I was having trouble understanding what the big rush was.*)

After loading the booty in my car trunk (*thank goodness for the large trunk in my old car*), I relented and let Chief Dulie drive home. The conversation on the way centered on hunting. Except for the apparent deception at the store, I had a good time.

Once home, both of the conspirators seemed to be in a rush to go do something else, somewhere else. We did, however, make plans to play golf with Reets, another buddy.

I checked the mailbox and had a rest before I started to unload the car trunk. I was greatly surprised to find that Chief Dulie had exchanged all of my mid-range priced items for the highest priced items. The sleeping bag was an extra-large bag designed to keep one warm down to zero. The one I had selected was only good to 10 degrees above zero.

The boots were now the best pair that was available. I had liked these boots but had decided to purchase a cheaper pair. Once a person has lived a frugal existence, it is sometimes difficult to spend money.

I had even purchased a portable solar powered GPS, which wasn't on my list. I was bewildered and confused. I leaned on the car a minute before I opened my wallet and took out the receipt. It was for $1,427.29 after the $100 coupon was subtracted. I was greatly confused about the good Chief's reasoning for the upgrade of my purchases, but I became both intrigued and engrossed by the GPS. I am technology challenged but this GPS appeared to be fairly simple. I loaded in the location of my home.

That evening, I watched the football game between the Rams and the Saints. As I watched the game, I decided not to make an issue of today's deception. In fact, I was not going to bring it up; maybe it was time to let them worry and squirm a little.

My preparations for the trip included both target and GPS practice. When Callie, a young lady I had mentored, called from her service in the Navy, we discussed the GPS. She was greatly surprised I found the GPS both easy and interesting since I am usually technology challenged.

I decided to leave a couple days early since I would be driving all of the way to Sudbury, Ontario, by myself. Chief Dulie helped me pack the car. He warned me to take ample breaks so that I would stay awake.

He still seemed to be waiting until I started a discussion about the purchase exchange, but I was determined not to do so. I wasn't going to give him the satisfaction. (*Actually, I now liked everything we selected.*)

The drive was uneventful. The car performed well as I expected it would. Bill, my late wife's cousin, keeps this car running well.

At Sudbury, I checked in a hotel. I made sure I loaded the hotel location into my GPS, which I had even used on the drive here. The GPS was quite helpful.

I had a good meal and a cold beer before falling asleep while watching a Canadian football game on television.

The morning of the flight found me at the water's edge, where a Beaver float plane would transport me to the hunting camp. I was excited since I had never flown on a bush plane before. I was assured my car would be safely enclosed in a locked, fenced-in area close to the dock.

I was wearing jeans, lightweight long underwear, a ball cap and a jacket. I had on waterproof hiking shoes. All of my cold weather and hunting gear was packed.

I met the pilot, one surly and grouchy Captain Bellivan. He suggested we call him Captain Belli or just Belli. He was short and stocky with a persistent sneer on his face. He wore a grimy baseball cap. I also met the other passenger.

She was a tall lady in her early thirties. She had on jeans, tennis shoes, a bulky vest and a knit pullover cap over her shoulder length blond hair. The weather was almost 50 degrees, which is fairly warm for early October in Canada.

The lady's name was Renie Ceena and she appeared distant or just distracted or maybe thoughtful. She had a high pitched squeaky voice; almost a little girl's voice. She had a straight thin nose. She explained she was going into Five Forks. She was going to be a substitute for a teacher who had been called away for an emergency.

There was something about her that didn't seem quite right as she seemed to be too watchful. I wondered if it was because she had never flown on a float plane before.

About the only similarity I could find between us was that we were both carrying a plastic bottle of water. I'm old, and frail looking and she was young, and tall.

Since Renie Ceena was to be dropped off first, we helped Captain Belli load my gear and rifle case into the back of the plane. Then we loaded Miss Ceena's two mid-sized bags. She declined Captain Belli's attempt to put her handbag in the back of the plane.

After everything was loaded, Captain Belli gave both of us an appraising glance. He scratched his chin before he grunted and then said, "Bear, is it, eh? Well, you do not look like a Bear. Anyway, you get in first. I want you in the back sitting on the right side. Miss Ceena, you get in the co-pilot seat. That should balance out the load. "

We climbed in the Beaver plane. Captain Belli called on the radio before he started the engine. He twisted this control, and turned that one before he pumped a handle a couple of times (probably to adjust the flaps). He instructed the guys outside to undo the tie downs and we were on our way. He tapped a gauge with his knuckle before he increased the throttle. He pumped the flap handle a few more times before he put the nose of the plane into the light wind. I never felt the pontoons leave the surface of the water. It was that smooth. The only distraction was the roaring sound of the motor.

It was quite enjoyable to be above the road, houses, water and trees. But soon there wasn't anything but trees and water below. The weather forecast called for a cold front to come in later in the day, which was supposed to cause the temperature to drop below freezing. Flurries were expected also, but now it was mostly sunny; just a great day to fly above the bush.

I watched Captain Belli as he turned this dial or that one. He tapped with his knuckle on the same gauge that he had tapped before taking off. I hope that gauge wasn't going to be a problem. I noticed he watched his compass a lot. What amazed me was he did not appear to have a GPS on board. Also, he seemed to be constantly turning to the left a little. It made more sense to me to just fly in a straight line to one's destination, but what did I know?

Due to the loud engine noise, I made no attempt to talk to the other passenger. Was her first name, Renie? Captain Belli seemed happy to just sneer at her sitting beside him.

One time he pointed down to the right and turned the plane down and said, "Now that is a real bear, eh" as he looked back over his shoulder at me. There was a black bear walking across some barren ground. What a sight! I was hoping to see a moose, but it didn't happen.

After we were flying for about an hour, Captain Belli leaned back and said he was going to set the plane down on the next lake. He needed to check out a gauge which was acting up. He did not expect it would take more than a couple minutes to remove and then reattach a cable on the engine. He tapped that pesky gauge again with his big knuckle. Then he grunted.

I turned to look at the lake in front of us before I realized that Captain Belli had tapped a different gauge this time. But before I could inquire, he nodded to himself before adjusting the throttle and pumping the flap handle and turned us down towards a lake in front of us. The lake appeared to be shaped like a classic dog-bone; it flared out into bays at both ends and was narrow in the middle.

The plane slowed as Captain Belli slowly reduced the throttle before he started to sit the plane down in the flaring end of the lake nearest to us. I didn't feel the plane touch the water. Captain Belli increased the throttle a little and we went skimming across the surface. I would have expected him to slow down, but it did not do so.

As we approached the narrow part of the lake, the left pontoon must have hit something in the water because the plane started to rise up so the right wing was closer to the water surface. The plane also appeared to be turning to the right. Captain Belli swore as he turned the wheel to the left to compensate. Right then, the pontoon was off of the obstruction so the plane settled back down and veered left and went sliding up on the gradual sloping bank.

The plane crashed into and through the bush with a lot of scraping and scratching and banging noises. Just like that, the plane shuddered to the left and stopped abruptly with an enormous ripping sound.

Then the front of the plane settled so that we were facing slightly down.

The crash landing had shaken me up quite a bit. My head was supported by the tightness of the seat belt and the shifting forward of the gear behind me, which was mainly my sleeping bag. I was glad it was something soft or I could have been seriously injured. I did not think I had suffered whip lash, but time would tell. I leaned around and pushed all of the gear back so I could sit more upright.

As I did, I could hear the sounds of the plane settling. There were also some pinging sounds so I unhooked my seat belt and leaned forward and turned off the ignition key. I thought that would shut down the electrical system and eliminate the chance of sparks being generated, which might keep the plane from exploding in a ball of fire.

I felt around my body to make sure nothing was broken. I thought of the old line "a fine kettle of fish" that Captain Belli had gotten an old Bear into this time. I didn't seem to be experiencing any pain so maybe nothing was broken although I would be quite sore soon.

I decided to check on Captain Belli, which was when I noticed the bloody pointed end of a snag sticking out of the back of the pilot's seat. I knew that Captain Belli wouldn't be making any more flights. I reached over and touched the blood. I rubbed it between my fingers and my thumb. There was no doubt about it, the blood was wet.

Just to be sure, I leaned forward and looked at Captain Belli, his chin was resting on his chest with a wicked looking solid snag going into his abdomen. I sighed before I decided to check on the other passenger on this ill-fated flight.

I pulled myself a little to the left and leaned around the seat before I reached over to try to find her neck to check for a pulse. That must have roused her because she squeaked loudly, "What are you doing? Keep your hands to yourself."

I pulled my hand back and said quietly, "I was just checking for a pulse to see if…."

She interrupted, "Of course, I'm ok. Why wouldn't I be?"

I replied slowly, "Because Captain Belli wasn't so fortunate."

There were a few moments of silence while she looked at Captain Belli before she screamed loudly and started to pull at her seat belt.

She appeared to be almost frantic until I said calmly, "Relax, relax, RELAX". I grabbed her shoulder and squeezed and kept repeating that word until she seemed to quiet some.

I continued, "We are both alive and probably unhurt. We will get out of this ok, but first we must access our situation. Are you hurt? Do you have any broken bones?"

She hesitated, before she replied, "No, I do not appear to have anything broken. How about you, Mr. Bear?"

"I am sore across the ribs from the seat belt but apparently did not suffer any broken bones, Renie." I was glad I remembered her name; that should help us get along. All of a sudden, I had to take a leak. Even in the midst of a plane crash, old guys still have to go pee.

"Renie, let's try to open the door. Getting out and stretching has got to help us." I probably should have told her the real reason, I guess.

I was surprised when the door opened easily, and Renie stepped down on the pontoon and pushed the seat forward and extended her hand to help me down. I took hold of Renie's hand and stepped down beside her on the ground. There was a little space between us and the bush on that side of the plane. I started to walk away from the plane a little distance as I fumbled with my zipper until I realized that Renie was following close behind me.

I said, "I gotta' pee."

I glanced back over my left shoulder to see her turn her back and walk towards the plane. I finally was able to start a weak flow of urine, which felt so good. I finished that task, zipped up and turned around.

"I apologize. I should have told you the real reason I needed to get out of the plane."

She replied, "Well, I guess I will water this same spot also, if you will give me some space, and not peek."

I turned my back while assuring her I wouldn't watch a lady perform her duties. I stood there for a couple of minutes until I heard Renie behind me.

She squeaked, "You didn't sneak a glance!" She must have watching me. She had an incredulous look on her face as she looked at me. She continued with, "Not even a little quick look!"

I shook my head side-to-side as I said calmly, "No, I didn't look". *(I decided I would wait until later to have the talk about our situation here.)*

I tried to defuse the current tenseness by asking, "Do you know how to work the two-way radio in the plane? It would be nice to send out an SOS. I'm very technology challenged."

She replied, "Yes, I know a thing or two about radios" as she walked towards the plane. She looked into the open door of the plane. She visibly shuddered and gasped as she looked at Captain Belli. But she climbed valiantly into the plane, leaned across the co-pilot's seat and tried to use the radio. She talked to me as she adjusted the dials.

I then remembered so I informed her, "I turned off the ignition to cut down on the risk of a spark setting off the fuel. So if you can't get the radio to work, try turning on the key."

I was standing directly behind her as she worked on the radio. I must admit the view of her shapely behind in those tight jeans was quite enjoyable. While I had made no attempt to look before, I must confess I did not turn my head away now. I may be old but I ain't dead yet. I still like to look at scenic views.

At that second, she demanded, "Just what are you looking at, Mr. Bear?"

As I turned my head to glance around at the sky, I murmured quietly, "Oh nothing in particular."

She cursed before she climbed back down. "It is no use, Mr. Bear. I tried all of the usual frequencies for emergencies. The radio is dead."

"Too bad that we do not have a satellite telephone."

Renie answered thoughtfully, "Yes, we did not think of that." (*We? Who is the we she was referring to?*)

A gust of cold wind blew from behind us. There were a few snowflakes in the wind. I glanced at my wrist watch. It said that it was now 1:30 in the early afternoon.

I suggested, "I'm going to put on some warmer clothes."

"Ok."

I walked over to the plane and pulled the co-pilot's seat forward and leaned into the plane. Right there in front of me was Renie's handbag, which she had refused to hand to Captain Belli when she boarded the plane. I lifted it to move it aside. It was heavy. I glanced over my shoulder to see Renie looking the other way. I opened the handbag. There was a revolver in the bag. I took it out. It was probably a 38 special or .357. This complicates things since it means that Miss Renie is either a criminal or an undercover policewoman. This is Canada after all; short guns are controlled here. I looked back at her again as I put the revolver back in her bag and slid the bag forward under the seat. I decided not to ask her about the gun now. There might be a better time later.

I moved stuff aside until I found my large duffle bag. I removed my heavy underwear, boots, waterproof outerwear, heavy socks, and a knit cap. I threw my ball hat in the back and put on the knit cap.

Stepping down into the wind, I walked over to Renie. "I'm going back in those cedar trees to change into warmer clothes."

She nodded.

Needless to say, it didn't take me long to change since it was getting colder by the minute. I carried my jeans, and shoes back to the plane.

"Now it is your turn to change into something warmer."

She replied matter-of-factly, "I am fine. I am wearing warm clothes. This is the heaviest clothes that I brought."

I stared at her.

With an incredulous sound to my voice, I asked, "Huh? You are standing there hugging yourself. You didn't bring anything warmer? No waterproof boots?"

She shook her head side-to-side as I glanced at her feet and legs. Then I remembered where I had seen a good pair of boots and coveralls.

"What size shoes do you wear?"

She replied, "Fives."

I gave her an incredulous look since if a woman answers a question about her body that requires a number, she will usually say a number a lot smaller for her weigh, her age, and her shoe size and a larger size for her bra.

While she could wear the shoes I had just removed, they would probably be too large for her. I may be frail looking and short but I have big feet. I assured her that I would be right back with boots for her.

I walked to the plane, leaned in across the seat, and looked down at Captain Belli's boots. They looked fairly new and serviceable and seemed to be about the right size for Renie to wear.

I started to remove the shoe laces from the right boot. I finally was able to remove the laces before I started on the other boot. I grunted and pulled before both laces were removed. Then came the hard part as I had to try and lift Captain Belli's heavy legs off of the floor before I could remove the boots.

The boots were in better shape than I had previously thought. They had some blood on them which I wiped on his pants.

I noticed something through the wide opening where the pilot's door used to be. There was some foil blowing back and forth in the wind. It looked like medicine. Interesting!

I slid out of the plane before pushing the seat up and rooting around in the back of the plane. I found the pair of Captain Belli's insulated coveralls I had noticed earlier. They were stained and probably a little short for Renie but they would be better than nothing. I also found some duct tape. Perfect.

I removed a pair of my warm socks from my duffle bag for Renie to wear under the boots. Even if the boots were a little too big, the bulk of the socks would help to cushion her feet. I also removed a big bag of my lucky candies. Even an old Bear needed a quick snack once in a while.

I walked back and tried to hand the boots, the socks, and the coveralls to Renie. She gasped at the sight of the blood-stained boots and promptly dropped them.

"Are those Captain Belli's boots? I can't wear them." She gasped again.

"Well," I replied, "he won't need them and you do need them. I intend on both of us surviving this little setback with all of our digits intact. So put them on now." I glared at her.

She shuddered but found a seat on a log and proceeded to put on the boots. She tried to avoid touching the blood stains, but she put them on anyway. She agreed they were a pretty good fit.

She took off her jacket and put on the coveralls. I used the duct tape to seal the pants legs to keep out the cold air.

Renie walked to the plane and pulled out a ski jacket, which she put on.

That was when I surprised Renie by offering her some of the lucky candies. She took a handful and we both proceeded to eat.

I asked, "Do you have any food with you?"

She shook her head as we munched. (This would have to keep our hunger at bay until we were rescued.)

I stopped both of our gluttony after two handfuls each even though I had another bag in reserve.

"Oh. It is the strangest thing but I thought I saw medicine or pharmaceuticals on the ground beside the pilot's side of the plane."

Miss Renie Ceena became quite serious. "Show me," she demanded in a shrill voice.

I was shocked by her attitude but I led her around the back of the plane. I leaned down and tried to show her the foil packs through the brush.

She informed me, "Wait here."

She was back in a second with the axe from the plane. She calmly and efficiently chopped a path to the medicine. She started to gather them up. She stopped and walked back around the plane and came back carrying her nylon bag (the smaller one). It was orange in color. She must have emptied her belongings in the plane because she put all of the pharmaceuticals in that bag. She even removed some from around the pontoon and from under the plane. I watched all of this in thought. (*Was this contraband she was shepherding to its destination or was it evidence to criminal activity? Was this why Captain Belli landed here; to drop off the illegal medicine? I decided not to ask but to just wait and see how this played out.*)

I left her to her business, whether it was monkey business or legitimate, and walked around to the other side of the plane. I found my half-filled water bottle and drank some. I located Renie's bottle and set it down beside the plane.

I took out my in-line muzzleloader and cleaned it after examining it to make sure it was still in good shape. I loaded it with 100 grains of the latest synthetic powder, followed by a 270 grain sabot. Just as I was putting the cap in the nipple to fully load the gun, Renie walked around carrying the bag full of medicine.

"What are you doing?" She demanded.

"I'm loading my rifle. We may need this to get food or for protection. You never know. It is an in-line – a modern version of the flintlock."

"I know what it is."

She grabbed her water bottle and drained it and walked away from me. I picked up my bottle and removed the label so we could tell whose bottle was whose.

I loaded five quick loads, which are plastic tubes with covers on each end. Once loaded, each one has the equivalent of one shot. I could reload using one of these in a little over a minute. I put all of my gun related items in a shoulder bag I would carry if we left this area.

I then had a brilliant thought. I took the GPS out of the gear bag and turned it on. I attached the solar charger as Renie walked back. She watched as I made the selection for the GPS to tell us where we were. I queried it to tell us how far that we had traveled from Sudbury. It listed that we had traveled 93 miles. I would have thought we had traveled farther than that.

Renie asked to use the GPS. Her hands flew across the screen, hitting that button and then this one. I thought I was fairly fluent in its use but she boggled the mind.

She finally shuddered and said, "There aren't any roads or towns near here; just woods, hills, lakes and more trees." She sighed.

I asked "How far is it to the village of Five Forks? You know, where you were SUPPOSED to work?" (*She didn't pick up on my sarcasm when I said the word supposed.*) She thought, hit a couple keys and typed in the words FIVE FORKS. She showed me the screen. The village was just over 22 miles away. Then she toggled back and forth between here and there. The GPS showed that there weren't any rivers between us but we would have to skirt around a lake if we did decide to walk.

It was now after three in the afternoon and the wind gusts were getting stronger and blowing more snow. It was time to prepare for our first night in the bush. I grabbed the axe from where Renie had dropped it and walked over past the urinal spot to a small group of cedars. I used the axe to cut some branches, which I arranged on the ground to make a bed. I went back to the plane and took out my sleeping bag, the air mattress, and waterproof tarp.

I blew up the air mattress until it was partially full; just enough so it would give with the various curves of our bodies, which Renie appeared to have a lot more of than I do. I placed the air mattress on the bed of soft cedar limbs. I put the sleeping bag over it, like a cover. This I covered with the tarp to keep out the weather. I propped up the inner side of the tarp with small cedar branches to keep it off of the sleeping bag. I secured the outside edges of the tarp with some heavy limbs so the wind wouldn't blow it around. It looked pretty snug. It was only missing pillows.

Renie had been watching all of this with concentration. She asked, "Who is sleeping there?"

"We are."

"We are?" She asked shrilly.

"We are." I replied calmly. "I can't allow you to stay outside in the freezing night air while I am warm and snug in there. Also, I cannot and will not stay outside while you are warm inside. So the only option is for both of us to sleep together. Keep each other warm. If we work together, we will survive this little adventure with all of our fingers and toes intact."

"The only question is should we take off our boots and outer wear when we retire?" I said light-heartily and with a wave towards the sleeping area. I wanted to take the edge off.

You could tell by the lady's expression she didn't think any of this was a good idea. She started to say something and then stopped. I almost made a wise crack about what a great opportunity it was for her to sleep with a Bear while she was camping in the wilderness, but thought better of it.

I carried more stuff to the camp site. Things like Captain Belli's big flashlight, my bag of gun supplies, and my rifle, which I laid close to the right side of the mattress. I was claiming a side of the bed, so to speak.

Renie did not miss a thing. She noticed everything but did not ask any more questions. She had a skeptical look on her face.

At dusk, I walked back to the plane, and took a piss. Back at the sleeping area, I used my hand to indicate that Renie should do the same. She walked to the other side of the plane to do her business. She came back carrying her handbag, which contained the revolver.

I sat down to remove my boots. I put them along my side of the sleeping bag under the tarp. I took off my coat and pants and rolled both up to form a pillow. I was now in just my long, heavy underwear, warm socks and a knit cap. I smiled at Renie, which probably wasn't the correct thing to do.

She sighed before she sat down to remove her boots, which she left outside of the tarp. She removed the coveralls, which creaked from the duct tape. She put her ski jacket under her head as she reluctantly reclined. She was now wearing her jeans, my socks, vest, and her knit cap.

"You better put those boots and coveralls under the tarp or they will be full of snow by morning," I admonished.

She sighed again but complied.

I was lying on the edge of the air mattress. I assumed that Renie was also. We were both on our backs with a space between us. That wasn't a good idea as that space would let cold air in. The sleeping bag could barely cover us when we were so far apart. Also, and more importantly, we were both NOT lying on the air mattress.

I tried sliding towards here. She in turn moved away from me. This wasn't going to work.

"Listen, Renie, the sleeping bag isn't big enough for us to sleep apart without touching. Also, the air mattress isn't wide enough either so slide towards me, please."

She sighed again but moved towards me. We then had room enough to be comfortable on the mattress and under the sleeping bag. It was a good thing that Bench and Chief Dulie duped me into buying this extra-large bag and air mattress.

I had a dozen thoughts in my head, but I refrained from asking them. Finally I asked her if she camped much. She didn't answer. So I asked if she had hunted or been fishing.

She whispered, "Fishing." She was really uncomfortable with all of this, I guess.

The wind was not only blowing the trees and limbs around, but it was also blowing snow and sleet around. There was quite a lot of noise. I asked her about her family and that got her talking, which seemed to help.

I had turned onto my back. I then said I do not sleep much on my back so I rolled on my left side facing her. She stayed on her back, but my right leg was cocked and partially on her legs. My head only came up to her shoulder so I had to place my face up at an angle; but it seemed to work. I put my right arm across her abdomen.

She scolded me coldly, "Watch where you put your hands, Mr. Bear."

I rolled over so my back was against her side. I asked her if she was sore or if she hurt anywhere as a result of the crash.

She informed me in a quiet, sharp voice, "A little, I guess." But she refused to tell me where; like discussing her body wasn't an option. I started to tell her about some soreness I was experiencing now that I was lying down, but she stopped me abruptly. This was also a discussion she deemed to be off limits.

I sighed and then said "Good night." I wondered if this sleeping arrangement would work as I fell asleep.

I slept a while before I woke up when she moved. I hadn't slept with anyone in many years so I was not used to having someone squirm around in bed beside me. Sometimes, I would need to pull the sleeping bag back over me when Renie pulled it too far her way. At times, it was almost too warm. Also, I often slipped off the air mattress and had to pull myself back on it.

I did not wake up at all due to my feet getting cold. I guess that since Renie is taller than me she probably kept the bottom of the sleeping bag pulled down far enough so my feet were warm.

I was surprised Renie hadn't wanted the big flashlight on all night. I was also surprised that I did not need to get up in the middle of the night to pee as us old guys are prone to do. That was one reason I had not filled up my plastic bottle from the lake and drank a lot of water. But we would need to do that tomorrow to fight off dehydration.

I awoke to find I was now on my left side facing Renie. She was on her right side facing me and we were entangled; arms and legs around and betwixt and between. I was having trouble breathing since her breasts were pushing into my throat. She may have removed her jacket but definitely not her bra. I moved my head to the side and gulped in the fresh air and then burrowed deeper into her soft body and fell back asleep.

She must have come awake in that unfamiliar position so she pushed me away and rolled over on her other side. I did the same while I pulled the cover back over me and we dozed a little more; back to back. It really felt good to have my back warm.

I awoke when she tried to sit up at dawn, which pulled the cover off of both of us. We got out of the communal bed.

I put on my outer wear as she did the same. We both put on our boots.

Finally, I finally managed to say a gruff, "Good Morning. Have you made the coffee yet?" She turned her head and looked at sharply. Then she responded by rolling her eyes and pointing at my water bottle.

"Thanks." I grabbed the water bottle and turned it up and pretended to drink the contents. I sighed contently.

I informed Renie, "The coffee is a little weak today. Make it stronger the next time."

She replied, "Of course, Sire. Whatever you want." (*So she was getting into the proper spirit of things*.)

I held my hand out so Renie could help me stand up. I really needed the assistance since I now had pain in my right side, probably as a result of the plane crash.

I remembered something so I said to Renie, "Wait a minute. I have a surprise for you." I walked to the plane and pulled out an almost full roll of toilet paper in a plastic bag. I figured it might come in handy when one is spending a lot of time in the wilderness. I threw it to Renie, who caught it with one hand.

"Thanks again. But where was this yesterday when I needed it?"

"I forgot I had packed that until just now."

I turned my back. Actually, it felt good to turn my back since the wind was strong, cold and blowing sleet. It was now hitting me on the back instead of in my face.

Renie said, "You can turn around now." So I did. I used the duct tape to close her coverall leg openings.

I asked her, "Are you in pain? I am. I hurt here and here and."

She interrupted me by waving her hands and saying a quick "Stop!" So any discussion about a body part was still not allowed.

"Ok. Now that that is finished, let's pack up and go. We have over 22 miles to Five Forks. But first, I have some pain pills in my bag. Do you want a couple?"

"We are walking there?" she asked quietly in her little girl's voice.

"Yes, we are. There isn't much chance of our getting rescued with this cloud cover. We would not be visible from the sky. Also, I checked the weather forecast before we left Sudbury. This same pattern is expected for the next few days."

I pointed up. Renie shrugged.

We loaded my backpack with the candies, binoculars and the air mattress, after we let the air out of it. We could mostly fit the plastic tarp in the backpack; some of the tarp still stuck out. I would have to make sure branches did not snag the tarp as we walked. I used some duct tape to hold the tarp in place. I helped roll up the sleeping bag and put it in its bag along with the toilet paper.

Renie said, "I can carry this."

We checked the lake water. It did not have a petroleum smell from the plane crash so we drank some water and I took a pill. We filled our bottles with more water.

I was ready to go. I was carrying my rifle, the shoulder bag of shooting supplies, the backpack, and the GPS (I put the charger in the backpack.)

Renie put her handbag on her back like a backpack. That sure seemed like a good design for a handbag. I noticed the handbag did not sag so she must have put the revolver in her jacket pocket. She was able to carry the sleeping bag over one shoulder.

It was time for a little test so I asked calmly and quietly, "What about the evidence? Are you taking it or leaving it?"

Renie stopped, hesitated, and answered, "I better take it along." She walked over and picked up the large orange nylon bag with the suspected illegal drugs, looped the handle around her other shoulder and proclaimed we were ready to depart. (*Well, that answers that question; she definitely was an uncover policeman since she did not object to my use of the word evidence. If she was assisting in the criminal movement of drugs, she wouldn't have thought of them as evidence.*)

Just then, I had to make a different kind of deposit. I informed her of that before I had to go through the ritual of laying everything down and ask her for the toilet paper.

Renie proclaimed, "I'll wait for you up ahead." She moved off. I took my pants down and tried to balance myself as I squatted down to relieve myself. I was able to manage all of this without falling in my deposit. I wiped and got dressed. I washed my hands in the snow. I made sure I had not forgotten anything as I loaded up. I was off. (*So, yes, Bears do crap in the woods. Just in case you were curious!*)

We shared some of my lucky candies. I turned on the GPS to get our direction, and we started. She led the way. She seemed to have the most awkward and bulky load since she had the sleeping bag on one shoulder and the bag of drugs on the other shoulder. I only had the rifle over my shoulder, the reloading supplies and GPS case on the other side, the backpack, and the axe and the GPS to hand carry.

It soon became apparent that Renie would set the pace so she took the GPS from me and led the way.

The walking was basically level but still uneven, sometimes you ended up stepping down into holes partially filled with a watery mush and sometimes your foot ended higher on a log. The logs were slippery and rounded so we had to watch every step. Also, we had to watch for limbs and branches so we had to duck our heads and manage our loads. I struggled to keep up. There did not appear to be a way for us to continue to talk since the wind still howled and blew snow around. The sky was overcast.

After a couple of hours, I asked Renie to stop. We found seats on a fallen log. I took off the backpack and we both ate a handful of the lucky candies. We both drank water from our bottles.

I tried to encourage Renie to talk but she seemed reluctant to converse until she said to me pointedly, "I'm watching you, Mr. Bear. Keep your hands and advances to yourself. I'm watching you."

I sighed as we got up, picked up our parcels, and off we went.

The next break came in the early afternoon. This time it was candy and water without any discussion. Renie refused to even answer questions. I was concerned about her. I was hoping we could handle this situation without having major issues. We set off again on our journey.

I checked my watch and called a halt at about four p.m., when I saw a few cedar trees. This would be a good place to camp tonight. There was even a small fast-flowing stream close by for us to refill the water bottles.

Limbs were cut to cushion the air mattress. Logs were cut or found to prop up the tarp and to hold down the edges. The lousy cold wind was still blowing snow flurries and sleet around.

We had had hiked over five miles so that put us that much closer to our destination. After taking care of nature calls, we quietly got ready to retire. We did it solemnly just like an old married couple. Of course, it was only our second night sleeping together.

We lay down with our backs together. It seemed to relieve Renie's sense that I was up to something sexual. I mentioned that if she heard something strange in the night, like a growl or howl she was to wake me up. I would get my rifle ready and she could shine that big flashlight on the target and I could shoot at the offending animal. My desire was just to scare the animals away and not kill or maim them.

She replied, "It better be since you do not have a hunting license yet and wolves and cougars are protected anyway." (*She definitely was an undercover Mountie; there wasn't any doubt about it now*.)

I awoke to find that I was directly on top of Renie. It was like sleeping on the softest, warmest and most comfortable mattress. I stretched out and fell back asleep.

A feeling of total discomfort made me come awake. I was on my side now. But I had to get up to take a leak. Somehow I found my little flashlight, pulled on my boots and pushed and pulled my way out of the sleeping area much to the consternation of Renie, my version of Duddly-Do-Right.

I walked a short way and relieved myself before climbing back in bed. We put our backs together and off to dreamland I went.

Dawn brought us more of the same weather, windy and cold and overcast. But at least we were able to keep toasty in our sleeping arrangements.

Just as we were about to pick up our gear and set off, Renie told me in her little girl voice that, "Your thingy was moving around last night. It moved quite a lot in fact. Are you active?" She looked at me in awe and wonder.

"Am I active? Of course, I walked over five miles yesterday."

"No, not that," she said. "Are you sexually active?"

That made me think, I finally said, "I wouldn't know. I haven't been for many years since my wife was sick and died. But I could be, I guess." (*I wonder if my thingy as she called it was actively moving about when I was sleeping on top of her or was that just part of a dream. I suspect I better not share any pertinent details of the maybe-dream just yet.*)

We ate some candies and drank water. The water bottles were now empty, but the GPS showed we would find a lake in our path in a couple of miles. We could get water there. We had enough lucky candy in the bag for another snack. Later I would have to open the second bag.

I had expected to feel some pain and discomfort from the crash, but I guess that the exercise yesterday helped to minimize any discomfort I may have felt. I didn't expect Renie to allow any discussion on this subject. I did wonder how her feet were holding up in a strange pair of boots. I was finding my new expensive boots to my liking since I had no foot or ankle discomfort at all. Also, my feet were dry even though we were walking in a wet, light snow cover and stepping in mud.

The weather was still the same, windy and gloomy. At the lake, we stopped and filled up the water bottles, or should I say that Renie filled up the water bottles. I was quite tired by then and I would have fallen head first into the water if I had to lean down. We both gulped the bottles empty one time before she filled them again. We finished off the first bag of candy.

Then we were off again.

We had decided that the shortest way was around the left side of the lake. I kept my eyes out for a cabin on the shore or a path or road, which would signal that humans came here a lot. But the only event was when we scared a cow moose and her half-grown calf away from the lake.

Renie asked, "Should we stop to hunt for a moose or travel?"

I replied tiredly, "Let's make tracks. While shooting a moose would fill our bellies, it would take a day for us just to be able to butcher the animal. We couldn't carry much excess meat anyway." However, the thought of fresh meat weighed heavily on my mind.

The travel was more difficult close to the lake since we had to walk around boggy areas. There also appeared to be more downed trees.

Finally, it was about four in the afternoon. We had somehow traveled over six miles so we had just about ten miles to go. We couldn't find any cedar trees so we set up a different version of a campsite. This time, we did not have cedar boughs to cushion the sides of the air mattress.

I did surprise Renie when I produced the second bag of candies though. We ate sparingly even though we were exceedingly hungry and very tired. We drank water from our bottles, leaving only a couple of swallows for the morning. We would need to find a stream or lake tomorrow.

The only event that night was when I had a leg cramp. I reached down quickly to rub the quite painful and tight calf muscle when I heard Renie shrill loudly, "I thought I told you to watch where you put your hands, Buster."

I sighed and said quietly and patiently, "I have a leg cramp; a quite painful leg cramp, thank you very much!" I proceeded to rub my leg and only my leg. While I was doing that, Renie squirmed around.

Finally, my leg was more comfortable so we assumed the non-threatening position of back to back and we both went to dreamland.

Dawn found the weather still the same; overcast with the wind blowing snow. We both got dressed and performed the toilet exercise before eating and drinking from our respective water bottles. We were off with Renie leading the way and weary, old, hungry me trying to keep up, step by step by step by step.

My stomach was really growling. Also, I started to experience bouts of gas. It was a good thing the persistent wind blew all of the smell away quickly.

We found a stream, which was a good thing because we drank our fill of water before we filled the bottles for later use. The stream was also a bad thing because we had to detour until we found a wide shallow area for us to cross. I would have had problems crossing without Renie's assistance.

This slowed us up so we only made five miles that day. I was really tuckered out by the time we stopped to prepare our sleeping quarters. We ate another handful of candies before we settled down for the night. I tried to get Renie to talk about how she felt, and whether her feet were sore or anything, but she did not even mutter an answer. We drifted off to dreamland back to back.

Just before dawn broke fully, we both heard it, the sound of snowmobiles coming in from behind us.

Renie jumped up and exclaimed shrilly, "Here they come to get their drugs and to shut us up. We gotta' get out of here."

She was busily putting on her outer wear and boots, while I tried to do the same thing. She kept urging me to speed up.

Finally, we were both on our feet (Renie had practically pulled me up). She wanted to rush off but I knew that we couldn't survive this wilderness without the sleeping bag so we hurriedly stuffed the sleeping bag in its cover. We folded the tarp and put it in the backpack, but not the air mattress; I would have to carry that. We were off as I tried to squeeze the air out of the mattress. Renie carried the sleeping bag and the evidence bag; maybe it would have been better to leave the drugs. They might have taken them and let us alone.

There was a rocky ridge to our left so we went in that direction. My heart was racing as we climbed to the top of the ridge. I noticed there was snow on the ridge that went down to the right but rocks on the higher left side. I stopped Renie and instructed her to walk down to the right. Once we reached rocks there, I showed her how to walk backwards in our tracks so it would look like we went that way. Then we clambered over the rocks to the left. The wind had blown the snow off of these rocks so we weren't leaving a trail here. My heart was still racing as we heard the sound of the snowmobiles getting louder. It was dawn now and the wind was still howling and blowing snow.

As we reached a slight plateau, two snowmobiles pulled into our camp site. Two big guys in snowmobile suits climbed off of the machines and looked around. They both had long guns slung over their shoulders. I couldn't tell what caliber or gauge they were and my binoculars were in the bottom of my backpack. With the wind blowing, I couldn't hear what they were saying but I could tell by their body movements they were getting ready to follow us on foot.

Renie whispered in my ear to pick out one guy and shoot him with my rifle. I considered the distance to be about 200 yards. I could aim about two feet high and hit my target, but I just couldn't shoot anybody. I was already in trouble with the man-up-stairs and did not want to add to that. But I could put a sabot into the motor on one of the snowmobiles. If I could reload fast enough, I could maybe hit both machines. A 270 grain sabot would do a lot of damage.

If I could disable both machines, they would be on foot but they were younger, well fed and in good shape. Therefore, they could easily hunt us down.

My heart was still racing.

Renie kept urging me to shoot with hand and face gestures.

Finally, I laid the rifle down gently on a rock and sighted on the snow mobile on the right. It was mostly out in the open. I sighted about two feet high. My heart was still racing. As I pulled the trigger and heard the loud bam, I woke up in a sweat and my heart was racing. This was all just a nightmare.

Renie asked, "Mr. Bear, are you all right?"

"Yes," I replied tiredly, "I was having a nightmare. Go to sleep."

I turned on my side and snuggled up to Renie. I stayed still until my heart rate slowed down and I fell back asleep.

The morning found us moving slower as we got ready to leave. We consumed the last of the candy and drank the last of the water. I used the duct tape to seal the bottom of the overalls and to repair rips and tears in Renie's ski jacket. It now resembled a patch work quilt. We set off again; just a little over five miles to go. I found that I could barely move my feet. But I tried to keep up with Renie.

Finally at about 11 a.m., I saw a fallen log and just sat myself down. I called to Renie to stop.

She informed me with much displeasure we had only walked about two miles and we had a little over three miles to go.

I noticed the log I was sitting on had a smooth end. It had been cut off. Also, there was a smooth path with straight edges through the bush. Only man and their machines make a road like that. At that instant, I heard the faint sounds of snowmobile motors. I couldn't tell if they were headed our way or not.

Renie kept urging me to get up and start walking. I shushed her.

"Listen."

She did. The motor sounds were getting louder. Although, the wind was still whistling and blowing snow and sleet.

We listened for about ten minutes and the snowmobiles were definitely getting closer. They were headed our way. As they came into view on the path, I slowly laid the rifle across my lap and I noticed that the good and always prepared Mountie put her right hand into her jacket pocket on her revolver.

The two snowmobiles pulled up and stopped. The first rider looked to be short just about my height. He turned off the motor and looked back over his shoulder at the other guy.

He looked at us and asked in a gravelly voice, "Where did you come from? A plane wreck, eh?"

I said slowly, "Yes, yes, we did. Some 20 miles back."

The guy got a confused look on his face, and said, "Seriously, eh?"

"Yes", Renie responded. "We are walking to Five Forks camp. Are you from there?"

The leader still looked confused. He hesitated before saying, "Yes, we are. Jack and I were out looking for moose sign. We have some hunters coming in next week."

He said, "Oh, I'm sorry. Where are my manners? I am Rory and this is Jack. We outfit out of Five Forks during the summer and fall."

I said, "Nice to meet you. In fact, it is really nice to meet you. I am Bear."

Renie added, "I am Renie Ceena. The plane crashed on the way to your town."

Rory and Jack kept giving each other glances.

Rory said, "Well, we can finish this scouting run later. Hope on the back of these 'mobiles and we will give you a ride back to Five Forks."

I was assisted on to the back of the snowmobile with Rory. Renie easily jumped on the back of the other one. She had put the two bags behind her shoulders. We both put our arms around the respective drivers and off we went. It wasn't too difficult to hold on but I sensed at times I was leaning one way while the machine was going the other way. (*I didn't fall off since I suspected Rory was going slowly.*)

As we approached the dwellings, which were loosely scattered around, Rory pointed out where everyone lived. He stopped at a log cabin he proclaimed "home". He somehow slid easily off of the snowmobile after I lowered my arms to my sides. I heard Renie and Jack talk behind me but I couldn't move. I figured then and there that they would just let me freeze solid and they could turn me into a skinny bear stature.

Renie was asking a question when they all noticed I wasn't moving. Jack and Rory came over and helped me off of the snowmobile. They practically lifted me and carried me into a small outer room, which Rory said was a place to stash stuff and remove wet and muddy boots.

Jack and Rory were still holding me by the arms as they piled all of my stuff in a corner. They sat me down on the floor and Renie removed my boots. She gave me a concerned look. They helped me off with my coat and knit cap before Rory held the door open. I was practically carried into the snug and warm confines of the cabin.

Rory introduced me to his wife, April, who was about as short and spare as Rory was. I expected to fall down at any second so I wobbled over to a rocking chair close to the cook stove and settled down quietly. Rory, April and Jack all looked at each other in a questioning manner before April asked if we wanted coffee.

She said, "It has been on the back of the stove since this morning, so it will be strong."

I replied, "Yes, please with milk and sugar."

Renie looked concerned.

She asked, "How strong is it? Oh, I'll have mine the same way, milk and sugar."

April didn't reply. She just poured the coffee into big, old chipped mugs. She added condensed milk from a can. Sugar was added also. She went to a cupboard and extracted a bottle of whiskey and added a shot to each cup. She handed us each a mug.

As I sipped the wonderful coffee, April scurried around and cut us each a big piece of cake. But it wasn't cake; it was a piece of date bar. It had a crunchy crust on both the top and bottom and a smooth layer of date filling in the middle

If there can be heaven on earth, it was that exact moment. Drinking coffee with whiskey and eating a piece of delectable date bar by the warm cook stove while sitting in a comfortable wooden rocking chair.

Rory and April talked to us. They kept asking questions about how far we hiked and how the sleeping arrangements were, etc, etc. I did not even answer. I let Renie handle that chore. I held up the cup which April refilled. I was getting lethargic. I must have dozed off. I remember someone taking the mug from my hand.

I awoke when April said, "Mr. Bear, it is your turn."

I looked up to see Renie drying her hair with a towel. She was wearing clean jeans and a flannel shirt.

"I borrowed these from Jack's wife. She is about my size. Now it is your turn. April has already laid out some of Rory's clothes for you."

Renie helped me stand up. My legs had really stiffened after all of the walking, the riding and now the sitting in the rocking chair. But it did feel good to stretch out my short legs.

I was led into a small bathroom with a sink, a commode and a shower stall. Renie showed me how to flush the commode using a bucket of water. She showed me the shower. There was a plastic bag full of water with a shower nozzle attached hanging high in the stall. The water was warmed on the cook stove and poured into the bag. I was to moisten my body first from the bag. Then turn off the water and apply liberal amounts of soap and shampoo before running the water to rinse off. For a quick shower which used a small amount of warm water, it felt so good!!!! So good!!!!

I put on an old pair of long underwear, a union suit, and a pair of work pants, a flannel shirt, and a pair of warm socks. All of the clothes had seen use but were clean and in good repair. I ran my hands through my hair and I was all warm, clean and toasty and as presentable as an old Bear can ever be.

As I walked back into the room, I noticed the sign over the rocking chair, which read "April's chair"; maybe that explained the looks between Rory, April and Jack, when I sat on it.

I walked over and sat beside the kitchen table. Renie was helping April set the table and prepare the evening meal.

April admonished me, "Mr. Bear, go sit in my rocker. You are being given special permission to use my chair anytime you want. I'll explain why later. Also, you are in the way here and now."

I apologized about using her chair, but she shushed me.

June instructed Renie to fill a mug for me with coffee, condiments and whiskey. The coffee still tasted so good.

Rory came back inside carrying wood for the cook stove, which provided the only heat for the cabin. He went back into the bathroom, to clean up.

He came back in and sat at the table. Renie, April and I joined him. We had a great meal of moose stew, and home baked bread along with more coffee. The small talk was about the camp, hunting, and our long hike. When our sleeping arrangements on the trail were discussed, Rory and April gave each other a quick smirk.

But Renie quickly steered the conversation elsewhere by saying, "I contacted the Mounties on the satellite phone. They are flying in tomorrow around noon to pick us up."

I replied, "Will that will take us back to Sudbury?"

"Yes".

Rory said, "I have used the same phone to contact the Meandering Moose Lodge, Bear. I sometimes contract with them when their camp is full. I can offer you a moose hunt right here starting tomorrow at no additional cost to you. There is plane bringing in hunters next Wednesday that you can fly back out on. It is going to Sudbury. I mentioned no additional cost, but you might wish to give the pilot a tip."

"Sounds good. But what about my stuff on the crashed plane?"

"Oh, I forgot to tell you, Mr. Bear, we are stopping at the crash site. We can drop off your stuff in Sudbury for you to pick up later", replied Renie.

"Fine, it is settled, I will stay here and hunt. Thanks, Renie. Thanks Rory and April for the hospitality and, especially, for rescuing us."

At the end of the meal, April plied us with more date bars, which this ole' Bear did not refuse.

She said, "I have a surprise." She walked over to a built-in book case and selected a paperback. The cover looked familiar. It was one of my recent books, entitled, "THE EDGER. I thought you sounded like someone I should know." Can you autograph it?"

I noticed a look of bewilderment on Renie's face as April handed me a pen. I sometimes draw a total blank when it comes to book signing. This was not one of those times.

I wrote "APRIL, A LOVELY LADY AND A GREAT COFFEE AND DATE BAR MAKER, DON'T FORGET THE WHISKEY, BEAR."

Yeah, I know, that was a lame. I can be quite creative in my writing, but have trouble with book signings. Sigh!

We finished the meal using candles. The generators were used sparingly since it was so expensive to haul in gasoline.

April reminded us, "We go to bed early here. Follow me." She led us into a small bedroom with a double bed that was covered with a brightly colored quilt.

She said matter-of-factly, "Since you slept together on the way here, I figured that you would want to spend one last night together in this bed."

She looked at me.

I replied with obvious glee, "Great. I know that I will get cold all by myself."

Renie looked aghast, and she finally shrieked, "In your dreams, Bear, in your dreams!!"

April looked at us and then she started to holler and laugh. She bent over and leaned forward as she tried to contain herself. By then I was laughing loudly. Finally Renie got the joke and she joined into the fray with her high pitched giggles. After the laughter subsided, April led me to a tiny bedroom full of bunk beds.

She said simply, "I guess you will have to sleep here." I noticed my sleeping bag and backpack were on the bottom bunk so she knew all along where I was sleeping. April had just put one over on Renie.

April said, "You can keep the door open a crack to leave in the heat from the stove if you want. But it will get cold come morning. I loaned Renie a sleeping bag so she will be fine. Here is a toothbrush for you to use. I loaned Renie one also." She smiled the biggest-dirty-old-woman smile at her prior joke on Renie.

Pleasantries like "good night" were exchanged. I took my small flashlight and walked into the bathroom, brushed my teeth and took care of other duties. I went back to the bunk bed and undressed down to the union suit and heavy socks, climbed on the bottom bunk and was soon asleep. I got up in the middle of the night to use the bathroom (thank goodness, I had a flashlight).

I awoke with some confusion the next morning, but after hearing April and Rory talk, I remembered where I was. I got dressed and went into the bathroom and took care of the various duties, which included brushing my teeth. It takes not brushing one's teeth over a few days to appreciate the clean taste after brushing.

April already had a mug of coffee ready for me as I walked into the kitchen and joined them.

Just then, Renie stuck her head out of the hallway and said a cheery, "Good Morning All" before she walked down the hall to the bathroom.

Breakfast was pancakes with real maple syrup and salt cured ham with lots of coffee (without the whiskey). We made small talk.

By about 10 or so, Renie walked out to wait for the float plane. I put on my boots and outerwear and followed her. The weather had finally cleared up but it was still gusty.

Renie was watching the horizon for the plane as I walked up to her. She glanced at me, then she looked back at the sky and then back at me.

She then sighed (*I get that a lot*). She said, "Mr. Bear, I owe you an apology. I just assumed that you being a man, that you would, well, take advantage of that situation and expect fringe benefits of a sexual nature. I do not like being taken advantage of to say the least. But you were nothing if not a gentleman and I was glad that you were on the plane with me."

I thanked her. I asked, "Are you going to tell Rory and April you are working uncover as a Mountie?"

Her face took on a look of utter disbelief, and she asked me in a high pitched squeaky voice (even for her), "Who told you? Er, how do you know?"

She looked around to see if anyone had noticed or overheard my question.

"Well, I kinda' figured it out by my little ole' Bear self. You carry a revolver, and you were very careful to take along the drugs when we left the plane wreck. It was like you mentally cataloged every package as you put them in the bag. If you were in cahoots with the drug dealers, you may have left them with the plane so they could have been picked up later. Also, you did not mention the teacher position when you arrived here. Little things like that."

"What? How? How did you know about the revolver?" She asked.

I just smirked. At that time, we heard the float plane in the distance so I wandered away from her. She continued to give me a look of total disbelief.

I met the pilot and co-pilot. They wore Mounties' uniforms. The co-pilot asked me if I would be available to answer questions when I got back in Sudbury.

He apologized. He said that they had to get back. They wanted to stop at the crash site to collect evidence before dark.

I said it would be no problem to stay a day or two in Sudbury at their convenience. I asked that he call Chief Dulie Andrews back home and tell him I was fine and I would be home in a little over a week.

He replied, "Sure thing."

Renie came over and gave me a big hug and kiss before she boarded the plane. She gave me a direct look as she climbed in the plane. I was thankful for the wool cap on my head 'cause I was blushing, again.

The rest of my time there was quite enjoyable, but anticlimactic after surviving a plane crash, a long hike and sleeping in the same bed with a pretty, sexy undercover Mountie.

Yes, I did harvest a nice mature bull moose. I must add that the weather turned sunny and fairly warm once we arrived at Five Forks. It was just the opposite of what we had previously endured.

I really enjoyed my time there and the flight back to Sudbury. I had promised Rory and April to send them a collection of my books. I gave Rory a generous tip. I suggested it included a finders' fee.

I was really happy to see my car in the fenced-in area as we circled the dock prior to landing. I thanked the pilot, who was young and pretty – totally unlike Captain Belli.

I gave her a big tip and a smile.

I spent two nights at the hotel in Sudbury. I answered a billion questions from the Mounties. They told me I might be asked back to testify, which I would be happy to comply with. Finally, they thanked me and released me. Release is quite the operational word.

They said they would also release a statement to the Canadian press about my assistance in shutting down the trafficking of illegal drugs in Ontario. I even allowed them to take a picture of me.

I should have begged them not to include my name and picture in the news. I should have! I should have! After all, I really did not do anything other than be on the correct flight.

I paid my bill at the hotel after a big breakfast. I stopped and picked up my frozen meat. I had taken along ice chests. The meat should stay frozen until I arrived in PA in two days. I programmed the GPS, which worked well; who says that I am technology challenged?

My big, old, customized car ran well all of the way to the border. I crossed back into the good ole' US of A without incident.

The trouble started when I stopped to spend the night at a hotel outside of a small town in upstate NY. It turned out to be my fault, of course. I should have signed the register with my given name and not with my assumed name of Bear. But I still persisted in using Bear, because of the stigma associated with my real name.

I thought the attendant would ask me for my full name but he didn't. He just glanced at the newspaper lying on the counter.

I asked him, "Is the restaurant next door a good place to eat?"

He nodded in the affirmative while seeming to be distracted.

I put my suitcase in the room and walked next door to the family restaurant to get my evening meal. I selected a stool at the counter and ordered. I was kinda' tired from the boredom of expressway driving and wasn't too alert to the surroundings as I sipped coffee.

The waitress just sat my plate of food in front of me when they arrived. They, you ask? They, as in all manners of reporters; print, television and whatever media walked in – in force. They stuck their microphones in my face and practically screamed while they asked me to confirm, deny, or explain about my role in assisting the Canadian authorities. I was surprised, aghast, and speechless as they pushed and shoved each other to get my response.

Right then, a savior appeared in the form of my youngish, petite waitress. She yelled something that sounded like "Robbie" and then she got herself in between that mob of reporters and me. She had a great set of pipes as she yelled at the reporters to shut up and get back; that they were disturbing her customers.

A young, fresh faced policeman in uniform appeared and demanded the reporters shut up. That quieted everything down. He asked one to explain. He knew the reporter's name.

The paparazzi explained I was the famous writer, Bear, and I helped to curtail drug related crimes in Canada. This reporter went on to practically beg for an interview with me so he could get the scoop on all of this.

The policeman held up his hand to keep the unruly crowd of reporters at bay and turned back to me.

He asked politely, "Mr. Bear, would you consent to give an interview or hold a press conference?"

"NO, to all", I said forcefully. "I just want to eat in peace."

The policemen informed the semi-quiet reporters, "You may stay as long as you order something but you are not to disturb Mr. Bear now or after he leaves this restaurant." He looked at me and asked, "May I join you?"

"Yes, please do."

He said to the waitress, "Serve me here please Angie."

She replied with a sweet smile, "Gladly, Robbie."

Robbie, the local policeman, who looked like he should still be in high school, told me, "I read the article about your crime fighting activities on the front page of today's newspaper. It even had your picture. I never figured to get to meet you or experience this." He pointed back at the reporters.

I sighed twice while I glanced back at the few reporters who stayed and sat at booths and tables. I just couldn't figure what to do when I left this place of protected solitude.

But Robbie had it figured out.

He asked, "Where are you staying or is this just a brief stop for supper?"

"Well, I checked in at the motel next door. The attendant must have promptly notified this rabble."

He replied confidently, "I'll handle this."

He walked to the reporters and explained, "Leave that man alone (he pointed at me). If he files a complaint, we will have to serve a warrant." The reporters started to complain about their rights but Robbie ignored it. He gave them a stern look, which seemed odd considering his youthful looks.

He returned and sat beside me. He said, "I would just check out and go to the next exit. I have a friend there who works at a motel. I will call him. He won't bother you."

We both finished our meals. I even ordered pie a la mode. I tried to order a piece for Robbie and offered to pay for his meal, which he declined.

Robbie accompanied me as I went next door to the motel. I demanded I be allowed to check out of the motel without any charges going on my credit card. The attendant didn't like it but he complied; thanks to another stern look from Robbie. Robbie told me the next exit number and the name of the motel I should find there.

I got my things from the room and loaded up my car and proceeded to drive away. I noticed Robbie was out in the road stopping all traffic so I wouldn't be followed by those pesky reporters. I couldn't help but think that I should do something nice for Robbie and Angie.

I was treated with respect at the next motel. The attendant even offered to carry my bags to the room. I told him I would gladly autograph one of my books for him but I didn't have one in the car and he didn't have one. I wasn't able to get any information about Robbie or Angie from him except that they were sweet on each other and had just gone out on their first date. I wished them nothing but happiness in my thoughts as I drifted off to sleep.

The rest of the trip was uneventful. I was one tired ole' Bear when I finally pulled into my driveway. I put the car in the garage and started to put the moose meat in the freezer. Needless to say, it wouldn't fit in my small freezer so I grabbed a cold beer and called my friend, Chief Dulie, the local chief of police.

I asked him to stop by and pick up some meat (*no, I practically begged him to take some*). He said he would stop by after his shift ended in about two hours.

I made the mistake of checking my messages on the home phone. I had 27 or so messages; a few from my worthless agent, and the rest from all of the pesky reporters wanting an interview – probably about the drug arrests in Canada. Of course, it doesn't help that I have been quite successful as a writer and have a checkered past before that, but I won't elaborate now.

I busily put clothes and stuff away.

Chief Dulie arrived bearing a pizza.

He said, "I knew you were probably too tired to get something to eat tonight."

I agreed and offered to pay for the pizza but he refused. As he was about to say more, there was a screech of tires out front. We walked to the picture window and looked out. Yeah, you know, it was a media van stopping on the street.

A pretty blonde reporter was getting out of the passenger door with a mike in hand while she encouraged the driver (and probably the cameraman) to get out quickly. Chief Dulie sighed and opened the front door and went out. He stopped by his cruiser and picked up a pad of paper.

He calmly walked up behind the van, flipped open the pad and started to write. The reporter came over and asked what he was doing. He replied about their van blocking traffic. The reporter asked about where they could park. He pointed to the parking lot of a local convenience store but mentioned the possibility they would then get arrested for loitering since Bear wouldn't be giving out any interviews, not in this lifetime.

They reluctantly climbed in the van and pulled away. The reporter was heard to issue an unladylike epitaph as she got in and slammed the door.

I walked out and put up all of my NO TREPASSING signs. I sighed twice.

Chief Dulie and I talked as we put a cooler of meat in his cruiser. He promised to come back on Sunday evening to watch the game. He would bring beer and I would barbecue moose meat. He wanted to hear about my adventures in the wilds of Canada. We also made arrangements to go golfing with my other buddy, Bench who was expected back in town with his main squeeze, one pretty and successful Jacky Mooney, a talk show host often seen on the boob tube in the afternoons.

Boy, can she play golf. I would probably lose again and have to buy at the nineteenth hole; it usually happens.

WOBBLE

I became aware of the sunlight coming in my game room and I slowly awakened. I was still in my favorite easy chair and still wearing my shiny lounge wear with the big smiling face in a circle on the backside (*this lounge wear has caused my good buddy Bench to go running out of my house in terror. Who would have suspected that someone as big and strong as Bench would be so easily frightened? It wasn't like I expected him to wear clothes like this*).

After checking the time, I grabbed the phone and called a number from memory (I only can remember three numbers and one of those is 911).

After three rings, the phone was answered by a distinct male voice, who said, "Good Morning, this is Hoarce at WRAX television. How can I direct your call?"

"Hello, Horsie, have you heard from Joyce?

"Joyce, who?" he replied.

"Why, Joyce who used to be the receptionist there, of course."

"I do not know her. How may I direct your call, sir?"

I answered, "I have a few comments."

"You mean complaints!"

"I guess they could be construed that way sometimes", I replied as sweetly as I could.

After a long period of silence, he finally said, "Ok, I'm ready. What are your COMMENTS?" He put the emphasis on the last word.

I said loudly, "Do you know that the your rated-X station interrupted the baseball game last night to present some SCIENTIST from some summit somewhere, who made some arcane statements concerning global warming?"

"Well, you know, sir, unless we slow up the progression of global warming, we could see premature ending of the world as we know it", he continued evenly.

"Yes, I know but at my age, I won't live long enough to appreciate the ending of the world, but I had waited all day to watch and enjoy that game. Because of the interruption, I missed the last 7 innings", I said maybe a little too hotly.

"That is too bad, sir. I'll pass on your comments."

When he hesitated, I asked, "It wouldn't be a problem though if you can just mail me a DVD copy of the complete game from last night. Your wonderful station would have it on file so it would not be a big deal for you to have a copy made and mailed to me, would it? Please. Please (*I hated to beg but some things are so important*)."

To which, he replied simply, "No."

He hung up.

I got up and changed into a pair of semi-clean jeans, tee shirt and a pair of ratty sneakers after brushing my teeth, washing my face and running my fingers through what is left of my hair (*proper hygiene is important, you know*). I picked up the newspaper off the lawn and removed the sports section before carefully folding the rest of the paper to read later. I put the folded paper in the slats of the rocking chair on my porch so I could savor it when I came back.

I set out to walk to the only restaurant in town for coffee and breakfast.

As I walked, I fumed a little bit about missing the game last night because there was a much anticipated matchup between the rising young hitter for the Astros, who was about to face the veteran hot shot pitcher of the Rays. I had waited all day for this face off. I was ready with my remote close by and a fresh cold beer in hand. I was seated in my favorite comfortable easy chair.

The camera concentrated on the veteran pitcher on the mound and it showed the sly old pitcher as he took his right hand back to his mouth for the second time just as I suspected. He was going to throw a spit ball and he knew just how to do it so the umpire wouldn't catch him.

At that moment, the television switched to a national news announcer, who said, "We are sorry to interrupt your regular show but there has been another proclamation by Dr. Jealously Page, the world renowned scientific expert on Global Warming. We go live to the United Nations Summit in Stockholm and to our person there, Lily....."

By then, I was fuming, fussing and cussing so much I dropped the remote. How could that station switch from the all-important game at the exact moment, which was going to prove that the Astros' multi-million dollar pitcher cheated? (All of my excitement and flaying around caused my beer to drop while spilling it on my chair. I had to push my legs back from the reclining position to grab the beer before it all gushed out and retrieve the remote and try to find the game on another channel before that moment of sports history was lost forever.) But every damn network was broadcasting the same thing, Dr. Jealously Page talking in a somber tone about the upcoming ending of the world.

I had to admit she is a striking figure of a woman. She has long cascading black hair, a willowy figure, a long pretty face and a long, graceful neck, but her voice sounded worse than fingernails on a blackboard. To top it off, she sounded very whinny like a boss I had in my formative years (*which are all those years I had to leave home to go someplace else and have someone tell me what to do and when to do it and how I did it wrong. Work, gasp!*).

I put the remote on mute which brought up the sub-titles so I could endure to watch her on TV. Her talk was just her paraphrasing with what has been said before by other experts. I fell asleep while watching her on TV.

By the time I re-examined that episode in my mind, I had arrived at Old Bob's Cafe. I went in and sat at the last stool at the counter as far away from everyone as I could get. The waitress, Alice brought me over coffee and waited while I read the menu. She hummed something that sounded like the waiting song from Jeopardy.

Finally I asked for two eggs fried over easy, an order of rye toast, and a slab of scrapple.

Relishing the taste of the coffee, I spent time going through the sports section line-by-line and there wasn't any mention (*not one*) of a spit ball controversy at last night's game. It seems not only had the umpires missed that crafty old pitcher throwing a spit ball, but also those worthless columnists missed it also.

Once Alice brought the food, I thanked her. Alice actually smiled at me (*I thank her all of the time. You know that I do! Not!*)

I always try to get her name correct or else I might get on Bench's bad side. I wouldn't want that. Also, Alice had been around and could handle herself and I wouldn't want her to bend me into a pretzel. It was frustrating, because there were so many natural choices for getting her name wrong such as Malice, Cowless, even Ballast, and especially Flatulence.

After finishing breakfast, I walked home. I made one stop to purchase laundry detergent since all of my clothes were in a state of unclean. I was almost just another college student as my clothes were all dirty. I lived on coffee, beer, and takeout food as I had little food in the house. But I couldn't remember the last party of any kind I had attended and I was a lot older than college students anywhere in the world, but we will not go there.

I threw some clothes in the washer and added detergent before switching on the TV to the all-sports-channel. There wasn't any mention of the suspected spit ball. None, nada, nothing! Everybody watching the game missed it including me due to the interruption. Who would know about that pitcher?

The rest of the day was spent as follows; move wet clothes to dryer, put more clothes in washer, take dry clothes out of dryer, and attempt to fold clothes. All clothes are made in such a way that it is impossible to fold them so shove said clothes in drawers. Repeat over-and-over again until all clothes are put away or in a pile on the floor. Boy, did I miss Callie, who I had mentored. She had helped me a lot with my laundry. But she was serving in the Navy so I was without her assistance.

The newspaper was consumed along with coffee on the front porch swing during the afternoon.

I was back in my chair that evening listening to the game on the local station. This would be the same chair that my now sometime neighbor and good buddy Bench and his new found love interest, the one-and-only, Miss Jacky Mooney of the Sunshine Show, had volunteered to retire. They wanted to buy me a new top-of-the-line easy chair to replace this one since they said my old, reliable chair not only looked disgusting, but also smelled musty and moldy.

But I threatened them with exposure. I told them I would tell the whole world (*especially the media*) they were sneaking down here to Bench's little house to continue their illicit, romantic affair in the peace and quiet of our town. Once the media got wind of it, Bench and Miss Jacky Mooney of the Sunshine Show would have to find someplace else to hide away. I won that battle.

At ten p.m., the game was going into the eighth inning on the radio (*old school, no less*!). After my team won, I switched back to the TV.

After about ten minutes of watching a rerun, the station interrupted the show. They switched to a perfectly-coiffed national announcer, who stated, "I am sorry to interrupt your regularly scheduled show, but there are startlingly new developments in global warming. We switch now to the Energy Summit in Stockholm and Dr. Jealously Page, the world renowned scientific expert on Global Warming."

Luckily I was able to find the remote and hit mute before she started talking. I managed it without spilling my precious beer. I was able to avoid hearing her voice, which could cause milk to curdle. How could anyone sound that bad and yet be so smart and look so good.

I was starting to get upset by having Dr. Jealously Page, the world renowned scientific expert on Global Warming, appear on TV two nights in a row and interrupt what I was watching. But I can be understanding and patient to a fault (*don't believe a word of it, do you?*). I tried not to get upset. I switched off the set and went to bed.

The next day was a normal day.
After my usual saunter for brunch, I came home to work on my next novel since I am a writer and I have won a couple awards. My agent was becoming a pest by urging me to please, please, and please finish this book.
Later in the day, I stopped editing my current manuscript to make coffee and have a snack. I turned on the local news to check out the weather since I planned to play golf tomorrow. The local weatherman just gushed about Dr. Jealously Page, the world renowned scientific expert on Global Warming. The weatherman was so excited he forgot to give the forecast for tomorrow.

After a long difficult day in front of the computer, I wanted to just relax in my easy chair, which has been customized by and for the comfort of my skinny butt. I wanted to enjoy a cup of coffee and a snack. Most of the channels including the sports and food channels on the idiot box were showing excerpts from the latest research by Dr. Jealously Page, the world renowned scientific expert on Global Warming.
On the food channels, she was shown out in the field talking about the possible effects of food production. On the sports channel, she talked about the possible consequences to golf courses if Global

Warming was allowed to accelerate. Her grating voice resounded in my head.

I tried to watch TV with it muted, but I couldn't stay awake so I fell asleep in my old chair. I dreamed about the upcoming Master's golf tournament. The announcer had this terribly grating voice like you-know-who. The pro-golfer looked like a slender woman in a green sports jacket, green pants, and a perky hat. Her long black hair hung down covering the back of her jacket.

The camera showed a face on the golf ball on the tee – it was my face screaming in terror just as the woman golfer smacked the hell out of the ball. The golfer turned and looked at the camera with a wink and a smirk on her face. Yes, it was none other than Dr. Jealously Page, the world renowned scientific expert on Global Warming, who had just hit the ball with my face a country mile. All of the time, the announcer kept talking in the screeching and annoying voice of the same Dr. Jealously Page. I awoke in a cold sweat and decided I must do something about this overdose of the good doctor of earth science.

After playing one of the worse rounds of golf ever in the history of golf-doom (*it's amazing I could attempt to play golf at all after the nightmare*), I went back home to contemplate the situation.

I decided to see what old GOOGLE could tell me about Dr. Jealously Page, the world renowned scientific expert on Global Warming.

Her bio stated she was born and raised in West Virginia in a coal mining family and became interested in the environment. I tried to find a web site or a way to contact her but while the web sites had loads and loads of data, there wasn't any way to contact her. I must admit to be web-site challenged since it seemed that these sites contained everything anybody could possibly ever want.

By then, I was web-site and computer frustrated. I imagined taking all the laptops to the sporting clay or skeet range. At these ranges, they have a thrower, which will fling clay disks into the air so shooters can shoot the disks with shotguns. What I contemplated was - throwing the laptops out in the air with a thrower and blasting the laptops to pieces with shotguns.

It would be possible to do the same with keyboards, but it would be more sporting because keyboards are rectangular and would fly more erratically.

For desk tops and monitors, you would need a catapult to propel them, like pumpkins. You would need something much larger than a shotgun to shoot them with though. A bazooka would be great, but it would take a lot of practice to get the trajectory of the rounds to match the trajectory of the computers and monitors.

But it would be great fun to turn all the computer hardware into scrap-ware. The software would probably drift upwards from the piles of scrap-ware. The software would turn into ghost-ware, which would look like a ghost with a logo. The ghost-ware could then be shot with a laser like a video game so the ghosts would shrink into a dot and disappear.

Then giant critters would appear and eat all the scrap-ware, which would be seasoned liberally with remnants of ghost-ware. This would pass through their alimentary canals and would be turned into pure and clean top soil, which would be great for growing barley and hops so that there would be more beer and no more computers!! Yes!!

I was getting grumpier and grouchier all the time with all that was happening to my life right now. For one thing, my buddy Bench was off traveling the world with his new love interest, Miss Jacky Mooney, of the Sunshine Show. Secondly, the weather was turning rainy and foggy so golf and stadium outings would have to be deferred. Thirdly, my book wasn't finished yet and lastly, an obnoxious scientist was on the TV all of the time.

Even I know that global warming is going to shorten the continued occupation of earth for us mere mortals, but I just had to divert the attention of Dr. Jealously Page, from her current pursuit, which was screeching at summits or other notable events. This put her right smack in the middle of the few shows I enjoy watching on the idiot box.

Ah ha, there is another important potential environmental problem in our future that even she had not yet considered, and I call it WOBBLE. Therefore, I planned to get her so busy investigating the WOBBLE theory that she would not have time for all these TV appearances.

Now would be a good time to explain my WOBBLE theory, I guess.

Wobble is based on the concept that the crude oil is located deep in the Earth for a reason, which is to keep the Earth spinning smoothly. The earth spins on its axis. It completes one revolution in one day or 24 hours. Scientists say the crude oil we are now pumping out of the ground is the result of the dinosaurs dying off and turning to carbon based oil. These same scientists speculate a meteor or some earth changing event caused the dinosaurs to die off but it could be that the earth had a wobble in its spinning way back then. The climate was changing a lot due to this wobble and the climate fluctuation caused the dinosaurs to die. They turned into the carbon based crude oil, which seeped into cracks of the earth. As the cracks were filled in, the earth started to spin more evenly. The even spin caused the crude oil to flow into the current location, which further stabilized the spin.

It would be possible to take this further by saying that the smoother spin helped to separate the super-continent called Pangaea, into the current continent placement. It might just take one little tweak of the Earth's weight distribution (like removing crude oil from strategic places) to start to add WOBBLE.

The question I could foresee Dr. Jealously Page, the world renowned scientific expert on Global Warming, addressing is whether enough crude oil has been removed to actually cause this WOBBLE to take place and what the possible effects would happen if the Earth did start to WOBBLE. Research like that could help her to win more awards and maybe stave off the future effects of WOBBLE. Also, and more importantly, it would keep her off TV so you and I can enjoy watching it in peace and quiet.

I contemplated the method I would use to get this new important theory in front of Dr. Jealously Page, the world renowned scientific expert on Global Warming. I did not know any people at any of the scientific journals or at planetariums or at museums so that was out of the question. I kept going back to this dilemma while I watched the Indians battle the Senators, which ended in the 14th inning with a balk.

I had an inspiration and grabbed the phone and called my agent, which is the other number I have memorized. I called on his super-secret-cell-never-call-me-there phone.

He answered, "Hello this is Cliff Loews, Agent to the Stars." Then he rushed into an admonition about calling him at this late hour.

I responded with, "Why I thought you told me to call you day or night, Biffy".

"Oh, it is you again Bear. Yes, I always have time for you", he said in his smooth never show emotion accent.

"You had better have time for me, Sir Lancelot, since you have made a lot of money as my agent".

"Well, there is that I suppose", he said with disdain now in his voice.

"I have a problem since I have written an inspirational theory on the Earth. It puts a different spin on the burning of crude oil. I would like to get a copy of this in front of Dr. Jealously Page, the world renowned scientific expert on Global Warming, for her to use her massive expertise to investigate and save us from total destruction. Here she comes to save the day," I gladly informed him.

"Let's see, you, Bear, who writes T R A S H F I C T I O N (*he actually spelled it*) has written a scientific theory that you want a well-known scientist to investigate. YOU, who hasn't finished his latest book, took the time to write this and NOW you want to publish it in such a way that it is read by someone like Dr. Jealously Page, the world renowned scientific expert on Global Warming. Also, you probably want to get paid for this article, I guess."

"You make it sound better all the time. What do you have in mind?"

"I have just the medium in mind, supermarket tabloids", he said confidently.

I thought a couple minutes and had to agree my agent's idea was brilliant. It was the ideal way to get her attention. She would see the headline as she reached for her favorite tabloid at the grocery store. I could see the front page by-line in big bold print "THE EARTH IS LOSING ITS SPIN". But I couldn't let my agent know I loved his idea that much.

I asked, "Do you actually think this would work?"

He said assuredly in his smooth practiced monotone voice, "It can't fail. It will BE the talk of the entertainment community just like your appearance on the talk show. Then it will be picked up by the news media, which will attract all the scientists in the world. She is bound to see it, and hear about it even after she reads it. Then I will be contacted since I am your agent."

I spent the better part of the next day writing and editing the WOBBLE article. This would run in the next issue of the bestselling tabloid, which is called THE BEST SELLING TABLOID (*catchy name, isn't it?*). I e-mailed it to my agent, who said he would send me the check just as soon as he received it and after he subtracted his considerable agent's fee.

After waiting two weeks after my article (*it was so good I would probably win an award for tabloid writing next*) was published, I decided to GOOGLE Dr. Jealously Page, the world renowned scientific expert on Global Warming, to see if she had picked up the on the World-ending-as-we-know-it-WOBBLE-problem. I figured she had probably made some announcement about it and was actively focused on resolving that issue. I knew she was so engrossed with WOBBLE now she had not had time to call me or my agent.

There wasn't anything about the announcement, but there was an article about an upcoming summit scheduled at a hotel in Baltimore. I made plans to go to the summit and present her with a copy of the article, just in case she had been in Outer Mongolia and had missed this latest scientific news item.

I wasn't able to get a seat at the summit. I guess they did not appreciate the magnitude of my recent contribution to the world of science. But I planned to wander around in the lobby until the opportunity presented itself. I just knew she would be lounging around waiting to be recognized or photographed or hounded by the slimy media.

On the day of the event, I slowly drove the tank, which is my gleaming non-descript giant of a sixties car to the light rail station. I drove two to three miles over the speed limit, which must have made the other drivers so appreciative they all waved at me with one arm or one hand or one finger. I took the light rail into the city while I read the newspaper and sipped coffee.

Since the summit had started, I wondered around the lobby waiting until the lovely but evil-sounding Dr. Jealously Page, the world renowned scientific expert on Global Warming, made her appearance. She did not show by lunch time. I left copies of the tabloid at various spots around the lobby.

When she had not appeared by 4 p.m., I wrote a note on another copy of the tabloid and handed it to the man behind the desk and asked to have it put in her box. I went home, expecting she would call by the time I arrived. But there wasn't a message.

Since I had stopped to eat on the way home, I switched on the sports box to watch the game of the evening. It was in the seventh inning in a hotly contested battle between the Twins and Rangers when the phone rang.

After saying an almost polite "Hello", I heard the caller say in the most agonizing voice, "Hello, Honey Bear. I have wanted to meet you since I watched that talk show episode. Also, I positively love your writing and to think you even know who I am. Little ole' me, Jealously, me!! How soon can you get here, Honey Bear?"

Yes, it was her and she sounded even more hideous on the phone. Plus she wanted me there at her hotel room tonight!! (*For what, I wondered?*)

"Not tonight, but I can be there tomorrow, if you are still staying." I replied while slowly trying to comprehend why she wanted me there and why she was sounding so sweet; why she almost sounded lovey-dovey.

"Oh, alright. I'll just stay here in the big 'ole room by myself and pout without my little Honey Bear. Be here as early as you can. I'll keep the room for the next couple of days just for us. Come right up to room 319, Honey Bear."

Honey Bear, pout, little 'ole me, big 'ole room all by herself, keep the room for us? I gotta' tell you I am befuddled, mixed-up and mightily confused. After all, I had never met the lady. Also, I'm not like my buddy Bench, who is the tall, muscular, silent type and a chick magnet. I'm old, gray, and frail looking. I'm nobody's expected stud-muffin.

So the next morning, I got up and got ready for another trip downtown. This time, I even showered and shaved before I left the house. I even smelled the clothes before I put them on to ensure they were clean or at least semi-clean. My usual hair grooming technique of running my fingers through my almost non-existent hair was replaced with an actual combing while looking in the mirror.

I made it to the train stop earlier than expected (*was it anticipation, I wondered*). I tried to read the paper on the train but I was distracted. I sipped my coffee and thought.

I approached her room with lots of trepidation and some fear since I had no idea what she had in mind. I knocked quietly but she flung the door open and stood there in a sleek pink and black frilly negligee and bunny slippers. Plus she had that long hair piled on top of her head, which I really enjoy seeing. Her neck looked so soft, warm, and creamy. She looked positively sexy.

I hesitated so she grabbed me and pulled me into the room while she was shrieking and moaning. She pushed me towards the extra-large king-size bed. She had the biggest dirty-old-woman-hungry-look on her face. But all the time, she was sounding more and more like a banshee in heat or in pain or both.

Due to an unbelievable ache in my ears from the sounds coming from her, I had to escape. I feinted left and started to lean down to take off my left shoe. That caused the lovely, beautiful, desirable, ultra-sexy, intelligent Dr. Jealously Page, the world renowned scientific expert on Global Warming, to slow up her advance. The break that I needed was at hand. I jumped right and put on a burst of speed which amazed even me. I was at the door and had it open before she could even react.

As I sped down the hallway, she opened her door and screamed at me in the loudest, most annoying and terrifying way. It echoed and re-echoed around the hallway.

"Bear, you little runt. How dare you toy with a ladies' affection. I have been awake all night waiting for you. I'll get even if it is the last thing I do."

Luckily, the elevator door closed at that precise moment so I couldn't hear what she was saying. But I could still hear the sounds of her screaming and ranting and raving while I was riding the elevator down to the lobby and while I slowly walked.

I looked up just like everyone else. Those scary sounds seemed to shake the hotel just like an earthquake. I did not want anyone to think she was making all that noise about me. Heck, I'll bet that her voice could be heard in other continents.

As I rode the train north, I thought a lot about what just happened. They say that "necessity is the mother of invention". Well, if there ever was a need for a woman to come equipped with a mute button and a screen that showed sub-titles; that woman was definitely Dr. Jealously Page, the world renowned scientific expert on Global Warming. This change would make her the world's most perfect woman!!

Now I had to put together a plan on how to protect myself just in case she tried to get even like she promised. Luckily, I was good buddies with Chief Dulie. But I would never live it down if he ever found out I ran in terror from an amazingly beautiful woman, who tried to seduce me. I guess the first step is to change my home phone number.

I slowly and thoughtfully opened the sports page, which I hadn't dropped in that melee. I soon found that there was a good game between the Orioles and Nationals on tonight. I would pick up takeout food on the way home so I was ready to watch the game. Tomorrow will be spent writing.

A BETTER BEAR

Well, I was here!! I couldn't believe it, but I was actually at a Un-holly-wood party. Me, here with all of these celebrities plus who-knew-what's.

It was a must show for me. I wasn't given a choice. I knew I did not fit in. I also wondered what the repercussions would be since I would say something or do something, which would have far reaching effects forever or even longer.

I was wearing a black suit, which wasn't wrinkled when I put it on but it was very un-kept now. Of course, all of the other men here were in tuxes and the women were in all manner of evening gowns.

I must admit I was shocked by the way that the hair of the other attendees were arranged; pushed, pulled, teased, made to stand straight up, shaved on one side, colored in blues, purples, oranges, etc. and that was just the men's. I couldn't even begin to describe the women's hair-do and I'm a writer, an award winning wordsmith!!! Hmm!!

However, I was starting to appreciate the grandeur of the great ballroom with the chandeliers, lights flashing and the glamour of everything including the squads of waiters all dressed identically in blue uniforms. Each of those carried a tray elegantly balanced on their fingertips. The trays were full of long slender goblets of champagne or tiny little pastries or snacks.

The beautiful people were all gabbing and gesturing to each other while they sipped the bubbly and dined on the tiny snacks.

One well known slim man was stuffing his face and washing it down with goblets of bubbly.

I was alone, of course. I wouldn't have known how to start a conversation or even to continue one. I was thinking about leaving when a cultured feminine voice said, "Mr. Bear. You made it here. I'm so glad-d-d!" She put an emphasis on the last word which she stretched out.

I turned to see a pretty slim brunette with long lashes and gracefully flowing brown hair smiling at me shyly as she appraised me.

"Y-y-yes, I d-d-did", I stuttered.

"I wondered if you would actually attend this time. You have been invited to all of these A-lister parties since you have been winning all of the awards for your writing. Also, there is your checkered past. We shouldn't forget that."

I hesitated before asking, "A-a-a-lister party? Like Allen, Ashe, A-abernathy, Arnold, Ava, or Abrams?" (*I had known I wouldn't fit in.*)

Her pretty face with the slightly sunken cheeks took on a quizzical look while she contemplated my attempt at a list. Then her eyes brightened and her face became a wide smile as she quipped, "No silly. Your name doesn't have to begin with A to be invited. You have to be a current celebrity or sports star or one of the pretty-in-people."

"W-w-who, for instance?"

She looked around and pointed with her chin at a tall man with an equally tall woman on his arm.

"He is a basketball player who played on last year's championship team. She won an Oscar last year. She vowed not to date until she could find a man tall enough for her. They made headlines when they got engaged recently."

She turned to look at me and said coyly and shyly, "and you know me, of course" as she turned around and looked back over her shoulder at me.

I was taken in by her lovely sleek and muscular back with those cute dimples above her backside. Her entire back was visible since the blue and gold sparkling gown was almost open in the back except for a collar around the neck and a portion below the waist that barely covered her butt. She stood there looking over her shoulder with an expecting smile on her face.

When I did not say anything and had a confused look on my face, she slowly completed the turn and looked me in the face and asked, "So you do know me, right?"

"N-n-no, I c-c-can't say that I do, but could you turn around again? I want to see those dimples again." I was becoming more brazen by the minute.

She pretended to pout with her full lips and sunken cheeks and said, "But I do not have dimples." I could tell by her sneaky smile she knew which dimples I was talking about.

"Oh come on, I am Grabrinia, the queen of the reality shows on TV. I have been in nine of them" as she pretended to count the shows on her fingers. "Now I am the personal trainer to a lot of the stars here."

"Like him?" as I trained my eyes on the slim, handsome man who was now sitting at a table full of snacks and goblets. He was still stuffing himself.

She grunted, "of course, dear. He really needs help."

At that moment, someone called something out and she turned to leave. I wanted to ask her a question about where a guy could get a beer but I had forgotten her name, just like that. Was it Gabby or something close?

She must have heard me utter that word Gabby because she stopped quite still. Her spine became even more erect and she turned slowly and moved towards me.

Her lovely jaw had taken on a rigid bearing as she uttered through clinched teeth, "Do not ever call me that. My name is Gabrinia."

Her entire look went from one of the most beautiful women with long flowing locks in a tight fitting gown to a cobra-look-alike sizing up her prey.

I usually do not dwell on things that happen or were about to happen, but I gotta' tell you she now appeared beyond lethal. Her hair seemed to fan out behind her head just like a cobra. Her eyes were dark and focused. The dress looked like just like a snake skin. She was scary looking to say the least.

She uttered quietly, "The last reporter to call me that is now working at a remote station in Alaska or someplace."

She turned slowly to leave as I inquired merrily, "Oh r-r-really, do you have his name and phone number? I need a contact up there to help me arrange a fishing trip."

By then she had turned around so her marvelous back with those great dimples were very visible to me. She stopped a second at my comment before she shuddered visibly and walked away.

I watched her leave. I looked around; there was a terribly profound vacant and quiet space around me as if I was infected with a terrible virus. This was a good thing 'cause I farted loud and long. It irritated my nose.

You hear talk about butterflies in the stomach, hell, my entire colon was doing backflips. If someone approached me from behind and patted me on the shoulder, I would have went through the roof. I was that jittery.

I kept watching all of these great and wonderful people interact. They were talking, joking, hugging and air kissing. They were eating those tiny foods and drinking glass after glass of bubbly while they were sneaking side long glances at me as if they couldn't figure me out. I was doing none of those things.

Looking around the room, I noticed a line of waiters in their short and tight dark blue jackets, light blue pants with red piping and red bow ties coming out of an entrance off to the right. Each one was carrying a tray of bubbly. Ah, that is where I might be able to get a beer. I headed over that way.

I entered a small bar area. There was a young man working behind the bar. He looked at me and asked, "May I help you, Senor?"

I answered, "Yes, could I get a beer please-e-e?"

He answered, "Of course, Monsieur," and he reached up towards one of those elegant long stemmed goblets.

I said, "Not in one of those glasses. Don't you have a stein with a handle that a r-r-real man can actually hold on to?"

He said, "da" and reached under the counter and found a beer mug. He turned around and filled it from the tap. I did not expect the beer to be my favorite, but I still expected to enjoy it.

He sat the mug in front of me as I leaned on the counter while putting my right foot on a foot rest. This was a real bar, after all.

As I sipped the beer, I heard a deep male baritone start talking in the ballroom.

The voice said, "Hello and welcome to one and all. As you know, I do not need nor want an introduction.... First, we will have a song fest from the Serious Seven, all of whom are quite famous in their own right. They are not famous for singing, but we will enjoy their versions of popular patriotic songs. Then we have a wonderful surprise. The famous or should I say infamous author, Bear, will read the first chapter of his next book, THE AVENGE OF DUSK." He kept talking, but I stopped listening.

I must have turned quite pale because the bartender said to me in pure upper Midwestern slang, "Are you ok, Mr. Bear?"

I muttered under my breath, "I c-c-can't. I just c-can't." I put my head down on my hand on the bar. I must have expected something like this to happen here, but I couldn't get in front of an audience and actually speak. I just couldn't do it.

The bartender said, "So it is correct what they say, that you suffer from stage fright?"

I nodded and said a pathetic, "Y-y-yes". I farted again, silent this time. It was silent, but it was not deadly, thank goodness.

He thought a couple of seconds before his face brightened. He said with conviction, "I'll do it for you. It might be the break that I need. I have been trying to get an acting job. My girlfriend is in the kitchen. She has been trying to break into make-up so together we can make me become you just like that" as he snapped his fingers.

He got out from behind the bar. He grabbed my arm and led me out a door. We went through a hallway and ended up in a private dining room.

He said, "Sit right here. " He pulled out a chair for me. "I'll be right back with Sally. I think she has her make-up kit in the car."

He turned to leave and stopped and looked back at me. I was still standing – in shock. He guided me into the chair and handed me the beer, which he had carried from the bar. "Drink some of this. I'll be right back. Everything will be ok." Then he patted me on my balding head and departed.

Before I knew what had happened, he was back with a pretty girl with blue and green fluorescent hair, which was straight on one side and braided on the other. He explained again what he intended on doing.

She gave him a quizzical look and asked, "But Carl, I can't do anything with your hair except shave most of it off to get you to look anything like him." She pointed her chin at me. "And, I love your hair. It is so full and lush."

"Do it – whatever it takes. This may be the break I need; that we both have been looking for. Make me look like Mr. Bear here."

Sally opened her case and took out her kit while Carl took off his blue uniform jacket, tie, shirt and pants until he was in his tight briefs. Carl sat in a chair beside me. Sally started to work on his hair with clippers and scissors. Carl's cut hair was flying about as I sat and watched. I even managed to listen to the singing coming through the walls. My stomach had settled a little by then.

At times, the music sounded pretty good. They now were singing 'AMERICA THE BEAUTIFUL' and Sally wasn't quite finished putting on the makeup to change Carl's complexion to match my gray shade.

Just as I started to worry they would not be done in time, the mc came on and said, "Let's have them sing another. What do you say folks?"

There was a cheer. I relaxed a little bit and actually sipped some of the beer. Sally stopped and shrugged as if to say "that is all that I can do now." So Carl turned and looked at me and asked, "How do I look?"

Well, his face looked pretty much like a younger version of me, I guess. But I am no expert on how I look.

"Good, good," Carl beamed.

Sally urged me, "Hurry up. Take your clothes off so Carl can put them on. I won't even look." She turned her back.

I started taking off my clothes until I was down to my boxers, which were old and wrinkled, of course. She turned around unexpectedly and looked at me and sighed. I farted again. Both of them ignored it or tried to. It almost made my eyes water.

She helped Carl get dressed. The rented suit fit him better than me except for the waist, which they had to cinch in. I guess I have been getting soft around the middle. I am frail looking and short and balding with a turkey neck and now, I am gaining a soft middle.

The pants were a little short since he was a couple inches taller than I am, but there wasn't much we could do about that. We made sure to retain our own wallets, keys and personal items.

Sally ran her hands over the suit and tugged and pulled until Carl looked great in my suit, better than when I wore it.

She patted him on the butt and encouraged him by saying, "go do it." Carl extracted papers from the inside pocket of the suit coat, which were the first chapter of my next book. I had been told to bring it along; now I knew why.

The deep voiced mc came on then. "Weren't they great? Let's hear it for the Serious Seven."

There was loud applause.

He continued, "Now let's bring Bear up here to read from his next blockbuster." There was lots of applause and whistles and cat calls.

Sally turned to look at me as I stood there in my wrinkled boxers, yellowing undershirt and sagging socks. Carl winked at me and turned and confidently walked out of the door into the ballroom.

Sally smiled at me weakly as she handed me Carl's blue pants with red piping. I sat down before I pulled the pants on. I tried to fasten them at the waist. I couldn't quite pull in my belly enough. I put on the white shirt. Sally helped me button it up. She stood behind me and tied the red bow tie on me.

I stood up as I pushed the shirt tail into the pants. I put on the belt and used it to hold the pants together since there was about a three inch gap. I put my shoes on. I grabbed my wallet and keys.

Sally had me turn around and then she guided me out of the dining room and into the hallway again. As we walked past a mirror, I glanced at my reflection. I looked like all of the other waiters in the blue uniforms with the white shirt, red bow tie and red piping.

I was led outside like a lamb going to slaughter. Sally signaled for a cab on the street outside the massive ballroom.

I finally thought to say, "P-p-please r-r-return that suit to the rental agency. The address is on the inside of the suit coat."

Sally assured me they would as she opened the back door on a yellow cab.

The cab driver just sat there. Finally, he turned around and asked, "Where to Mac?"

"Oh, I n-n-need to go to a hotel."

"Which one? There are lots of hotels here."

He sounded impatient.

I finally remembered where I was staying so I told him.

He started to drive as he asked, "Did you get fired? Is that why you are leaving now?"

It dawned on me, finally. He thought I was a waiter because of my attire.

"N-n-no, they need another waiter. One called in sick."

The driver grunted in understanding and concentrated on driving in that maddening traffic and through and around the walkers, bikers, joggers, sightseers and more of the beautiful people in Un-holly-wood.

As I saw my hotel come into sight, I noticed another installment of that popular restaurant chain directly ahead. Since I hadn't eaten anything at the event, I directed the cabbie to drop me off there. He told me the fare was only $12. I mindlessly gave him a twenty, but it was too late to ask for change since the cab was pulling away.

I went in and ordered a full meal of proper Bear chow; a big burger, fries with catsup and a mint flavored milk shake. I sat and relished my evening meal as I watched current events on a big flat screen television.

The main event, of course, was me reading the first chapter of my book at a charity party of A-listers. I couldn't tell how Carl was doing since the TV was muted and I couldn't read the sub titles. It looked like he was doing an ok job of being me. I finished up the meal and walked quietly back to my hotel while sipping the shake.

I tried to enter my hotel but I was stopped by the doorman who wasn't about to let a waiter, who was sipping a shake from a fast food place enter into this exclusive manor.

I finally said, "I a-a-am staying here. My clothes were r-r-ruined so I had to borrow these." Finally, I slipped him a five which he reluctantly accepted; guess he wanted a twenty or a fifty.

I stopped at the front desk to pick up my room key. The guy behind the counter did not seem too thrilled to give a waiter a key, but he did anyway.

The food and being away from that party definitely helped to settle my stomach. I felt fine now.

Once in my room, I switched on the set and looked for a ball game. That would farther settle my nerves. I found one; the Phillies were playing the Dodgers right here in California. I would have enjoyed being at the game instead of at the silly party and that's for sure.

I awoke in the middle of the night. The TV was still on. I was in Carl's waiter uniform. I had spilled some of the shake on it. I went into the bathroom to clean up, brush my teeth, and what-have-you before getting ready for bed. I turned off the TV and opened the curtain so I could watch the fancy lights while contemplating my day. I actually slept well until the full sun hit me in the face through the opened curtains.

I closed the curtains and showered and put on my own clothes. I decided not to shave since I had shaved yesterday. I noticed the waiters' uniform piled in a corner of the room. What should I do with that? I looked it over and found it had the same rental agencies name and address as my suit. I hung up the waiter's suit and left it in the room.

I walked down to the same fast food restaurant for a breakfast fit for a Bear. I enjoyed sitting there and sipping coffee and watching the people either scurry off to work or loiter like tourists like me. I wandered around in the nice sunshine.

I went back to the hotel. It is too bad that my buddy Bench wasn't in town; if he had been, we could have taken in the ball game today. But I did not feel like going by myself. As I walked into the hotel, I was looked at quite skeptically since I was sipping from a cup with a big red M on it.

I stopped at the front desk and asked if they could have the waiter's suit returned to the rental agency. I was told, "certainly Monsieur". I wondered how much that would cost me. I walked over to a nice plush chair off of the lobby proper and picked up a copy of today's newspaper. Why buy one when one was there just waiting?
I read the sports page first, the comics, and finally I noticed the entertainment and society section. The paper had one, of course, since this is supposedly the capital of all that nonsense.

The caption that caught my eye was about last night's big fund raiser. It showed a picture of the Bear-stand-in, Carl, reading the first chapter of my next book. I won't bore you with the critique. It wasn't bad, except it did say that the look-alike probably did a better job at reading than the original Bear would have. I started to sigh before I realized that the article was correct. I am sure Carl did a much better job than I could have. Heck, I may have fainted or frozen stiff while up there on stage.

I went up to the room and changed into shorts, golf shirt, sun glasses and a wide brimmed hat before leaving the room. I sauntered around the streets in the sun looking at the people and enjoying the hustle and bustle.

Finally, I walked back to the hotel and had a seat by the pool. I was barely seated before a young and pretty waitress in a tiny outfit was beside me asking me if she could bring me a libation.

Without thinking, I asked for a cup of coffee. This led her to go into all of the flavors, roasting styles, creamers, etc, etc, etc that were available. After about five minutes, I finally was able to order a regular coffee with just a hint of chocolate and some flavored creamer.

She said, "Oui, Senor" and departed loudly on her high heels.

She was back in a couple minutes with a tall elegant see-through coffee cup which was topped with whipped cream (which I did not ask for).

She set it down with a flourish and then handed me a bill while encouraging me to just charge it to the room.

I declined as I glanced at the bill. I was surprised as it was over a ten spot for a cup of Joe at this hotel. I took a twenty out of pocket and handed it to her. She said "domo" and left. I tried to stop her to ask for change but she wasn't to be deterred. I had just spent $20 for a cup of coffee and last evening, I spent the same amount for a short cab ride. This really galls an 'ole Bear, who is frugal with his money. I fumed a couple of minutes before I allowed myself to just sat back and relax in the sunshine. I had noticed this waitress continued the trend of using multiple languages to converse, just like Carl, the Bear stand-in.

The rest of the trip was uneventful except for the long security lines at the airport, the weak coffee on the plane, the meager bag of nuts provided, non-talkative seat mates who concentrated on their pc's or iphones the entire ride, etc.

I was picked up at the airport by one of the Deputies of the borough police force. It was Deputy Doug, who happened to have a day off and seemed eager to make some spending money by acting as a chauffeur. We exchanged small talk about sports on the way home. It was great to be home and have that toxic event finished.

About six weeks later, I was eating brunch at old Bob's Café when Chief Dulie walked in and joined me at the counter. He placed his order with the grumpy waitress, Alice, who actually smiled at him.

After sipping his coffee, Chief Dulie glanced at me and waited. When I did not react as he expected, he asked, "What are you doing tonight at nine?"

"I expect to be watching a ball game, I guess, unless the Cardinal-Philly's game is rained out."

"You're not watching that new reality show on MBCI?"

"No," I replied, "I'm not really into those dribble shows".

He hesitated before saying, "even one called A Better Bear."

He smiled and then returned to concentrating on his coffee.

When I did not respond, Chief Dulie asked, "Aren't you even interested in this show; after all it will have contestants trying to imitate you – to be a better bear than you?"

My mouth popped open and I looked sideways at the good Chief. All that I could manage to say was, "Moi?"

He shook his head yes as he said, "It is a reality show. The contestants will try to win by pretending to be you. They will have judges and everything. Surely you have heard about this."

When I didn't respond, he replied, "Or not!"

We both thought about this as my food was delivered by a smiling Alice (not her usual facial expression when she lays a plate of food in front of me). I started to eat while Chief Dulie sipped his coffee.

He finally said, "Listen, why don't I pick up Reets and bring some food and we will come to your house and watch this show. It might actually be good."

Even though I couldn't think of a good reason to waste time watching a reality show about me, I agreed. It must have been a weak moment.

The day progressed much too fast since I was distracted – I guess that I was wondering about this show.

Chief Dulie, Reets and I settled in front of my newfangled flat screen television. We each had a cold brew-ski. I was apprehensive, to say the least.

The screen started by showing a series of bear images as a deep, male voice started to talk about me and my accomplishments. Then the voice said, "Here is the mastermind behind A Better Bear, the queen of reality television, Gabrinia."

The screen faded out slowly and melted into the image of Gabrinia, who was standing there in a tight fitting evening gown. Her hair was cascading fully around her lovely face.

She smiled and said, "Thanks, Bill, for that great introduction." She then winked at the camera, "Of course, you know him as The Larynx". Then she chuckled before saying, "We will have seven shows; each show will have seven contestants. The contestants who does the best imitation of Bear, the famous, and reclusive writer of books, short stories, and articles will win. Tell them about the prizes, Larynx."

The deep distinctive voice came back on and explained the prizes. I was amazed at the amount of money that was being awarded for contestants to pretend to be me. This wasn't missed on Chief Dulie and Reets, who both gave out cat calls when all of the prizes were announced. Reets, of course, had been doing the same cat calls since he first saw the beautiful hostess, Gabrinia. (*I didn't add to it by telling him about her wonderful dimples!*)

The announcer piped in by saying, "Now let's introduce the judges. She is the renowned talk-show-host and all-around actress and celebrity, Miss Jacky Mooney of the Sunshine Show. Her cojudge is the love of her life and constant companion, Bench. They are both good friends of Bear. Also, we would be remiss if we didn't mention they are both donating their compensation to Bear's favorite charity, the Cancer Society, in honor of Bear's wife, Mide, who passed away many years ago." With that the camera showed both the lovely Miss Jacky Mooney, and Bench, who was holding his right hand up to his face as if he was talking on a phone. He mouthed the words "call me", which was obviously intended for me.

I noticed both Chief Dulie and Reets gave me a questioning look after that. They probably expected me to issue profanities since two of my friends, part of my limited inner circle, would appear on this farce of a show. I guess I was too shocked to have a reaction.

Well, the show proceeded as well as it could. They had seven men dressed up like me. They wore rumpled old-style clothes. They had little or no hair. There were three white guys, two black guys, one Hispanic, and one Asian.

They first had to read a recent short story I had written. They each put emphasis on different parts of the story. Then they had to give a speech at a lectern. They pretended to be afraid to be in front of an audience. They gave an interview, which was designed to be similar to ones I have been forced to give.

After a long break, the contestants had to ad-lib – they were put in a situation and they had to act like they thought I would act. There was a traffic accident, a rough pat down by a woman at a security line at an airport, a restaurant bill that was too high, a drunk that spilled his drink on me, and a prostitute who was trying to sell her services.

I was really not entertained or amused by this show, which seemed to take forever. At the breaks, I kept changing the station to watch the ball game. Finally, the guys relented and we watched a great Phillies game. This was much better than dribble television.

Before they left, Chief Dulie tried to gauge my reaction to the reality show. Just like the remote, I switched the conversation back to the game.

Over the next week, I endured having people stop me on the street or interrupt my breakfast at Old Joe' Cafe or walk up to me in a store to tell me about watching the reality show.

The second show had women made up to be me. The third was a dance competition by my look-alikes, both men and women. It looked strange to see me dancing with me.

The fourth show was a sports competition. The fifth was a version of a popular question and answer show. A talent show followed. The last show was the winner's derby to determine the ultimate champion. I only watched these shows when Chief Dulie and his deputies stopped by with beer and forced me to watch. Reets was usually there then; was it because of my apparent discomfort or the free beer or both?

Callie, a wonderful young lady I had mentored, must have been worried sick about me and my reaction to this show because she called me every day or so from her duty station, where she was taking flight training. I assured her that the show wasn't worth a flea's bite on an elephant's butt. She was still quite concerned about me. No one had been that concerned about me since my late wife died. It really felt good, in a way.

The really good thing was Miss Jacky Mooney and Bench was the judges on only the first show. After that, the other judges were my money-hungry agent, Cliff Loews, Agent to the Stars, and Carl, the original Bear stand-in.

I did not call Bench. I did not have any contact with him until one day when he walked into my little house with his main squeeze in tow, the lovely Miss Jacky Mooney of the Sunshine Show. They had bagels, cream cheese, and lox in hand. They both looked tentative, as if they did not know how I would treat them. I guess they thought maybe I felt they had done something unforgivable by being judges on the reality show.

I let them squirm a little by not looking directly at them and by trying to watch the boob tube before I asked them, "Where are your clubs? How can you come here without giving me a warning? I coulda' made a tee time." They looked at each other and then both of them looked out the window at the rain mixed with hail and then looked at me with raised eye-brows.

I smiled and said, "I got you!!!!!"

After a good laugh, I made coffee and we shared great bagels, cream cheese and lox. Since I was between books, I spent the next couple days with them. We even played golf one day. We made plans to go visit Callie in Florida, when she was scheduled to graduate from flight school.

I make a point of thanking them both for honoring my late wife by donating money to find a cure for cancer. My adoring wife had died many years ago after suffering from cancer.

Everything got back to normal. I now ignored all calls from my agent; let him sweat a little, I thought.

I made plans for the fall hunting season. I even spent some time at the rifle range making holes in paper at long range. I also finally came up with a script for my next book, and so it goes.

THE ROOT

The phone started to ring so I got up from my very comfortable old recliner to answer it.

"Hello".

"Mushi, mushi, Kuma-san", the voice said. (*Hello Mr. Bear in Japanese*).

"Kenji, how are you? I'm so glad that you called", I replied. (Kenji is the exchange student that stayed with us years ago. He really clicked with my late wife, Mide).

"Kinky des, Kuma-san. O'kinky des ca?" (*I am fine, Mr. Bear. How are you?*).

"I am fine, Kenji. How are Junko and the kids?"

"We are all fine. Please excuse me, Mr. Bear, but do you want to catch some salmon? If so, I can meet you in Vancouver at the company house for a few days."

After I confirmed the dates he had in mind, I said, "Those dates should work for me. It will be good to see you again and catch some salmon. Is Connie still working there at the company house?"

"Yes, he is still there. He will be glad to see you also. I'll see you there, goodbye Kuma-san."

It was great talking to Kenji, but it was an interesting phone call. Maybe I should call it a strange phone call. Kenji did not even give me an opportunity to inquire about the health of his parents, Junko's parents or their grandparents. Also, he did not talk about his lovely and charming wife and their kids. He usually gushed about them. He did not ask how I was getting along without Mide or about having read my books and stories. Lastly, an important part of fishing is the anticipation of catching fish. The talk about kinds and sizes of the potential catch is often the best part of fishing. Kenji did not even take the time to discuss the type of salmon. Strange, stranger, and strangest!

I turned off the sports tube and logged on to the internet to make an attempt at scheduling my trip to Vancouver using one of those travel web-sites. (*Whatever happened to calling an agent who could make your travel arrangements with efficiency, cheerfulness, useful suggestions and a spot of humor!*)

This time it went pretty well, however. I decided to use this trip as an opportunity to ride the Canadian railroads from Vancouver to Montreal on the way home. I would ride the Rocky Mountaineer to the Canadian Rockies and then transfer to the Via Train. I could edit my book while I enjoyed the sights and sounds of riding the rails across Canada.

I now had the money to travel as I wanted, which is a result of the revenues from my books and stories. I also receive Social Security, and a government stipend. (*I'll explain about the stipend in another time and place*). It is too bad I did not have this income while Mide was still alive; we made do and scraped by a lot back then. Oh well!

The best flight would put me in Vancouver a day before Kenji arrived. I expected that would not be a problem at the company house.

The flight was uneventful, thank goodness. I tried to read the paper, and sip coffee while riding on that tube full of people hurtling through the atmosphere, but I kept thinking about Kenji's phone call. I could not arrive at any conclusions.

After arriving on friendly terra firma, I went to pick up my luggage off of the carousel. I noticed a man in a dark suit holding a sign with the outline of a bear on it. I should have known Connie would send a car for me and not make me catch a shuttle into town. Connie must know my given name since I have to use it to fly. I did not let him know which flight I was on.

The driver was friendly and talkative as we rode into town. He was from a limo service so I gave him a tip after he dropped me off at the company house.

Conyers (who I call Connie) is a short solid stocky guy. He is late middle aged with graying hair and glasses. He has Japanese ancestry. I do not know where his name came from. It is definitely not a Japanese name. Conyers is like the sergeant-major of this company house. He seems to be everywhere and does everything.

Connie greeted me at the door with a bow so I bowed back.

We went through the same greeting of Konichi-wa (Good day). He took my luggage and led me towards the elevator as he asked me politely about the trip and my health. I was glad to see him and I inquired about his family. Everyone was fine.

The estate rooms in the company house are really spectacular. They usually have two bedrooms and a great bathroom with a sauna.

After a relaxing bath, I got dressed and rode the elevator down. Connie had on his sports jacket and was ready to escort me around the city. He introduced me to a young guy who would fill in for Connie in his absence. Connie would have considered it an affront if I objected to his accompanying me. We spent a nice evening meandering around the pretty city of Vancouver after enjoying sushi, which Connie insisted on paying for. The only down side was that the beer was a Japanese brand and not my favorite. Close but not.

I noticed the change as soon as I arrived in my room. All of my usually rumpled and semi-clean clothes were freshly laundered and folded. I never knew if it was part of the usual service or a special benefit arranged for me. I got undressed and put on a kimono and watched the sights from the patio. It was a warm night without a cloud or rain in sight, not typical here on the Pacific.

Breakfast and a couple newspapers were delivered to my door. Both arrived as soon as I woke up; did they have the bedroom bugged? I lounged around and took a short walk outside until Kenji arrived.

He is tall and a good looking guy. He really seemed happy to see me. We spent the rest of the day walking around and filling each other in on current events. Kenji had brought me pictures of his family. He seemed to relax as the day wore on so maybe I had been imagining things about the phone call.

We got up early and had a small breakfast before riding a limo to the boat yard. There I was introduced to the captain and mate on the fishing ship. The captain was an old salt by the name of Captain Bandi and she (yes, she!) is certainly easy on the eyes. She is a blonde with curves in all the right places. She did not seem old enough to be a captain on her own boat. Also, she did not smile much at me so maybe she is street smart, also. (*I wouldn't trust me either*).

Kenji and I sat in the back in the fighting chairs in the sun and mist as Captain Bandi and her mate piloted the little ship out to the fishing grounds. There in the privacy of the water and over the roar of the motor, Kenji told me a story. It went like this.

"I have been fortunate to have a job with a good international company. I have been moving up the ladder and can provide a future for my family. I have two great kids. I have also been lucky in love; my wife Junko is both beautiful and smart. Junko has had some success as an aide to an influential member of the Diet. Junko is preparing for a run for a seat in the lower house of the Diet.

"But we have a problem. It seems that Junko's great-grandfather was a member of good standing in the war machine in World War II. We suspect he stole funds from the Japanese government. We do not know why he would do so unless he thought that it would be good to have an emergency fund in case Japan lost the war. On a trip to Europe to meet with German officers, he was able to sneak into Switzerland and put money in a secret bank account.

"If any of this about her great-grandfather's thievery ever comes to light, Junko's career in politics and my corporate career would be in jeopardy. We would be greatly ashamed. Both my family and Junko's family would be tainted, probably forever. Our kids could forget going to college, any college.

"We cannot go to the authorities to explain; that would be as bad as or worse than if it came out some other way.

"You are the only non-Japanese person that we know and can trust. We would be grateful if you could help to arrange for that account to disappear. We do not want any of the money. We just want the account to be emptied by a non-Japanese person.

"Here is the information that we have." He showed me a slip of paper, which was in plastic to keep it dry. There was a bank name and two series of letters and numbers written on it.

"Kenji, how did you find out about all this?'

"Junko's grandmother passed on this secret before she died. It would have been better if this secret had died with her. Now it is our all-consuming worry."

We lapsed into silence as we both contemplated the consequences of my helping or not helping with this problem. The fishing was sporadic, but we did catch some silver salmon.

Also, even though I kept thinking about the Swiss bank account, I still managed to keep my dirty-old-man eyes on Captain Bandi. I was trying to think of a way to ask her out on a date before I left Vancouver. But she was very adept at maintaining her proper distance from me. She may have read my mind or else she did not find this skinny, frail, old Bear attractive at all. It was too bad I couldn't let her know I was about to become wealthy thanks to a Swiss bank account. (*You knew I couldn't let this pass by, didn't you?*)

On the way back towards the dock, Kenji and I agreed on a code that would indicate the account was taken care of.

The rest of our time together in Vancouver and my anticipated train ride across Canada were over-shadowed by my thoughts in planning the money-moving caper. There was some book editing accomplished, not near enough.

The first day at home, I started to implement my plan to rescue the unused funds from a Swiss bank. After coffee and a bagel for breakfast, I jumped in my car, the tank, and proceeded to visit graveyards in the area. I concentrated on graves of people who had served in the military and who would have had a birthday close to mine. I was selective. I wanted someone who had died young so he probably did not have a surviving spouse or kids. (*You will see why later*).

The day wore on without having too much success so I quit for the day and stopped at Old Bob's Café on the way home for supper. That evening I tried to edit my latest book. Finally, I succumbed to the lure of a baseball game between the Giants and the Mariners on the sports screen and a cold beer. Ah, it was good to be home and in my recliner, stains, musty smells and all!

The next day, I varied my schedule by stopping to eat breakfast before I continued my grave site searches. I took my time in selecting my breakfast; I started doing that a long time ago to aggravate Alice, the waitress, but now I do it out of habit. (*But it still does aggravate her so it is still a worthwhile endeavor*).

I did find a couple perspective candidates but a GOGLE search later eliminated both of them.

I called Callie, my pupil, who is serving in the Navy to find out if she had a day off in her schedule and if she could meet me in the Washington, DC area. She told me she could be on a flight into the DC Metro area late on Friday, which would give her Saturday off. She looked forward to seeing me again.

I asked her to jump on mapquest.com and get the directions to Arlington National Cemetery. She knows me quite well so she did not ask why I wanted to go there. (*I had a lie made up in case she asked; it is good to save a well-thought-out-lie though since I might need it later*).

Saturday was a pleasant, sunny day as I drove the large, old, comfortable, nondescript car, the tank, leisurely down to meet Callie at Andrews Air Force base.

Callie looked really sharp in her dress white Naval uniform (*I never told her how much I like to see women in a uniform*). We made small talk about her life in the Navy. Also, we talked about how her mother was adjusting to Callie being away while we drove. I really missed having Callie around, but I couldn't tell her.

We spent quite a bit of time walking around and looking at all the graves of our heroes, who have served their country. (*These are true heroes; not like all those celebrities our national media likes to try to turn into heroes*!) Now I was about to give one of them another chance to serve. I would draft one for his name only.

I recorded about twenty possible candidates in my notebook before we went to see the eternal flame at President Kennedy's grave, and to the tomb of the Unknown Soldier. Callie looked so pretty in her dress whites; I hoped she would not cause the guards there to miss a step or a motion. But they maintained their composure. They are really good!

It was a great day; the weather was sunny and bright and I got to spend time with Callie at such a historic site (*for such a selfish reason*). I purchased Callie a late afternoon meal at a good seafood restaurant. Callie hugged me as I dropped her off at the base. I promised to find a way to watch her fly her first solo.

At home the next day, I GOOGLED the candidates. Now for step two.

After breakfast, I made a long out-of-the-way drive to a Halloween shop. I needed to change my appearance. I wanted to look like a more dignified old man, something like the Colonel of fried chicken fame. I needed a mustache, a wig, dark framed glasses, and a cane. I stopped at a consignment store and purchased a dark, lightweight suit and a used dress shirt, which were a little big for me. I had the other items I needed at home already.

I got dressed the next day in my newly purchased suit and shirt, and put on the mustache, wig and glasses. I had to put a small pillow around my middle to fill in the unused space. I drove to a small post office in Maryland. I selected one fairly close to where I live but not close enough so someone might recognize me, or so I hoped.

I parked down the street from the post office. I watched until the post office was empty before I donned a pair of light leather gloves and walked jauntily up to and in the post office, while holding the cane in my left hand.

I had to remember to open the door with my left hand, which wasn't easy since I had to hold the cane with that hand also.

I walked up to the counter and told the lady working there, "I want to obtain a post office box please."

"Surely, can you fill this out?" as she handed me a form.

I struggled to fill it out with my left hand while holding my right hand down at my side. Finally, I asked her, "Could you fill it out please? I can't write very well with my left hand since the stroke, you know."

She replied, "Can do".

I gave her my new name of Jake Brownie. I had his name and birth day all ready in case I was asked.

She then said, "That will be $35.00 for a year and I need to see some identification".

I handed her the money. It was a struggle to get the money out of my right pocket with my left hand.

I informed her, "The ID is why I need this box. I turned in my driver's license after the stroke so I do not have any ID now. Before I apply for that other identification, my family thought I needed an address of my own. I spend most of my days moving from family member to member so we picked this post office since it is smack dab in the middle of all the places where I hang my hat. Actually my living arrangements aren't bad. It is better than living alone. That isn't any fun." I gave her a questioning smile.

She did not even hesitate as she said "Ok. I do not see any problem with that."

She gave me my post office box key and opened the door of the post office so I could leave. I slowly walked down the street while using the cane in my left hand. I walked past my car. I stopped and looked back to see other customers entering the post office so I got slowly in the tank and drove away. Old people must be more believable, I guess, since she could have asked to see a Medicare card, but she did not.

At home that evening and over the next couple of days, I ordered free pamphlets, which I had mailed to my new post office box.

I searched the web and found a cruise that left from Baltimore and stopped at The Cayman Islands, which is a good place to have an offshore account or so I have read. I wonder how many of our elected officials have illegal accounts there. It is too bad that I couldn't query a bunch of those bums to get a recommended bank to use, but they wouldn't tell me the truth anyway. They never do.

I made reservations for the cruise.

Before I left, I got dressed again as Jake Brownie and rode down and picked up my mail at the new post office box. I went in after hours. I made sure to use my left hand and to keep my right hand at my side. I knew that I would need the practice later. I wore the gloves again. Best not to leave any finger prints while I was doing this.

The cruise was pleasant. I really enjoyed the sea air and the relaxing atmosphere. I kept reflecting back on my first cruise, but that is another story. The food was great. They even showed ball games on large screen televisions, but they did not have my favorite beer. Close but not the same.

Upon docking in The Cayman Islands, I slowly left the ship with a gym bag. I proceeded to a major hotel where I entered the lobby as quietly as possible. I found a large men's room and entered the handicapped stall. There I removed my rumpled Bear clothes and put on my Jake Brownie get-up complete with gloves. I realized I had forgotten the cane. Oh well, I would have to do without it this time.

I left the hotel quietly by a different door. I did not have to walk far until I found a large bank. I entered and looked around. Off to one side was a desk with a pretty dark skinned Caribbean lady sitting behind it.

I approached it and said, "Excuse me, ma'am. I'd like to open an account."

She glanced up and gave me a dazzling smile and said in an English accent, "Of course, Sir. Have a seat."

I used my left hand to pull out the plush chair and sat down easily. "I want to open an off-shore account, if you know what I mean?'

I expected her to say "No problem, mon" but she replied very formally, "Yes sir. How much do you want to start with?"

I handed her a wad of cash, which totaled $1500.00 and said, "Let's start with that. I expect to add significantly more money. I assume that the funds can be wired here. Will you show me how to do that?"

"Yes, I can, Sir. May I please have you fill out this application with your name and address?"

I handed her an address label for Jake Brownie and his new post office box; courtesy of junk mail.

"I had a stroke and I do not write well with this hand. Could you do the writing for me, please?" I showed her my gloved left hand.

She took the address slip and entered the name and address. She asked, "Do you want us to send you a statement to this address?"

"No, I will check it on-line if that is ok. Can I do withdrawals on-line also? Oh and what is your interest rate?"

She agreed she could show me how to do everything on-line and she told me an interest rate. The password I gave her was a combination of my late wife's name and birth date. As soon as the tutorial on accessing the account was finished, I asked her to show me again to ensure I had it down. I had her record the bank's name and the account number on a card so I wouldn't forget both. I thanked her and left the bank slowly.

I went into a different hotel and a different men's room to change into my wrinkled Bear skins before enjoying the rest of the day and the rest of the cruise.

At home, I sat in front of the laptop and searched for senior tours that had a stop in Zurich so I could access the Swiss account. I couldn't find any but I did find one due to leave for Paris in a couple weeks. It had an enjoyable itinerary. I signed up for a single. I made the air reservations so I would have two pre-tour nights in Paris. I finished the reservations by arranging lodging in Paris at a nice hotel for those two nights. All was set now.

The flight to Paris was smooth considering I was packed shoulder-to-shoulder, knee-to-knee with people I did not know and probably wouldn't like and we were all in a giant tube that was being propelled through air at an unbelievable speed while the Earth was spinning on its axis. Also, the plane was probably being piloted by a computer while the pilot and co-pilot were talking about their golf games or napping or flirting with the stewardesses.

I checked in at the hotel and tried to stay awake until evening so I could get my body cycle on local time. I took a walk around the hotel since the weather was sunny. I stopped at a bistro and tried to order something I would enjoy. I finally settled on soup, roll, a fancy pastry for dessert and coffee. It wasn't bad, I guess, but I wasn't used to such good food. (*It is no wonder since I usually frequent greasy spoons back home, like Old Bob's Café.*)

Early the next morning, I purchased an all-day ticket on the Euro-rail and got on the train to go to Zurich. I got off the train and walked outside of the terminal to a large hotel to change into Jake Brownie's clothes again. This time, I had remembered to bring along the cane. I wanted to have that dignified look down pat this time; dark wig, dark full mustache, dark framed glasses, suit with tie (large size filled in with pillow around my middle), cane and thin leather gloves. Can anyone say special recipe?

I waved down a cab and gave the driver the address of the bank. He gave me a funny look and drove about two blocks before he stopped. I included a large tip.

I entered the bank using my left hand again. I asked a guard there where I could open an account. He directed me to the elevator and told me to go to the second floor. I was met there by a well-dressed lady who took me to a desk where another attractive well-dressed lady introduced herself. She said her name fast in a French accent. Of course, I completely missed it.

Instead of asking her to repeat it, I just said, "I'd like to open an account please". I went through the same procedure as I used in The Cayman Islands; I used a different Jake Brownie address label and a different password, which was based on a mix of numbers and letters from my wedding day. Again, I wasn't asked to show identification. I used $1,000.00 of greenbacks to deposit in this new account.

This bank employee was every bit as attractive, stunning and cheerful as the one was in the bank in The Cayman Islands. I could just see them as bookends for me – what a threesome that we would make; especially since I had pictured both of them as long legged, gorgeous with long wavy hair and I am short, balding and frail looking.

I was beginning to wonder if the person at the withdrawal desk would be like a drill sergeant, husky, loud-mouthed and mean. Pretty and pleasant to accept your money but just the opposite if you want to take it out!

I thanked her and left. Outside of the bank, I walked down the street, and went into an American burger chain restaurant I had noticed. I lingered over the food.

I went back out and into the same bank. This time, there was a different guard posted, which was good since I did not want to be noticed too much. I inquired about needing help to service my account. The guard asked me for the first two numbers of the account. I told him the first two numbers from the information Kenji had provided me. I was directed to the same elevators, but I was to get off at the fifth floor this time.

There was another pretty lady there in a tight, business suit who led me to an office. Sitting behind the desk in the office was a sharply dressed middle aged man. His name was on a plaque on his desk, which said Pietr Gauche. He asked me to sit in the chair opposite the desk.

He gave me a big smile as he said in English, "How may I help you, Mr. ....?"

"My name is Jake Brownie and I need help with an account."

"Certainly, Mr. Brownie", he said in perfect English. "What do you require?"

"I need to make some changes to my account." I gave him the number.

He entered it into a keyboard and turned the screen so that I could see it. I read the amount as he said, "You currently have a little over 1.8M Euros in your account." (It was exactly 1,834,569.40 Euros).

"I need to have some money wired to another bank."

"Certainly, just enter your password," he said as he slid the keyboard across his desk to me.

It took an effort but I entered the password with my gloved left hand. The screen blinked and then Mr. Gauche said, "That is fine sir. What do you require now?"

"I would like 2,500 in cash; half of that in American fifties and the rest in Euros of mixed denominations."

He entered something on the keyboard and lifted the handset and spoke for a minute. He said, "It will be ready in about five minutes. Would you require something else, sir?"

"Yes, how much is left?"

"That is 1,832,069.40 Euros.

I took out the card from the bank in the Caribbean. I gave him the bank name, the routing number and the account number of the bank in The Cayman Islands, and told him, "Please wire half of the money there. The other half, I want transferred to a different account here" and I gave him the new account number at this bank. "Then close this old account. "

He repeated all the information to ensure he had it correct. I asked him to print everything on paper and he did. I read and re-read all the amounts and accounts and told him to finish the transactions, which he did.

There was a knock on the door and the same attendant I had followed into this office handed Mr. Gauche a small, neat package of money. Mr. Gauche handed it to me and I almost reached for it with my right hand but at the last minute, I took the package with my left hand.

Mr. Gauche asked, "Will you require privacy to count it?"

"No counting required. Thank you, sir. Good bye"

He said, "Thank you for continuing to allow us to be of service," as he handed me his card. He tried to shake my right hand but I declined. He almost had caught me at my deception.

I went to the elevator, where the same attendant held the door open for me. Then she pushed L and sent the elevator down to the first floor. En route, I slipped the money package and papers inside my shirt on the right hand side and moved my right arm tight against my body to keep the package from slipping.

I walked jauntily out the door and away from the bank. It wasn't long until I entered a lobby of another major hotel. I waved and smiled at the desk personnel as I walked to the elevator and got on alone. I pushed button 5 at random. I got off the elevator and looked around. I saw a cleaning lady with her cart, which was perfect. I moaned as I approached her and grabbed my stomach and acted like I had a stomach ache and needed to use the bathroom soon, like right now. Not seeing any patrons, I moaned even louder and asked to use the water closet. I grabbed my stomach and leaned forward as if a cramp had just hit me.

The cleaning lady looked at me and tried to explain where the public water closet was, but I moaned again and said, "No time, I have to go now" in a loud, demanding voice. She turned and used her pass key to let me into a room, which was not being used since there wasn't any luggage or clothes in view.

I looked back and said, "Thank you so much."

I groaned again and went into the bathroom and quickly removed the false clothing, which I had worn over my usual rumpled Bear clothes. I flushed the commode and ran the water in the sink. I left on the wig and mustache so I could peek out of the room door.

I said, "Could you get me a soda please?" I handed her a 10 Euro note and said, "Thanks again. Keep the change". She looked relieved as she pocketed the money and she left. I left right after her. She went right towards the stairs and I went left towards the elevator. I had put the extra clothes and money into a thin nylon bag. I was in luck as the elevator arrived before the cleaning lady was in sight. I relaxed as I slowly walked into the lobby and meandered around.

I found a soda machine and purchased a soda. While doing that, I dropped the now empty money package in a trash can. I went into the men's room and examined all the money. Holding each bill up to the light, I could not find any hidden chips or homing devises. It felt safe to leave now. I had figured the cleaning lady would take her time getting the soda since she would not have exact change. She would now inspect the room and find it was still clean so she would think that the incident was strange but probably not report it to the authorities.

It had been hot wearing the extra clothes, but now it felt refreshing. I took my time meandering hither and yon until I made it to the train station and got on the train and went back to my hotel in Paris. I got off the train at a stop. I dropped the Jake Brownie disguise in a trash can and purchased a coffee-to-go before getting back on the next train to Paris.

I might have been followed, but I was pretty sure that my hotel escapade would have fooled any followers, especially since I entered the hotel in a disguise and left looking different. Now the fake clothes and disguise was history also.

Paris was an interesting place to rest up and sight-see on my own. Then I joined the tour. There were a few pretty, ladies I happily joined at meal times. I would even volunteer to buy them glasses of wine and souvenirs. After all, I had some extra Euros I had to spend. I didn't worry about an exact conversion.

After enjoying the tour of four countries, I was still glad to be home. That evening, I called Kenji. There is a 13 hour difference between the East Coast of the US and Japan. So calling in the evening here at 9 p.m. meant it was 10 a.m. in Japan the next morning.

We went through all the usual preliminaries; asking about the health of parents, grandparents and kids.

Finally I was able to break into the agreed to code.

I told Kenji, "I will not require that loan now. My finances are quite healthy. But thanks for asking the last time we talked." (*To signify the original account was empty. I was to say I did not need a loan now*).

He said happily, "Oh that is wonderful. I'm so glad. I'll let Junko know. She will be happy for you also. Let's get together to fish some more."

I replied, "Yes. But this time I want to fish for halibut off the coast of Alaska. Halibut are huge and I want to catch one or more."

"Good idea. I'll bring my son, Akio. He has wanted to go fishing for a long time."

A day later, I wrote two identical letters;

Mr. Jake Brownie and all veterans are proud to be able to give money to your great organization to provide assistance to veterans-in-need. The donated funds are in off-shore accounts; see the enclosed data. While it is often felt that MONEY IS THE ROOT OF ALL EVIL, the money in this account was obtained legally. Feel free to make use of it.
Bear

With one letter, I put the name of the bank in The Cayman Islands and the account name and password. In the other, I put the name of the bank in Zurich with the appropriate account name and password.

I addressed two envelopes, one to the state commander of the VFW and one to the state commander of the American Legion. I wrote a note that said (to the state VFW or American Legion Commander, open after my death, Bear). I put both envelopes in my safe deposit box.

I chuckled. I wanted to be a mouse in the rooms when the officers of the VFW or the Legion tried to decide if they could accept this gift. Also, it would be interesting to see how those people would handle getting money from an off-shore account. People do not make decisions easy especially when there may be circumstances they do not understand.

I made sure that Callie would know where my safety deposit key was and that she had signing privileges. She could access my safety deposit box in the event of my death. Then I contacted my attorney, Maude, to change my will. I was going to leave everything to Callie, except the tank which I was leaving to Bill, the mechanic who kept that car running smoothly. Callie is an officer in the Navy and she took an oath of office. I did not want to burden her with these off-shore accounts. No sense putting her in a bind about them.

The Check

I was on a roll. The ideas and words were really flowing when there was a loud knock at the front door. I ignored it and tried to concentrate on writing my next blockbuster book. The knocking started again, only louder and more persistent.

I got up and went to answer the door. I hoped it wasn't any slimy reporters, who keep hounding me for interviews. For some reason, I did not grumble and yell as I went to answer the door, which is my usual attitude when interrupted.

It was only a delivery man at the door. He was dressed like I was, in pants and long sleeved shirt, except his were pressed and neat while mine was rumpled and wrinkled as usual.

When I opened the door, he looked at the address on the slim package and at me and back at the package. He looked very confused. He started to say, "Are you Mr. Harv?"

I interrupted him and said "Yes, that is my given name, but I now go by Bear."

He replied, "I thought so, I recognized you as Bear from your PUC appeal for proper military recognition and reporting. I served in the Middle East with the Marines. I want to thank you. Sign here for your package from a Mr. Cliff Loews in NY. You may sign as Bear, if you want."

The last comment was too late as I had already drawn a crude outline of a bear for my signature. I asked him if he wanted to come in for a cup of coffee, but he refused citing his tight schedule.

Time is money to all those delivery services. I waved at he jumped in the van and drove away.

I was left holding that slim package from my agent, one suspicious-obnoxious-money-grabbing Mr. Cliff Loews, Agent to the Stars.

I laid the package on the glider on the front porch and went inside to get a cup of coffee. I took my time returning to the porch. I watched the wind carry my newly delivered package away towards the East. I launched my frail, weak old body to catch that package before it went the way of Dorothy and Toto. After retrieving it and catching my breath, I sat on the glider on the porch and enjoyed the warm, sunny and sometime windy last days of winter.

I was shocked beyond belief when I opened the package and found an advance check for one million dollars, as in a 1 followed by 6 zeros, made out to my given name. This was a first for me, my first million dollar payday. It was for something I hadn't written yet (*even though I was working on it now or at least, I was before I was interrupted*).

The package also contained a new contract, written in lawyer-ezze and was about ten times the length it needed to be. This new contract probably contained all kinds of requirements for me, more personal appearances, more book signing, more exposure on national talk shows and who knows what else. This was designed to sell more of my books so my sleazy agent would make more money.

All in all, it seemed to this ole' Bear as if they were trying to buy me completely for a million dollars. My life becomes theirs. By now, you probably know not only do I detest all of the theatrical stuff but I also have a fear of speaking in public and in front of cameras, etc.

Also, the check was for exactly a million dollars, which is unusual since the fine print in my current contract has a formula for determining the agent's compensation. Royalty checks are usually in uneven amounts. This shows something weird and maybe even contract breaking went into the negotiations for this advance.

Also, for something this monumental, my agent would have called me first and gushed about it in his newly practiced nasally French sounding accent, which he delivers quite smoothly. I could see him standing in front of a mirror and rehearsing.

Now back to the check and new contract as there were a lot that couldn't be right about all this.

Maybe I will make my agent wait and worry since he would expect me to call immediately after I received the check. He also expected me to be so taken with the check I would just sign the contract without reading it or just cash the check, which would probably be the same as signing the contract. Lawyers can easily put clauses in contracts like that.

Yeah, like that is going to happen as I do not trust anyone, as in anyone, except of course, for my small inner-cadre of friends.

I put a copy of the contract in an envelope addressed to my lawyer, Maude. I wanted to put the check for a million fat ones in a plain envelope with first class postage, and mail it to the publisher's address in the Big Apple. But if the check got lost or misplaced in their mail room, they might claim I cashed it. I might end up being stuck with a new contract or pay a lot in lawyer fees to get off. I put the check in the gun safe until I could get the delivery service to stop by and pick it up.

I put the contract in the mail to Maude on my walk to Old Bob's Café for brunch. I had stopped work anyway so I might as well eat my main meal of the day. As I walked, I contemplated my proper reaction to the check and the new contract. Own me, huh? Well, we will just see about that.

At the café, I joined a buddy of mine, Reets at the counter. He knows how to push my buttons so he started the conversation with, "Who you?"

"I'm still Bear." (I *should know better than to answer his questions, but I was still thinking about that check!*)

"You do not look like a still bear. Bears are big and plump and furry; you are skinny, short and almost hairless. Heh, Heh. But you are close to being still as you move so slowly in your aged condition." The rest of the conversation went downhill from there.

The banter obviously brightened Alice's day since I bug her by taking a long time to order and by selecting strange combinations not on the menu.

Reets and I made plans to go play golf that afternoon. Reets dropped me off at my house to pick up my clubs and shoes.

I refuse, flat out refuse, to tell you about that golf outing since we were paired with two ladies. Reets beat me as he usually does even though he is older than I am, much older, like over 85. The two ladies, who are approaching early senior status, also beat me. They even lured us into betting a quarter a hole and an additional dime for each birdie. It aggravates me to no end to have to pay off golf gambling bets. I'll remember the $3.40 I had to pay as long as I live! I added that to my list that I keep; now I have lost $139.89 at golf. Someday, or somehow I will win at golf, if I live that long!

My bad temper was assuaged by drinking a cold beer with pretzels and nuts while I watched the Red Sox get beat by the White Sox that evening. (*I wonder what color sox the umpires wore?*)

I received a number of phone calls, which I suspect was from my agent. Since I was not quite ready to talk to him, I let the calls go to recording. I called and the delivery service stopped by and picked up the check, return to sender. I did not even have to pay for postage or insurance. Whew, it was good to get that out of the house.

I called Maude, my lawyer. After I identified myself, she began talking in her sharp voice.

She said, "Bear, you will not like this contact. The publisher will have complete control of you. For instance, they can fly you from Miami to Tokyo and then to Hong Kong for personal appearances or book signings, all in three days if they want to. I only gave you some of the bad parts."

"I suspected. I returned the check yesterday."

"Good. Cashing that check was the same as signing the contract. It is too bad you felt you had to return it. It sure is a lot of money."

We said good bye and I called my agent on his super-secret-do-not-call-me-there-ever cell phone number, which I obtained using stealth and treachery. It is one number I will never forget.

He answered, "Hello, this is Cliff Lowes, Agent to the Stars."

"Hi-lo Biffy." I said.

"Oh. Hello, Bear. It is so good to talk to you," he answered. He sounded so happy to talk to me, which only increased my suspicion about all of this recent activity. Usually he is quite reserved and reluctant to talk to me. I became silent. I wanted to force him to talk, which he did.

"How did Bear like that big fat check?" he swooned.

"It sure is great to finally receive a publisher's check that is tax-free, work-free, and agent-free. Finally, I have it made; I can retire to Tuscany and sip wine while chasing pretty Italian ladies. No more work for this old Bear! Thank you! Thank you!" I said laying it on thick.

"Wait-a-minute, Bear," he exclaimed. "That is just an advance for your promised book. You can't quit now and you still have to pay taxes on it."

"Ok, should I send you your agent's fee?" I asked to get him to divulge information.

It worked. He said, "Oh no, I received my check already for two hundred...." He stopped.

I had the impression he knew he had said too much.

"So Buffer, you received a check for $200K, huh? Let's see that makes the total payout for this advance at a cool $1.2M. Per our current contract, you are entitled to a lot less. You owe me at least $80K. I will be happy with that amount. Put it in the mail please or deposit it in my working account right there in the Rotten Apple"

"No, Bear, the new contract allows me to negotiate a fee commensurate with my effort so I can keep all this $200K." (*I* wasn't going to tell him quite yet I did not sign the last contract but only attached a note on the front, which said how happy I was with the new contract. Therefore, it was not in force. I had expected to get flack about the lack of a signature but never did. The person filing it must have read the note and assumed that I signed it.)

"I do not think the contract supersedes our original contract so I expect to receive the check by Tuesday or I will have to sue you for breach-of-contract Jif 'ole boy! To make matters worse, I have stopped work on my next book. Maybe I can put the publishing out for bid. Wouldn't that set the publishing world on its cultured ear?" I hung up with, "Guess that I will soon be in the market for a new agent".

My almost-fired agent called back a couple days later. I answered the phone with, "You have reached the Bear cave. Do not leave a message. Call someone else."

Cliff said in a pleading and desperate voice that lacked his usual practiced accent. "Bear, what have you done? You returned the check. You can NOT do that. I worked tirelessly to get you the check and the great new contract. Now I will have to try to re-negotiate a new amount. Oh no!!!"

"Listen, Stuffman. Calm down or not. Did you actually think I would accept the new contract? It is even worse than the old contract. I demand you send me that $80K you still owe me. Also, you better return the $200K to the publisher since you are not entitled to it, or have you already spent it?

"Of course, you have. You bought some fancy gadget like a new beamer and now you have to return the money. You are one naughty boy, Cliff! So bad, I am firing you as we speak and filing a lawsuit against you for breach of contract." I said the last very quietly and meekly not like that gizillionaire on television. I hung up. I had even gotten tired of changing his name to test him so at the end I had used Cliff.

Also, I felt like a big weight had been lifted off of my shoulders. For a long time, I had suspected that my agent was behind most of the unexplained events that happened to me. He was fired now. But would I need to look for another agent? That would be a question to ask my attorney.

I called Maude and explained the circumstances. She agreed to start legal action.

Two days later, the telephone woke me from a nap. I groggily answered the phone with a soft "Hello" and a yawn as I had just dozed off while watching the noon news and weather, which often happens.

I heard a feminine voice say, "Good day to you, Mr. Bear. Please hold for Vice President Rindoshunt."

One click later and I heard, "Bear. I have been authorized to negotiate with you for your next book. Did you really return a check for one million dollars?"

"Yes." Yawn.

"That is amazing. Anyway we can proceed. I have our lawyer here. May I introduce Mr."

"Stop now," I cut in. "If your lawyer says anything on the phone, then I have to have my attorney on the phone line and with those two mouth pieces talking, we will never accomplish anything." I heard a slight commotion in the background so I did not expect to hear a peep from the company lawyer.

I asked, "Is this call being recorded?"

"No" Rindy said firmly.

I was awake now so I said, "My book is almost finished. It is as good as you suspect. I will take an advance of only $1.1 Million, which will save your company a hundred thousand from what you were prepared to pay through my now-fired agent.

"I'm proposing a new contract. I will only do limited public appearances and book signings and only the ones that I agree to do. Also, I get my usual royalties and half of the amount paid to turn my books into a movie. Take it or leave it."

I thought I heard a muffled protest in the background, which sounded like someone trying to talk while a hand was held over his mouth. It must have been the company lawyer, who was not used to not hearing his own voice postulate for hours on end.

Rindy came back on and said, "We will talk about it and get back to you. Is that new book worth that kind of money?"

"There is no doubt about that. I hope that your lawyer recovers soon."

Rindy laughed and said "Good bye Bear."

Two days later, I received another phone call at the exact same time as the last call. Again I was taking a siesta like an old Bear. I slowly answered the phone.

I heard, "Hello, this is Betty Lou. Vice President Rindoshunt has instructed me to tell you. We here at HIHO Publications accept your conditions. If you can give me your lawyer's name and fax number, I will fax your lawyer a draft copy of the proposed contact. All that would be left is for you and your attorney to come up for the contract signing ceremonies."

I had her wait while I looked for Maude's card so I could provide the fax number.

I asked, "What contract signing ceremonies?"

She replied, "The signing will be in front of the reporters at an elite restaurant to get the maximum press coverage. The publisher wants to start this book off with a bang to use the Vice President's own words."

"I want Rindy to know that I prefer an isolated meeting in your offices with no media present. However, if this ceremony is mandatory, I will attend these ceremonies under protest, strongest protest. Also, I will not be liable if they do not go as Rindy and HIHO Publications expect."

Betty Lou hesitated and said, "I do not understand. What could go wrong?"

It is obvious she does not know me.

I added, "Just pass my comments on to Rindy. He may understand." I said all this as I started to make plans on how to change the ceremonies if the publisher still proceeded with them.

I called my lawyer, Maude, to tell her to expect the fax and to plan a trip to the core of the Big Apple, if the contract looked fine. I reminded her about my conditions.

Maude called back the next day at the exact same time as the two prior calls from the publisher. These calls meant that my nap had been interrupted three days.

She said, "This contract meets the requirements. They gave us an option of three possible dates to go to New York City." She gave me the dates and we selected the second one. I had her secretary make Amtrak reservations from Lancaster to New York City and back. Maude called to make arrangements with the publisher.

On the day of the meeting, I met my lawyer at the train station in Lancaster. I made an attempt to look presentable. I was wearing gray dress slacks and a dark blue sports jacket over a clean shirt and no tie. (*After all, it was only one-point-one million so a Bear shouldn't get too excited*). The coat and pants were clean but somewhat wrinkled. I even shined my shoes; not spit shined like we did in the army. It was unseasonably warm for late winter. I did not anticipate requiring a heavier coat and hat.

We sat together and sipped coffee and munched on donuts as the train left the station.

Maude asked me, "How are you going to handle these signing ceremonies? Are you planning on disrupting them?"

I said innocently. "What would I do? I love the press", which I said with as much affection as I could muster and without gagging. (*I couldn't wait to put my plans in motion; it would be the talk of the entertainment and news world. HIHO Publications and Rindy wouldn't look too bad, or so I hoped. But who cared!*).

"Yeah, right!" she replied.

As the train rumbled on, we conversed about the weather, the economy, and golf. She plays a couple times a week. But I suspected that I was not in her league. In fact, I wasn't in anybody's league.

She glanced around before she whispered, "Have you made plans on how to handle all of that money?"

"Yes, we will stop at a branch of my bank in the city and deposit it before we leave so I do not lose the check. There is a branch close to Penn Station. I guess I need to find a financial planner to make proper arrangements for investing."

"Both are good ideas," she replied.

We arrived at Penn Station on time and hailed a cab to take us to the downtown offices of HIHO Publications.

The cab driver dropped us off after a ride, which was not dangerous at all. He managed to miss all the other cars, pedestrians, and bikers. I just do not know how he missed every single one of them.

Maude paid him before I could reach my wallet. I do not know how much of a tip she gave the driver. But I would probably find out later when she listed it on her bill, another sneaky lawyer trick.

After entering the lobby, we were admitted to the building after identifying ourselves. I was pleasantly surprised when the elevator operator, who was a tall gray haired man with a slight paunch, stood at attention and saluted me as he saw us approach the elevator.

He said, "Thank you for supporting the veterans and the military so much, Bear. I served in Vietnam with the Army. I am proud of my service and I am grateful to you."

"I thank you also. Are you from here in the Apple?"

This got me a stern look from Maude. She obviously expected me to say something not politically correct. I changed the topic and made small talk about the time we spent in the Army.

He stopped the elevator and held the door as we exited. I went straight to the men's room, while Maude went into the ladies' room to freshen up.

While in the men's room, I contemplated my plans for the signing ceremonies. It involves a buddy of mine, Bench, who lived most of the time here in the city with his main squeeze, one Miss

Jacky Mooney of the Sunshine Show. As soon as I knew where the ceremonies were to take place, I would call Bench to have him bring the props (*like a clown, a trained pot-bellied pig, a marmoset, and other assorted non-living items*) to the restaurant. I couldn't wait! This would be my best ever!

I stepped out as Maude exited the ladies room. We walked into the anteroom. Miss Betty Lou was a round faced middle aged lady, who was wearing glasses. She dropped the glasses on a chain around her neck and smiled at us and welcomed us to HIHO Publications. She got up and led us into a small private meeting room off to one side.

She opened the door and we were ushered in. There were two men standing there. One was a little taller than I am and very broad across the chest and shoulders. The other was quite large and graying.

The short, broad man smiled and walked my way while extending his hand and said, "Bear, it is so good to see you. I am Rindy." His voice was even deeper in person. The introductions included Maude and the company mouth piece, whose name I missed.

We were offered coffee and doughnuts but I refused, which surprised Maude as she looked at me with raised eye brows. We sat down and the two lawyers started to discuss the contract, which the company mouth piece handed to Maude, who asked, "Is this the same contract that you faxed me?"

The big company lawyer who looks more like a bear than I do replied, "Yes, it is. You can read it while I attend to a minor problem." He left the room.

"Yes, that will be fine," she answered as she started to read the contract.

Since I wasn't needed, I accompanied Rindy to get a cup of coffee after all. When I got up from the plush chair, I noticed that there was a divider in this conference room. The divider was closed and I hoped that they were not videotaping everything we did.

Rindy directed my attention out of the window by saying, "Look at the view, Bear. That is the Empire State Building there." He kept pointing out the landmarks here in the Big Apple. I was listening closely as I expected he would include the location of the exclusive restaurant where we were going to meet the national media for lunch and contract signing. But he did not bring the subject up. Weird.

I did think I heard something rattling in the other half of the conference room and I know I smelled something that had a hint of fried hamburger in it. No, couldn't be.

Rindy and I talked about the sights as the mammoth-sized company lawyer came back in.

Maude said, "Bear, this is the same contract so you may sign it."

She gave the other legal eagle a wink and a sly smile. She probably tried to be sneaky so I wouldn't see it, but I did. I couldn't help wonder what was about. I did also notice that Rindy and his lawyer had wry smiles also. Nothing was making sense now.

Rindy stepped to the door and opened it and leaned out and said something to Betty Lou that ended with "now" as I had a seat at the conference table.

As Rindy was sitting down, the divider was pulled open and there stood my buddies, Bench and Miss Jacky Mooney of the Sunshine Show. They were both dressed as if they worked at a famous hamburger chain. They had on black slacks, striped shirts, red hats and red aprons. They were beaming and smiling and holding food bags. Behind them were a couple younger people dressed the same way. Betty Lou came into the room and put a big board behind me with the words "BEAR CHOW" inside the outline of a bear.

I was given my meal in a bag. I opened it to find a big burger, fries and a chocolate shake. (*Ah, definitely food fit for a Bear!*) Rindy, Maude, and the company mouth piece were served identical sacks of food.

Betty Lou stood in front of us and said, "Smile". She held something shiny in her hand. It looked about as big as a postage stamp.

I asked between bites, "what is that?'

Rindy answered, "That is the latest in digital cameras. Meet the distinguished photographer of today's contract signing, my assistant, Betty Lou."

Bench and Miss Jacky Moony joined us at the conference table and opened their bags of food. We were all having burgers, fries and shakes, and we were all being photographed. So this is what the winks and smiles were about. They wanted to make sure I did not disrupt the contract signing. They were in cahoots about this, Bench, Miss Jacky and Maude. They really got one over on me, you just never knew what to expect.

After we finished with cherry pies from the same restaurant, we proceeded to the contract signing, which was done in front of the thumb-nail sized camera. Bench and Miss Jacky Mooney of the Sunshine Show signed as witnesses. I was presented with a five foot long check, which would show up nicely on film.

Miss Jacky Mooney had to leave early since she had some filming to do. She said "chow baby" as she kissed me on my expanding forehead, much to Bench's delight. I pointed at him and mouthed "call me" as they departed. They looked happy together. Bench looked even more chiseled. He certainly had the strong-silent type down pat. Miss Jacky Mooney was still pert, pretty and vivacious.

Rindy said, "Bear, HIHO Publications has signed a contract for advertising this new book. The fast food chain may include a CD copy of some of your short stories, books and articles with their meals as soon as all the details can be worked out. That should explain this setting. We hope that you did not mind staying here for burgers."

He sounded so smug, but I had to admit. It went better than I could ever have planned it.

I was provided with a folded check for $1.1 Million, which I put in my inside jacket pocket and Maude was given a copy of the contract, which she put in her slim, designer computer case.

I took one of the empty bags and helped myself to some of the un-eaten doughnuts from the spread, much to Maude's chagrin. Rindy only chuckled.

It was safe to do that now since Betty Lou had departed. If not, she may have photographed me helping myself to those doughnuts, which would not be a good thing to have posted on the web. So we departed after the handshakes were given and goodbyes said.

On the street, we hailed a cab. I held the door open so Maude could get in. As I climbed in, I told the driver to take us to Penn Station. Since the driver resembled the other driver except this one wasn't wearing a turban, I asked, "Where are you from?"

He replied "Brooklyn" in a Middle Eastern accent. Maude hissed at me so I did not make any comments.

We had the driver drop us off at the bank branch, which was close to Penn Station. We went in and paused. I saw a lady at a desk off to one side so we walked over there.

She stood and said, "May I help you?"

"Yes, I would like to make a deposit." She pointed at all the tellers as she sat down, "they can help you".

I held out the chair for Maude to sit and sat myself. I made a show of taking out the check, which was made out to "Bear" and an outline of a bear, and handed it to her.

"Oh," she said as I handed her a deposit slip. She asked, "Do you want it all deposited?"

"Yes. I do not want to lose that check."

She instructed me to sign it and write deposit only, and my account number on the back. I even put a drawn outline of a bear after my signature.

She was back soon with my deposit slip. Maude and I left after thanking her. We walked slowly to the train station since we had some time to kill anyway. Maude carried her slim designer case and I carried a bag of leftover doughnuts in a fast food sack. How appropriate!

We had a brief wait in Penn Station in New York until we boarded the train for the trip to Lancaster so we both had another cup of flavored coffee. (*It wasn't from that famous and expensive coffee place but from another fast food place. I am still cheap even though I just received the check of a lifetime. I prayed the restrooms were not closed on the train because I would be going there often after consuming all of this coffee*).

As soon as the train pulled out of the station, Maude turned on her laptop and started to check emails or do work. I dozed off in spite of all that caffeine. We had pretty much exhausted our full allotment of small talk on the way to the Apple anyway.

I was awake by the time we pulled into the station at Philly. I made another trip to the men's room before the train left for Lancaster.

While we were waiting, I asked Maude, "Do you want a doughnut?"

I received a scowl back from my own lawyer. Can you believe it?

The train was moving slowly in the suburbs of Philly when things started to look crazy on the streets. There was a severe auto accident at an intersection and only two men were standing looking at the cars. I would have expected a crowd to appear to check it out. Also, shouldn't there be emergency or police cars present by now?

After going past a fence that blocked our view, there was another accident at the next intersection. It looked like at least five cars ran together. Probably the traffic lights weren't working. Here there wasn't anybody standing around or walking on the sidewalks or even sitting on the front porches. But I thought I did see a few bodies lying on the sidewalks or on porches. This was strange. Beyond strange.

The weather was sunny and warm on this late February day. I still had a warm glow from receiving the check and the signing ceremonies. I didn't usually win!

At that time, Maude complained about something and closed her laptop. I heard similar noises on the train.

"What is wrong?"

"I lost the service to the internet."

I told her, "That is not all that is wrong. Look there," and pointed out the window as we watched a small foreign car slowly run into a light pole. The car just came to a stop.

Maude looked at me and started to say, "What is going on?"

"That was about the fourth accident I have noticed. The crazy thing is there are no people on the sidewalks or porches. These accidents would probably draw a crowd, but not today. Also, I did see bodies lying around in odd places."

We watched the extraordinary events, which included more car accidents and bodies lying around. We saw where a car had run into a porch. The porch fell on the car. To top it off, no one was there checking it out. Cars and trucks were parked at weird places, in the middle of the street or off to the side of the road or in yards or against houses. One car was almost on the train track. But the train slowed down and managed to proceed without touching the car. As we moved past it, I could see the driver slumped forward over the steering wheel.

The streets were now entirely devoid of moving cars and the sidewalks were devoid of people, dogs, birds or anything that moved. We were in a train car in the late afternoon crossing a still, quiet world.

I heard a hard thud from the seat across the aisle and one row forward so I got up to check it out. A businessman wearing a suit had just fallen over and his head had hit the window loudly. He was sprawled out and was not moving at all.

The woman in the window seat across the aisle asked quietly, "Is he all right?"

"No," I said solemnly as I shook my head side-to-side.

She let out a little scream so Maude got up and looked at the slumped man. She reached over to check his pulse when I stopped her hand and shook my head again. I walked forward to check the other passengers. I found seven non-responsive. They either had their heads down on their chests or at an angle or had fallen over.

At that time, a young lady started to lose control as I walked past her.

She yelled, "Sean, wake up. For god's sake, please wake up." She shook the man sitting beside her. His body just shook loosely so she grabbed and hugged him and sobbed in his hair after his body toppled over onto her. That brought more shrieks and yells of terror in the train car.

In total disbelief, I walked back and sat down beside Maude. She was speechless and her face was white. I suspected that mine was also. I took out a doughnut and munched quietly in reflection while I looked out of the window at the strange world and listened to the scary sounds inside this train car. Maude was squeezing the hell out of my right arm with her left hand. She was too shocked to talk, I guess. We both were probably searching for some sign of normalcy. It would be great to see people walking around or cars being driven. There was also a lack of police or emergency vehicles.

By now we were out of the suburbs and going through farm land. There was a herd of black and white Holstein cows in a green pasture. Only one was standing up quietly chewing its cud. All of the rest were sprawled out, slumped down or had collapsed with legs askew. It did not take a veterinarian to figure out that these cows were dead, except for that lonely one that was still standing.

I asked, "Is your cell phone working? Call your office and find out what is going on?" Maude did not move so I said forcefully, "Do it now."

She called and listened before saying, "The answering machine just came on. That can't be as our offices are always open later than this." She tried her laptop but she could not get service.

"Bear, what has happened?"

"I do not have the foggiest idea, Maude. Not one clue."

The train car went totally silent as the train moved past an Amish horse and buggy on the road outside our window. The horse was slumped down to one side, and appeared to be dead, which pulled the buggy down on that side also. The off side wheel was in the air. There was an Amish man in black pants and a wide brimmed hat standing there looking at the sight. He was the first living thing we had seen since that lonely cow back down the track a ways. All of the other farm animals we passed like horses, sheep, and cows were sprawled over or had fallen down.

I said to Maude, "I hope they have been knocked unconscious and they will recover," but I did not believe it at all.

All of a sudden, the conductor came into the front of the car. He started to speak, "Ladies and gentlemen." But he was speaking too softly as he contemplated his shoes so he coughed and raised his head up and started to speak louder. "Ladies and gentlemen, as you are probably aware, there has been a terrible, er, disaster. According to the communications we have received on this train, people are dying everywhere. I'm sorry but I couldn't think of a better way to say it." He hung his head down as there were gasps and screams in this car.

He brought his head back up and stared towards the back of the train car.

He continued, "There had been announcements about staying inside. People should find someplace to get off the streets until the authorities and the medical professionals can determine what is happening.

"All communications stopped about fifteen minutes ago and we can't reach anyone on any frequency. Also, the AM and FM radios are silent. Therefore, the engineer, who is feeling well, has made up his mind to continue to the Lancaster train station, which is usually only about twenty minutes away. The engineer is proceeding carefully so it might take us longer to get there. There are no other trains on the tracks headed this way. If he sees any vehicles on the track, he plans on pushing them slowly out of our way. Lastly, are there any medical professionals in this car?"

Not getting an answer in the affirmative, the conductor started to walk towards the next car when the young lady who was holding her companion's body asked the conductor in a pleading tone, "Can you do something here? Sean isn't moving at all."

The conductor shook his head no and slowly left the car. An older woman moved up and tried to provide some comfort to the shocked young lady.

Maude and I exchanged glances and were quiet as the train slowly moved down the tracks into the station. This took over an hour. The sights outside the windows were quite terrible, calm and quiet.

The train slowly stopped and the doors opened. People, who would usually be in line and rushing to detrain, now took their time getting up and organizing their belongings or just remained seated since they did not know what to do; go or stay. They were afraid of this new world. We all were.

I told Maude, "I am going to try to get home. What are your plans?"

"That is what I intend on doing. Home sounds so good to me."

We got up and got our things. Maude had her thin fancy leather monogrammed briefcase with her laptop and my new contract inside and a designer leather coat and I had leftover doughnuts in a fast food bag. I also had just deposited one-point-one million dollars in my bank account. I knew it would be a cold day in hell when I became rich, but I never expected this. No one could have!!

We slowly walked past the young lady who was still holding her companion's body while she cried.

I leaned down and asked, "Where do you live?"

She replied, "Lebanon", which was in the opposite direction from where we were going.

The attending lady said, "Go, I'll help her. I live here in town. She can come home with me." After we wished them well, we slowly left the train. There wasn't anything we could do to help them now.

We walked to our cars in the parking lot beside the station, past the attendant in the booth, who had fallen completely off his chair head first. I looked in the booth. His body was crumpled and not moving.

As I reached my massive old car that I call the tank, a new luxury sedan squealed its wheels and plowed right through the barrier that blocked the exit. The driver was probably scared to death and was trying to escape all of this madness or rushing to get home to his family or both. The speeding car turned left at the corner on two wheels. I was expecting to hear a loud, scary crash as the car collided with some obstacle.

But it just got quiet again. I hung my head and got in the tank and started it up. I sat there a minute and tried to think before putting the tank in drive and waited until most of the other cars left the lot before slowly driving towards the exit.

I tried the radio but could only get an intermittent message on a couple stations that kept repeating, "Stay inside. Do not have contact with anyone until the medical authorities can determine if the danger of farther exposure has stopped." That is not exactly what was said but it captures the essence of the message. I wasn't thinking too clearly at the time. The fire sirens would blast for a while, go silent and then blast again.

Maude's little foreign car was stopped at the entrance. I pulled alongside. She rolled down her passenger side window and we talked.

Maude said, "Follow me. I will go slowly. We need to go around all the blockages. Are you up to trying?"

I shook my head yes and said, "Let's do it. I'll blink my lights at you if I want to stop for any reason." It was dark now but the street lights were on so it did not look too strange or foreign, except for the lack of movement or noise.

Maude nodded, rolled up her window and pulled out of the lot and made the turns to go north towards Route 30 West. She had to maneuver past a crash before she could turn right and proceed north. I followed but not too closely since you never knew when she might have to stop or back up.

She was able to get around the next accident by pulling her car partway on the sidewalk on the right. As I followed her, I noticed two bodies lying side by side on the lawn on my right. One was of a lady and the other was of a boy, probably mother and son. It scared me even more as I pulled my eyes back to the cluttered street.

Maude drove slowly avoiding the obstacles. There were single cars that just ran into parked cars, and there were multiple car crashes. There was a body in the street Maude almost ran over. She stopped and backed up and went around on the other side of the street. I followed her thankfully. She was my only link to another person now, which is a scary thought.

Maude only had to detour one more time, which was only over one street. She couldn't get past the mangled cars so she turned right, went one block and turned left. She turned left again and right at the north bound street. All of the streets on that detour were devoid of car crashes.

As we finally reached Route 30 West, I blinked my lights at Maude. She stopped and we both got out of our cars. I started shaking. I needed a rest. I was not feeling well at all. I leaned down against the front fender of the tank.

Maude said, "Bear, are you ok?"

"Not too well, please get me a bottle of water from the back seat."

She opened the door and handed me the water bottle. I drank about half the bottle before I opened the car door and sat on the side of the front seat a couple of minutes. Feeling a little better, we started again.

Maude made the left turn on Route 30. We found it was easier on the four lane road since there was a median strip and a shoulder on both sides of the road so that we could find a path around the impediments. We even had a clear path on the bridge over the Susquehanna River. But we did not proceed at too fast a pace anyway.

As we were approaching my turn to go south on Route 24, I blinked my lights again to Maude. She slowed and then stopped her car. We both got out and talked.

I said, "I am going to leave you here and head south to home. Are you going to ok?"

"Yes, I'll make it home. You be careful, Bear."

As I started to walk to my car, she yelled at me, "Is your cell phone on?"

"No, I forgot all about it."

"Well, plug it in so that it charges and turn it on."

"Ok. Oh Maude, would you like a doughnut? I got them at a good price."

She laughed. It was so good to hear such a normal reaction from her. It helped since we were going to be separating. We would both be traveling alone in this quiet, still, crazy-crash-filled world. It left an empty feeling in the pit of my stomach.

We walked towards each other and hugged for the longest time before Maude slowly and reluctantly got in her car. She waved at me out of the window and drove straight ahead while I went on the ramp and turned left towards home.

I was able to get around a tractor-trailer and car crash at the intersection with Market St. by going left onto the north bound ramp and then going down the north bound portion of the street. That was the most difficult part of my journey until I came to a newly constructed convenience store. I realized I could use some gas in my car and should eat something.

I pulled up to a pump and proceeded to fill my gasoline tank after inserting my credit card. I even got a receipt.

I walked into the brightly lit but quiet store. I did not see anyone until I looked over the counter at the crumpled form of a youngish cashier. Her skin had a very dry look to it. It was not a pleasant sight. I glanced down an aisle and saw a customer lying partially against the side of the display as if he had collapsed there. I grabbed a candy bar and started to eat it as I checked out the coffee stand. All of the coffee pots were almost empty so I turned the burners off. No sense burning up the pots. I selected a container of chocolate milk from the coolers. The candy and milk helped to make me feel better.

I decided to help myself to supplies, which might be needed to keep me alive. I went out and backed my car up to the door, which I propped open. I proceeded to loot the store and, yes, I know I was committing a crime. I selected mostly snacks, water and soda. I loaded up the expansive trunk and back seat of my car before going to the cooler and helping myself to packs of lunchmeat, cheese and bread to make sandwiches. I added milk and other assorted cold products.

I pulled the now fully loaded car to the side of the parking lot and ate a sandwich and drank another container of chocolate milk. I sat there thinking about the big check I had just received. I wondered if I would get to spend any of it.

All of that in the Big Apple seemed like it happened a lifetime ago, and now I was a looter. Getting comfortable in the seat and being totally exhausted, I fell asleep until the cold woke me up. I got out of the car and took a leak before starting the car and continuing on the trip home.

I couldn't help but think of the sixties song entitled Mr. Lonely about a young man who didn't have a girlfriend. I hummed the tune as I drove. The next town was Leoberg, which was a total mess. All the streets were blocked. There is kind of a narrowing of the main road there in Leoberg anyway, but it still looked like all of the commuters were in their cars at the time the disaster happened.

I backed up and looked both ways at a cross street. Accesses were blocked so I backed up to the intersection. It looked clear on the right so I tried going that way. I made it to the next intersection, but the way south was blocked again. I backed up and proceeded west. I kept trying and trying streets until I found a way that went towards a small mall. From there, I drove across the parking lot until I found the narrow road that went south so I could make it back to route 24. I hated to take that road since it was downhill and narrow, but thinking what the hell, I took it. It worked out fine as all the unfortunate drivers who went that way had their cars slide off of the road. I was able to drive in the center of the road.

I was now humming Silent Night to keep my thoughts positive and to keep from crying. I had not seen another living thing since I left Maude back on route 30. I hoped she made it home fine and would survive all of this madness. I was glad it was dark outside because I couldn't see into the cars and witness the ghastly sights of the bodies.

I turned right on the road to go back to the main road. Now I was going up a hill and was finding the same thing as I just left. All of the cars were parked or stopped on the sides of the road.

Once on route 24, I encountered more accidents, but I was able to work my way around the crashed cars and trucks. I even drove through some fields when I had to. I wondered what Bill, my mechanic, would think if he watched me drive this car (that he babied and kept in perfect running order and even waxed) through fields and over rough terrain. I also wished Bill and his family well. It would be tough to find all of my friends and relatives were gone now. I coughed and then stopped to munch on a candy bar and to sip some soda.

I was almost home at the last S turn before the straight away into the borough. I left my foot off the brake and gave the tank some gas and proceeded when I noticed a borough police car pointed at the road. As I passed, the lights came on in the car and it pulled out to follow me. I was praying he would pull me over and give me a speeding ticket. I so wanted something normal to happen.

When the police car was beside me, I looked over and saw in the pre-dawn light that it was my buddy, Chief Dulie. Thank goodness! I felt almost alive again; a friend survived. We waved at each other and he put his right arm up and waved it forward as if to say "follow me."

He sped up slightly and seemed to know the way around and through the accidents so I followed him right to my house where he parked in the middle of the street. I hit the garage door opener and pulled my car into the garage.

Chief Dulie walked into the garage and noticed I was having problems moving.

He said, "Here Bear. Let me help you out" as he opened the driver's side door and took my left arm and provided much needed assistance for me to get out and stand. I had seen a lot and been through a lot since I received that check in the Big Apple.

I leaned against the car and was almost overcome with emotion. I asked, "What happened, Chief? Was it a terrorist attack?"

He shook his head and replied solemnly, "It is not known now. It might have been something released by terrorists or not. All we know is that it is not nuclear-based as that could be detected so it is probably bacterial, viral or chemical. But it has taken the lives of untold numbers of good people". He sighed.

I had regained my strength some so I said, "Let's go inside and have something to eat. I'll make coffee."

He started to agree when he noticed all of that stuff piled in the back seat of the tank. "What is that?'

"I stopped for gas at that new convenience store north of Leoberg so, I well, I kinda' looted it. I figured I would need supplies if I was to survive for an extended period of time. Are you going to arrest me?"

He laughed and said, "That was a good idea. Maybe I'll stop on the way home and make sure the supermarket here in town isn't looted first."

"Will I get in trouble for looting?" I asked.

"No, probably not. The store has a video camera but it recycles so it will only record the latest looter. I expect the store will be looted many times before someone in authority will ever look at the video."

I said a stupid thing. "I'll send in a check to pre-pay before I am caught."

Chief Dulie said, "Bear, there isn't any mail service. There aren't many people left. We are in a quarantined area. Soon there won't be phone, cable, electricity or any utility service."

He glanced at his shoes and shuddered.

Of course he was right. I tried to think of all the consequences but all I was able to think of was coffee and food.

I said, "Let's at least have coffee."

Inside, I made coffee with water from the spigot. We made sandwiches and ate slowly and contemplated the current madness. He thanked me and prepared to leave.

I asked, "Do you need any supplies?"

"No, I'll stop and pick up a car load on the way home."

He walked out the door to the garage when I had a terrible thought. I called out to his back, "Did you lose anybody in your family, Chief?"

He stopped and hung his head down before slowly opening the car door and driving away. Did I hear him make a gasping sound? This was all too sad, too bad for words!! He had a lovely wife who accepted me for who I am, and two smart kids, a boy and a girl; a quite beautiful family. Or it was.

The front door opened and he stuck his head back in to tell me, "Load up a couple of guns. Take the plug out of that shotgun of yours so it holds all five rounds. Keep the guns close in case we are invaded. Also, watch for looters. Keep your wits about you, Bear. I'll stop by."

With that he closed the door and left. I went and closed the garage door before I put the cold food in the fridge. Then I sat down on my old, worn and stained, but very comfortable easy chair and fell asleep.

I came slowly awake. There was somebody shaking me and saying over and over again, "Wake up Bear. Wake up."

I became aware enough to realize that it was Chief Dulie, who was in the room. My eye sight was blurred but slowly I was able to see more clearly.

Chief Dulie asked, "Are you awake now? You had me scared there for a minute."

I tried to move the chair so I was sitting erect instead of reclining. Chief Dulie helped me change the chair setting. He kept encouraging me. I felt the need to go to the bathroom to pee but I almost fell when I tried to stand. Chief Dulie helped me to get up. I was so dizzy.

I asked him, "please escort me to the bathroom", which he did. I shook off his assistance as I used the walls for support to go into the bathroom. I do not remember if I closed the door or not. But I did wash my hands and face after urinating. It seemed to help clear my head.

After I finished, I walked out of the bathroom fairly erect and walked without support. "What time is it?"

He replied, "It is after 7 now."

That confused me so I asked, "But it is dark."

"Yes, Bear, it is after seven in the evening. Did you sleep all day?"

"Hmmm. I must have. Let's make coffee and sandwiches again." We did.

I asked, "Is there any more news available about this calamity?"

"Not really. We lost so many of the first responders that even the emergency communications are down. The police network is down, 911 is down, cable television is down, etc. It is difficult to determine how many people survived since everyone is encouraged to remain in doors and avoid contact with other people since there is a fear that everyone else may be contagious. It is a bad situation all around."

He continued talking as we ate sandwiches, cookies and drank coffee.

"I have tried to clear the two main streets through town so emergency vehicles can travel unimpeded thru the streets.
h the streets. I have been moving cars where I can. It is tough to do since I know a lot of the people that live here. If the cars will start, I

push the drivers over onto the passenger side and start the cars and park in driveways or on the sides of the street. If the cars won't start, I take them out of gear and try to push the cars aside by hand or with the cruiser. I wear rubber gloves and a face mask just in case.

"But I came across something unusual today. When I went to push a man's body off the driver's seat, his body cracked and snapped. It slumped down as if it was coming apart. It scared the life out of me especially when his left hand broke off at the wrist and fell on the floor. I put that hand in a zip-lock bag and froze it in the freezer at the police office. The skin on the bodies appears to be dry and the bodies do not have an odor. It has been getting colder again but I would still expect to smell something. Their bowels and urinary systems did not even release as they died. Totally weird and frightening! Do you have any ideas Bear?"

"You got me Chief. I am speechless."

He asked, "Are you feeling ok Bear? You look so pale."

"I guess that I am fine. Yesterday was a long day. It must have taken a toll on me physically and the events have shaken my mental facilitates also," I admitted.

We talked some more. He did not bring up his immediate family but I did ask about another buddy of ours Reets.

He shook his head and replied, "Reets did not make it. I stopped and checked his house. I found his body. I wish I had someplace to put all of these bodies but other than using a back hoe and making a huge communal grave, I do not know what to do.

"I found how Reets got his nickname a while back. He was a chubby, red faced kid with reddish hair so the other kids called him Red Beets, which got shortened to Reets over time. That nickname followed him as he grew into a tall lanky guy. He was in the clandestine service for all those years before he retired here."

Chief Dulie sighed heavily and we said good bye. He left.

I tried to get service on the television and radio, but all I could get was a message about staying indoors until the threat had passed. The telephone system appeared to be down also. Both the old landlines and the new cell phones were not working since I tried to call Maude to find out if she made it home. I logged on to the non-internet-connected computer and recorded all of these events.

  I sat there on my easy chair in the dark thinking and worrying after the electricity went out; until sleep came. I covered myself with a blanket.

TOI

The weather was cold, windy and spitting sleet. It was not an evening to be outside. The house did not feel much better since the furnace was set low to conserve fuel. Of course, the furnace only kicked on when the electricity was on since all the controls require electricity to function. I had said the hell with it and raised the setting of thermostat. When the furnace came on, it would feel warmer, maybe comfortable. Yes, I was wearing multiple layers of clothing including a knit ski cap.

I heard the furnace come on while the swag light over the dining room table glowed faintly. I had everything else turned off to conserve electricity in case the power did come on. I usually keep a candle burning so there was some light in the house; as long as the candles lasted.

I got up to fix myself a cup of tea. I was glad to have something hot. I walked over to look out of the living room window. I didn't expect to see anything since there wasn't anything moving outside due to the disaster. But it was something I did out of habit.

I did not try to watch television or listen to the radio since all that was broadcasted was usually just a repeated message advising people to stay indoors and off of the roads until things could get sorted out.

There was a brief newscast I was able to watch one time. The usually well-groomed and wide-eyed newsman looked disheveled. He eyes did not even look at the camera. He provided no additional details about the disaster. It was an unidentified virus, disease or poison. It had affected a lot of the Northeast. An untold quantity of people had died or been infected. Many of the gallant and hard-working first responders had perished. Therefore, all hospitals, police, ambulances, EMTs and fire departments were under-staffed and overwhelmed.

I made a cup of tea in the microwave while I had power (I added some rum and honey to it for flavor) and then carried the cup over to the window. I made sure that my cell phone, laptop, and flashlight were plugged in so that the batteries would charge while the electricity was on.

I should have started to heat up a can of soup while I could. But I appreciated the warm glow from the tea.

The street light was flickering softly. There was a small figure below it. Was that a child there huddled against the light pole? It couldn't be. Not now.

The little figure moved. The thought of a child being outside in this cold and sleet was too much for me. I set down the cup and put on a coat and shoes. As I got closer I could see it was a child, who was clutching a coat tight around its body with little hands.

I approached slowly and started to talk quietly, "Are you ok? I won't hurt you. Come inside to get warm." I could see a turning of the head my way but there wasn't any other movement.

I leaned down and a pair of scared wide eyes looked back at me so I said, "I'm not going to hurt you. Come inside where it is warm." I lifted up the child who was light in my arms. Now I am a skinny, old man, who is getting weaker all the time so if this child was light to me, well, she must have been small.

I took the child inside and put her on the sofa. I started to hand my cup to the child until I remembered the rum kicker.

"Just a minute, I will fix you a hot cup of milk."

I opened the door to the cold garage and grabbed a gallon of milk that was approaching the sell-by date. Hopefully the milk was still good. I sniffed it first. It seemed ok so I put a cup of milk in the microwave to warm and opened an old box of ginger snaps, which were still good, just stale. I do not throw much out that doesn't spoil.

The habit has come in handy since there isn't anything available to purchase.

I took the milk and cookies back to the child and helped her (yes, it appears to be a little girl) sit up and then I handed her the cup. She sipped slowly at first and then faster as if she was starved. She really attacked the stale cookies. I watched her eat before going to run some water in the tub. It was barely warm to the touch, but it would have to do.

I helped her stand up and took her into the bathroom while saying soothing words about getting her clean. (*My late wife and I never had kids. I was never around kids much so this was a whole new experience to me*). I helped her undress and lifted her in the tub. She didn't need assistance with washing her body lightly and shampooing her hair.

I used a clean soft towel to rub her dry and I put her in one of Callie's old sweatshirts she had left here a long time ago before she went off to the Naval Academy. I rolled up the sleeves as much as I could so it would fit better. I found a pair of clean socks of mine to cover her feet. Those socks covered her legs all the way up. It was too bad I did not have anything that she could wear for underwear, but she couldn't put hers back on since all of her clothes were wet and filthy. She had to be more comfortable since she was clean.

However, she looked a little funny wearing all those ill-fitting clothes, like wearing Momma's clothing. I chuckled at the sight of her, which may have helped because she smiled slightly. I just dropped her dirty clothes in the bath water and soaked them. They would be cleaner that way. I planned on keeping the water in the tub to rinse our clothes as needed.

I made more of the milk warm and she drank it and ate a few more cookies. I covered her with a couple blankets and she curled up and went fast asleep on the sofa. I ran my fingers through her hair and thought about her. Who was she and where she came from and sadly, what had happened to her family. She hadn't spoken a word.

I had a seat on the other end of the sofa and watched her sleep while I sipped more tea until it hit me. I had to tell the authorities about her.

Luckily, Chief Dulie survived. I used the cell phone to call his cell phone. He answered so the cell phone service was now working.

"Hello Chief, this is Bear. I may have done a dumb thing."

Knowing me as well as he does, he said firmly "What did you do NOW BEAR?" He emphasized the last two words.

"Well, there was a little girl out by the streetlight so I brought her inside and gave her milk and cookies. I cleaned her up and she is asleep on my sofa in the living room. I know all those warnings about staying inside and keeping away from other people because they might be contagious, but I just couldn't let her stay there and freeze. I am not on the best terms with the man-upstairs anyway....."

He hesitated and said sadly and slowly, "OK. I understand. You couldn't resist. It isn't too much of a bad thing anyway. I'm on patrol so I'll stop by and see her".

"Come in the front door. The heat is on now so we will be on the first floor."

I fell asleep on the sofa in the warmth of the house until I heard the front door open (Chief Dulie has a key to my house), and in he walked. He is an average sized guy and usually seems happy but all of this has taken a heavy toll on him since he has witnessed so much death and suffering. I suspected he had lost family members also, but he will not talk about it.

He held his finger up to his lips for silence as he inspected the girl's sleeping face. I followed him into the dining room to talk. It was now after 11 p.m.

"Can I make you a cup of tea or coffee, Chief?" I whispered.

He shook his head yes so I put a cup of water in the microwave. We do not talk much until we both have a cup of tea with rum and honey and were seated at the dining room table.

"I just couldn't leave her there Chief."

He replied "I wouldn't expect that you could, Bear. What can you tell me about her?"

"Well, she was wet, dirty, cold and hungry. She almost finished all of my milk. She appears to be in good shape but I would need someone with more medical experience than I have to examine her. She did not say anything, but I did not ask her. Her clothes are hanging above the bathtub to dry. They were dirty and wet so I rinsed them out while I had water."

Chief Dulie stepped into the bathroom to check the clothes for clues and said, "I'll try to call 911 and report it, if they answer. I might also call that social worker you like so much, Miss Jones. You might get to see her again," as he gave me a sly smile, but he did not add the unspoken words, "if she survived!"

He continued, "I'll drop off some kid's clothes tomorrow. Do you have food enough for a few days?"

"Thanks for the clothes. That was a good thought. Yes, I have enough food since I had good luck while hunting. The freezer has been running enough to keep everything frozen. I hope that she likes ground venison because I have quite a bit of it. I'm about out of the stuff I looted though."

Miss Jones, Miss Jice Jones (*rhymes with nice Jones*) was the social worker who became involved when I was mentoring Callie. Callie has finished at the Naval Academy and was reassigned to flight school or was she on active duty? I forget so easily now. I had not been able to contact her since all of this started.

Chief Dulie had stopped by to check on Callie's mother. He had found a pile of dust with bones, long hair and women's clothing all mixed together. We assumed that had been Callie's mom since that was how this was affecting some of the people. Their bodies were turning to a gritty sand-like substance or into dust. The same thing was happening to farm animals. It was probably happening to wild animals but no one had the time to check. Of course, we were not seeing any birds flying around or squirrels looking for acorns. Strange, weird and crazy!

Some people had gotten unheard of symptoms but appeared to be getting better. I had some days I could barely get out of bed myself due to dizziness and weakness.

Chief Dulie left so I turned off the light and went back in and sat at the foot of the sofa. I was still there the next morning since I fell asleep. I awoke stiff and quite cold as the furnace apparently quit working towards morning. I looked up and saw the girl quietly looking at me with her wide innocent eyes.

"Do you want to go the bathroom?" I said as I slowly stood up and helped to pull back the blankets. She got up and went into the bathroom after trying to rearrange her off-sized clothes. I listened at the door and heard the sound of her peeing. Good, she would not wet her clothes later.

I got the rest of the cold milk from the garage and made us some cereal for breakfast.

I asked her, "Did you sleep well, honey?" She only looked at me. "What is your name?" Again no answer. "How old are you?" I said as I got up to put the dishes in the sink. I glanced back to see her raise five fingers. She was five years old.

I watched her look around until her eyes fell on a toy figure of a bear on a shelf. I had bought it as a joke for my late wife when she was in the hospital years ago. I had used it as a cute gift to try and cheer her up. I went and took it down and handed to the girl. She ran her fingers over it and set it up on the table.

"That is my name, I am Mr. Bear. Can you say that? Can you say bear?" as she just gave me a blank look. "What is your name?" She did not respond.

There was a knock at the door so I went to let in Chief Dulie, who had a box of clothes in his hand. "Most of these are boy's clothes from my son, but they are clean and dry. Sorry that I did not have any girl's underwear in her size, but she can wear what is here until we can get her better clothes."

We handed the girl some clothes and asked her to go into the bedroom to get dressed since the sweatshirt and socks she had slept in were too big for her to walk around in.

"I called 911 and reported her. But there have been so many people dead and missing that it is impossible at this time to even begin to identify her. Your girlfriend, Miss Jones might call you to check in. She survived, thank goodness." Chief Dulie said quietly. "I forget to bring you any toys for her. I was only thinking of necessary things, I'm afraid."

She came back in. She looked so cute in clothes that were a couple sizes too big, but at least they were closer to her own size. I figured she could wear her own shoes. Her old clothes would soon be dry so she could wear them if needed.

Chief Dulie only stayed a short time since he was on duty. I removed some ground venison, bread and mixed vegetables from the freezer so we could have a good lunch. I used some rain water to flush the commodes, which I collected in buckets outside. We would be ok as long as it kept raining. I had purchased water in plastic bottles a while back for use in emergencies and looted some, but the water would not last long now.

I used the grill to cook the venison burgers. She seemed to enjoy it as long as it was covered with ketchup. She even nibbled on the vegetables.

I kept talking to her since I figured that the sound of a friendly human voice would probably help. Her world was now suddenly silent since the electricity service was sporadic, which meant no television or radio noise.

I remembered a toy car that had been in a cereal box. I found it so she could play with it. She seemed to like running it around on the floor until she dozed off. That was when I decided to call her Toy (but I would spell it Toi). She would at least have a name. I took a nap also since I was unusually weak myself and had been ever since this calamity started.

The electricity and water were off again when we woke up so we had some cold leftovers before we both went to the family room in the basement. I had some dried fruit, which was dessert.

I burned a candle since I did not want us to fall asleep before 7 p.m. The basement is a lot warmer since it is below grade.

I moved the furniture around so we could sleep side-by-side on some exercise mats on the floor. I gave Toi the sleeping bag my late wife had used infrequently over the years. I would use my big old (too warm) sleeping bag, which had saved my sorry butt in Canada. It is too bad the air mattress developed a leak. It would make the sleeping more comfortable.

I showed Toi where the bathroom was and instructed her to awaken me if she needed to go to the bathroom since I only had one rechargeable flashlight, which I would need a lot since us old guys gotta' go pee frequently at night.

Now to address that concern of yours; yes, even an old Bear has exercise equipment. It might not get used as much or as often or as vigorously as yours does, but I still have it and I do use it some. A buddy from work stated all exercise equipment will outlive us all!

Sleep didn't come easily for me tonight so I went back upstairs using the flashlight after making sure that Toi was fast asleep. I went into the living room and looked out of the picture window. It was like I was in an isolated wilderness as it was totally dark outside (and inside too). There wasn't a light showing anywhere, and not a sound to be heard; no television or radio or stereo was blasting away. There was not a car moving, nor were there any people about. Sometimes in the calm of the night before this calamity, I could hear the truck rigs bellow as the drivers downshifted to slow down as they approached town. That sound would be welcome now. As would the sound of motorcycles as they were being accelerated down the street. It was like Toi and I were the last two people still alive on this planet.

It was early spring now so there should have been birds flying around and starting to chirp and sing to attract mates. There should have been geese honking as they flew overhead on their migration north. Usually I watch squirrels and rabbits run around my lawn. But there weren't any. None. Zilch. Zero.

I could just imagine how all of this was affecting Toi. She went from a world with a loving family with lots of people around – from an environment with television, lights and sounds to one of dark, quiet and an 'ole Bear. It is no wonder she looked at me with that innocent wide-eyed serious look. I have trouble dealing with all of this, but it must be a totally changed and scary world for her. Oh well, we will get through this. It's too bad that I couldn't think of ways to get her mind off of all this.

    I used the flashlight to go back downstairs before she woke up alone again. I ran my fingers through her hair before climbing down on my mat beside her. I worried about my health for a while since I hadn't been feeling the same since all this started. Also, there was a dry paper-like place on the inside of my right ankle that was worrisome. However, sleep finally came for me.

AND MATT

The next morning, we went upstairs to eat breakfast. Since there wasn't any electricity, we both had cold oatmeal with raisins. It wasn't very tasty at all. It was also lumpy. The oatmeal, fresh drinkable water and dried fruit weren't going to last long since I had another month to feed. We would not have a way to wash the dishes so we would have to eat off of dirty plates covered with all kinds of bacteria and germs. Also, the house was bitterly cold.

I am normally a quiet person, but I tried to remember to say reassuring words to Toi; to keep her mind on more pleasant things. I talked about the first flowers of spring, the arrival of birds and the weather would soon be warm.

I couldn't help thinking about what I would give for a cup of coffee; a hot cup of coffee like I used to make. Before this all happened, I would wake up and make coffee and lace it with flavored creamer. I would savor the coffee and watch the world go by outside my picture window or read the newspaper before writing for a couple of hours and then walking to Old Bob's Café for brunch. I would write some more on the laptop or nap after I got back. If I wasn't working, I would be playing golf or going to a stadium to watch a game or doing yard work.

I must have been missing my caffeine or maybe I was just feeling poorly or both. My mind was in a total fog as I stepped out of the back door to get a bucket of rain water to flush the commode. I failed to see an impediment in my way until I went flying over it. I just splashed down on the deck. I pushed myself up on my hands and knees and turned around so my face was within inches of a dog's muzzle. It was a big, ugly, shaggy, scruffy dog and it was looking directly at my face from a distance of about six inches. My head was pounding and I was beyond being shocked. I just couldn't even begin to wonder where this dog had come from. I started to pull my face back slowly when Toi came out and walked over and started to pet that monster of a dog.

I got up and took inventory of my old, frail body. It didn't seem like I had any major pains anywhere; so probably nothing was broken. I was fortunate I went down like a wet towel because if I would have tried to stop my fall with an arm or hand, I would have probably broken something. As it is, I would still be bruised and sore for a few days.

I turned around and went to get the bucket while starting to get some dignity back. I had to step over that huge dog to carry the bucket inside to flush the commode. I know that it probably wasn't the best situation but we had to conserve if we were to survive.

Back in the kitchen, I watched Toi walk into the house with her arm over the back of that dog. I chuckled sadly and said, "Just bring him in, I guess. We will enjoy having him here." (*Who was I kidding, I did not want to have a large dog here but it seemed like Toi had made up her mind about keeping him. I was going to have to think of a way to get dog feed. A dog that size would eat like a horse and we couldn't waste people food on him.*)

I walked over and slowly reached out to pet the dog on the head. It pulled its head back as if it didn't want to be touched. But I admonished by saying "Stand still" and it did. I raised its ears and looked it over. It seemed in good shape except its ribs were showing. It probably hadn't been eating much. It was a male dog.

I guess that the fall had shaken my brain as I just had an idea. The new neighbor at the second house down the street had had two mid-sized dogs so she must have dog food there. Just maybe, she had some extra– if she was still alive. I had not seen anyone at all except for Toi and Chief Dulie.

I told Toi, "Bring that mutt outside while I check next door to see if they have any extra dog food. We do not have enough people food to share with that mutt. Keep him in the back yard." (*I had pronounced mutt with 'a' sound instead of a 'u' sound so the dog had a name now; he was Matt.*)

After putting on my gun belt and a .22 revolver, I walked slowly down to the second house. I approached the side door cautiously and knocked. I remembered anyone inside might have been expecting terrorists and/or looters so I stepped to the side and knocked again (like they do on the cop shows on television). The front, side and back doors were all locked.

I yelled, "Hello is anyone home?" at all the doors. I peeked through the side of the windows. I did not want to stand right in front of the picture window in case someone was inside with a shotgun and they were scared. They could easily shoot me. But there wasn't any noise or movement inside. As I walked around that house, I glanced over and saw Toi with her arm around Matt. They were both quietly watching me.

I tried lifting the garage door and it came up easily. (*I kinda' expected this since I suspected the garage door lock had never been fixed.*) The single car garage had the usual assortment of buckets, trash cans, and stuff. Plus it contained a car so the owner was probably here at her home. I walked around checking everything out until I opened a large trash can which was over half full of dog food. Good, that should feed that hound for a couple of days. There was also a half case of bottled water, which would also come in handy.

I stood off to one side as I opened the door into the house. The smell hit me right between the eyes. It was strong and ripe, and it made me gag. It almost made my eyes water. I knew I have never smelled anything that rank before. I held my sleeve over my nose and walked into the kitchen.

There on the floor was a large unshapely pile of clothing, with bones and putrid flesh with yellow or orange rivulets of something leaking away from it. The smell was coming from that. It was apparently the lady that had lived here. I moved into the living room and found two piles on the sofa. One pile had bones, fur and a dog's skull resting on its front paws looking towards the kitchen.

The head was partially covered in fur but was missing its eyes and part of its muzzle. All of that was in the middle of granular clumps. It looked like the dog fell asleep with its head on its front paws as it waited on its owner to move. The other pile just had some fur and one leg bone sticking out of dust. This was way too strange for me.

Thinking of something important, I went back into the kitchen and rummaged through the cabinets. I found bread and a couple bagels in a bread box. They seemed ok since it had been a cool spring.

At a hunting camp, someone forgot a loaf of bread in the winter and the bread was not moldy in the spring when we went to open up the camp. There was not any heat on so it was like the bread was in a freezer.

I found more people food, both canned and dry. The dry consisted of flour, corn meal, pancake mix, jello, pasta of assorted styles, and pudding mixes. All of that would really come in handy for us. I then found plastic shopping bags under the sink along with two more bottles of water. I put the food in the shopping bags, which I took to the back door. I sat the bags outside before checking the rest of the house. There was the usual assortment of stored things in the basement. None of which I could use to prolong our survival, except for one important tank full of fresh water that I may access later.

I covered my face up to mask some of that horrific smell and started to leave the house when I thought of something so I went to the refrigerator. I opened it and found the usual assortment of food stuffs, most of which were probably spoiled, except for some ketchup, mustard and pickles. They were vinegar based. I hoped they would still be edible. Taking the condiments with me, I went into the garage and carried the dog food and two big plastic bowls outside.

I had another thought so I went back into the house of the terrible smell. I went downstairs and found the circuit breaker panel. I proceeded to turn off the master breaker. After a quick search, I found where the public water came into the house and turned off the water valve. Now if the electricity came back on, it would not be wasted in case some appliance might still be turned on. It was the same with the water, if it started to flow again, it would not run in this house. Covering my nose, I left quickly.

I waved Toi over to help carry the looted food and water to our house. She helped without asking why. Just as I lifted up the dog food container to carry it home, Chief Dulie walked into the backyard of my house.

He called to me "looters can be shot, Bear." He chuckled.

"Not funny. I had not thought about what may be in all of my neighbor's houses until he showed up". I pointed around my house just as Toi and Matt walked into view.

Chief Dulie asked, "Where did that dog come from?"

"I do not know. I tripped over him this morning. Toi seemed to like him so I guess he is a fixture here. I remembered the lady that lived there had dogs so I went to find dog food." Lowering my voice, I described what I had found there. I ended with telling how ghastly and smelly that it was.

Chief Dulie remarked, "That is strange. Everybody I have found did not have any smell and are all turning to dust."

I filled one plastic bowl with water from a bucket and one with dog food. I expected Matt would just charge over and devour all of that dry dog food very fast as dogs usually do. But he just sat there looking at us until I said, "Eat Matt." He got up and walked over and started to eat slowly. It wasn't done with the usual dog gusto.

I asked, "Do you have idea where he came from? Have you seen a dog like that around here?"

"No."

I then told Chief Dulie about what I found in my neighbor's house.

"There are 35 gallons of fresh water in the basement. All of the houses will have the same thing. It is in the water heater, which should be full of fresh water we could use. Also, I turned off the electricity and water so when it comes back on, it will not be wasted in an empty house."

"Good idea, Bear. I had not thought about the water in the water heaters. Also, that is a good idea to turn off the utilities so they do not get wasted. But you need to be extra careful. You could get shot going into any house that has a frightened owner there."

"I know but I intend on going into the other houses in the immediate area to check for food; only the houses I haven't seen activity in. Has the markets and stores been looted much?"

"Yes. I have looted some but I can tell other people have been there also."

I then asked, "What about that feed store over your way? Do you think there would be any dog food left there? Also, I could use charcoal for the grill."

"I'll check on the way there today. If there is any dog food, I'll drop some off tomorrow."

"Would you like some ground venison Chief? I'm not sure how much longer it will stay frozen."

"Yes."

I went and got him a couple packs of frozen meat. I took a pack out for our supper.

Toi was now playing chase with Matt so Chief Dulie and I conversed about the current quarantine of the area.

He said, "I think it covers most of Pennsylvania and parts of New Jersey, Eastern Ohio and some of New York and maybe Maryland. At least, the authorities are working on the emergency communications so that is a start. But I do not have any idea when people will be allowed in to provide assistance. They are still not allowing airplanes to fly over this area. If they could, they could drop off medicine, food and water, but no such luck."

We had grilled venison burgers again on bread I had found in the neighbor's house. We opened a can of baked beans. Yum. That was followed with canned peaches. Toi really ate a lot of the burger as long as she could smother it with ketchup. We gave Matt some more dog food but he still refused to eat unless he was told to.

Since there was daylight left, I went on a key search. My neighbor across the street, Mrs. Shaw, had given my wife a spare key. Now where would it be, I wonder. Ah, this is it.

I told Toi to play with Matt in the front yard as I walked across the street. They stopped to watch me. Toi still looked at me with those large innocent yet somber eyes. I wonder if she would ever be able to talk or smile again.

I was still wearing the revolver. I approached the house cautiously. I knocked on the doors while standing at the side of the doors; all of the doors were locked. I yelled, "Hello Mrs. Shaw. Sharon. It is Bear. Are you ok?"

Hearing no reply, I tried the key in the lock on the front door. It took some jigging and shaking, but the lock opened. I walked in slowly and looked around. I found a pile of dust mixed with women's clothing in the dining room. I suspected I had just found Mrs. Shaw. This was still something I would never understand.

I looked around her house and went down the stairs. Her freezer had quite a collection of meats, breads, and baked goods. I removed some of the cakes for us to eat. Since the food in the freezer was mostly frozen, I did not turn off the electricity but I did turn off the water valve.

Back on the first floor, I searched the cabinets and collected canned food and dry food in shopping bags. I set the food in the living room by her front door. I found some more condiments in the fridge including the new red gold, ketchup. Plus there was an unopened bottle of red gold in the cabinets. Toi would continue to eat good now if I could find some charcoal. There wasn't anything useful in the garage.

I walked home. I was exhausted. I stretched out and took a nap after encouraging Toi to stretch out on the floor beside Matt. I was getting weaker or so I thought. I came awake just before darkness was falling so Toi and I ate banana bread, which had thawed out. We sipped some grape juice. Toi accompanied Matt outside so he could do his business.

We went down in the basement and got ready for bed. Toi put on boy's pajamas, which were a few sizes too big while I put on my micro fiber shiny ones.

We placed an old rug on the floor for Matt to sleep on. She put an arm out and fell asleep while she was stroking Matt's head. He was always quite close to her.

I pulled my sleeping bag over me. I lay there a while before I fell asleep. Everything was in total darkness and it so quiet that it was scary. I could really use a beer now. It would not have to be my favorite. I stick to it since I met my wife while I was drinking it, so many years ago.

We had some electricity the next morning so I made sure that my laptop, cell phone and rechargeable flashlight was plugged in to get a full charge.

I made us pancakes with frozen strawberries, which I had found in Mrs. Shaw's freezer while Toi watched Matt do his business in the back yard. I also made coffee, which tasted so good even though I was out of flavored creamer.

Chief Dulie stopped by early in the day. He backed the cruiser in the driveway and unloaded five big bags of dog food he had looted from the feed store.

I said, "Thanks, Chief. Was there any more dog food there?"

"Yes, there should be enough to hold even that dog a while."

He gave me a bottle of whole milk from a farmer that had survived. The farmer had looked around and discovered two milk cows were alive on neighboring farms. Their udders were fully packed with milk so the farmer milked them and was throwing the milk away since he had no way to use it or save it. But now Toi and the other survivors would get fresh milk.

"Thanks, Chief. That was good thinking. Do those cows give beer?"

He chuckled and replied, "No, unfortunately. But I do have some more good news. That same farmer has found a few chickens also. So he might soon have eggs. Plus more people are coming out of their houses now. I guess they were getting tired of hiding and of being scared. I have told them of your plan of raiding their neighbor's houses for food and water. They thought that turning off the utilities was a good idea also. I plan on making a list of those people and then having a meeting to discuss our common problems."

"That is good news. If you have time, let's go check out Bench's house now."

"Fine with me." I called Toi and instructed her and Matt to follow us. We left them in Bench's backyard to play ball while we entered the house.

I knew where a key was hidden. We were soon inside the house. We did not find much in the way of food and drink since this house was now just a secret getaway spot for Bench and Miss Jacky Mooney of The Sunshine Show. We did find some beer and coffee. We turned off the utilities.

I asked Chief Dulie, "Have you heard from them, Bench and Miss Jacky?"

"No, I have not. Phone service has been spotty at best."

He replied, "I need to go now to pick up my daughter, Deen. I left her with a young school teacher, Miss Rasher. Miss Rasher is planning on moving into town and living in her aunt's house on Main Street. Miss Rasher plans on opening a room in the elementary school building for the kids. It will be like the old time one room school with all the grades in one room. It will be good to give the kids some structure and something normal in their lives."

"Good, lots of algebra homework will take their minds off of their other problems." We laughed a little at my joke.

"I have been hoping to receive a call from Callie but she is busy there in the Navy, and like you said, telephone service has been spotty at best."

As we walked back to my house carrying the beer and coffee, Toi and Matt ran ahead of us so it was a good time for Chief Dulie to warm me about looters.

"They have been hitting some houses. They are probably taking valuables, like money, guns and jewelry. So you need to be extra careful at night, but with big Matt here, you should be fine."

"Do you want any of this beer, Chief?"

"No, I'm finishing off Reets' supply." (*Now who would have suspected that my good buddy, Chief Dulie, would hoard beer and not share with me? Not I? Humpf.*)

The not-so-good Chief laughed at the humor in this beer disagreement and got in his cruiser and drove off after waving at me. Humpf again!

I waited until Chief Dulie left before I went back to Bench's house and raided his shed. Bench likes to shoot off fire crackers at special occasions and he had a few remaining ones. I took the fuses and the fire crackers back to my house. I put longer fuses on a couple, medium length on a couple and a short fuse on one. I then put them in my shed; just in case.

That night, I had a couple semi-warm beers after supper, which tasted so good. But the beer wouldn't last long and I really hated rationing beer and coffee. I wondered if I could get Chief Dulie to make a beer raid at the local distributor. Fat chance of that happening!

Chief Dulie stopped by the next day.

He asked, "Are you interested in going pig hunting? Farmer John has found a couple of pigs, which are running around not far from his place. Those pigs have gotten a taste of freedom and would be difficult to catch but we might be able to go hunting to bag one to share fresh meat with everybody before the weather warms up.

"Also, I found a couple partial bags of charcoal."

"Do you need the charcoal Chief?"

"No, I have quite a bit now."

He shared the bags of charcoal with me. At least I have charcoal to continue to cook outside if the electricity was off. I should have planned ahead for this and had a wood stove installed, which would have provided heat for both warmth and for cooking. But it was too late now for that.

Chief Dulie reminded me about the opening of school by saying, "Bring Toi up to room 3 at the school house on Monday at 9 am. That is the planned date for the opening of school."

He got in the cruiser and started to back out of my driveway, but I waved at him to stop. He rolled down has window and I yelled at him, "What day is today?"

He laughed and replied, "Today is Friday, Bear."

He shook his head at my expense and backed up and pulled away with a wave.

It was now time to loot another house for supplies and to turn off the utilities. I selected the first house on the street. I had to break a window out of the door to gain access. I did not find much there except for some appreciated coffee. There wasn't much food. I suspected they had eaten out a lot. There wasn't any sign of dust piles so they probably did not make it home from work before the disaster happened. I again turned off the utilities.

At home, I stopped in the shed and grabbed a board to cover the broken window. After making that repair, I stopped and moved the firecrackers with fuses into my garage. I put them on a high shelf.

I made pork barbeque using a looted pork roast and sauce on the grill. I put some frozen vegetables in a pan to make them warm – at best. It is difficult to cook on the grill but at least it gave us hot food. Dessert was frozen cake from Mrs. Shaw's freezer.

Toi really was eating well but she still did not try to talk. She usually played with the big hairy dog, Matt. They were inseparable. He was definitely a one kid dog and he did not seem to like adults. He did not let me get too close and he made no effort to approach Chief Dulie.

It was in the middle of the night in the basement, when I was awakened by Matt's low growl. I used my flashlight to look at Matt, who had his lips pulled back in a grimace. I got up quietly so not to wake Toi and put on warm clothes over my pajamas and went upstairs quietly. I shielded the light from my flashlight. It was good because I soon saw lights flickering around in the house across the street. The looters had reached my neighborhood.

I slipped quietly into the garage and retrieved the firecrackers. I walked quietly down the street using the dim moonlight. But I could pretty much find my way. I placed all of the firecrackers on the east side of the house. I hoped to direct their flight away from my end of the street. I hid behind the nearest house.

I gave them an opening to run. It was west away from my house. I lit the fuses. I moved back against the side of the house just as the short fused cracker went off with a loud bang and lots of light, which bounced around the houses. That was followed by the sounds of crashing in the house. I heard swearing next from inside. I just had time to cover my eyes before the medium fused firecrackers exploded.

I heard doors slam at the back of the house as the looters left amid yelling and cussing and flashlight beams roaming around. They ran away from the house, towards the west as the long fused firecrackers exploded.

I suspected they departed the area; hopefully to not appear again. There weren't any sounds or flashes of light. They must have departed hastily.

As soon as my eyes adjusted to the partial moonlight, I walked home. There weren't any sounds now in the darkness. Inside on the first floor, I listened for sounds from the basement, but I did not hear anything. Toi may have awakened due to the sounds of the firecrackers, but she was fast asleep again curled up almost on Matt.

I hated to put her through that scary episode but I did not have anyone to watch her while I set off the fire crackers. The other alternative was to be forced to shoot the looters to protect us and I could not do that. I was not about to take another life if I could help it.

It took me awhile to calm down in that total darkness, but I managed to fall back to sleep.

The next day, I went looting again. I approached and entered the house cautiously. I found piles of clothing interspersed with dust. I was getting used to the idea of people dying and turning to dust. I had Toi help me carry the food, soda and useable bottled water. I continued the practice of turning off the utilities.

Chief Dulie showed up later in the afternoon. He gave me some news by saying, "The farmer, John, heard some noise last night. It was so calm the sounds really carried a long way. It was squealing, and was probably made by the escaped pigs. So we investigated. We found where a fight between dogs and the pigs probably took place. There was one dead dog there; a little one, probably a terrier of some kind. So the pigs were probably chased far away by now. But they put up a good fight. I also heard some sounds of shooting last night here in town."

"It wasn't shooting. It was me putting off firecrackers to chase away a couple of looters. Do you want to check out the house that was being plundered?"

After telling Toi to play in the front yard with Matt, Chief Dulie and I walked over to the looted house. We found where the door had been broken. The inside of the house were in disarray. We found where clothes and jewelry were strewn about. The looters probably dropped everything as they ran in terror after the crackers went off. We straighten up a little. We helped ourselves to the food and water and turned off the utilities. Chief Dulie and I nailed boards over the door to secure the house.

On the way back, I said, "I expect any surviving dogs to get into packs to try to survive. They may have gotten used to eating corpses before the people turned to dust; combine that with their associating people with food makes then quite dangerous. You better alert all the remaining people and Farmer John to maintain proper safe guards."

"I will. I will also keep a closer eye on my daughter."

Chief Dulie did not stop by on Sunday. It really was not a concern because I spent all day lying down. I was quite dizzy and weak so we ate cold food from cans and some left over pastries from Mrs. Shaw's freezer. I was getting worried, though, about my deteriorating condition. Toi just played with Matt and watched me with those big thoughtful eyes. She did not speak at all.

On Monday morning, I was feeling a little stronger. We had a breakfast of cold oatmeal and canned fruit. Again, I did not have any coffee, which I really missed. I could have made cold instant coffee but I wasn't going to have any coffee if it wasn't steeping.

Toi took a bath using water I had left in the bathroom sink overnight since the water pressure was greatly reduced. After she brushed her long hair, I handed her some clean clothes, which she put on. Then it was off to her first day in class. I put my revolver on just in case. As we walked, I watched for any activity and sounds but there wasn't any. It was still so calm and quiet.

We arrived at the school and walked in the front doors and followed a boy into the first classroom. There was a small gathering of people there, six adults and seven kids of various ages.

A tall woman smiled at us and walked over and introduced herself by extending her hand. "I am Miss. Rasher. Welcome."

Then she knelt down and said, "And this is Toi. Welcome to you and Matt, also." Miss Rasher extended her hand and Toi solemnly shook hands with her new teacher.

Miss Rasher' clothes were a couple sizes too big for her. She had obviously lost weigh; probably most survivors had experienced the same thing. Introductions followed.

I waited until I could talk to Miss. Rasher alone. I asked her, "Do you have a gun? Have you ever used one?"

She looked alarmed and asked, "Why?"

"Well", I began, "There is the possibility any dogs that survived would form into a pack. The pack mentally would supersede their normal behavior. Also, they are hungry and may have already consumed human remains. So attacks are possible since there isn't much for them to eat. I intend on leaving Matt here at the school to help protect you and the kids. Matt doesn't tolerate adults much but he loves kids." Then we both looked over to see the kids fawning all over that big, fierce-looking Matt. He just loved it.

Miss. Rasher replied, "I was raised in the country. My father taught my brothers and me how to hunt; so yes, I can shoot." Then her face got sad as she was probably remembering all of those loved ones who did not survive. She looked at her feet.

She raised her head after a brief period and said, "I moved into my Aunt's house here in town; to be close to other people. Anyway, my uncle's pump shotgun is in the house. I will keep it handy."

"Put shells in the magazine but I wouldn't keep one in the chamber. Carry that gun with you or keep it handy until we know differently. One dog by itself shouldn't be a problem but I wouldn't trust three or four in a pack until I could see their intentions."

I had forgotten to pack Toi a lunch, but then I smelled fresh bread. One of the ladies had baked it for the class, probably in the oven of a wood stove. I would have to make sure I gave all of the extra flour and baking supplies to the baker, especially since I was given a sandwich bag of fresh bread for my lunch.

As class was about to get started, I bend down and told Toi, "Be good. I'll be back to pick you up after class. Matt will stay with you also."

She nodded and gave me a hug, which surprised me. I hugged her back.

I walked home while keeping a watchful eye. I walked down the street and looted another house. There were a couple cases of soda and water. We would appreciate that. I was quite tired by the time I lugged all of that stuff back home but I still made sure to secure my entry point. I had turned off the water and electricity in the house. At home, I munched on the freshly baked bread and some canned fruit. So good!

I removed more of the ground meat from my freezer since it had thawed out and would soon spoil. I would pass it out to the other people when they came in to pick up the children. I started to let myself drop into my old easy chair but I feared I would fall asleep and miss picking up Toi at the end of school. So I carried the meat in shopping bags up to the school. It was a cold day here in early spring so I figured the meat wouldn't spoil if I left it in the shade.

I grabbed a chair and had a seat in the sun. I fell asleep and was still there until Toi pulled on my sleeve to wake me up. I managed to be awake enough to pass out the ground venison. Toi, Matt and I walked home but my mind was in a fog. I just couldn't seem to see or to think clearly. Somehow I got the charcoal in the grill started and put burgers on the grill. It took a real effort to finish preparing the meal. Toi now knew enough to get the ketchup and cover her meat and mine before we ate. I opened a couple cans of cold baked beans. We both enjoyed sodas; these were the first we had in a long time. Toi remembered to feed and water Matt.

I slept like a log. Toi finally awakened me in full light. I helped get her breakfast before she cleaned herself, brushed her teeth and hair and grabbed her back pack (now where did that come from?) and walked off to school with Matt after giving me a hug. I went in and fell asleep in my easy chair, despite the cold in the room.

The cold temperature finally caused me to wake up. I felt better so I made myself some lunch by opening some cans of vegetables and Vienna sausages before walking up to school. This time, I took my shotgun along. Since it was early, I made a long loop in the neighborhood. It felt like I was walking guard duty, which in fact I was. I was trying to get a sense of impending trouble, but I did not see any nor did I sense any.

I was feeling better as I approached the school. I talked to people about the weather and about the current living conditions. One popular topic was when we would get relief from outside the affected area and when the electricity would be coming back on. On the latter topic, Chief Dulie was convinced the electricity just needed to be rebooted, like a computer. I thought about all of this and remembered how it used to be; rabbits, squirrels, and birds flying around. There were many people, traffic and shows on television and on the radio. If you wanted something, you just went to the many stores and purchased it.

    Time moved forward. Toi and Matt would walk to school. It was decided that school would be for six days with a church service on Sunday. Electricity and water service were still off. Rain water and creek water were being carried to school to flush the toilets although the pipes going to the sewerage treatment plant would soon fill up and then, we would have to build outhouses for the kids to use. Someone donated a kerosene heater so the classroom wasn't too cold. The heater was used sparingly to conserve kerosene. It would have been great to have both electricity and water on so that we could wash clothes, take baths, wash the dishes and clean the house.
    I had been keeping my notes of my daily activities on paper now. I wanted the power to come back on so that I could recharge my batteries in the laptop, cell phone and flashlight.
    I was feeling a little better, but the dryness was slowly expanding on my body. I used a moisturizer but it did not appear to help much. I would walk on guard duty around the school since I felt I might be able to intercept some trouble before it could happen. I kept looting houses. I now was collecting water from water heaters for our consumption. Food was starting to get even scarcer. The good thing was the ladies were able to still make fresh bread and Farmer John was now providing whole milk and eggs. Talk about a real treat. The good food and the school routine were having a positive effect on the kids. They actually smiled now and played. Toi, however, remained her solemn, serious, quiet self, even while she was playing. I forgot to ask if Toi talked at school.
    I had propped open my freezer lid since I did not want mold to form.

In mid-morning a few days later, Chief Dulie stopped by. He had his concerned police face on so I suspected that something had happened.

He hesitated before he said, "Billy is missing since early this morning. He went outside to take a leak and hasn't been seen since. You know him, he is about seven but short for his age. Tomas, the man who took him in and has been caring for him finally tracked me down to inform me. Do you think that Matt could help us track Billy?"

"I do not know. He seems to be well trained. Let's try it." I grabbed my shotgun and a water bottle and a slice of bread.

We rode in silence to the school. We interrupted Miss Rasher's dialogue and called her outside the classroom. She also was worried about Billy, who should have been in class. She agreed to our decision. She called Toi outside the classroom. I got down in front of Toi and said slowly, "We need to borrow Matt for a couple hours. I will bring him back. Miss Rasher will take care of you if I am a little late. But don't worry, we will be fine. Ok?" I hugged her.

She only nodded her same quiet and solemn wide-eyed way. Miss Rasher took her back inside the classroom.

I called, "Matt, come."

He got up and slowly walked over to us. He stopped and looked back at Toi. Then he walked out with us.

I opened the back door of the cruiser and said, "Matt, get in." He did.

The trip to Billy's and Tomas' house was quick. Tomas was sitting on the front porch with his head in his hands. He looked up at us with anguish and tears on his face. The Chief tried to put him at ease but it did not help. Finally, Tomas got us some of Billy's clothes. Tomas went to get his jacket to go along, but the Chief insisted that Tomas stay there in case Billy came back. Chief Dulie brought along his deer rifle and I carried my shotgun.

We had Matt sniff Billy's clothes.

I said, "Matt, find."

Matt did not react so we started to walk a circle around the house. I had instructed Matt to walk with us. Matt showed nothing. We made a longer circle around the property. Then Matt sniffed the ground and turned off to the Northeast. We followed. We found a shoe a while later. It was a boys' sneaker. We then knew we were on the right track. But it scared us. We now worried more about what had happened to Billy.

Matt was in the front and Chief Dulie was close behind him. I was lagging behind. I just did not have the stamina in this old body like I did before all of this happened.

I saw the Chief slow up. He told Matt to stop. That was when I saw the dog-like form run out a little ravine into a field and stop and look back at us. The Chief raised his deer rifle and aimed and fired. The gray dog fell over.

I walked up to Chief Dulie and then we walked on to Matt. Chief Dulie told Matt "stay, Matt", which he did. We walked over and looked into the carnage at the bottom of the ravine. There was blood and boy's clothes everywhere. Chief Dulie hung his head. I was in total shock as I tried not to look.

Chief Dulie started to walk around the scene so I followed. He walked slowly up to the animal. It was a coyote and it was nothing but skin and bones. Obviously, it was starving so it took the only prey that was available.

We left the coyote lay there. We walked back to the body, which had been partially devoured. It was difficult for the Chief but he put on rubber gloves and started to collect the body parts and wrap everything in the clothes. He tied the sleeves and pants together to form a bag. We should have brought a bag but who could have expected this. I tried not to look, but I knew that we both had tears running down our faces.

The chief carried the body and I carried his rifle back to the house. I did not relish having Tomas see this but there wasn't much that we could do about that now. I told Matt "walk" so he stood up and walked along with us.

I cannot begin to even describe the grief Tomas showed at the sight of Billy's body. We spent some time with Tomas before he started to calm down. Arrangements were made for a brief graveside service. Chief Dulie would make a wooden casket and Farmer John would get drafted to dig a grave with a back hoe. This was one of my worst experiences since all of this started.

We put Billy's remains in the trunk and started to drive through town to the school. Right there on Main Street, Chief Dulie quickly stopped the cruiser and jumped out and pointed at the sky. I realized why.

We had both heard the honking of Canadian geese as they flew overhead. There was a large V shape flock flying towards a farmer's pond just north of town. This was the first sign that we had of things getting back to normal. Birds were moving in and not dying or so we hoped.

Chief Dulie had a smile on his face. I did too.

Chief Dulie said, "Maybe the threat of further contamination is over. Then they might lift the quarantine. Hooray." We both cheered. We both danced and cheered. This was our first look at the end of the tunnel and it came after the horrific events we had just endured.

We stopped at the school just as class was about over. We told Miss Rasher everything and reminded her to pass on the word about Billy and to remind everyone to exercise caution.

The funeral service was brief and solemn. It was held in a graveyard in the borough. For us, it was the first burial service we had had since this started. Lots of other people had died and they just turned to dust. We conducted this service for Billy and for all of the other people who had died. The kids had collected spring flowers blossoms like snow drops, and crocuses, which they dropped on the casket.

As we left the graveyard, there was another positive sign, both of spring and the disaster was ending. A flock of robins had found a shrub, which was full of red berries. The birds were gorging themselves on the berries and some were looking for worms in the partially frozen ground. Someone remarked more geese were showing up all of the time. Hope was again in the air on this solemn occasion. Toi still hadn't talked or smiled.

HELLO

Hello. My name is Lieutenant Callie Bonnet. I am currently serving as a pilot in the US Navy aboard the USS Ronald Reagan, a carrier on patrol here in the Atlantic. Yes, I did pass flight school just as my mentor, Mr. Bear, encouraged me to do. He was the first to believe in me, sigh!

I have Mr. Bear's laptop here on board ship. This is the same laptop I organized so Mr. Bear could write his stories.

Since I have some time when I am not on call or actually flying, I have compiled all of the stories you have been reading. I think I have them in their proper chronological sequence just as Mr. Bear lived them. He usually recorded everything on this laptop whenever he had time, including all that happened during the national disaster in the Northeast.

Now, I guess would be a good time to tell you about the rest of the saga of Mr. Bear. I have talked to everybody who was there and survived and can provide you, the reader, with the following events.

Here goes;
Chief Dulie's cell phone rang. He glanced at the caller id before answering. The call was from Bear's cell phone.
"Hello".
There was silence and he heard a little girl's trembling voice say, "Mr. Bear won't wake up."

Stunned, he didn't say anything at first until it became clear in his mind.

He asked gently, "Toi, is that you? Where is Mr. Bear? Is he in bed?"

There was more silence until he heard, "No, he's sleeping on his 'puter. But he won't wake up."

"I'll be right there Toi. It will only take me a couple minutes."

Chief Dulie did not expect to see any traffic on the streets and roads since all of this weirdness started so he did not use the siren. He just swore a couple times quietly as he made a sweeping U-turn and sped to Bear's house.

He jumped out of the cruiser and went running into Bear's house through the living room. Matt growled; that was the first and only time the Chief had heard Matt growl. So Chief Dulie slowed up his pace and looked over a very solemn and still Toi, who stood there with her arm around that giant of a dog.

Chief Dulie asked, "Please take Matt outside so he can go to the bathroom." He told me later it was the only thing that came to his mind then. He needed to find something to occupy Toi while he checked on Mr. Bear. Toi slowly did as she was instructed.

Chief Dulie walked into the computer room and found the slim, fragile body of Mr. Bear slumped over his computer, well, over this computer (sigh!). His head was at angle so his left cheek was on the keyboard and his eyes were open staring at Chief Dulie. Chief Dulie knew that Bear was dead but he checked for a pulse anyway. Chief Dulie did not find one.

Bear's skin was so dry, just like paper and there wasn't any smell. Mr. Bear succumbed to the same illness that took many other lives. Now the Chief was faced with a dilemma, what to do with the body. He had hand dug a grave for his wife and son, who had died on the first day the terror had happened. But he couldn't physically bury everyone, so he had left their bodies as he found them and they had all just turned into dust. Also, he would have to make sure that Toi had proper care, and let's not forget, Matt.

Chief Dulie heard the sounds of Toi and Matt coming back into the house. He walked into the dining room to have a most difficult talk with a little girl, who did not have anyone else. He got down on one knee so he was at her eye level. He put his hand lightly on her shoulder and said, "Mr. Bear has gone to heaven."

He was greatly surprised by Toi's response since she pointed at a picture of Bear and his wife on the wall and said, "Is Mr. Bear with her? He often said she was in heaven now. He loved her very, very much."

Chief Dulie related to me he almost totally lost his composure, but he remained in control for both Toi's benefit and for his own. Toi never missed a beat as she pointed at my picture in my Navy dress white uniform and said in a positive tone, "I will live with her now, Miss Callie."

Chief Dulie couldn't figure where she got that idea but he wasn't about to dash the hopes of a little girl who just lost not only her family, but also an almost adopted father and who probably did not have anyone else.

He instructed Toi to get her clothes ready so she could move in with Miss Rasher, the teacher. He hoped she would take Toi and Matt since Chief Dulie's daughter was still having mental problems adjusting to everything. He called the teacher, Miss Rasher, on his cell phone. He explained about the death of Bear and asked, "Can you take Toi and Matt in until other arrangements can be made?"

Miss Rasher agreed immediately. Chief Dulie helped Toi to gather her clothes and toys. He put Matt's dog food and dishes in the back of the cruiser with Toi and her clothes and dropped her off with Miss Rasher.

Chief Dulie finally was able to get a message to have me call him. I did. The call went something like this.

"Is this Miss Callie Bonnet?"

"Yes, it is. Who is this?" I replied. I was expecting bad news since everyone I knew lived in the quarantine area and only bad news seemed to be coming from there.

"This is Chief Dulie. I hate to tell you this, but Bear passed away today. It looks like it is associated with the disease that has killed millions here in the area. I am so sorry."

I finally regained my senses so I asked, "What is going to happen to Toi?" I had already had conversations with Mr. Bear about my Mother and Toi and Matt and, well, everything.

Chief Dulie slowly said with a hesitation in his voice, "I do not know about any long range plans but right now she is living with a school teacher, who has started school again for kids. For some reason, Toi, well, she seems like she expects to live with you."

My heart soared as that is what I wanted. But I never could remember later why I wanted it. I was just a few weeks short of finishing up flight school and would probably soon be serving on a carrier at sea, with little or no money and no family. But I still asked "Do you think that I could adopt her? I will be at sea a lot and everything."

"I don't know but I will call your social worker, Miss Jice Jones, and give her the facts. She had survived the initial attack so maybe she is still around. I'll give her the facts and your phone number."

At the next opportunity, I asked to see my flight training commander. I was escorted into his office so I saluted and made the statement of "Ensign Bonnet reporting, Sir", which is required even though he knows who I am.

"Sit down, Ensign. What brought about your request to see me?"

I began, "Sir, I need a leave to go home as soon as the quarantine in the Northeast is lifted. I lost both my mother and my mentor, who was like a father to me. Now there is a little girl back there who I may need to adopt. It is kinda' complicated, Sir."

"We have time so explain, Ensign."

So I took him through an abbreviated but thorough coverage of my story. I explained how Mr. Bear was so helpful to me, a girl being raised by a single parent. I explained about Toi and how she was taken in by the same man.

My commander said my leave would be granted as soon as it was possible for me to travel into the area. He asked me to talk to the Chaplain. Then the commander did something out of character. He winked at me and told me to ask the Chaplain about Heck and Martha. Well, I must have looked confused so he said directly, "Heck is a retired Master Petty Officer. His wife is Martha. They live right outside of this base and they have an apartment in their house they rent out to Navy personnel. Their kids and grandkids live all around the country and I'll bet they would just love to have a young family move into that apartment. Martha would probably love to have someone to bake cookies for and to be a mother to. She has given up on changing cranky old Heck." Then he chuckled.

I met with the Chaplain and then I went to meet with the Heckarsons. They were pretty much as I was led to expect. Heck was a wiry younger version of old Bear. He loved to fish, and tinker or fix stuff but he abhorred the idea of playing golf. Martha was a plump, apron wearing military wife, who had followed Heck around the world and had lived through it all and seen even more. She was quite the no non-sense mother and grandmother. It's too bad that we couldn't elect her to be President; the country certainly needed her in charge.

Since the apartment was available, I rented it immediately. I did not want to miss the opportunity. Also, I still did not have a car and I could walk to this apartment. It would give me someplace to escape to anyway, if all of my new plans did not work out.

The call came in from Miss Jice Jones. I answered, "Hello."

"Hi, Callie, this is Miss Jones from York. How are you?"

"I am fine. I am so glad that you survived, if I may say it that way?"

"You may, and thank you. I was sorry to hear about Bear. He was a gem in his own way."

"Yes and he really liked you," I replied to lighten the mood.

She laughed and changed the subject by asking, "You want to take in Toi? It is quite an undertaking for a single person serving in the Navy."

"I know. I have a couple weeks left here in flight school. When I finish, I may get assigned on a carrier and be at sea. I just don't know how I would handle it all. On the positive side, I have met an older couple here that could help, I guess. They are retired Navy, but I do not know if I could ask them to help out. It is almost too much to even consider."

"The problem I have is there are not many families or people who could take in a child of that age. The courts could look favorably on allowing your guardianship if you could work out the details."

I met again with the Chaplain and both of us went to see the Heckarsons. We both explained the problems I could face and they instantly volunteered to help although Heck wasn't as enthusiastic as Martha was.

The quarantine was lifted in a week so my leave was granted. The military tries not to interrupt flight training but this was an extreme situation. I was able to fly as a co-pilot in a fighter, yes, a real live fighter, all the way to Paxtauent Navy Base in Maryland. I called Chief Dulie on my cell phone and informed him of my arrival time.

He asked, "Would you be staying at your Mother's home or at Bear's house?"

"I was thinking of staying at Mr. Bear's house, if I could."

"Yes, you may. I'll prepare it for you." I did not know what he meant but he explained it to me later.

After Mr. Bear's death, Chief Dulie accepted the responsibility for care of Mr. Bear's remains. He had carried Mr. Bear's body out to the cruiser. Mr. Bear's body had started to degenerate into dust and was quite light in weight. He then drove to the graveyard, where Mr. Bear's wife was currently residing peacefully. He had recruited Farmer John who had a back hoe to dig a grave and they buried Mr. Bear in a handmade box beside his wife.

The house now needed a little cleaning, especially the dust that was lying upon Mr. Bear's chair and computer. Chief Dulie ran the vacuum and cleaned up the house a lot.

Upon landing, I met a Petty Officer whose assignment was to drive me to Mr. Bear's home. I was so happy the Navy did this for me since I do not drive cars well at all. I have taken and passed the driver's test but I do not have a car, hence, I have never practiced driving much.

My leave was a blur; upon arriving at Mr. Bear's house, I called Chief Dulie, who brought his very shy daughter to meet me. I met the bright-eyed and very pretty Toi, and Matt. I was very surprised by his large size. Toi seemed fairly well adjusted in spite of everything she had lived through in her young life, while Deen, Chief Dulie's daughter looked like she would require a lot of therapy.

I stayed in Mr. Bear's house. Toi asked if she could stay with me. I agreed tentatively. It was quite an awkward couple of hours while we adjusted to being around each other. Also, Matt added in another dimension. He was really more like a giant cat as he did not bark or growl. He just followed Toi around and did what she instructed him to do. I called the Heckarsons and explained about Matt.

They said, "Just bring him along."

That first night, I cleaned the house as much as time allowed. I changed the sheets on Mr. Bear's bed so that Toi could sleep there. I planned on sleeping on the couch but Toi surprised me. She lugged an old exercise mat up the stairs from the basement. She went back down and brought up a sleeping bag and an old rug. She then ran water into the bathtub and jumped into the tub and took her bath, just like someone a lot older would do. She dried herself off and put on pajamas before she left Matt outside with an admonishment about "staying in the yard". She brushed her teeth and then let Matt back in. She gave me a big hug and she climbed into the sleeping bag, which she placed on the exercise mat on the floor of Bear's computer room. Matt lay down on the rug beside of Toi. I went in and sat beside them both and we talked about a few random and non-serious things as I stroked Toi's hair until she fell asleep. I got ready for bed and I slept in Mr. Bear's bed. It was a very surreal experience; one that I would never have expected to do.

We held a memorial for Mr. Bear at his grave site. Toi and I both cried at the thought of not seeing that cranky old tenacious Mr. Bear again.

I met with Miss Jones and we discussed all of the possible scenarios about Toi. I filed all of the paperwork that was required by the courts. Miss Jones wasn't sure when the government could find someone to man the court system to review all of the paper that was being generated to resolve issues like this.

The next day, Chief Dulie presented me with another surprise when he suggested, "When you get a chance, look in that top drawer of Bear's desk for his last will and testament". As soon as Toi was asleep that night, I found the will. It shocked me into next week, when I read that Mr. Bear had left everything to me, except for his car, the tank, which he had left to Bill, the mechanic who babied it. Mr. Bear had hand written instructions that Toi and Matt should always be cared for. This part wasn't witnessed but that wasn't a problem as I intended to make sure that they were both well cared for. He also left me instructions there were documents in the lock box at the bank that would require action.

The next day, I started to search for an attorney to probate Mr. Bear's will. This would take a lot of time due to the same problem I encountered with Toi's guardianship. The attorney agreed to contact all the institutions like Social Security to provide notification of Mr. Bear's demise.

One day while Toi was in school, I rode my old bike out to my mother's house, where I was raised. I let myself in using a hidden key I often had used when I lived here. The house was musty. I found it, well, I found a pile of dust with Mom's clothes mixed in. This was what remained of Mom's body. I just sat on the sofa and contemplated it.

Finally, I made up my mind. I took the broom and swept up Mom's dust and put it in a shoe box. I put Mom's last dress in the box also. I kept Mom's wedding ring she had worn every day since Dad had left us. I put it on my middle finger of my right hand to remember Mom by.

I carried the box up on the ridge a little above the house where the view was best. I dug a small hole as deep as I could with a shovel. I buried the box, which now contained my mother's remains. I said a few words that ended with 'dust to dust'. I wiped the tears away and went back into the house to clean up. I would need to find a cross or a monument to mark the spot.

I expected that Mom did not have a will, but, I guess, I now owned this house also. I cleaned and organized some things. I emptied the refrigerator; everything just went into a trash bag, which I would stop by and pick up later. I unplugged it and left the refrigerator door open. I went through Mom's clothes, while keeping an eye out for jewelry and anything of value. I turned off the water pump and opened the faucets to drain out the lines. I took Mom's jewelry and closed and locked the door. I looked up at the new burial site there as I rode back into town to be there when Toi came home from school.

My leave was almost over and I needed to make plans for both Toi and Matt. It was finally agreed by both Miss Jice Jones and Chief Dulie I should pack up Toi and Matt and take them to Florida in the tank. The thoughts were the courts would probably approve my guardianship sometime in the future. Miss Jones wrote me a note explaining everything about Toi. Also, Chief Dulie couldn't find Bill, the new owner of the tank, so Chief Dulie wrote me a note I could show to prove ownership of the tank. I called an insurance agent in Florida to get insurance for the car.

With Chief Dulie's assistance, I started up the tank. It kicked right over. I backed the car out of the garage and practiced driving it around on those empty roads. I was a very tentative driver, who was about to drive 1000 miles to Florida with a girl about five years old and a large dog.

I had things to take care of in Mr. Bear's house first. Mr. Bear's most valuable items were his guns so Chief Dulie helped me take the guns, and the gun safe to his house. You could have knocked me over with a feather when I found a big wad of cash in the safe. Chief Dulie just raised his eyebrows when I removed that money.

He only said, "That should help you pay some bills until the will is probated."

I started to protest but he just walked away from me. He continued carrying some guns out to the cruiser. (I now know where the cash came from, after reading the story called THE ROOT.)

I also found more jewelry of Mr. Bear's late wife. Chief Dulie wouldn't take any nor would he allow me to give any away, so I added the jewelry to the gun safe now at Chief Dulie's house.

The house was cleaned and closed with the pipes drained and the electricity shut off. There were still a lot of Mr. Bear's clothing and personal items like his golf clubs and fishing tackle, which we left in the house. I must admit I forgot Mr. Bear's awards and his Emmys. I will need to find all of that stuff when I get back on leave. Maybe I can find a corner at a VFW or Legion hall to arrange a display honoring Mr. Bear. He was always so supportive of the military personnel.

I put the will, check books and papers in a box that went in the trunk along with the laptops and a printer. The oh-so-helpful Chief Dulie agreed to check the house once in a while and keep the grass mowed. It was time for me to go on the next adventure, the long drive south.

There was a small group of people there to see us off; Toi's teacher and classmates, Miss Jones, and Chief Dulie and a few other people. We said our good byes and waved as we drove out of town and started south.

There wasn't much traffic for the first 50 miles or so. Then we hit normal traffic in the unaffected areas. Toi's eyes went big as she saw all of the people and cars in Maryland. She soon adjusted to it.

I drove close to the speed limit and stopped often so that we could stretch our legs and so Matt could do bathroom breaks. He seems so relaxed; just like he rode in a car every day. The weather was dry most of the way south, I was thankful for that.

The Heckarsons welcomed us into their house and their lives. Toi became a student in first grade. The letter from Miss Jones was used as Toi's identification until we could come up with a birth certificate. Toi even got her required shots. Matt and Heck developed an alliance of sorts, while Toi was in school. Matt was the only dog allowed to walk without a leash. It amused the local police to see him walk alongside Toi or Heck as if Matt was on a leash, which he was not.

I went back to flight training since Martha and Heck helped with getting Toi off to school and when she came home from school.

It was a month later we heard the official announcement from the government about what caused the calamity in the Northeast. It seemed that a couple of do-gooder scientists were responsible. One was a micro-biologist and the other was a physician. They had met while working on developing a new chemical weapon. They were amazed to realize that the world was about to develop the perfect weapon. One that was air borne and would kill people quickly and turn their bodies into dust so the aggressors could deploy the weapon and then wait a while until it dissipated. The houses and the property would be there waiting to be lived in. There wouldn't be much of a mess to deal with. The people would have turned into dust. Just vacuum it up and take over.

Anyway, these two scientists combined their talents to create an antidote before the weapon was finished. Well, they were successful in creating the antidote but they had to test it to be sure that it worked. So they swiped a tiny sample of the chemical weapon and put it in a special containment vessel, which was buried in the ground beside their laboratory.

But there was a small earthquake in their area. It caused the weapon to be released into the air on a day with swirling winds so many people in a wide area were affected. The weapon killed most of the people immediately. It also killed most of the air breathing birds and mammals. The pattern of the deaths was what made it possible for meteorologists to finally determine where it all started. They put the death rate and the wind direction and speed into computer generated models.

I guessed that Mr. Bear and some of the train occupants were protected somewhat by the train cars and the direction that the train was going.

Well, my training was almost complete and I still hadn't heard any official word about Toi's papers. I was expecting an assignment at sea. I was wrestling with making a decision about what to do; option one was to just resign my commission if I could and find a 9 to 5 job, and option 2 was to ask the Heckarsons to become Toi's official guardian while I was at sea. But I couldn't do that. I just couldn't. I was pretty much heart sick with worry. I was losing weight and I couldn't sleep.

Finally, I put in my papers to ask for an assignment on shore, which meant I would not be flying. I was in the Navy after all, which traveled the world's waters, not on shore. I did not feel any better.

I had just got home to the apartment we lived in after dropping off my papers when my cell phone rang. It was Miss Jice Jones.

I opened my phone and answered, "Hello."

Miss Jones said "Callie, this is Miss Jones. I have some news for you."

"About Toi?"

"Yes" she hesitated before she said "It is not good news, I'm afraid."

I worked on my courage and said, "Please go on."

"Toi has an uncle in Connecticut, who has filed a lawsuit to adopt Toi. He just found out she was still alive when he was contacted about picking up his sister's car. That apparently gave him some idea where she might be so he called our offices and faxed me a picture of Toi. It is her.

"I checked about him, Callie, he appears to be a nice guy with a family. Toi has three cousins. I'm so sorry."

"What is her name, her real name?"

"Oh, I forgot. Her name is Anna. She is six now. I explained about Matt. They have a cat but they agreed to take Matt also."

I thought a few minutes before I asked, "Was Toi and her family living in York County?"

"No, they were traveling from their home in Virginia to visit when the disaster happened."

"So they were probably on interstate 83. How did Toi get from interstate 83 to Mr. Bear's house in a late winter day? That is at least five miles."

"No idea. Are you okay with this, Callie?"

"I guess I will have to be. Mr. Bear would have told me to just suck it up and make it happen." I was heartbroken but arrangements were put in motion.

I asked, "What is her uncle's name so that I can tell Toi?" "His name is Ben, Toi's, no, Anna's Uncle Ben."

I took Toi out for pizza for supper. While there, I waited until she was glancing at some kids.

I said, "Anna". She reacted to that name by turning her head back to me so that was her name. I told her, "Your Uncle Ben wants you to live with him. Do you remember him, Anna? Do you remember him and your cousins?"

She was quiet as he thought. She said, "Uncle Ben" with a quite solemn face. She shook her head yes while she smiled and tears flowed down her pretty cheeks.

She replied, "But I will have to move away from you and Matt."

I said, "Oh, no. Matt goes with you."

She smiled and said, "I'll miss you Miss Callie. I want to be in the Navy when I grow up to be just like you."

That is the way that it happened. Toi, now called Anna, and the large scruffy dog, Matt, went on a long drive north with her Uncle Ben and his family. They made a lovely family.

I call Anna as often as one aboard a carrier can or she calls me. She appears to have adjusted just fine. I am setting up a large 529 college fund for her as Mr. Bear would have wanted. I plan on visiting with her as often as I can. When I can find the time, I want to take her and her cousins to Disney world. I hope to keep flying in the Navy and maybe someday have a family of my own. Then retire to Mr. Bear's house.

I shouldn't forget about the money that Mr. Bear rescued from Switzerland; the same money he wanted to go to the VFW and the American Legion. Well, as an officer and a lady, I decided to handle this with the sensitivity that was required, so I turned this over to the Chaplain. He made it all become a problem for the VFW and the American Legion and their lawyers.

The Chaplain also helped me meet with a financial advisor for proper handling of my inherited money. I am now quite rich and, also, thanks to Mr. Bear, a pilot, living my dream. Oh, I am also meeting lots of young, and talented single pilots and sailors so who knows who may happen in my future.

The unique, one-of-a-kind car, the tank, is another story. Heck wanted to keep it so he could drive it and baby it, but I did not want to sell it. Finally, I gave in and rented it to Heck. As for the title of the car, well, that is so confusing since it was left in the will to Bill, but I have possession of it. Bill apparently died in the calamity along with so many in the Northeast. The title to the car and probate of the will plus the house titles are in the hands of an attorney, who lives in Maryland but is licensed to practice in Pa. Someday all of this will be straightened out.

As I organized all of these stories, I noticed that Mr. Bear didn't include some of the conflicts that arose between the two of us. He didn't include those confrontations so I won't elaborate about those incidents either.

After I joined the Navy, I soon became aware why Mr. Bear demanded that I be on time and follow instructions. He was preparing me for the realities of Navy life.

I really miss Anna. But I know this is for the best. I also know that both of us will never forget one grumpy and feisty old man, who we called Mr. Bear.

COMING SOON

POLITICAL CIRCLE
The making of an American Original

The first book in the Bear saga will be available soon. And, yes, Harvey Most
is a Presidential Advisor, maybe the MOST trusted advisor of the newly elected President. Of course, he is a quite reluctant advisor. Not long after leaving that role, he becomes the MOST wanted escapee. Or is he?

DF Garland

Contact info: dfrgarland@gmail.com

Made in the USA
San Bernardino, CA
11 September 2013